SARAH T

Anna's
F-Plan

CRANTHORPE
MILLNER

First published by Cranthorpe Millner Publishers (2022)

ISBN 978-1-80378-008-5 (Paperback)

www.cranthorpemillner.com

Cranthorpe Millner Publishers

About the Author

Sarah T. Wright is an author and photographer from
Northern Ireland. Anna's F-Plan is her debut novel.

www.sarahtwright.com

Facebook: Sarah T Wright
Instagram: sarahtwrightauthor
Twitter: @sarahtwright

1
Fait Accompli

I was listening to the calming classical music – a captivating composition by my favourite composer – when suddenly the lift stopped mid-sonata and in sauntered a tall, dark-haired angel. Although he didn't look like one. He wasn't wearing white. Here in heaven everyone wore white.

"The maestro that is Wolfgang Amadeus Mozart," I heard him, say as the lift re-started its ascent. I watched as he began to wave his hands in the air, pretending to conduct the musical masterpiece. "He's fantastic live."

I knew that as I'd recently seen him perform at a concert organised to entertain the troops. There should have been a headline collaboration with Beethoven, but it was cancelled due to 'artistic differences.' Apparently, they had been caterwauling at each other like two alley cats backstage and Beethoven had stormed off in a huff. Mozart did have a reputation for being a bit difficult, but his music was divine and his performance was amazing.

"I saw him in Vienna in '82. Fabulous show. Wild night!" he told me.

I didn't want to engage with the dishevelled angel who looked like he'd just come back from a wild night in the 1980s as opposed to the 1780s, wearing tight black trousers, unlaced boots and a long, dusty coat. He continued to conduct the complex concerto with his hands.

I didn't know which celestial department he belonged to, but whichever one it was, standards were slipping. I straightened the jacket of my uniform, stood with my shoulders back and stared straight ahead.

Maybe he wasn't from heaven, I thought while continuing to ignore him. *Maybe he was from down below*? If he was from the other place, what was he doing here? *Maybe he was a spy…* Thankfully the lift came to a stop and I side-stepped past the demon double agent, being careful not to dirty my feathers on the way out.

"Nice wings," he called after me as the doors closed.

I admired their magnificence as I stretched them out, checking that every perfectly preened feather was in place. I was so proud of them, and of the uniform I wore. I was proud of my work, my medals and yet another successful mission in the Middle East. There was no question I had done a brilliant job. I had led my battalion in a campaign that crushed an uprising of local insurgents.

Puffed up with my own self-importance, I marched into the boardroom, confident that I'd been called here today to receive another commendation or possibly a promotion. I stood to attention in front of my commanding officer who was flanked on either side by two high-ranking officials. To my mind, their presence only confirmed my suspicion that I was to be decorated. I saluted my superiors who sat behind a long white desk.

"Lieutenant." The colonel addressed me but didn't look up. "I want to congratulate you on your recent tour of duty. Great job."

"Thank you, sir."

It had been a difficult operation. We'd been subjected to a persistent and prolonged siege by the enemy but in the end good had triumphed over evil and we were victorious.

"The reason we've called you here today..." He glanced at the deities dressed in white suits who sat either side of him, "Is to tell you that you're going to be..."

In the expectant silence that followed I prepared for my promotion.

"You are going to be..." The colonel paused for a second time, keeping his gaze fixed on the papers he held in his hands.

The suspense was killing me. Technically I wasn't alive but still, I couldn't wait any longer.

"Yes, sir?" I prompted.

"Lieutenant," he said, looking me in the eye, "You are going to be…"

I drew in a deep breath. *Here it comes! He is finally going to tell me I've been…*

"Transferred."

Wait! What? "Transferred?" I parroted in disbelief.

"Yes, transferred." The colonel shifted uncomfortably in his seat.

"No!" I protested. "There has to be some mistake."

My mind was reeling, my head was spinning. This wasn't happening. This couldn't be happening!

"There's no mistake," one of the superiors said.

"You are being transferred to the Guardians." The other one informed me of my fate.

"No!" I cried out again. "Please, colonel," I said, pleading with my commanding officer. "I'm a good soldier. I've fought on the front line. I've done back-to-back tours of duty. I belong in the EAA."

He sat in stony silence.

The EAA (Elite Angel Army) was heaven's equivalent of the SAS; a sword-wielding crack team of highly trained operatives sent into battle to fight against evil, for the glory of God. I loved being in the army. It was my life. It was more than just a job to me – it was my reason for being.

"I'm a fighter, not a… a… a…" I stammered and stuttered, unable to even say the word. "Guardian," I finally spat out.

"The Guardians are an elite force too, Miss Frost." The other official addressed me by name, stripping me of my rank. "They are entrusted with personal protection."

"I'm a lieutenant in the army, it has a responsibility for protecting whole nations!" My pleas were ignored.

"Your new post will begin immediately," it was pronounced.

"I don't want to go!" I wailed, as I was sent without further delay to the Guardians' headquarters.

I leaned my head against the cold glass door. I'd been dismissed, deported and deployed in a heartbeat. In heaven there is no measure of time, there are no weeks or years. We are not bound by days or hours. I'd forgotten about time but standing there, it all came flooding back and I knew that every second in this place would feel like an eternity.

"No! No! No!" I said as I banged my fist on the glass.

Suddenly the door opened and I fell forward, landing unceremoniously face down on the floor at the feet of a pair of familiar boots.

"The door was open," the owner of the dusty leather boots told me.

I looked up to see the dark angel from the lift.

"It's you!"

"The one and only. Here, let me help you," he said, as he reached out a hand.

I didn't move.

5

"It's what we do here." He smiled. "We help people."

So he was a Guardian, not a demon, although, in my opinion they were the same thing.

"I can manage," I snapped, and he stepped back. However when I tried to get up, I couldn't. Something was wrong. I struggled to move and started to flap about like a fish on the floor.

"Allow me."

He reached down, lifted me up and carried me inside. My embarrassing entrance attracted everyone's attention and work in the busy office stopped. Guardians left their desks and gathered around.

"Put me down!" I ordered the angel who held me in his arms.

He did as he was told and I was relieved to find that I was finally standing on my own two feet, although they felt odd. I looked down and shrieked when I saw what I was wearing – my combat boots had been replaced by white pointy stilettos, and the restrictive white bandage skirt that bound my legs together was the reason I hadn't been able to stand up.

"Oh my God!" I cried out. *What was I wearing?*

A chorus of hallelujahs and amens rang out from the surrounding angels who thought I was praising the Lord; every single one of them wearing a variation of what I presumed was my new uniform.

"Welcome, welcome," a tiny, tinkly voice greeted me.

6

The crowd of hosts parted and I saw a petite, buxom blonde angel teetering towards me, taking lots of little steps in heels that were too high and wearing a dress that was far too tight.

"You must be Anna."

It crossed my mind to deny it and just run out the door, but before I could she had captured me in a suffocating embrace.

"I'm Zelda," she hugged me hard, introducing herself to my breasts. Addressing the crowded congregation she continued, "Anna was an Avenging Angel."

I still am! I wanted to shout at everyone who was in awe.

"And now she's a Guardian."

No, I'm not! I wanted to scream.

"And she was so eager to get in, she was beating the door down," the dishevelled angel divulged to the entire workforce.

I turned and glared at him.

"Leonardo, at your service." He made a sweeping bow.

"It's so lovely to have you join our little family," Zelda enthused.

The feeling was far from mutual.

"Holly's going to show you to your desk," she told me before tottering off.

The welcome party returned to work although I

wasn't sure exactly what that entailed. I knew they watched over people and tried to keep them safe; they did little things like helping old ladies cross the road and stopping children from falling off their bikes; trivial things that I was sure wouldn't be terribly taxing on either my talents or the very short time I intended being here.

Holly appeared beside me; her voluptuous figure squeezed into a standard issue white dress which she had accentuated with a wide red belt.

"Mince pie?" she offered and pushed the plate under my nose.

"No," I recoiled.

"Are you sure? They're delicious!"

"Absolutely sure."

My body, ethereally speaking, was a temple. It had to be, for my job – my *proper* job. Holly's, on the other hand, appeared to be less temple and more waste disposal. She devoured a mince pie and immediately picked up another.

"*Hmm*, I really shouldn't, but they're so good!" she said as she stuffed it in her mouth. "Oh, I'm so sorry," she apologised, having spat crumbs all over me. I brushed them off as she looked for a place to put her plate.

"I'll take that," Leonardo swiped it from her hand.

Holly tried to grab it back but he held it high above her head. *Definite demon behaviour*, I thought. I still had serious reservations about the strangely dressed dark angel.

"Don't eat them all," she warned him.

"Of course not," he promised as he picked one up and, with a twinkle in his eye, put it in his mouth.

Holly was not a happy angel but a quick stop at the coffee machine soon cheered her up. She was salivating as she shared the long list of drinks, which could be dispensed from the state-of-the-art contraption, while making a gingerbread and caramel macchiato with cream and chocolate sprinkles.

"This is heaven," she said, breathing in the sweet smell. Pepped up by a new sugar rush, my Guardian guide introduced me to everyone en route to my desk. She shouted names, which I had no intention of remembering because soon I would be gone.

Then Holly grabbed me and screamed; a shrill, high-pitched shriek that made me jump.

"What's wrong?" I tried to assess the situation and ascertain the danger.

"Listen!" she squealed.

There were no alarms, no distress signals, no gunshots, no encroaching threat that I could detect, although it was almost impossible to hear anything in the noisy office.

"Christmas music!" Holly shouted like an excited child before starting to sing at the top of her voice, *Deck the halls.* She giggled and then, pointing to herself, sang, "*With boughs of Holly.*"

It wasn't funny and was even less so when she tried to get me to join in. There were manoeuvres that I could have, should have and was sorely tempted to use on her, to get her to stop before we finally *fa, la, la, la, la'd* our way to my desk. I'd never been so happy to see an inanimate object before – this small space would be my sanctuary, a safe place away from all the madness; somewhere I could plot and plan a way to get back to where I belonged.

"We're desk buddies," Holly cheerily chirped, and pointed over to what I presumed had once been a desk before it had been transformed into a flashing, festive shrine. Every inch was covered in twinkling lights, tinsel and Christmas tat. "Obviously yours needs a little decorating." Before I could stop her, she'd dashed over to her desk and brought back a bobblehead Santa, a small fake tree and a musical snow globe.

"Isn't that better?" she said, setting them down.

I looked beneath the desk for a bin.

"And there's more."

"No!" I shouted but she completely ignored me.

She quickly returned carrying a box.

"This is more than enough," I said, picking up the little snow globe and shaking it.

An oblivious Holly was now sticking tinsel to the edge of my desk and I was horrified when I saw her bring out a string of lights. There was no stopping her.

All I could do was sit back and watch my desk disappear under a mass of baubles and sparkly stuff.

"Don't you just love Christmas?" Holly gushed as she garnished.

I didn't answer. Finally, after she had pinned, positioned and put everything in its place, she stood back and clapped her hands with delight.

"Come look." She dragged me up to admire her handiwork.

I cringed when confronted with the decorations she had crammed onto my desk.

"It's too much," I told her, but Holly disagreed.

"You can never have too much of Christmas. There's no such thing as too many reindeers or trees or lights." Her excitement grew as she said, "Or too much holly!" She laughed as she pointed to herself again. I was already tired of her joke and I had had enough of Holly and all her festive good cheer.

"After all, we are Christmas angels."

"We're what?" I hadn't got my head around being a Guardian and now I had to try and wrap it around this fresh hell!

She beamed with pride, and pointing at the two of us said, "We're Guardians *and* Christmas angels."

Could this day get any worse? It was bad enough being demoted from the army and sent to the Guardians, but now I find out I'm a Christmas angel and my partner's the Sugar Plum Fairy! There were no words. I couldn't believe how far I'd fallen and just how fast.

"We're CIA," she whispered conspiratorially.

I was fairly sure she didn't mean the covert, Secret Service agency.

"Christmas Incident Angels," she confirmed.

I stood there open-mouthed with shock.

"We're a special task force, just like the EAA."

The Elite Angel Army was the crème de la crème of God's armed forces – a specialist missions unit sent in to spearhead any attack. We led and the legions followed. How on heaven or earth did that compare to a Christmas incident team? What major incidents even happened at Christmas? Were we deployed to help Santa find a parking space for his sleigh? Or sent to fix fused Christmas tree lights? This was a farce! I was catatonic with rage. Surely this couldn't be true? Then I watched as Holly reached into a box and brought out a long, brass plaque that she placed on my desk. I picked it up and read, "Anna Frost, Christmas Incident Angel."

So it was true. I had no idea what I'd done to deserve this, but whatever it was I had to find out and fix it fast.

"What does a Christmas Incident Angel even do?"

"We're sent down to help anyone in despair," Holly told me.

I was in despair!

"Down where?"

"I'll show you."

She walked a few feet from my desk and pointed

down. I stood beside her and gasped when I saw we were standing on the edge of a huge circular opening. I glanced around and saw that other Guardians were also looking down. Below was Central Park, the beating heart of New York City. There was a constant pulsating ebb and flow from concrete arteries that spread out through avenues overshadowed by soaring skyscrapers. Perfect soft snowflakes fell silently past us, falling down to earth. They sprinkled over the park like fairy dust, transforming the ordinary and every day into something magical. I'd forgotten how beautiful life was.

I watched families build snowmen and children make snow angels. Dogs barked and lovers walked hand in gloved hand. All were lost in the fairytale winter wonderland, and for a moment I too was lost in the bittersweet memories it brought back.

"This is our jurisdiction."

There was a buzzing sound.

"I have to take this," Holly said, as she unhooked a pager from her belt and waved it in the air. "Back in a tick."

I kept looking. This had once been my playground and childhood memories came flooding back. I saw myself playing hide-and-seek in the forest, skating on the ice rink and running under the wisteria-covered pergola. In the spring, cherry blossom would fall like confetti and I would walk under branches, imagining it was my wedding day.

I was always dreaming of my wedding; designing my dress, planning every detail of what I knew would be the most important day of my life. I believed in the fairytale, the promise that one day, when I did grow up, my prince would come. He would sweep me off my feet and we would marry. It would be the happiest day of my life. Yet that day never came, and that life ended.

"What do you see?"

I jumped; I hadn't realised Leonardo was standing beside me.

"I see Central Park," I replied, stating the obvious.

"Yes, but what do you *see*?"

I looked down again, "I still see Central Park."

I began to wonder if he was seeing something else. Leonardo hunched down beside me and stared intently at the scene below. Maybe he needed glasses?

"Look closer." He invited me to kneel down beside him with a wave of his hand.

"It's okay, I can see perfectly well from here."

"Look closer," he insisted.

"Fine," I said, as I tried but failed several times to sit down beside him. Eventually I hitched the tight skirt up above my knees and knelt down. How I missed wearing trousers!

"Now what do you see?" Leonardo persisted.

I peered over the edge and looked closer. I saw a lonely figure, sitting huddled on a bench. The snow fell and covered him in a blanket that brought neither warmth nor comfort. I saw others too seeking shelter in the park. For those unfortunates there was no fairytale, only a cold, harsh reality. A mounted policeman, wearing a waterproof cape patrolled the pathways. A reminder that thieves, rapists, murderers lurked in the shadows; watching, waiting, ready to pounce on the innocent and unsuspecting who were spellbound by the fairytale; forgetting that where there is good, evil is never far away. Somewhere soon the pure snow, which covered the pretty park, would be stained red. An oozing, thick stream would seep into a deep, dark, crimson pool.

"I see darkness."

I didn't look through rose-tinted glasses anymore and wasn't deceived by the false promises and beauty of the snowy paradise below. I turned to look at Leonardo who was sitting on the edge. Leaning forward, he rubbed his hand through his tousled hair, his coat fanning out behind him like a superhero's cape.

"What do you see?" I asked the dark-haired angel.

"I see despair," he replied, staring at me with such an intense gaze it seemed to pierce my soul.

I looked back at the fairytale setting and nodded.

"So do I."

"Anna," I heard Holly call my name and turned to see her trotting towards me carrying a cake in one hand while waving papers in the other.

Leonardo reached out a hand to help me stand up and

this time I took it.

"Anna!" She sounded excited. I was sure it was because she had cake.

"Let me take that for you," Leonardo offered as she tried to catch her breath.

"No!" she barked, pulling the iced Christmas cake out of his reach. "I mean, no thank you," she smiled sweetly, firmly holding onto the festive, fruit-filled cake. "These are for you," she said, handing me the papers while keeping a wary eye on Leonardo. "They're your orders – your first case – and you're being sent down."

"Down where?"

"Down there," she replied, pointing to the park.

"No!" There must be some mistake (yet another one!). I'd only just been demoted to the CIA. I wasn't ready for whatever Christmas incident was happening in Central Park.

"Yes!" She beamed. "I'm so happy for you Anna! Shall we celebrate with cake?"

"No!"

There was nothing to celebrate. I didn't want to be a Guardian! I didn't want to be in the CIA! I didn't want to go down to Central Park, and I definitely did not want cake! Holly just smiled before taking a big bite and I watched as she waddled off with the plate, leaving me to read through my orders.

2

Frippery, Flattery and Flying by the seat of your pants

I sat down beside Leonardo and dangled my feet over the edge.

"There is a young man in despair," I read aloud. "He has lost everything. Tonight is Christmas Eve. At nine p.m. he will be at Bow Bridge."

Panic started to set in.

"I can't go, I'm not trained for this type of situation," I said, waving the papers in the air. "They need a professional. They need Clarence Peabody," (or someone who had at least taken his class in angel training. This was his department, his speciality. It was how he got his wings in the first place). "I'm trained to fight," I reasoned, looking at Leonardo in desperation. "I wouldn't know what to say or do."

"You'll be fine," he tried to reassure me, but it didn't work.

I wasn't prepared for what I was being asked to do. I looked again at the orders but before I could read another word, a strong gust of wind blew the papers out of my hand.

"No!" I jumped up and tried to grab them but they flew out of reach. "Well, that's just great! What am I supposed to do now?"

"Meet your young man on the bridge."

"And do what?" I couldn't follow orders if I didn't know what they actually were.

"Wing it," Leonardo said, being anything but helpful.

That was exactly how you could lose your wings.

"I don't even know his name, or why he's in despair. I don't know what I'm supposed to do or how I'm supposed to help him."

I needed orders – I followed orders. Angels in the EAA didn't 'wing it'.

"You'll figure it out." Leonardo was being blasé. "Well, we better get you ready to leave," he said and stood up.

I looked down at Central Park. The sky was turning a deep shade of blue. Lights were going on in the towering skyscrapers, which from here looked like tiny specks.

"You need to get changed," Leonardo informed me. "You can't go dressed like that."

That was the first bit of good news I'd had all day.

I followed Leonardo to, what I presumed, was the

wardrobe department for the Guardians. A dapper young angel dressed in a three-piece suit was busy sorting through rails of clothes. He stopped what he was doing when he saw us come in.

"Leo darling, how lovely to see you," he said as he danced across the room. "You look divine."

He embraced him, air kissing both cheeks.

"I should do. After all, it was you who dressed me," he cajoled the foppish angel who flounced over to me, waving a frilly cuff in Leonardo's direction.

"Yes darling, but that was way back in the Fifteenth Century. I dressed him in 1480 and he hasn't changed since," he told me.

That explained a lot.

"It was the height of fashion." Leonardo admired himself in the mirror.

"Five hundred years ago!"

"It still is," Leonardo said, defending his attire. "It's a timeless classic. Just like me." He flashed his most charming smile at the dandy young dresser.

"You're incorrigible," he told him before turning his attention to me. "And who have we here?"

"I'm Anna," I introduced myself as he looked me up and down.

"Sebastian Alexandre Victor Le Braseille at your service," he said, holding out the tails of his frock coat as he curtsied. He continued with his introduction: "I'm from a long line of French couturiers. I've dressed kings and courtesans, dukes and duchesses."

"And a lot of queens," Leonardo interrupted.

"You're so naughty," Sebastian scolded. "Isn't he naughty?"

He was giggling like a schoolgirl.

"Yes, very," I agreed, playing along.

"We need to avail of your great talent and expertise once again," Leonardo began.

"Flattery will get you everywhere," Sebastian said, fluttering his eyelids at the handsome angel.

"Will it get a lovely new outfit for Anna?" He winked at the dressmaker as he sashayed across the room to me. "It's her first time," he said putting his arm around me and giving me a reassuring squeeze. "She needs something…" Leonardo bit his bottom lip before mouthing, "'special'."

"*Absolument*!" Sebastian said, clapping his hands excitedly.

"Oh, thank goodness! I can't wait to get out of these clothes!" I told him.

"Ooh la la! Someone's excited."

I was!

"I have just the thing for you. It was a favourite of Marie's," he called out, as he disappeared into a closet.

"It will be perfect," he promised.

I couldn't wait.

Sebastian reappeared with a bodice in one hand and swinging cream stockings from the other.

"No!" I cried out. This was going from the frying pan into the fire!

"But King Louie loved them," he said, looking hurt.

"If I wear that, I'll catch my death," I told him truthfully (although maybe that wouldn't be a bad thing if it would speed up my return to heaven).

"This liaison is outside," Leonardo clarified.

"*Mon Dieu!*' Sebastian looked horrified.

"Yes, on a bridge."

He let the lingerie fall to the floor.

"It'll be really cold, so something warm would be great."

Sebastian was staring at me open-mouthed.

I explained: "I might have to stand around talking to him but hopefully not for too long. I plan to be in and out, as quickly as possible. Still, I don't want to get frostbite."

"*Mais non,*" Sebastian mumbled. "The times, they are a-changing." He picked up the sexy lingerie and walked away.

"I think I might've upset him," I said to Leonardo, who seemed to find the whole thing very funny.

Not confident that Sebastian was going to choose the right clothes, I decided to take matters into my own hands.

I went on a reconnaissance mission of my own, rummaging through the rails until I found the perfect outfit.

I returned with an armful of clothes at the same time as Sebastian, who was holding a long, black gown.

"Do you think your young man will like those?" he asked sceptically, casting a disapproving look at what I'd chosen.

"I don't know, but I love them!"

"Don't you think he would prefer something a little sexier, like this?" and he held up the elegant evening dress.

"I really don't think he'll care what I'm wearing," I reassured Sebastian. "Trust me, he has other things on his mind."

"I know!" he said, "That's why I think you should make a little more effort. It is a very 'special' night."

"No. It doesn't matter what I put on. It won't stop him doing what he's going to do."

Sebastian looked concerned.

"You don't want him to do it?"

"God no! Of course I don't! I'm going to do everything in my power to make sure he doesn't do it."

"Leonardo, you can't let this happen!" Sebastian declared, running over to the dark angel who was trying his hardest not to laugh.

I didn't get the joke and obviously neither did Sebastian, who was becoming very upset.

"I'll just go and get changed" I told them.

I couldn't wait to get out of the clingy clothes I was wearing.

In the changing room, I quickly peeled off the skin-tight skirt and blouse, kicked off the uncomfortable high-heeled stilettos and pulled on a pair of combat trousers, a big baggy jumper and boots that reminded me of the ones I wore in the army. I finished off the ensemble with an oversized coat. That would surely keep me warm.

"Will I do?" I asked, as I pulled back the blue velvet curtain.

"No!" Sebastian cried.

It was my turn to be offended.

"Please Leonardo," he begged. "You can't let her go. This is not right!"

Well, it might not be to his taste but really, he was being a tad over dramatic as he was now openly weeping. Leonardo ignored Sebastian's histrionics and walked over to me. Putting his arm around me he asked if I was ready.

"I'm going now?"

In my excitement about swapping my CIA regulation uniform for a more comfortable civilian alternative, I'd completely forgotten that I was about to become a civilian.

"No time like the present."

I begged to differ, as did Sebastian, who was now praying for me.

"Shouldn't I ask Holly if she has a copy of the orders?" I asked, stalling for time.

"There's no time," Leonardo informed me.

"I'm sure she read them," I said, dragging my heels. "I'll just run back quickly and ask her."

Leonardo kept a firm hold of me as he waited for the lift doors to open.

"It's time to go," he instructed as he pushed me inside.

I felt trapped as there was no escape.

"Don't worry, you'll be fine," Leonardo reassured me as he reached in and pushed a button.

Sebastian was waving me off with a lace handkerchief he'd pulled out of his sleeve.

"But—" I wasn't ready. I didn't have my orders and I didn't know what I was doing. I didn't want to go. However, I didn't manage to say any of those things as the lift doors started to close before I had the chance.

"See you down there," Leonardo called out.

"Wait! Are you coming too?"

He had no time to answer. The doors closed and I was on my way down. My last lift journey had ended in disaster and I had a sinking feeling that this one would too.

3

Fools rush in where angels fear to tread

I stepped out into the park and looked up at the night sky. There was no sign of heaven but I knew it was there. Walking along the path, I wished again that I'd taken Clarence Peabody's class. At least then I would've known what to say to the man who was waiting for me on the bridge.

I tried to prepare as I walked along but I had no idea what to say to someone in despair. I was no good with words. I was good with a sword. I could swing and slash my way out of any situation, but I didn't have my sword. Even if I had, it wouldn't help me here. I was going to have to take Leonardo's advice and 'wing it'. I just hoped and prayed that I'd still have mine after tonight.

Ahead of me lanterns lit up Bow Bridge, which arched across a body of deep, dark water. Silhouettes of snow-covered branches stretched up into the night sky and illuminated skyscrapers stood like silent sentinels, watching over the park. I could make out the figure of a man leaning against the side, his head in his hands. Thank goodness I'd made it in time.

"Stop!" I shouted as I ran onto the bridge.

The man jumped but thankfully not over the side. Rather, he jumped back from the edge and stood with his hands above his head.

"I don't have any money," he told me.

After the exertion of running I needed a moment to catch my breath.

"I don't have any either (I thought that might make him feel better). It's not... worth... dying for," I told him between gasps. I was struggling to breathe; I couldn't understand why because I was in great shape. Or at least I had been before I left heaven. I felt a sudden, sharp pain in my chest and reached inside my coat.

"Don't shoot!"

The man was grappling to take off gold cufflinks that peeked out from under the sleeves of his expensive overcoat.

"Take these," he said, holding out his hand.

I wasn't here to hurt him; I was here to help him. He looked scared as I staggered towards him. My heart was racing, and I felt faint.

"No," I said, as I grabbed his arm and gasped for breath. "I was sent here for you." That was all I managed to say before another sharp pain bent me double and brought me to my knees.

"Help!" he started to shout.

"No, stop!" I grabbed his trouser leg and hauled myself back onto my feet, my head spinning. I stabbed a finger in his direction and said, "You have no money?" I was trying to establish what he'd lost, in between gasps.

"I have no money on me," the man corrected me.

"You've no job?"

"No, I have a job," he said, looking confused.

"You've no house then?"

"No, I still have all of them too."

He hadn't lost any of his houses. How rich was *he*? None of this was making any sense and then I realised my mistake.

"Oh no!" I cried out. I'd got it wrong; this wasn't my man! I ignored the pain in my chest and jumped up onto the stone railing that ran the length of the bridge. The man on the bridge was panicking now and calling out for me to come down. Unlike most humans, angels don't have a fear of heights. I walked along the edge, searching the darkness for any sign of him but there was no movement in the water.

"He's gone," I said.

"911," the man was calling for help. "Yes, ambulance."

"It's too late, he's gone."

"Please come down."

"You don't understand. A man's dead because of me," I told him and turned to see the colour drain from

27

his face.

"Police too," I heard him tell the emergency operator.

I crouched down and stared into the darkness. I was meant to be here. I was meant to save him, and I'd failed. There was no sign of life in the cold water below me.

"I know what it feels like to lose everything."

"What have you lost?" the man on the bridge asked.

"I lost my job today," I told him, "I loved my job."

"You can get another one." He was trying to be comforting.

"I have another one!" I wailed, thinking I was about to lose that too. "I'm not cut out to be in the CIA."

"You're in the CIA?" the man asked, shocked.

He wasn't the only one. I still couldn't believe I was a Christmas Incident Angel.

I was getting really upset now. It had been a *long* day. "I never wanted to leave the army. I was a great lieutenant," I told my confidante.

"I'm sure you were."

"I fought on the front line," I sobbed.

I could hear sirens in the distance.

"You know there are people here who can help you. People you can talk to."

"There's no one here who can help me," I sniffed as I wiped my eyes with the sleeve of my new coat. No one on earth could help me. "Okay, enough!" I declared, I had to stop wallowing in self-pity. I was here to do a job.

I was too late to save him, but I could still find him. "Talking isn't going to bring him back." However, *I* could. I stood up and took off my coat.

The man on the bridge pleaded with me, "Please, you don't have to do this!"

"Yes, I do."

I had to do my duty and with that, I jumped off the bridge.

4

A front

"Anna," someone was calling me.

"Anna," they called again.

Everything had gone black when I hit the water but now there was a light.

"Open your eyes," the voice told me as the light became brighter.

I tried to open them but I couldn't. The light was hurting them.

"Open your eyes," the voice coaxed again.

It sounded familiar. I slowly prised them open and saw Holly's face before bright beams, from the torch she was holding, bore into my eyeballs, forcing me to close them again.

"Thank heaven, I'm home!" I said, as I tried to sit up.

"Not quite," she confirmed as she shoved me back down. "You're in hospital," she said merrily, as if that was a good thing. "And it's Christmas day. Happy Christmas!"

Holly walked to the end of the bed.

"Why are you dressed like a doctor?" I asked her.

"Because I am your doctor, silly."

There was another bed in the room, occupied by an elderly lady who wore black-framed glasses. She was staring at me. She nodded at the machine I was attached to, beeping in the background.

"Did you have a heart attack too?"

"A what?"

Holly rolled her eyes at me and set down the chart she'd been reading.

"You'll have to excuse us Mrs Di Maggio," she said and pulled the curtain around the bed for privacy.

Holly sat down on the edge of my bed and proceeded to bring out a gingerbread man from her white overcoat pocket, biting his head off as she played with her stethoscope.

"What am I doing here? And why am I not—," I pointed up above.

Holly lay back and looked up.

"That's the male renal ward. Trust me, you don't want to be up there."

"You know what I mean."

"Well..." Holly sat up and started swinging her stethoscope around. "Things didn't exactly go according to plan."

"You think?" and I held up my hands. One was attached to a monitor and the other to an incessantly noisy machine. I started to get flashbacks from the night before. "I didn't have my orders. They blew away before I could read them and then Leonardo said I had to go, but when I got to the bridge, the man was gone. I'm sorry," I said, "I was too late."

I realised now how precious time here was. Holly reached into her other coat pocket and handed me a folded-up piece of paper. I opened it and read the orders I had lost the night before.

"There is a young man, in despair. He has lost everything. Tonight, is Christmas Eve. At nine p.m. he will be at Bow Bridge. His name is Nathaniel Banks. Nathaniel is a professional golfer. In the last year, he has lost every match and every tournament. He has lost his ranking, his confidence and his self-belief. He has lost hope and lost faith. It is your job to help him find it again."

'I thought he was going to... I thought he had..." *jumped*. I'd got it all wrong.

"The good news is," Holly said, as she finished munching a mouthful of the decapitated and now armless gingerbread man, "You weren't too late. You met Nathaniel last night on the bridge."

She stood up. "The bad news is, he thought you were going to kill him..."

I cringed.

"...after you had mugged him." She reached down and switched on a flashing Christmas tree badge that was pinned onto her doctor's coat. She walked around the bed before saying, "Then, he thought you'd killed another man and dumped his body in the lake."

I slid further down the bed and under the covers.

Holly pulled them back. "And then he thought you were in the CIA. Isn't that funny?"

There was nothing funny about it.

"When you—" Holly mimed diving off the bridge. "He was convinced you had done what you thought he was going to do."

I was mortified.

"And you were both wrong."

I groaned. This was a mess.

"When the police arrived he told them that you were a veteran, who he thought was suffering from Post-Traumatic Stress Disorder after several tours of duty. Soooo, that's what we're going to use as your cover – you're an ex-Army vet. Which ironically is the truth."

I didn't want to be reminded of that nor did I want to be reminded of any of the events of the last twenty-four hours.

"Why do I need a cover?"

"Because you're going to be here for a while," she told me as she walked to the end of my bed.

"How long is 'a while'?" A while was an indefinite amount of time and I wanted to know exactly how long. A day? A week? A couple of weeks?

"For as long as it takes to complete your orders."

This was a nightmare.

"Let me get this clear in my head (which was throbbing) – I have to stay here, on earth, until I teach this Nathaniel Banks how to play golf?"

"Mr. Banks knows how to play golf and he plays it very well."

"Well clearly not otherwise I wouldn't have to be here at all!"

"He's lost his faith, not his ability."

"But I don't know anything about golf. I don't think I'm the right angel for the job."

Holly ignored me and handed me an A4 manila envelope.

"Your orders, ID, passport and everything else you'll need for your stay." She smiled sweetly and said, "Try not to lose them."

I reluctantly took possession of my new identity while Holly read my chart.

"And while you're here, you can't tell anyone you're an A-N-G-E-L," she quietly spelt out the word. "You don't have any celestial powers. You're human now, so look after your body," she warned. "You only get the one."

The one I'd got ached from head to toe.

"And I probably should tell you that it's had a few teething problems."

"What kind of teething problems?" I watched as Holly read my medical report.

"There were a few teeny, tiny, mechanical problems but it's nothing to worry about."

I remembered how I'd struggled to catch my breath the night before and the searing pain in my chest.

"What problems?" I wanted to know. "Holly!"

She kept her eyes fixed on the clipboard and mumbled something under her breath.

"I didn't hear that. Tell me what's wrong," I insisted.

"Oh, very well," she agreed, putting down the clipboard. "There was a problem with your heart, which wasn't detected before you left, but I fixed it, so yay!"

There was a buzzing sound. Holly's beeper had gone off again.

"I have to go," she told me as she pulled back the curtain.

"Wait!" I had so many questions, but Holly was already walking towards the door.

"I'll be back for you shortly Iris," she said to the old woman on her way past. "Merry Christmas," she called out and then she was gone.

Iris was still staring at me.

"Are you CIA?" she asked in a broad Brooklyn accent. "Look, my ticker might not be working but there's nothing wrong with my hearing."

"No, I'm not in the Central Intelligence Agency."

"FBI?"

"No, I'm not in the Federal Bureau of Investigation either."

Iris sat up in bed and pushed the huge round frames further up her nose; the thick glass magnifying eyes dulled with age but her mind was still razor-sharp. She reeled off different other secret service organisations I'd never even heard of and I denied involvement with them all.

"I'm ex-army," I told her, just to shut her up.

"And what's your interest in Nathaniel Banks?" Iris interrogated me.

"That is sensitive information that I'm not at liberty to discuss."

That was the wrong thing to say.

"I knew it!" she said, pointing a spindly finger at me. "I knew you were on a case. Is he being investigated? Is it fraud? Drugs? Money laundering?" Iris's imagination was running wild.

'No! It's none of those."

"Oh." She sounded disappointed that Nathaniel Banks wasn't a hardened criminal. I watched as she drummed fragile fingers off the bedspread, a network of blue veins clearly visible through thin, delicate skin. Wisps of white hair framed the fine features of a now frail face.

"It's a protection detail," I said, to prevent her accusing the young Mr. Banks of any more heinous crimes, which she was in the process of conjuring up. Her interest was piqued again.

"Has he been threatened? Is his life in danger? Is it a

criminal organisation? The Mafia?" She was getting excited and the numbers on her machine rose; the peeks heightened as the beeping became louder and faster.

"No, no," I insisted, as I tried to stop her.

"Is it from his wife?"

"Nathaniel Banks is married?" I was surprised; it was a revelation I wasn't expecting.

"Divorced," she drawled, re-positioning the pale pink cardigan she was wearing over her night dress. "Shouldn't you know that?"

"I have his paperwork," I waved the white envelope. "I just haven't had time to read it yet. Do you know Mr. Banks?"

She seemed to know everything about US national security so I was hoping she could impart some information about my charge that might help me.

"What can I say? The boy can swing a stick. At least, he could before his divorce. She was a piece of work." Iris proceeded to berate the former Mrs. Banks. "Never out of the tabloids. *Pah*, he's better off without her. It's that floozy's fault he can't play now."

I was intrigued to hear more, and Iris didn't disappoint. She launched into a full-scale character assassination of the blonde bombshell who had broken the young golfer's heart.

"Ran off with his caddie," she said, shaking her head.

"Really?" I listened to her every word, gripped by the unfolding drama.

"His best friend," she continued, as though this were a soap opera.

"Never!"

"Who does that? And then they sold their 'love' story to every trashy tabloid. Love – they don't know the meaning of the word," Iris said vehemently.

I was beginning to better understand why Nathaniel Banks had lost faith. There was a lot more to his story than Holly had revealed and it wouldn't be so easy to fix. I needed to speak to my CIA comrade-in-arms, and quick! I threw back the covers and groaned when I saw what I was wearing – bright red fluffy pyjamas emblazoned with a large Rudolph whose nose lit up. Beside the bed were white slippers with Christmas pudding pom poms, and to top it all off, a green dressing gown was draped over the back of a blue armchair. No doubt I had Holly to thank for this wardrobe choice.

"You a big Christmas fan then?" Iris remarked when she saw me.

"Huge fan," I lied, as I freed myself from the machines and went in search of the good doctor.

I walked along empty corridors, past a deserted nurses' station. The whole floor was eerily quiet. There was no sign of Holly, or anyone else. I took the lift down to the next level. The doors opened and I stepped out into a bright, crowded reception area decorated with tinsel, lights and a large inflatable snowman. If Holly was anywhere, this was where she would be.

"Hurry, Santa's coming!" shouted a nurse dressed as an elf, the little bell on the end of her hat ringing as she ran past.

A loud, "Ho! Ho! Ho!" sent excited children running after her, screaming with delight. I turned to see a large man, dressed as Santa walking slowly up the corridor, carrying a huge sack that I presumed was filled with presents.

"Quick!" The same nurse ushered me into a room filled with little children all looking expectantly at the door. "He's coming," the elf-nurse told them, and they squealed with delight.

I watched their eyes widen with excitement when they heard another, "Ho! Ho! Ho!" and just for a moment, when Santa walked through the door, I forgot how sick they all were. I didn't see illness, disease, wheelchairs, drips or oxygen tanks – I saw happy, smiling faces. Santa left his large sack in the middle of the floor.

"Is Mary here?" he asked, his loud voice seeming to fill the room.

A hairless little girl with swollen cheeks sat shyly on her mother's knee. Santa walked over to the small child and knelt beside her.

"I know you've been a very good girl all year, so this is for you," he said, handing her a present wrapped in pink paper. Her face lit up as she held it close.

It was Jimmy's turn next, then Gemma's. Susie sat

on the floor with a nurse dressed as a fairy. I watched her chest rise and fall in time with the oxygen being pumped through the two tubes inside her nostrils. She was too weak to open her present, so the Christmas fairy unwrapped a beautiful doll on her behalf. I saw pleasure take away pain, and happiness bring hope. I saw light where there had been darkness and joy where there had been despair. I saw Christmas through their eyes, and it was magical.

Torn paper lay all over the floor, the children were playing. I was about to leave the room when I heard Santa say, "And the last present is for Anna." He reached into his large sack and I waited to see which child had the same name as me. Then the man with a big bushy beard in the red suit walked towards me.

"This is for you," he said, and he handed me a cylindrical-shaped present.

"There must be some mistake." I wasn't a child, and I wasn't even meant to be here.

"Santa doesn't make mistakes."

I sheepishly took the gift.

"Merry Christmas," he boomed. "I'll be back next year."

As everyone clapped and cheered, I wondered how many of the little souls would still be here then.

"And I'll see you next Christmas, Anna Frost."

I didn't know how he knew my name but I was guessing Doctor Holly was behind this. There was one thing for certain: I most definitely *would not* be here next year.

"Thank you for the present," I called out to the man dressed as Santa, and with another "Ho! Ho! Ho!" he was gone.

5

A Festive Feast

A nurse dressed as a snowflake invited me to join everyone for Christmas dinner.

"That's very kind but no thank you," I politely declined. I had to find Holly.

"You can't miss it! There's turkey with stuffing and roast potatoes and buttery carrots with parsnips. And then for afters there's Christmas pudding with custard and cream." She sounded almost as enthusiastic about food as my feathered friend.

"On second thoughts, I will join you." I might not be able to find Holly but she would definitely be able to find food. I knew if she was still here there would be no way she could resist the temptation of that festive feast. "Lead the way," I said to the young nurse.

I followed Snowflake to the dining room, down a colourful corridor decorated with children's drawings. Parents, children and staff were starting to take their seats at large round tables, which filled the room, but there was no sign of Holly. I went back out and smells of roasting meat led me to the hot, steamy kitchen. Turkeys sat resting, waiting to be carved, their skins crisp and crackling. Trays of vegetables laced with rosemary were kept warm on oven shelves, as piping hot soup was ladled from large saucepans sitting on the stove. Holly wasn't in the kitchen either, so I followed the waiting staff carrying the bowls of soup and crusty bread back into the dining room. Snowflake met me at the door and showed me to my seat.

"This is Jack," she said, introducing me to the little boy sitting beside me at the table.

"I'm very pleased to meet you Jack." I reached out my hand in greeting but he kept his head down and his arms folded.

"I'm sorry," his mum apologised. "Jack," she tried, in an effort to coax her son, but he didn't move or speak.

"I'm afraid Jack missed seeing Santa earlier and he didn't get a present," his father explained.

"Oh no, that's terrible." I was genuinely upset for the little boy who looked up at me and I could see he'd been crying.

"Everyone got a present except me," he said, fighting back more tears.

"I'm sure Santa had a present for you," I said, but my words were of no comfort to him. "Here, you can have mine," I said, as I offered Jack my un-opened present sitting on the table. For a brief moment he looked happy but then Snowflake snatched it back.

"No, no, no," she scolded. "This is your present."

I scowled at the nurse. She then turned her attention to the little boy, tears now flowing down his face.

"I have a message for you," she told him.

A message wasn't wrapped in pretty paper. You couldn't play with a message. A message wasn't a toy!

"It's from Santa."

Now she had Jack's full attention.

"Would you like to hear what it is?" she teased.

He was vigorously nodding his head.

"He said that if you were a good boy and ate up all your dinner, he would come back with your present."

Jack sat up in his chair and started shovelling the soup into his mouth as fast as he could. I leaned over and whispered in his ear, "I knew he wouldn't forget you."

The turkey dinner with all the trimmings that followed the starter was devoured at the same speed. I kept my eye on the door as I chatted to Jack's parents, but Holly didn't turn up. There was no way she would've missed this if she was still here so I had to assume she'd left the building. I only hoped she hadn't left the planet.

"You don't happen to know anything about golf do you?" I asked Jack.

His spoon, now heaped with Christmas pudding, stopped in mid-air.

"Jack lives for golf," his father answered.

"Do you play?" I asked the little boy.

"I do. I did. I don't play anymore."

"You don't play at the moment," his mother corrected him. "You'll soon be back on the course."

"And back on the circuit. Jack was Junior State Champion last year," his father proudly told me.

"Jayden is State Champion now," the little boy said.

"Well, he won't be next year. You will be champ!" and his father stretched over to ruffle his son's hair. "My boy's a fighter."

It must've been very hard for him to watch other boys he'd played and beaten, now racing ahead while he was in hospital.

"Do you have many trophies?" I asked.

"Lots," he smiled widely.

"He has a trophy room," his father told me.

"Wow! You have that many?" I was impressed. "And who's your favourite player?"

Without hesitation he replied, "Nathaniel Banks."

"Really?" I was surprised.

"He's the best golfer in the world."

That wasn't strictly true. If it was, there would be no need for me to be here.

"He's not at the moment,' I corrected his biggest fan. "But don't worry, I'm going to fix him."

Jack looked surprised. I leaned over and kept my voice low so only he could hear, "I've been sent here to help him win again, like he did before."

Jack's eyes were wide with wonder. He sat for a moment then asked me, "Can you fix me too Anna?"

"No, Jack," I took his hand. "I can't fix you and do you know why?"

He shook his head.

"Because there's nothing to fix. You're perfect." He gave me a big smile. "Our Mr. Banks, on the other hand… Well, where do I start? He's going to take a lot of work."

"But he's brilliant!" Jack defended his hero.

"*Was*, he's not brilliant now," I told him, taking another mouthful of custard. "He's mediocre, at best."

"What's mediocre?" Jack asked.

"It means he's playing very badly and is why he's losing everything."

Jack mulled this over as I helped myself to more Christmas pudding.

"*Hmm*, this is delicious!" Holly would never miss this, and I concluded that she had definitely left.

"How long will it take you to fix him?"

"I don't know exactly," I answered truthfully. "But I hope not too long."

We were nearing the end of our dessert and my thoughts, like Jack's, returned to his present.

"Did you ask Santa for something to do with golf?" I thought he might have wanted a new bat or stick, or whatever the thing you played golf with was called.

He was nodding, "But I don't think I'll get what I asked for." He was sad again.

"What did you ask for?"

He looked at his mum and dad, "I can't say."

"Can you whisper it?"

He thought about it for a little while and then leaned over to whisper, "I wanted to meet Nathaniel Banks."

I was so disappointed for him. I knew for certain Santa did not have a Nathaniel Banks-shaped present in his sack. Jack would be devastated when he opened a toy train after he'd finished his Christmas pudding.

"What did you ask Santa for?" Jack quizzed me.

"I didn't ask him for anything."

Jack was eyeing the present Santa had given me.

"What do you want the most?" he asked me.

I wanted my old job back; I wanted to be a lieutenant in the EAA. Yet that wasn't what I wanted the most.

"Right now, what I most want is for Santa to make your Christmas wish come true."

Jack blushed.

"I like you," he said, with childlike honesty.

"Well Jack, I like you too."

Snowflake appeared to clear away Jack's empty bowl.

"Do you hear that?"

He listened for a moment and then shook his head. "I don't hear anything."

"Listen again," she said.

This time we all heard the distinctive, "Ho! Ho! Ho!"

"Santa!" Jack shouted excitedly as he waited for him to appear.

This was awful; he was going to be so disappointed. There was another, "Ho! Ho! Ho!" and then the door opened to reveal a much slimmer, slightly taller Santa than the one before. Either the other Santa had gone on a crash diet and had lunchtime liposuction, or this was another impersonator. Jack had been rendered speechless as he sat staring at the man dressed in a baggy red suit, standing in the doorway. It was Snowflake who led him to our table.

"I'm very pleased to meet you," Santa said, reaching out his hand.

"I'm Jack," he said.

"And I'm Nathaniel." I watched in amazement as the golfer pulled down his fake white beard to reveal a face I'd last seen before jumping off the bridge the night before.

Jack's mum was in tears; his dad had stood up and was shaking Nathaniel's hand. Meanwhile I was sitting in shock.

"And this is Anna," I heard Jack introduce me.

"Are you okay?" Nathaniel took my hand and kept hold of it. I could feel my face flush.

"I'm absolutely fine, couldn't be better," I said, breezily.

Nathaniel looked concerned. "I was worried."

I tried to free my hand but he kept a tight grip on it.

"I called the hospital to check how you were."

"Honestly, I'm great! There's no need to worry." I wanted him to let go.

Jack looked confused.

"You didn't tell me you knew Nathaniel," he said, sounding hurt. I felt like I'd betrayed the little boy.

"I don't know Nathaniel. We met very briefly, like for a second, last night and I didn't even know who he was." I was relieved to see that Jack believed me. "And anyway, Nathaniel isn't here to see me, he's here to see you."

Snowflake pulled up another seat and Nathaniel sat down beside Jack.

"I hear you're a great golfer."

"I was but I'm not now," Jack told his idol. "Now I'm mediocre." He looked very pleased with his use of the big word. I couldn't help but smile.

And then I spat out my pudding when I heard him add, "Just like you."

"Jack!" his mother said, aghast. "I'm so sorry."

"So, you think I'm mediocre?" Nathaniel looked bemused.

"No," Jack told him. "Anna does."

All their attention turned to me.

"But don't worry, she's been sent here to help you."

Oh my God! He was going to repeat everything I'd said. This was a disaster! I was quite sure that God, the

CIA, the Guardians and every other celestial department were not going to be happy. That information was probably classified.

"Anna's going to fix you."

I looked across the table at his parents who were glaring at me. I had managed to insult their son's idol and was in the process of ruining his Christmas wish. I was waiting for Nathaniel to get up and storm out. Nervously, I glanced over in his direction and saw he was smiling back at me.

"Anna's right," he told Jack and I could hear his parents breathe a collective sigh of relief. "I haven't been playing well and I do need help." He kept staring at me for what seemed like an age before saying, "And if you think Anna is the right person to help me, then the job is hers. It's your decision Jack."

I could see his little chest puff out with pride. I looked at the young boy who held my fate and Nathaniel's future in his hands. If he said no, then I'd fail in my task.

"Yes, Anna's the right one." He hadn't let me down.

"Congratulations Miss Frost, the job's yours," he said, smiling. "And Jack, I have something else for you." He reached inside his jacket and pulled out an envelope. Jack tore it open.

"Wow!" was all he could say.

"What is it?" I was curious.

"It's VIP tickets for Jack and his family to come

watch me play at the Open in June, and a two-weeks' stay at my academy where my team can help him get back on form."

"I'm going to see you win the Open!" Jack was so excited.

He believed in Nathaniel; he believed he would win. Sadly, I didn't see the same self-belief in Nathaniel's eyes. It was going to be hard work. What I needed was a little divine help from up above, in the shape of Holly.

"If you'll excuse me," I said, leaving to go in search of my fellow angel. "It's been a pleasure to meet you all, especially you Jack. Enjoy your Christmas present."

The little boy beamed, "I will."

I turned to go but he called out after me, "Don't forget yours Anna."

Santa's present was still on the table. I had forgotten all about it.

"Open it Anna, please! I want to see what you got."

I couldn't resist those big, brown eyes of his. "Okay then," I agreed, gently pulling back a piece of the paper.

"Rip it! Rip it!"

I tore it off and looked at the long cardboard tube.

"There's something inside. Look inside!"

I reached in and pulled out a rolled-up sheet of paper.

"What does it say?" Jack asked.

I couldn't believe what I was seeing. I was holding transfer papers from the CIA to the EAA on completion of my task. All I had to do was submit them. How was this possible?

Jack stood up on his chair so that he was face to face with me.

"Did Santa get you what you wished for?"

"Yes, he did," I told the little boy who threw his arms around me.

6

Fending for yourself

There was no doubt in my mind that Holly was behind this. I left Jack with Nathaniel and went in search of the elusive Christmas angel.

"Holly," I called out as I walked along the corridor, but there was no answer. "Holly?" I opened a door and called into the darkness but I was met with silence. Surely she hadn't just left me here? Then Snowflake appeared, pushing a medicine trolley.

"Could you page Doctor Holly for me?" I asked the nurse.

"We don't have a Doctor Holly, Anna." She was looking at me strangely.

I had been wandering around the corridors, calling out for an imaginary doctor, which I realised didn't look good.

"I'll just go find Jack," I said, and quickly stepped past her before she had someone come to examine me.

I continued my search but there was no sign of Holly

on the children's ward, so I decided to go back upstairs. I remembered she had told Iris she would be back later and this was later. Stepping out of the lift, I heard laughter coming from my room.

"Holly?" I called out.

"Surprise!" Leonardo said as I ran into the room.

He was lying across my bed, eating chocolates out of a large red box.

"What are you doing here?" I asked him.

"Charmin," Iris piped up. "Your good friend comes to visit you on Christmas Day and all you can say is, 'What are ye doin' here?'," she managed to mock and berate me at the same time.

"Leonardo," I said through gritted teeth. "It's so lovely to see you."

"Can you tell yer face that!" My response had done nothing to appease Iris who was brutally blunt.

Leonardo jumped up.

"The lovely Iris has been keeping me entertained while I've been waiting for you. She's been fabulous company."

Iris gave him a big smile. He was such a charmer!

"We've been reminiscing about the good old days," he told me.

"You broads these days get it easy. Back in my day…"

I felt I was about to be lectured and I was right, as Iris launched into a diatribe about how hard it was in the dark ages. Women didn't go to work; they stayed at home to look after their man as well as doing all the cooking, cleaning and bringing up the children. From the way Iris was looking at me, I think she was expecting me to run out, get married, give birth and tie myself to the kitchen sink. I was sorry to disappoint her but I had no intention of abandoning my profession to pander to the needs of any man either in heaven or on earth!

Leonardo on the other hand, was loving her verbal attack on me. I'd deal with him later. I edged towards the door as the diatribe continued.

"Oh look, there's Holly," I said. "Holly!" I called, and stepped out into the empty corridor.

Leonardo ambled out after me, bidding *adieu* to his new best friend.

"Where's Holly?" he looked confused.

"She's not here," I whispered crossly, taking his arm and dragging him out of Iris's earshot. "I've been looking everywhere for her. Have you seen her?"

"I've just got here," Leonardo said, as he leaned against the wall. "I thought I'd call in and see how your first assignment was going."

"It's going great! Everything is just tickety-boo!" I said sarcastically.

"So, what is it?" Leonardo was grinning from ear to ear.

"What's what?" I was distracted, wondering where

on earth Holly could be.

"Your assignment."

"Oh yes, that. I have to help this guy who has 'lost everything'."

"And I take it he hasn't?"

"Well he has… and he hasn't," I answered honestly.

Leonardo looked puzzled.

"Remember when I left, I thought he was going to jump off the bridge because my orders had said that. It turned out that was just where I was supposed to meet him."

"So, what happened?" He was curious.

I really didn't want to tell him.

"There was a bit of a misunderstanding and I jumped off the bridge," I muttered under my breath in the hope he wouldn't hear. Unfortunately for me, he had better hearing than Iris and he roared with laughter.

"You jumped off the bridge?" Leonardo was in hysterics.

"It's not funny!"

I stood with my arms folded, waiting for him to stop.

"Oh, but it is! Are you sure he's not the angel and you're the one who needs help? This is priceless." Tears of laughter were rolling down his cheeks.

"I told you I wasn't cut out to be a Guardian. Anyway, I won't be one for much longer. Look, I've got my papers."

Leonardo eventually stopped laughing long enough

to look at my transfer papers.

"Did Holly give them to you?" he asked.

"No." I knew my admission was going to send him into another fit of laughter but there was no avoiding it so I said, "Santa did."

"Santa?" he howled. "This is the gift that just keeps on giving!"

"Obviously it was someone from up above, dressed as Santa," I tried to explain. "The point is, I have my papers. Now, I just need to find Holly. I need to know how long this job will take so I can get back to file them. I thought I'd only be here for a few hours."

"You still haven't told me what it is you have to do."

My official orders were to help Nathaniel Banks who had lost everything and by everything, I mean on the golf course rather than everything in his life. He still had all his money, his job and his great big property portfolio. Whoever wrote these orders needed to be much clearer. He was in despair because he'd lost all faith, hope and self-belief, along with all his matches and every single tournament he'd played in last year. I had to bring him back from despair, be a shining light and help him find his way again. I paraphrased the orders for Leonardo's benefit.

"There's a guy down below, who was once a great golfer. Now he's crap and I have to help him win again."

"When you say, 'down below'…?" He waited for me to clarify.

"He's down there," and I pointed down to the floor.

"He's in hell?"

"No! He's downstairs in the children's ward."

"He's a child?"

"No, no." I obviously wasn't explaining this very well. "He's a grown man, visiting a child. So, how long do you think this will take?" I was desperate to know.

"Well, that depends," Leonardo said. "It could take a few weeks or a few months. Maybe even a year."

"A year?" I shrieked. "I can't be here for a year!"

"Don't worry, the time will fly by," Leonardo tried to reassure me but failed.

"No, it bloody well won't! Up above it would feel like that but down here, it will feel like a year. A very *long* year." I had to find a way out of this. "Could you put my papers in for me?"

I was hoping and praying he would agree. If Leonardo filed them, then once I got my transfer, they could send someone else.

"I'm sorry but no. You have to do it yourself."

"Are you sure?" I was hoping for any shadow of doubt.

"Positive."

"Bugger that!" (I'd discovered that as a human I could swear).

"You will just have to help your young man improve his game and help him win again."

"Shit! Bugger! Damn! Fuck!"

7

A foot in the door

In a less than good mood, I left Leonardo and ran back
to the lift. I was hoping that my young man, unlike
Holly, hadn't left the building, although hope faded fast
when the doors opened and I saw that the children had
returned to their rooms and family and friends had gone
home. Then, as if by magic, Snowflake appeared.

"Anna." She seemed pleased to see me. "I'm so glad
you came back. Jack hasn't stopped talking about you!
It's all *Anna this, Anna that, Anna's wonderful!* Anna's
the best thing since sliced bread it seems!"

It made me very happy to hear that.

"Would his new 'best friend Anna' like to take him
his drink?"

"I'd love to," I replied, and Snowflake handed me the
mug.

"His room is the first door on the right."

I carried the hot drink carefully up the corridor.

"Knock, knock," I said, walking in.

"Anna!" he smiled when he saw me.

"Did someone order hot chocolate with melted marshmallows?"

"Me! Me!" he called out.

I walked over and sat down on the bed beside him.

"Did you have a nice Christmas?" I asked.

"The best Christmas ever! I got to meet Nathaniel Banks!" He still sounded in awe.

"I know, and you're going to go to his academy. Isn't that great?" I expected him to be excited about that too but he was quiet.

"When am I going home Anna?"

I didn't know what was wrong with him, and I felt guilty that I hadn't asked.

"Are you feeling better?"

"Much better," he said, sipping his hot chocolate.

"Then I think it will be soon. Are you ready to go home?" It was a stupid question – he was in hospital, away from his mum and dad, his family and friends. He was away from golf so of course he wanted to go home.

"I'll miss everyone here."

"And they'll miss you too," I told him.

I'd only met Jack today and I was going to miss him. It would be hard for the doctors and nurses to say goodbye. I could see how fond they all were of him, especially Snowflake.

"You can come visit."

"Can I?" he sounded excited.

"Of course you can!" However, the truth was that once this door closed, his memories would fade. He might want to come back initially but he was just a child who'd move on. His time here would become a distant memory and then disappear forever. "But you might not want to. Not once you're on the golf course again!"

He gave me a big smile.

"Will you come see me?" he asked.

"Try and stop me."

"Nate said he would come too."

"Nate?" I said, raising an eyebrow.

"His friends call him Nate." He grinned at me.

"Do they indeed? Well, I might need some help with your friend Nate. Would you like to help me?"

"Yes!" He looked pleased to be asked but before I could say any more about the important task at hand, Snowflake appeared at the door.

"Okay, young man, it's time for bed."

I stood up to let the nurse do her job. I watched her check his vitals and make notes. Jack looked small and pale lying on the bed in the neon light of the darkened room. It was nighttime but monitors and machines still flashed. No hospital room was ever in darkness. There was always light.

"Did you have a lovely Christmas?" Snowflake asked the same question I had, as she tucked him in.

He nodded his head.

"And what was the best bit?"

He looked over at me then said, "Meeting Anna."

"Goodnight Jack," I said, as I blew him a kiss from the doorway. "Sweet dreams."

When I walked back out into the corridor, I was surprised to see Nathaniel standing by the nurses' station.

"How's Jack?" he asked when he saw me come out of the room.

"He's going to sleep," I told him. "It was very kind of you to come visit him." I didn't think many celebrities would give up their precious time to fulfil a young boy's wish, especially on Christmas Day.

"I actually came here to see you." He looked a little awkward. "I wanted to check you were okay… after last night," he admitted, shifting from foot to foot.

Silence followed.

"That was a misunderstanding, and honestly, I'm fine," I reassured him.

"I'm really glad to hear that, and I'm glad I got to visit Jack too. When Nurse Aitkens saw me, she told me I had a big fan in the hospital. She said it would make his Christmas if I visited him."

"And it did," Snowflake (Nurse Aitkens) said as she appeared beside us. "He's sleeping now," she said in a hushed voice. "Thank you, both of you, for making it such a special day for him."

We said goodnight to the young nurse and I walked with Nathaniel back towards the lift.

"I know who you are." He kept his voice low, looking around to check no one else was listening.

"I don't think you do." I was sure of that.

"Your commanding officer told me."

Oh, holy crap! The colonel was here?

"What did he tell you?"

"*She*," Nathaniel corrected me.

Unless the colonel had had a sex change since I left heaven, I was certain my commanding officer was not a 'she'.

"Lieutenant Colonel Holly."

"Oh, the lieutenant colonel." I was amazed she hadn't promoted herself to commander-in-chief!

"I saw her earlier today when I came to the hospital. She wanted to explain what happened last night."

"And what exactly did she tell you?" I was curious to know just how much she had divulged. If she'd told him I was an angel I was going to kill her! It didn't matter that she was dead already. It was against the law for Nathaniel to know that.

"She told me that after the army you worked in the field as a CIA operative, but it wasn't for you."

Technically, I couldn't fault her for telling him the truth.

"I think that what you do is great and you're obviously passionate about your job. You cared so much when you thought that man had jumped last night, you were prepared to risk your own life."

I felt bad that Nathaniel was getting the wrong impression of me. It made me feel uncomfortable. I was on that bridge so I could save him and get back to heaven – back to the EAA – as quickly as humanly possible. It was a self-serving act, not a heroic one.

"The lieutenant colonel said that you still did consultancy work for the CIA but that you were now working as an independent."

An independent what? I wondered.

"Life coach," Nathaniel told me.

So, that was my cover.

"She spoke very highly of you. Said that you were the best in the business."

I thought it was Jack who'd got me the job with Nathaniel, but it appeared that wasn't the case.

Nathaniel talked on: "I meant what I said earlier — about the job. I'm sure you're in great demand and I don't know if you have the time but I'd really like it if you could help me. You were right last night. I have lost everything. I just didn't know how much until I met you. Can you help me?"

"Absolutely!" I assured the golfer.

Nathaniel Banks realised that he needed help and he wanted help. This would be a piece of cake! And speaking of cake, first thing in the morning I would resume my search for Holly. At least now I knew she hadn't abandoned me. Once found, we could come up with a battle plan to fix the young golfer and before I knew it, I would be back in heaven where I belonged.

8

Far, far away

"*Bonjour, bonjour,*" Leonardo greeted, as he flounced into the room carrying a handbag and wheeling a suitcase. "*How are we this morning?*"

I knew he was speaking French, but I didn't know what he was saying.

"Sorry, I forgot that you don't understand other languages down here."

"What do you mean, 'down here'?" asked Iris who missed nothing it seemed.

"We're from way up," Leonardo said quickly, having been caught off guard.

"North," I affirmed, helping him out.

"Yes, way up north, where they speak French." Leonardo hoped this would satisfy the old woman. How wrong he was!

"You're from Canada?" she drawled.

"Yes, Canada," Leonardo lied. "Land of mountains and Mounties. I could see myself as a Mountie, riding around all day with men in uniform. *Hmm*, heaven. Speaking of which, courtesy of Sebastian."

He dragged the heavy suitcase up onto the bed and pulled the curtain for privacy.

"Get changed," he told me. "It's time to go."

"She doesn't sound like she's from Canada," Iris said, talking about me as though I wasn't in the room.

Leonardo rolled his eyes.

"She's an alien," he called out before hauling me up and then out of bed. "Chop, chop," he said as he clapped his hands.

"My family came here during the war," I heard Iris say as I started to change. "We were one of the lucky ones. So many gone. My aunt, my cousins, my sister, all gone." I could hear her voice cracking with the emotion of painful memories.

"Gone to a better place," Leonardo said, but his words were of no comfort to the old woman.

"Came over on the boat…" Her voice sounded far away, and I sensed that she was thinking back to when she was on the deck of the ocean liner, which had carried what was left of her family safely across the sea. "Did you come over on the boat?" she shouted at me.

Iris seemed to be under the illusion that I was hard of hearing.

"No, I flew."

"My father was in carpets. Started his own business in '49. They never went back… no one ever goes back."

Iris raised her voice again, "Are you going back?"

I pulled back the curtain.

"I'm definitely going back Iris!" and I meant it. "Okay, I'm ready for action."

"Put this on first, it's cold outside," instructed Leonardo, handing me a long cashmere coat. "Iris, it has been a pleasure." He picked up the old lady's hand and gently kissed it. Blue veins rippled under paper-thin skin.

"Go on, get outta here," she said, shooing us out of the room.

"*Adieu, adieu,*" Leonardo said, as he left with a flourish.

Iris peered at me through rimmed glasses as I walked towards the door.

"Let me tell you angel, here's a nice place to live."

I couldn't tell if angel was a term of affection or if the wily old woman had seen right through me...

"Bye Iris," I smiled and stepped out into the corridor. "Have I time to see Jack before we go?" I asked Leonardo when we were in the lift.

"There's always time," he said.

I saw Nurse Aitkens as we stepped out into the children's ward.

"Perfect timing," she greeted us. "Jack is just waiting for his parents to arrive."

He was sitting on his bed, dressed in jeans and a hooded top.

"Look at us, all dressed up," I said, as I walked in.

"I'm going home," the little boy told me.

"I know." I sat down beside him on the bed.

"Are you going home too Anna?"

"Not yet," I told him, "I still have work to do."

"I'm sad you're not going home."

"Don't be," I said, squeezing his hand. "I'll be going home very soon."

"Do you want me to wait for you?"

"That's so thoughtful but I want you to go back with your parents. Remember, I have to help Nathaniel first and then I can go home too."

"You'll fix him Anna."

"Keep your fingers crossed," and I smiled when I saw him cross his fingers on both hands. "I think I hear your parents," I said, as I heard them outside talking to Nurse Aitkens. "Come give me a big hug." I kissed the top of Jack's head and hugged him hard. "I'll see you soon."

"Promise?" He looked up at me with his big, brown eyes.

"I promise. I'll see you at the academy."

I left him with an ecstatic Paul and Nancy, who were delighted to be taking their son home.

"I'm so happy you got to say goodbye," said the young nurse who was dressed in pale blue scrubs as I stepped back into the corridor. "I'm going to miss him. He's been a little ray of sunshine the whole time he's been here."

"How long has it been?" I asked her.

"Nearly a year."

I had no idea he'd been in hospital for that long.

"Jack had a brain tumour and it caused paralysis. He's put up quite a fight this last year. He's had operations, chemotherapy and a lot of physiotherapy. He is in remission but the paralysis has left a muscle weakness on his right side, which means he won't play golf again. At least, not at the level he was playing before, which is a shame because he was really good."

I was so proud of the little boy who held his mother's hand as he left his hospital room for the last time. I wished that I could've fixed him so that he could play golf again, like he used to, but that wasn't what I was here to do. Those weren't my orders. Yet I could fix Nathaniel for him. Jack was a fighter and he reminded me that I was one too. I was on a mission and I was more determined than ever to succeed. Mr. Banks was about to go to golf boot camp. I waved to Jack and blew him one last kiss.

"See you soon little one," I said, and with that, I left.

9

Flight of the Falcon

Leonardo whistled for a yellow cab and we jumped in.

"Where are we going?"

"My place," he told me.

I was shocked.

"You have a place *here*?" I didn't just mean in New York, I meant on earth.

"A little *pied-à-terre*, for whenever I'm in town."

I watched from the window of the cab as it weaved its way through the wide arterial avenues which pumped life around the city. Its wipers went back and forth, clearing soft flakes of snow. I thought of the little snow globe on my desk, and tried to see beyond the tops of the towering buildings, but I couldn't.

Instead, I cleared condensation from the small viewfinder and observed life in the Big Apple as it passed me by. Native New Yorkers walked briskly along busy sidewalks; their energetic pace and sense of purpose propelling them at speed towards their destination. In contrast, we drove slowly along Fifth Avenue until finally we stopped in front of an impressive stone building.

Our footsteps echoed on the marble floor of the lobby. I was engulfed in an aroma of white lilies emanating from a huge floral arrangement perched on top of a stone plinth. An operator dressed in a green tailcoat pulled back metal grills and Leonardo and I stepped inside the lift. This one was the most luxurious yet, with plush carpet, a brass rail and mirrored glass. A concerto accompanied us on our ascent.

"The maestro," Leonardo winked, as Mozart's music played.

The operator straightened his jacket and stood in silence, with his shoulders back. He stared straight ahead as we went all the way to the top.

"Welcome to my humble abode," Leonardo said, as we stepped inside his magnificent home.

"Wow!" I said, as I surveyed the sumptuous interior of the large penthouse.

Leonardo walked over and stood statuesque in front of a huge fireplace. He watched as I took in my surroundings. There were hand woven Moroccan rugs, ornate cornices and exquisitely carved Chippendale furniture. Beautifully painted works of art hung on the walls; timeless pieces that took me on a tour through history – from the Orient, along the spice trail, through Italy, France and England, to the new world. A grandfather clock chimed.

"Let me show you the view." Leonardo opened wooden-framed glass doors and I followed him out onto a spectacular roof terrace. Cream-cushioned sofas surrounded a tiled table. There was a firepit in front of a bar, and a swing seat rocked back and forth in the breeze. A falcon flew down.

"This is Nightshade." The bird of prey gave a shrill call. "Isn't she beautiful?"

Leonardo fed her a piece of meat. She held it in powerful talons and tore at the flesh with her razor-sharp beak. Tense and alert, her eyes moved constantly. Then, with a final cry, she opened her wings and took flight. Transfixed by the acrobatics of her aerial display, I watched as she soared and glided, then spun and dived in the skies above Central Park. I looked heavenward. Somewhere up above there were angels. I no longer had my wings, and I envied the falcon.

"Once you have tasted flight, you'll forever walk on the earth with your eyes skyward, for there you have been and there you long to return."

Leonardo was right but I couldn't return, not yet. I had a job to do first.

"What if I can't help him Leonardo?" Doubt had started to creep in. "I might never get back."

"You'll get back to where you belong," he said, putting a reassuring arm around my shoulder.

Soft snowflakes started to fall again. I looked down

on Central Park, just as Leonardo and I had looked down on the same scene a few days before.

"What do you see?" he asked me again.

Everything had changed; my position, my perspective, my sight. I was human now and could no longer see with angel eyes.

I looked down at the huge expanse of park covered in a blanket of snow and I remembered my childhood. I saw myself laughing as I ran under a tunnel of trees. I had to be fast before they reached down to tickle me. Bronze statues came to life and shared in my adventures. The Mad Hatter would count to ten as Alice and I went to hide. We were easy to find; our girlish giggling always gave us away. Balto, the lovable husky dog, faithfully followed me everywhere. Sometimes we'd be stalked by the cougar who was always on the prowl for prey. Then we would run to the fountain, where the angel of the waters watched over me from on high. I always knew she would keep me safe. Those were happy times.

"What do you see?" Leonardo asked again.

"A playground," I told him.

"Well then, let's go play."

"Wait!" I stopped him in his tracks. "I need to get to work."

"There's plenty of time for that."

No, there isn't!

"I have a job to do." The sooner I got started, the

sooner I'd be finished and on my way back home.

"I know but it's Christmas and no one works over the holidays."

"I do. Remember I'm a Christmas Incident Angel? Ergo, I work at Christmas."

"And you should remember that all work and no play makes Anna a very dull little girl indeed."

I wasn't a child, and I didn't need playtime.

"I need to get home." It was all right for him – he could go home any time he wanted.

"You will get home." He tried to reassure me. "But you can't start work until the new year."

"What?" I wailed.

"I'm going to try to not take offence that you don't want to spend the holidays with me."

"I'm sorry, but that's such a long time."

"Nonsense, it's a few days, and just think about all the fun we can have."

All I could think about was putting on my uniform and picking up my sword again, but clearly that wasn't going to happen any time soon. I was just going to have to be patient (although I'd never been very good at that). I think when God was handing out patience, I was at the back of the queue. To be honest, I don't think I was even in the queue.

"I can show you what life is like in the city that never sleeps."

"*Hmm.*" I wasn't convinced.

Leonardo launched into a rendition of Frank Sinatra's 'New York, New York' in an attempt to try and entice me to see the city.

What was it about Guardians and singing?

Oh, dear God please make him stop! I prayed as he continued to belt out the classic.

I gave in, "Okay, I'll go but only if you stop singing."

"Deal," said Leonardo, and he ceased immediately.

"So where are your *vagabond shoes* going to take me first?"

"Let's start down there."

I had to admit it would be nice to revisit old haunts, without anyone knowing who I was or where I came from. I would be an inconspicuous ghost going over old ground, walking in the footsteps of my past.

"Lead the way," I said to Leonardo, and we set off on a trip down memory lane.

10

Federico and a Fluffball

Leonardo and I walked along the Mall in Central Park, under a snow-covered canopy of intertwined trees. Light fell through their vaulted branches and cast long shadows on the wide avenue. These majestic elms were the tickling trees of another time. I remembered weaving my way around their trunks, dashing and darting from one to the other. I was lost in the memory and oblivious to all that was going on around me. It was someone continually calling out, "Lucy!" that finally alerted me to the oncoming danger. However, by then it was too late.

I looked up to see a large, brown Labrador bounding down the Mall. She was charging straight for me with her tongue hanging out. I had no time to think, let alone react. In an instant she was airborne and in the next, I was lying flat on my back; the lovable dog licking my face as I lay on the ground.

"Lucy!" Her owner caught up with her and pulled her

off me. "Bad girl!" she scolded the dog, who looked baffled.

"It's fine," I said as I scrambled to my feet. I gave Lucy an affectionate pat and her tail wagged wildly.

Her owner eyed me suspiciously.

"Come Lucy," she commanded.

There was no sorry nor asking if I was okay. She simply turned around and haughtily walked off, dragging the big brown dog behind her. Lucy took one last look before lumbering off behind her snooty owner.

"What was that all about?" I asked a bemused Leonardo.

"It's a side effect," he said.

"Of what?"

"Of being here."

That didn't make any sense.

"Well, why didn't Lucy knock *you* over?"

"It's different for everyone who comes down."

I was sceptical until a spaniel brought me a ball and a German Shepherd came to heel; a retriever wanted me to play fetch and a pit bull lay down on the path, refusing to move until I'd rubbed its belly. Their owners looked confused, annoyed and even angry that their loyal companions were betraying them. These public displays of affection for a complete stranger were out of character. I could see that they blamed me, but it wasn't my fault that I was the Piped Piper of pooches.

I watched as one small fluffball bounced across the

snow, a pink bow and pink tongue appearing and disappearing as she hopped towards me, closely followed by a young girl wearing spotted Wellingtons and a red velvet coat. She skipped along behind the runaway dog, abandoning her parents and the half-finished snowman they were building. I knelt down to pet the little dog who gave me her paw.

"What's her name?" I asked the young girl who was studying me intently.

"Ella Wella." The bundle of fluff ran back and forth between us, "It's short for Prunella."

"That's a very pretty name," I told her. "And what's yours?"

"Clarissa Veronica Amelia Huntley," announced the little girl who wore her hair in pigtails, which were visible beneath her red velvet hat. "What's your name?" she asked me.

"Anna."

She waited for a moment, "Is that it? Just Anna?"

"Just Anna. And this is Leonardo."

Leonardo bowed but Clarissa kept staring at me.

"What are you?"

That caught me off guard.

"*Um*, I'm a life coach," I answered, trying out my cover story but she didn't seem convinced.

"What do you do?" she continued to interrogate me, and I wondered for a moment if she was related to Iris.

"I help people."

"Are you an elf?" she carried on, quizzing me.

"No," I told her, and she looked disappointed.

"Elves help Santa," she explained. "They report back if you've been good or bad. You should be an elf."

I'd had quite enough career changes lately; I certainly didn't want another one.

"We had an elf," she informed me.

"Really?" I was surprised to hear that.

"Yes, he comes every year. Normally he sits on the shelf but this year, do you know where I found him?"

"No." I had a feeling she was going to tell me.

"In the bath with naked Barbies and a bottle of Prosecco."

Her elf sounded as if he should be on Santa's naughty list.

"He's gone back to the North Pole."

Probably for a detox and some sex therapy, I thought.

"Clarissa," I heard her name being called.

Clarissa picked up Ella Wella. "I have to go," she announced and off she went, back to build a snowman.

I stood watching the young family as they played in the fairytale setting. Once upon a time that was what I had wished for – a husband, a child and a dog.

"They can see that love," Leonardo said, as though he could read my mind.

I linked arms with the dark angel whom I was growing very fond of. We continued on our walk; the first of many over the coming days.

I experienced the sights, sounds, tastes and smells of this amazing city with my celestial companion. We ate hotdogs dripping with onions on street corners, under massive neon signs. Leonardo shared his passion for art as we wandered around both the Guggenheim and the Museum of Modern Art. We took the ferry across to Ellis Island and sailed past the Statue of Liberty. A towering symbol of freedom, she had become a beacon of light and hope. I looked out over the city from the top of the Empire State building and poured maple syrup over pancake stacks as we sat in a New York diner.

It was like being re-born.

I needed this time with Leonardo to get used to life on earth. There were limitations, restrictions and rules I needed to learn, and Leonardo was a great teacher, a great guide and great company. However all too soon, my time with him was coming to an end.

The following day I was to fly down to start work with Nathaniel. I would fly, by plane, from JFK to Miami, Florida. Apparently, this assignment necessitated a new wardrobe. So in the absence of Sebastian, Leonardo had engaged the services of a personal shopper called Federico who had spent most of the afternoon running back and forth from the shop floor, bringing various outfits for Leonardo to vet.

Federico had returned with yet another armful of clothes, which he was now hanging on a rail, in preparation for Leonardo's inspection. This particular consignment was from Bloomingdale's sports department.

"Yes, no, no, yes, absolutely, definitely not," I heard Leonardo mutter as he passed judgement on each of the outfits.

"*Hmm*, I don't know about this one."

"I love it!" Federico enthused. "It's a Pippy Polly Paavola."

"I'm not sure it will work." Leonardo clearly had reservations.

"It will," said Federico, who was convinced by the creation.

"It's the colour that's concerning me."

I opened the drapes to see Federico holding a bright yellow dress with a frilly skirt which would barely cover my modesty let alone anything else!

"I am not wearing that!" I hadn't been asked for my opinion but on this occasion they were getting it.

"It's a statement piece," Federico declared, defending the dreadful dress.

"Well, I'm making a statement," I told him. "I will wear that when hell freezes over!"

"We'll take it," Leonardo told him.

Federico took the couture creation with a smug look in my direction.

I was fuming.

"That will be all," Leonardo said, as he ushered him out of the room before I vented my anger on the annoying personal shopper.

"Have everything packed and sent to me this evening."

"Straightaway sir." He left, delighted to be of service and no doubt thrilled at the prospect of the huge commission coming his way.

"I am going to Miami but Pippy Polly what's-her-name's dress is not coming with me," I said as the shopping attendant wheeled my new wardrobe of work clothes out of the room.

Leonardo called for Federico again and I assumed it was to tell him to ditch the diabolical dress.

"Sir?" Federico eagerly hurried back into the room.

"Have you sent the dress I asked for earlier?"

"It's already been delivered," he told him.

"Grazie," and Leonardo dismissed him for the second, and I hoped, last time.

"What dress?" I asked.

"Tonight Cinderella, you are going to the ball."

"Has Pippy Polly Pavlova designed the dress?" I asked. "Because if she has, no I'm not going."

Leonardo laughed.

"No, she hasn't designed it."

I still had reservations about what Leonardo had chosen for me; his taste was not to be trusted. I decided I would wait to see what the gown looked like before I agreed to go anywhere. If it was anything like the

Pavlova palaver from before, Cinderella would be staying at home!

11

Forbidden Fruit and Fireworks

There was no need to worry. When we got back to the apartment, I found laid out on my bed a fabulous, fairytale frock fashioned from the finest fabric. It was simply stunning. I held it up against me and did a twirl as I stood in front of a full-length gilded mirror. Smells of lavender and patchouli rose up from steamy waters that filled an ivory bath. I walked across the warm oak floor to where it sat on gilded feet and, letting my robe slip down, I stepped into the hot, sweet-smelling water, through the rose petals covering the surface. As I soaked in the scent-filled bath, I thought about how much my world had changed in such a short space of time.

I had been devastated when I'd been transferred from the EAA. The army was who I was; I excelled at being a soldier. I'd been to earth many times before with my battalion. I was given my orders and I carried them out – without emotion, feeling or connections ever made. However, this time it was different. I thought about Jack and the battles he had fought so bravely in the short time he'd been here. He deserved a medal for the courage he'd shown, and I wished again that I could help him; that I could fix him.

A cool breeze blew in through the open window. The long, white, sheer voile curtains flew up and floated in the air. They reminded me of angel wings.

I was reluctant to leave the warm water but there was no more time for reverie. I had to get dressed. The night air was cold against my skin as I stood in front of the huge, ornate mirror that leaned against the bedroom wall. As I pulled on white stockings, I wondered if Sebastian had sent these down.

I put on the couture creation Leonardo had chosen for me and was amazed by the alluring apparition reflected in the mirror as I fastened the final few buttons. From below a fitted bodice, flounced a skirt brimming with black and white hand-sewn roses. I swept up my hair and pinned in a few small white roses, which lay on the dressing table. Eyeliner enhanced my eyes; so too eyelids that were coloured with a shimmering gold powder. I blended blusher into high cheekbones and applied a lip gloss before stepping back to study the finished result.

I found Leonardo sitting on the wall of the roof terrace. He'd changed out of his dark jeans and into leather trousers. His black silk shirt was open, revealing a leather necklace and a silver cross hanging on a chain.

The alabaster skin of his bare chest looked like sculpted marble in the moonlight.

"You look beautiful Anna," he told me as I lifted up the hem of the full skirt and taking silent steps in satin slippers, I walked across the terracotta-tiled terrace and took a seat beside Leonardo. Above us thousands of twinkling stars sparkled in a vast, velvety blackness. I looked up but I couldn't see what I knew was there.

"You see everything differently here," Leonardo said. "It's a different world."

I thought of the one we'd left behind; the world I wanted to go back to. My world was the army. It was all I'd ever known; all I'd ever wanted. It seemed so far away now and completely out of reach.

"I can't see it," I said with a longing.

"You don't have to see it to know it's there."

I wondered if Holly was watching us. I wondered if I'd ever get back. I wondered where my battalion was and in what war they were fighting. I wondered about Jack and wondered what the new year would bring for him. I looked out across the skyline sparkling in the night sky.

When I'd looked down before I saw only the bad that needed fixing; I looked for any reason to wield my sword. Those people and places were still there and no doubt the EAA was taking care of business, but there was also good in the world and I was learning to appreciate the beauty of life and what it was to live. I'd never expected to enjoy myself here or be moved by life itself, but by meeting Jack and spending time with Leonardo, something was changing – I was beginning to get lost in the fairytale.

"It's magical," I said.

"It is," Leonardo agreed. "And here's to a magical night," he toasted.

We each took a sip of the cold, crisp champagne, which fizzed and bubbled in our long-stemmed flutes.

"So, Cinders, shall we go to the ball?"

He stood up and held out his hand.

"Yes," I said to the dark angel.

I felt like a fairytale princess as I stepped into the black limousine waiting downstairs. Hordes of partygoers had taken to the streets, but we weren't joining the revellers heading for Times Square. We drove out of the city, past a streaming sea of car lights, past flashing neon advertising signs, and from Long Island the illuminated skyline of Manhattan receded into the distance.

As we drove along the coast, I wondered what the night and the new year would bring for me. Mine was a story still waiting to be told and I marvelled at the mystery and meaning of life as I looked up at countless stars, shining in an infinite space stretching far beyond my imagination. Both my vision and perspective were restricted by the human form I'd taken. I tried to rise above it, but it was impossible. I would never again see through an angel's eyes until I had *shuffled off this mortal coil.*

"Put this on," Leonardo said, handing me a delicate, black bejewelled mask, as we approached our destination. "It's a masquerade ball." I watched as he pulled on a full face mask.

"What is that?" I was horrified when I saw it had two huge protruding horns.

"I'm a horny devil," came his muffled reply.

Well, that was beside the point.

"God isn't going to be happy," I said, as I slid over towards the door. I wanted to keep a safe distance from the thunderbolt I was expecting to strike Leonardo down. Thankfully, there was no divine retribution and we made it to the party in one piece.

"This looks very grand," I said, as Leonardo took my arm and led me up the steps of the magnificent mansion.

Black and white harlequins danced up and down, serving champagne to the arriving masses.

"The car will pick us up again, just after midnight. If we get separated, meet me here and don't be late. You have an early morning flight."

"Copy that," I said, acknowledging his orders.

"And try not to sound like GI Jane," Leonardo said, as we were ushered inside.

I was tempted to salute him but I didn't. Instead, I took in my opulent surroundings – a stringed ensemble playing in the huge entrance hall, two enormous paintings hanging either side of a sweeping staircase, at the top of which I caught the briefest glimpse of a stained-glass window, the tiny pieces of coloured glass illuminated by a colossal chandelier suspended from the high ceiling. When I turned around again, Leonardo was gone.

Left to my own devices I wandered through rooms filled with glamorous guests and priceless works of art. Masterpieces of the Renaissance hung beside modern pieces. There were artefacts, ornaments and objects every museum in the world would want. Seduced by a sensual sculpture, I reached out to touch the cold marble of a muscled male nude, marvelling at the delicate detail carved into an unforgiving stone.

"It's a Bernini."

A figure was standing beside me, wearing a porcelain mask and white cape. He too reached out to touch the powerful nude who held a diaphanous-dressed girl in his arms. His fingertips pressed into flesh that looked real.

"He breathed life into every piece he created, and everyone I look at takes my breath away." He continued to caress the carved couple. "He was a master of seduction."

"It's exquisite," I agreed.

A waiter stopped to offer me a canapé, served on a silver platter. It was delicious! I found that I was really starting to enjoy food (although not quite as much as Holly). I don't think it was possible for anyone to enjoy food as much as her but still, I was developing a much greater appreciation for the local cuisine.

I followed the tray of tasty morsels out into the garden. Fairy lights flickered, and flames rose from torches illuminating the lawn. A jazz band played, and everyone was dancing wildly on a custom-built dance floor, on the grass and on the tables. A passing waitress, her body painted to look like a leopard stopped to offer me a cocktail. I took a tall glass filled with an orange liquid and watched as she continued to prowl through the masked revellers, carrying colourful concoctions to the partygoers. I sipped the sweet spicy drink through a straw. It tasted so good! I finished one and promptly took another. This next one was bright green and came with a sparkler.

I hadn't come across Leonardo, or any other horny devil on my travels, so I decided to go back inside in search of him. I continued to snack on the finger foods being carried on large platters as I wandered through rooms. Finally, I found myself back in the front hall. I walked up the wide staircase to look at the large stained-glass window. Squares of burnt sienna, Venetian red and burgundy burned in the light beside sun-baked terracotta and earthed ochres. Turquoise and ultramarine, azure and cobalt blazed beside crimson red, orange and yellow. It was a marvellous melange of glorious glass.

From below I struggled to see the picture as a whole

but now I saw the splendid scene spread out before me – a mosaic of bronze and gold melded into the toned torso of a magnificent angel. He wore a breastplate and belted tunic, the straps of his sandals laced up over strong calves. I stood spellbound by the beauty of spectacular wings in shades of silver and grey. Fine fragments of light and dark fell over the city he surveyed as the sun set.

I followed his gaze through cobbled streets crammed with contrasting colours and out over rooftops, finally coming to rest on the dome of St Peter's, which dominated the skyline. The Eternal City whose very foundations had stood through time; Rome, which rose up by Romulus' hand, built on the blood of his brother. I recalled the fable of the she-wolf and of Remus, doomed to die, slain by his own kin. He died so Rome could live, and as my eyes lingered on the Eternal City time could not touch, I suddenly felt a wave of nausea wash over me. I stepped back and into someone standing behind me. Turning around I saw steely eyes staring back at me.

"I'm sorry," I said to the cloaked man, who wore a golden mask.

Draped in red velvet he continued to peer down at me.

"Have you been to Rome?" he asked, as he waved a gloved hand over the vista, the mask distorting his voice.

"No, I haven't."

"Ah." The sound was sinister.

As I stood in front of the menacing masked man, I felt another wave of sickness and I clasped my hand over my mouth.

"Are you okay my dear?" the hooded figure asked as he reached out and grabbed my arm. His touch sent a shiver down my spine. I needed fresh air. I ran down the stairs and out of the front doors; fleeing the party and the frightening figure who watched me from the first-floor landing. Stumbling on the stone steps, I lost one of my shoes and fell straight into the arms of another masked man who bent down and picked up my satin slipper.

"May I?" he asked, and then gently slipped the shoe back onto my stockinged foot.

My head was spinning, and I was finding it difficult to breathe. My heart was beating fast.

The stranger said, "You can't leave now. It's nearly midnight."

Oh, thank goodness, I thought, *Leonardo would soon be here.* I'd just wait on the steps for the limousine, or at least that was my plan. Yet the stranger took my hand and, ignoring my protestations, led me back inside. I looked up to see the robed figure was still watching from the balcony. I tried to free myself from his grasp, but he held me firm, and I had no choice but to blindly follow him back through the crowded rooms, until finally we came to a stop at the entrance to a beautiful ballroom.

It was magical and everything I imagined a masquerade ball to be. My every sense was suddenly satiated in the stunning surroundings; the sight of all those who filled the floor, all the fabulous frocks and flowing fabrics. Swirls of silk and satin, velvet and velour, lamé and lace, danced before me in a delightful display. Their steps slowed as they moved in time to the mellifluous, musical medley. Waves of sound now washed over me, carried on a sweet-smelling air. I breathed in floral notes from an aromatic arrangement of narcissi, peony and lilies, laced with lavender, rosemary and mint. Standing there beside the striking stranger I was lost in the fairytale.

"After you," he said softly, as he placed the palm of his hand on the small of my back and together we stepped over the threshold.

"Dance with me," he said, as he took me in his arms.

We waltzed as one and I lost all my inhibitions as he swept me along at speed, in strong arms. My fingertips rested on a bicep, the like of which Michelangelo could have carved from Carrara marble; skin pulled tight over a toned torso beneath his tailored tuxedo. I looked at our reflection in the mirrored walls of the ballroom as we revolved as one; a becoming vision in black and white. I was the delicate flower he held in his powerful hands. Suddenly we stopped and I heard a countdown begin.

"Ten, nine, eight..." the dancers shouted out.

"…seven, six, five, four," they chanted.

I wasn't moving but my head was still spinning, and I felt faint.

On the count of three, I was aware of masks being removed.

"Two, one" was followed by a chorus of "Happy New Year!" Fireworks went off, the band began to play *Auld Lang Syne*, and then the dark stranger kissed me. I put my hands up to his chest in a feeble attempt to break free, but my mind and body were weak. I let myself get carried away in the fairytale and just for a moment I forgot everything else. And then I remembered Leonardo was waiting. I ran through the crowds, made a beeline for the front door and for the second time that evening stumbled down the stone steps.

Leonardo, who'd been leaning against the black stretch limousine, opened the door.

"You're late," he said, as I got in.

I turned around as the car pulled away and saw the handsome stranger standing on the stone steps. I wondered if our paths would ever cross again…

12
Face the Music

"Time to get up," Leonardo shouted, as he pulled back the curtains.

Bright light streamed into the room, waking me from my beautiful dream.

"Why are you screaming?" I asked. His voice sounded like a pneumatic drill pounding in my head.

"I'm not. Now get up!"

"No, I can't." My head was throbbing, and I was feeling sick. Obviously I was coming down with something. "I'm not feeling well." I was lying face down, sprawled out on top of the bed.

"I know," Leonardo said. "It's called a hangover."

"I didn't have that much to drink. I'm really sick Leonardo." I pulled my head out from under the pillow and looked up at him with bleary eyes. "I think I might be dying." My stomach hurt, my head hurt, my eyes hurt – my whole body hurt.

He handed me two small tablets and a glass of water.

"Take these. They'll make you feel better."

I eyed them with suspicion.

"I don't do drugs," I told him.

"They're headache tablets," he reassured me. "And don't worry, I'm not trying to poison you. You did a good enough job of that yourself with the amount of alcohol you consumed last night."

What nonsense!

"I had a couple of cocktails, that was all, and anyway, how would you know? You disappeared as soon as we walked through the door and I never saw you again for the rest of the night," I said, reminding him that he had abandoned me.

"Oh dear, it's worse than I thought," he said. "Not only are you suffering from a hangover, you also have amnesia."

In my present condition I couldn't remember what amnesia was, but it sounded a suitably serious affliction.

"Yes, I probably do."

Clearly the cocktails weren't the culprit but maybe I'd eaten something that was rotten. I did have a seafood canapé and decided that was what had caused it.

"I have salmonella," I self-diagnosed. If Holly could be a doctor then so could I. "You should take me to the hospital," I informed Leonardo.

"I'm taking you to the airport."

Considering his profession, he wasn't being very

caring.

"You're a Guardian," I reminded him. "You're meant to help."

"Yes, and I'm going to help you get up."

"No!" I cried. "I'm so ill."

"And it's all self-inflicted."

Rubbish!

"You don't know what I did or didn't eat and drink last night. You don't know what I did or didn't do. You weren't there!" I accused him. It appeared he had conveniently forgotten that he had deserted me as soon as we'd walked through the door.

"Do please enlighten me," he said, sitting down on the bed. "I'd love to hear what you think happened last night."

I knew what happened; there was no thinking involved.

"When we arrived at the party, you vanished," I began, reminding him that he was a terrible escort, and therefore everything that happened after that point in time was entirely his fault. That established, I continued to recount the evening's events: "I looked at the art, nibbled on a few canapés and then I took a walk outside, where there was music and dancing. I had a cocktail before I went in search of you but you were nowhere to be seen!" Leonardo was listening but showed no signs of remorse. "You left me on my own, a young, vulnerable girl stranded in an unfamiliar place with a lot of strange people. Do you realise how dangerous that was? Anything could've happened to me. Someone could've attacked me or abducted me, or worse." I looked over to gauge his reaction but still, nothing.

"I couldn't find you downstairs, so I went upstairs to look for you. There was a beautiful stained-glass window of an angel. Just so you know, an angel is a heavenly being who watches over and protects people."

"What happened next?" Leonardo simply asked. There was no contrition, only a curiosity. Honestly, had he no conscience?

"I needed some fresh air, so I went outside. My shoe slipped off and a handsome stranger put it back on for me. He asked me to dance. Then the clock struck midnight and I remembered my carriage awaited. So, I said goodnight and left."

Leonardo had listened intently to my rendition of the evening's events.

"I'm really sorry Anna," he began, and I presumed at long last he was going to apologise for his very un-angel-like behaviour. "But that wasn't what happened last night."

"For a start, I didn't abandon you. You ran off after a tray of canapés which you single-handedly devoured. So, I'm not surprised you're feeling a little squeamish this morning. That was a lot of food."

And a gross exaggeration!

"You then had one cocktail after another until you

decided that you wanted to go outside and 'bust some moves' – your words, not mine – which you did, on top of a table before shouting, 'Watch me, I can fly!'"

Nonsense!

"You got a little upset when you remembered that you couldn't actually fly. There were a few tears, and you ran back into the house bawling that someone had stolen your wings. You finally found the culprit at the top of the stairs. The angel in the 'purtty glass picture' and you got very upset with one of the guests who tried to stop you taking them back. I've been assured that he'll make a full recovery…" he paused to let that detail register.

He was making all this up.

"You then went outside for some fresh air where you did indeed lose your shoe."

Now he was telling the truth.

"However, your shoe did not slip off your foot. You staggered out, stumbled down the steps and off came your shoe, which a handsome stranger rescued and re-attached to your little tootsy wootsy," he reached over and wiggled my foot, "Right after you'd thrown up the contents of your stomach in the Bougainvillea bush by the front door."

He let me digest all of that before telling me I had then taken my rescuer's hand and dragged him back inside chanting 'dance, dance, dance,' like a demented drunk. I didn't know why Leonardo was lying.

"As the clock struck twelve, you obviously remembered your carriage was waiting and, like Cinderella, you came running down the steps. I opened the door and you fell head-first into the car, where you promptly passed out and snored all the way home."

"It's not true." I refused to believe his ridiculous story, which he'd clearly made up in order to make himself feel better about abandoning me.

But then he reminded me, "An angel never lies."

"Oh, heaven help me!" I cried out, as I realised that he was right.

"It's a bit late for that, I'm afraid. You can't turn back time."

I was well aware of that!

"But the beauty of life is, while we can't undo what is done, we can learn from our mistakes and we can change."

"I'm very glad you see it that way." I hoped that he had learnt his lesson and wouldn't make the same mistake again. "This was all your fault!" That was what I'd learnt from this latest disaster.

"Of course it was. Because I was the one who made you drink all those cocktails," Leonardo said sarcastically. "You do know it's wrong to give into temptation? God doesn't like it, not after the whole Adam and Eve escapade. And he definitely doesn't like any angel being drunk and disorderly. That bad behaviour can get you a transfer down below."

"I'm not an angel," I pointed out to Leonardo. "I'm human, for the time being at least, and God is very forgiving." *So there!* "And I will *never* drink again!"

I had learnt my lesson that drinking was bad. If a couple of little cocktails could make me feel like this, I had no intention of ever letting another drop pass my lips for the rest of my time on earth.

"Yes, well, you're not the first human to say that." Leonardo doubted my resolve.

When I made up my mind to do something, I did it. I'd show him. I got up and staggered to the bathroom.

"It's still all your fault," I said, before slamming the door shut behind me.

I stood under a steaming-hot shower and washed away all thoughts of the previous night. There was no point dwelling on it. What was done was done and I took comfort in the fact that I knew no one there and no one knew me. If what Leonardo told me was true it was embarrassing, but on the plus side, I'd never see any of those people again. I'd just forget all about it and start the new year afresh.

Leonardo was making pancakes in the kitchen. I sat up at the breakfast bar and put on the dark sunglasses he handed to me.

"I'll take you to the airport and then I have to go," he told me, as he put bacon in a pan.

Holly had gone – I didn't want him to go too. I wasn't ready to be left on my own.

"What am I going to do if something goes wrong?"

"You'll be fine."

I wasn't so sure about that.

"Where are you going?"

I was hoping it wasn't far away.

"I'm sorry but that information is classified."

"Can I at least call you?" For humanity's sake and Nathaniel's in particular, I hoped the answer was yes, but it was not. "So, I'm going to be all alone?"

"No," he said, surging my hopes again.

"You'll be with Nathaniel." They came crashing back down. "He's really nice, don't you think?"

To be honest, I hadn't given him much thought.

"I suppose. I don't really know him."

"I think up above will remedy that. You'll have plenty of time to get to know him over the coming months."

I felt like I'd been given a life sentence but at least Leonardo had said months rather than years. He stacked my plate high with pancakes, topped it with streaky bacon and drenched it all in maple syrup.

"*Bon appétit*," he said, as he served me the ginormous breakfast. "It's a great hangover cure."

Sadly, Leonardo's miracle cure didn't work, and I was still feeling sick, sore and tired by the time I got to the airport.

"Time to fly solo," Leonardo said, as the car pulled up in the drop-off zone. He took my case from the trunk.

An impatient driver behind who wanted our space was blaring his horn.

"Goodbye lieutenant and good luck." He saluted me before jumping back in his car.

My rank reminded me of why I was here. I had a job to do, to get back to the job I loved, and I was ready for action.

"Goodbye Leonardo."

The dark angel stuck his hand out of the window and waved as he drove away.

13

Felipe's Flight

The busy terminal was full of people returning home after the holidays, pushing trollies stacked high with suitcases. Small children sat on top of some, others ran riot around commuters who waited in long queues. I was glad when I finally got my boarding pass and left the chaos of check-in behind. A huge digital board told me I would be leaving from Gate 52, which was a twenty minutes' walk from the departure lounge.

I joined the mass exodus of passengers, on the last leg of their journey through the airport. Some had a long distance to walk before reaching their designated gates while for others, it was only a short walk. Some struggled to cope with all their baggage and theirs was a slow road. Some were given assistance, electric cars, silently speeding them along to their final destination. Boarding had commenced by the time I arrived at the gate and the airline assistant took my ticket.

"Thank you. Have a nice flight," she repeated to

everyone before shepherding them onto an enclosed airbridge.

"Good afternoon," an air steward greeted me when I finally reached the door of the plane. Then I heard a familiar female voice say, "Welcome on-board sir, if you would like to follow me?" I turned to see my Christmas Incident Associate leading a well-dressed man in the opposite direction.

"Holly!" I called but she didn't turn around.

"Could madam please take her seat?" The prissy flight attendant sounded peeved that I was holding up the boarding process.

"But—" I was just about to explain when the woman behind me snapped.

"Butt on seat girl!"

I watched Holly disappear behind a curtain.

Reluctantly, I shuffled along to 13A, a window seat, which I wasn't happy about. It would make it more difficult to get out if anyone sat beside me. Right on cue, a man dressed in a bright blue suit squeezed into 13B.

"Hello little lady," he said, as he stretched out his hand over a bulging belly. "I'm Bob and this pretty young thing is my wife, Dorinda."

"Oh Bob!" Dorinda laughed. "Pleased to meet you," she said in a slow Texan drawl.

"Anna," I replied, introducing myself to my travelling companions.

I kept watch for Holly as I listened to Bob telling me

his life story. By the time the airplane doors had closed I knew he was an ex-professional rodeo rider who had been forced to retire at the tender age of twenty-five after he broke his spine in four places. However, he turned his misfortune into opportunity and went from rodeo to ranching. He opened a chain of steak houses and was a millionaire before thirty.

"I've gone from riding to rearing to roasting," he chuckled, and clearly he was laughing all the way to the bank.

I wondered why he was travelling economy but I supposed he didn't want to make others rich at his expense. It didn't matter if you were rich or poor, in first-class seats or coach – we were all going to the same place.

"Good afternoon ladies and gentlemen," came Holly's voice over the intercom. "And welcome on-board United Airlines' flight 173 to Miami, Florida. The flight time today will be three hours and thirty-five minutes. Your cabin crew will shortly be giving you a safety demonstration. It would be greatly appreciated if you could please give them your full attention. In other words, no talking!" she ordered.

Bob mimed locking his mouth with a key that he then pretended to throw away.

"Okey-dokey then, sit back, relax and enjoy your flight everyone."

There was a ripple of chatter and laughter, but the

plane fell silent as air stewardess Holly arrived to give the safety briefing. I desperately tried to make eye contact, but the infuriating angel refused to look at me. Instead, she launched into a demonstration that was less United Airlines and more Broadway musical, theatrically waving her arms in the direction of the nearest emergency exits, before taking exaggerated breaths as she placed the oxygen mask over her nose and mouth. A loud piercing blast of a yellow whistle left a ringing in my ears.

"Useful for attracting the attention of nearby vessels or attractive sailors," she ad-libbed to the delight of everyone.

A round of applause sounded out as she finished her performance and began to make her way down the aisle, checking seat belts, making sure hand luggage was safely stored under the seat in front and soaking up the adoration of her adoring public. I expected her to stop beside me, to say something, to acknowledge me but she simply smiled and walked on.

Aargh! She was so annoying.

I consoled myself with the knowledge that at least she couldn't go anywhere for the next three hours and thirty-five minutes. Once airborne, I was going to have a talk with my CIA comrade whether she wanted to or not.

As the plane taxied out to the runway, Bob began to tell me about his great love for deep-sea fishing and how wonderful it was off the coast of Miami. He was giving me a step-by-step account of how he had caught a huge marlin 3.2 nautical miles north of the city. I wasn't quite sure why he was giving me the exact coordinates – it wasn't as if I was going to go deep-sea fishing and even if I did, the marlin he had caught wouldn't still be there. I knew that for a fact because Bob had had him stuffed and mounted on the wall of his Florida home for all to see and admire. As fascinating as Bob's fishing story was, I had bigger fish to fry. So, as soon as the 'fasten seat belt sign' had been switched off, I went in search of Holly.

Four cabin crew were preparing trays of food and stacking drinks trollies in the galley, but Holly wasn't one of them. Even though she'd done the safety briefing in economy class, she was obviously attending to passengers on the other side of the curtain. I pulled it back and stepped into what I presumed was business class.

"Gotcha!" I said, as I saw her taking drinks orders.

She'd taken off her jacket and was wearing a bright red apron over her navy skirt and white blouse. I was about to walk up and confront her when I felt a hand tap me on the shoulder.

"I'm sorry madam, but you can't be in here." It was the rather pompous flight attendant from before.

"Felipe," I said, reading his name tag. "I'll just be a moment, I have a friend I need to speak to." I politely informed him.

"Of course madam has," he said, although he clearly didn't believe me. "But I'm afraid you will have to wait till Miami to speak to your 'friend'. This is business class and you are in economy." He was being deliberately demeaning, and I could feel myself getting angry. "So, if madam could please return to her seat…" He stood back and gestured for me to leave.

"No, madam could not," I informed him. "I have to speak to—" Yet before I could say another word, he'd grabbed hold of my arm.

"I'm afraid I'm going to have to insist," he said, his voice having now risen an octave.

That was a red rag to a bull, and Felipe was about to discover I was more dangerous than any beast in Bob's beloved rodeo. I wrenched my arm free, and the condescending little man took a flight of his own, courtesy of EAA Airlines. He flew through the air and landed right in front of Holly, who had just returned with a Bourbon and coke for a business class passenger. She took a large swig of the drink before setting it down on his tray table and turning her attention to the now hysterical Felipe.

"*She*…" he howled, stabbing his finger in my direction. "She threw me!"

I was delighted with my new superpower. At last, a side effect I could put to good use.

"Don't be silly," Holly told him. "We hit an air

pocket. Didn't you feel it?"

The wide-eyed attendant wasn't listening.

"I was there…" he pointed behind me. "And then I was here," he explained, as he traced his trajectory through the air with a finger. "It was *you*!"

Everyone turned to look at me and I was expecting a round of applause, but they looked terrified.

"You hurt me!" he bawled.

There wasn't a scratch on him. The only thing I'd hurt was his pride. Holly, however, was placating the big baby, making a fuss of him as she ushered him out of the cabin.

"Let's get you a little sit down and a nice bit of cake. That'll make everything better, won't it?" I heard her soothe the sobbing Felipe.

"Bollocks," I muttered under my breath, as I watched Holly disappear through yet another curtain. Oh well, I'd just have to wait here until she came back. It was then that I realised everyone else in the cabin was still staring at me. They looked afraid, like I was about to assault them too.

"Hi," I said, raising my hand in greeting.

I wanted to reassure them that I was quite harmless, at least most of the time anyway.

"Anna." I heard my name being called and was so happy to see a friendly face.

"Come join me," Nathaniel Banks said to the consternation of the rest of the cabin, who were none too happy to have a potentially violent attacker in their midst. I didn't need to be asked twice.

"Excuse me," I said, as I clambered over the well-heeled occupants sitting in the seats separating us. I could have passed through one curtain and back in through the other but there was a risk I would be intercepted, and we didn't need another incident occurring.

"That was quite a performance," he said, as I sat down beside him.

Unlike the other passengers who looked terrified, Nathaniel was impressed.

"CIA training?" he asked in a hushed voice.

I nodded. The good old CIA. Clearly Nathaniel hadn't recognised my commanding officer in her new guise.

"Did you do anything special for New Year's?" he asked me.

"I went to a party in Long Island," I told him, "And you?"

"Me too."

What were the odds of that? Yet Long Island was a big place, and I was sure there was more than one New Year's Eve party going on there.

"I was at Villa Margherita," he told me.

"I was at a masked ball," I said, although I had no idea where it had been held.

"Me too!" My face grew pale and I sunk down in the

seat. "It was a great night! Very memorable."

"Happy New Year!" I wished him in the hope it would prevent any further questioning or discussions about the previous night.

"Happy New Year Anna," he said, and he slowly leaned over.

Oh no, he was going to kiss me, what was I going to do? There was nowhere to go – I was trapped. I braced myself and squeezed my eyes shut.

"Although we really need a drink to toast that." I opened them again to see him smiling at me as he reached up to ring the bell.

Flight attendant Holly appeared again from behind the curtain.

"What can I do for you sir?" she asked, as she brushed crumbs from her apron.

Clearly Felipe wasn't the only one having a slice of cake.

"Can I have a bottle of champagne please?"

I protested. "Oh no, really, I'm okay." I'd sworn I would never drink again. I might even have promised God I would stay away from the demon drink.

"I'll be right back." She completely ignored me and tottered off.

I wanted to get up and follow her into the galley, but Nathaniel kept me talking. In a moment, Holly returned with a bottle of Bollinger and two glasses. She was smiling inanely at us as she popped the cork.

"Congratulations," she said, as she filled our flutes.

That's a bit premature, I thought, *we hadn't even got to work yet.*

"I hope you'll be very happy together."

Well, I didn't know about that, but I was hopeful we'd work well together.

"We're not engaged," I heard Nathaniel say.

Wait! What? I glared at the cheery flight attendant.

"Of course, we're not!" I protested, as I felt my face flush with embarrassment.

"I'm sorry, it's just you make such a lovely couple, and you look so happy."

I raised my eyebrows.

"Really?" I look happy? I was furious!

"I'm sure you'll be getting that ring very soon."

What was she saying?!

"We're not a couple," I explained, wanting her to stop.

"Are you sure?" she persisted.

She bloody well knew that we weren't a couple! If she didn't stop going on, I would do a 'Felipe' on her (that was what I'd named my new superpower.). "Very sure!" I stated clearly.

"You look so good together."

I was fantasising about wiping that broad grin off her face.

"Enjoy your champagne!" With that, she trotted off up the aisle.

For once, I was glad to see the back of her.

"Sorry about that," I muttered.

Nathaniel was smiling. "Here's to making a great couple," he toasted.

I was taken aback.

"… On the course," he added.

"Yes, cheers to that." We clinked glasses.

"And Happy New Year to you Anna, I hope it brings you everything you wish for."

If we did make a great couple, on the course, it would bring me exactly what I wished for – a one-way ticket back to where I belonged.

"Happy New Year Nathaniel."

I took a little sip of champagne as it would have been rude of me to refuse. I was sure that God would understand; He was a stickler for good manners after all and it was just one little sip. However, one little sip followed another and another and two bottles of Bollinger later, I heard Holly's voice announce that we would soon be commencing our descent into Miami Airport.

Oh, holy crap! While I'd been drinking and chatting to Nathaniel I'd forgotten that I needed to speak to her. I excused myself and quickly went in search of my fellow angel. I found her filling in paperwork while tucking into a tray of pre-heated food.

"Anna!" she smiled, as she saw me walk into the small galley.

"Don't 'Anna' me! What was all that about earlier? 'Oh, you make a lovely couple'," I mimicked her.

"Well, you do," she said.

"You're not here to matchmake," I informed her. "Actually, why are you here?" It suddenly occurred to me to ask the real purpose of her visit.

"To observe," she told me, as she spooned in another mouthful of chocolate torte. "Don't you just love the uniform?" she said, before I had the chance to ask what it was she was here to observe. "I think we should consider neck ties. They really add something."

I refused to be drawn into discussing outfits. I wanted to get back to the business in hand. "How long do I have to be here?" I was eager to know.

"About another twenty minutes," she told me.

"Really?" That was great news!

"Yes, we'll be landing at half past."

"Not here on the plane," I said exasperatedly.

"Here on…" and I drew a big circle in the air.

"Oh, goody!" Holly squealed with delight. "I love charades! Now, don't tell me, let me guess – how many words?"

"One." I was convinced she was being deliberately infuriating.

"*Hmm*, it's a circle…" she said, taking a moment to think. "One word …"

This was painful.

"OK, give me another clue."

"It's not heaven!"

"Oh, that's good. I'd never have guessed that," she conceded, and went back to filling in her paperwork and securing trollies for landing.

"So?" I pressed her.

"So, what?" She looked vague.

"How long do I have to be here, *on earth*?" I spelt it out for her, so that there was no doubt about what I was asking.

"For as long as it takes."

"*Aargh!*" We were going around in circles; all I wanted was a straight answer. I tried another tactic: "How many games does Nathaniel have to win?" It was a straight-forward question. Or so I thought.

"I don't know dear."

It was something that my commanding officer *should* know!

"My orders were to help him become successful again. How many games does he have to win to be successful? One? Two? Three? Ten?" I was hoping multiple choice would make it easier for the lieutenant colonel.

"I don't know."

"You don't know much." I thought Holly would have all the answers; I thought she could help.

I heard a *ding*.

"I do know that we'll be landing in ten minutes," she said. "You have to go back to your seat."

"But I want to know how long I have to be here," I moaned.

"For as long as it takes."

Not that old chestnut!

"Enjoy it. Nathaniel's a lovely young man, and you do make a cute couple."

"Stop that!"

"It's just an observation," she winked, as she picked up a clipboard and started to write.

"I give up!" I wasn't going to get any answers from Holly.

As I turned to go she called out, "And Anna, try not to hurl anyone else through the air. It's not very human."

With those parting words of wisdom, (which I had no intention of taking on board), I returned to my seat in preparation for landing.

14
Filthy Rich

The airplane doors opened to reveal a bright blue sky, and we walked out into warm air. *This was a much nicer climate to work in*, I decided on my way to the terminal. As we were standing around waiting for our baggage, I heard a loud, "Howdy doody!" and turned to see Bob striding towards us. "So, you're the one responsible for spiriting off our adorable travelling companion," he said to Nathaniel, as he held out a hand in greeting. "Bob Brown – in beef," he introduced himself.

"Nathaniel Banks – in golf," he replied, shaking Bob's hand.

"I know who *you* are! I'm a big fan of the sport," he beamed.

"And I'm sorry for stealing Anna away," Nathaniel apologised to the ex-rodeo rider.

"No need for that," Bob said, grinning from ear to ear. "Far be it for me to stand in the way of young love."

Oh my God! First Holly, and now Beefhouse Bob

thought we were together. I had meant to clarify quietly that we were not in a relationship but instead I ended up shouting, "We're not a couple!" Dorinda jumped and Bob held up his hands.

"I'm sorry little lady. It's just that—" I stopped him before he could launch into why he thought we were romantically involved.

"We work together," I explained, trying to recover my poise following my embarrassing outburst. I was aware that Nathaniel was staring at me, but I kept my eyes fixed on Bob.

"My apologies again for jumping to the wrong conclusion." Bob doffed his Stetson just as I spied my suitcase come crashing down onto the conveyor belt behind him.

"Excuse me," I said, as I pushed past and attempted to pull it off. However, I didn't get a firm enough grip to remove it fully and it dragged me along. I stepped on feet and stumbled over other passengers as I struggled to heave it off the moving belt. Thankfully, Nathaniel stepped in and lifted it off the carousel. I watched as he started to wheel it towards the exit.

"What about your baggage?" I called out after him.

"I don't have any."

Red-faced and flustered, I followed Nathaniel outside.

"Welcome back Mr. Banks," his driver greeted him.

I slipped into a soft leather seat and a comfortable

silence, as the driver pulled away from the curb. I looked out at passing palm trees swaying in the ocean breeze. The sun shone in a cloudless sky and beyond a sandy beach, the sea stretched out towards a hazy horizon.

"Is this home?" I asked Nathaniel.

"I have other houses," he replied, and I was reminded of his property portfolio. "But this is where I call home.'

"It looks beautiful."

"You've never been to Miami before?" He sounded surprised.

"No, never."

The EAA were deployed to war-torn parts of the world, and while I knew there was violence and crime in most cities, it wasn't our department to deal with inner-city conflict.

"I'll have to give you a guided tour."

"I'd like that, but we really should get to work."

"First thing tomorrow, we'll get started."

The driver slowed down as he waited for the electric gates to open. A sweeping driveway led up to a beautiful single-storey Spanish-style home. Nathaniel jumped out and opened the door for me.

"Let me show you around."

Inside was light, bright and white, which made me feel right at home. From a large living room with an open-plan kitchen, glass doors opened onto a terrace, and the whole house wrapped around a spectacular swimming pool.

"Your home is beautiful," I told Nathaniel.

"This is the guesthouse and your home, for as long as you're here." He handed me the keys. "I'll leave you to settle in. The driver will be back for you later."

I wondered how big Nathaniel's house was if this four-bedroomed bungalow was just the guest accommodation. Each one of the bedrooms had a view of the pool and all had large ensuite bathrooms; one even had a sunken bath. That was the one I chose. I ran the taps and let hot water fill the tub.

"Heaven," I said, as I stepped in and lay back. I thought of my own home and hoped that I would be going back very soon.

After a long soak, I pulled on a robe, walked back into the bedroom and hauled my heavy suitcase onto the bed. I pulled out a summer dress and rummaged around until I found a pair of sandals and a denim jacket to go with it. My footsteps echoed on the tiled floor as I walked back through the lounge in time to hear a knock at the front door. I opened it to see Nathaniel's driver, who had ditched his suit and Sedan in favour of a short-sleeved shirt and a golf buggy.

I got in and he drove me up to Nathaniel's house – a magnificent white mansion stretching out either side of a colonnaded entrance. As we pulled up, the front door opened, and Nathaniel stepped out. He had changed into white trousers and a blue sports shirt, which brought out the colour of his eyes.

"Welcome to my home," he greeted me.

I followed him inside the palatial property that he was excited to show me around. He was eager to show off the expensive art, valuable collectibles and state-of-the-art technology. I could see how proud he was of everything he owned. They were an expression not only of his wealth, but of all that he had achieved. Like the trophies on display, all this was a status symbol.

I thought of the villa where we had both celebrated the New Year, full of priceless objects but also full of people. I felt an emptiness and loneliness as we walked around here, and a silence that wasn't restful. This house and everything in it were like a mask he wore to hide his pain and failings. His marriage had ended, and his meteoric rise and stellar career had crashed and burned. The house was a visual reminder of all he had once had; the love and success he had lost.

Outside, steps led down from a large terrace onto a landscaped lawn dotted with exotic palms and filled with plants. Statues of nymphs and goddesses, perched on plinths, looked down on the shimmering blue water of an Olympic-sized swimming pool. It was a perfect place to entertain guests and I wondered if the former Mrs. Banks had ever hosted parties here. Nathaniel had fallen silent and seemed lost in thought.

"Penny for them," I asked.

"I'm sorry," he apologised. "I was just thinking…that it's time I showed you the city."

I knew he hadn't been thinking that, but his tone and mood seemed to lift at the thought of the tour.

"Great, I'm looking forward to it," I told him.

He grabbed a set of keys from a kitchen drawer, and we walked back outside. There was a beeping, flashing lights and the doors of a bright red, convertible sports car opened.

"Ready to see Miami?" he asked, as he revved the engine.

"Yes, very ready."

With a warm wind blowing through my hair, we set off on a sightseeing tour of the city Nathaniel called home. We drove past magnificent mansions with moorings on waterways, which weaved their way inland. As the sky became a deep blue, lights illuminated the soaring skyscrapers dominating the business district of downtown Miami. Large high-rise hotels and apartment blocks lined the peninsula, and a huge white sandy beach ran its entire length.

Nathaniel slowed down as we turned onto Ocean Drive, giving me time to take in the iconic architecture. We drove past pastel-painted hotels and candy-coloured restaurants. The Art Deco buildings were abuzz with a vibrant mix of tourists and locals alike, who had come to enjoy the rhythm and beat of South Beach. Finally, we came to a stop in front of a cream-coloured building emblazoned with neon pink lighting. Diners sat on the sidewalk under white umbrellas. Outside, delicious smells of food tickled my taste buds but inside, *all* my senses came alive.

We followed a waitress through the crowded restaurant, dodging trays of food being carried to hungry customers. She showed us to a small table on the upstairs balcony. Below us a band played, and dancers swung their hips in time to the Latin American music. I watched barmen juggle bottles and jiggle cocktail shakers in front of mirrored glass, reflecting the entire, effervescent scene.

Nathaniel had ordered drinks and I was horrified when the waitress set down a Mojito in front of me. I couldn't drink another cocktail! God only knows what would happen (and I didn't want God to know.).

"Cheers," Nathaniel said, as he waited for me to pick up my glass.

I got a lovely aroma of mint and lime as I clinked glasses with the young golfer, who looked much more relaxed than he had at the house. I was about to ask for water but then I remembered it was bad luck to toast with water, and I didn't need any more of that. I weighed up my options and decided the polite thing to do was to take a sip of the delicious drink.

It was at that precise moment I fell off the wagon and downed the mojito. A sweet pina colada followed the sour rum concoction. Spicy food and salsa dancing were also on the menu.

"Can I take your photo?" Nathaniel asked, as we

walked to the dance floor.

"Sure," I said, and posed for the picture he then showed me on his phone.

Oh shit! There I was standing in my summer dress and I had wings! I spun around but there was no sign of them. Oh no! I had heard the phrase 'a camera never lies' but I didn't think to take it literally. Now Nathaniel would know I was an angel! And God, who was already pissed off with me for giving into temptation, would be furious when he found out I'd broken the cardinal rule of revealing my true identity to a human.

Fuck! Fuck! Fuckety-fuck!

Oh, and He wasn't going to be very happy with my swearing either!

"They're fantastic!" Nathaniel couldn't stop staring at the photo.

Admittedly, I did have a lovely set of wings.

"You're a beautiful angel," he said.

My cover was blown and very soon I was going to be a wingless angel, permanently! I would probably be demoted, yet again, to something even worse than a Christmas Incident Angel. Like a… I couldn't actually think of anything worse than that. I was about to cry when Nathaniel handed me the phone and asked me to take his photograph.

And then I saw them: two painted angel wings on the wall behind. Thank the Lord, it was only a mural. I was so happy! Nathaniel posed for his picture and I said a silent prayer of thanks that my secret was still safe.

15

Five Iron and Feathered Friends

Smells of cooking wafted into the bedroom. I stretched out muscles aching from salsa dancing, and opened eyes sore from a lack of sleep. My head was throbbing too, probably because I'd had a third cocktail and then two shots of Tequila. So much for vowing to be teetotal! It was only the second of January and I'd already broken my New Year's resolution not to drink. This was not an auspicious start, and I only hoped I'd have more success with my resolution to help Nathaniel.

I liked him and wanted him to do well in his career, so I could get back to mine. I still didn't know how I was going to fix him, but I'd have to come up with a plan promptly because today was the first day of 'life coaching'. What I knew about life could be written on the back of a postage stamp. Coaching, on the other hand, was a different matter; I had, after all, trained an army of soldiers. How hard could one golfer be?

Although I really should have made more of an effort

to learn about the game, I thought as I stretched again. However, I would surely pick it up as I went along. We were going out on the course this morning, so I would have to get up and have breakfast before he arrived. I was looking forward to whatever was cooking in the kitchen.

Then it dawned on me – I was here on my own, so who was in the kitchen? I fell out of bed and looked around for my suitcase but it was nowhere to be seen. I couldn't very well go out and confront whoever it was in my underwear. I ran over to the closet.

"*Ah-ha!*" I saw my case and grabbed it but it was empty! How had that happened?

All my clothes had been unpacked; everything was neatly folded and hanging up in the dressing room. I put on a pair of tracksuit bottoms, pulled on a t-shirt and made my way into the kitchen, where a maid wearing a pale pink uniform was arranging pastries on a baking tray.

"*Buenos días*, Miss Anna," she said, her jet-black hair pulled neatly back into a ponytail. "*Señor* Nathaniel sent me to look after you. If there is anything you need, you just ask Rosaria," she told me.

She sashayed her hips as she walked from the oven to the hob, where she cracked, whisked and poured beaten eggs into a pan.

"Please sit," she said, as she pointed to the table set for breakfast.

I'd no sooner sat down than she asked me in Spanish, "*Quiere usted café?* Sorry, coffee?" she explained, as she carried a two-piece silver coffee pot to the table and set it down beside a jug of fresh orange juice. Next, she brought a basket of freshly baked croissants, which she served with butter and a choice of different preserves. In between, she stirred and spooned creamy scrambled eggs onto a plate and placed them in front of me. I looked at the feast of food; enough to feed an entire army.

"You like?" The young maid looked very pleased with herself.

"It all looks lovely."

In stark contrast to the food and Rosaria, who looked stunning, I looked a mess. I had no makeup on and I hadn't even washed my face. God only knows what was happening with my hair.

"So, you working with *Señor* Nathaniel?" she asked me, just as I'd placed a huge pile of scrambled eggs into my mouth.

I tried not to choke as I answered, "Yes."

"*Señor* Nathaniel is a very nice man," she said, as she scrubbed a pan.

Somehow, she made even that look sexy.

"He is going to help bring my family from Cuba."

I listened as Rosaria told me how she had come to Florida on a boat. She lapsed back into Spanish as she spoke passionately about the hardships the Cuban people still had to endure.

"*Mi gente.* It breaks my heart," she said, pointing to her chest as tears filled her eyes.

I walked over and put my arm around the young girl.

"It'll be okay," I comforted her.

"*Gracias* Miss Anna."

"Just Anna," I told her.

There was a knock on the door.

"*Señor* Nathaniel!" Rosaria squealed, and had opened the door before I could escape to the bedroom.

"Morning Anna," Nathaniel called out, stopping me in my tracks.

"Dammit!" I muttered under my breath.

I didn't want him to see me looking like this. Nathaniel, Rosaria and another young man stood by the door.

"I'm sorry I'm not ready, I was having breakfast," I said, as I made my excuses.

"*Mmm*, croissants." Nathaniel made a beeline for the untouched basket. "I do love Rosaria's croissants."

"Oh, *Señor* Nathaniel," Rosaria giggled. "Let me warm them for you." She grabbed the basket from Nathaniel and walked seductively back to the oven.

"It's fine," he said, as he tried to protest.

"No, no, no." She wagged her finger at him. "I make them hot, just the way you like them."

"I'll have a coffee," said the other man, who sounded surly as he sat down on the sofa.

"Anna, this is Duke."

"Hi," I said.

He raised his hand but didn't reply.

"My caddie," Nathaniel explained.

I wanted to ask what a caddie was, but I didn't want to seem ignorant. Also I needed to get changed. I excused myself, leaving Nathaniel to his croissants, Duke to his coffee and Rosaria to her flirting. After a quick shower, I picked out one of the golfing uniforms Federico had chosen for me, put on some lip gloss and tied up my hair.

"Okay," I said to my reflection. "Let's get to work."

Nathaniel and Duke were having a heated discussion when I walked back into the room and Rosaria, who'd been plumping cushions, had to put a hand over her mouth to stifle a snigger.

"What on earth are you wearing?" Duke asked.

According to Federico, I was wearing the height of fashion on earth. I looked down at the pale blue pleated skirt paired with a white polo shirt, finished with a matching diamond check vest and knee-high socks.

"What's wrong with it?"

"Everything!" Duke snorted.

"I think you look great," Nathaniel said, defending me. "You might even start a new trend."

"Right then, let's go," I ordered.

There were more important things to worry about than what I was wearing. I marched past Duke who was shaking his head. Nathaniel held the door open for me.

"Thank you," I said, and left his grumpy caddie to bring up the rear.

I expected to see Gerry, the driver, waiting with a car, but a golf buggy was parked outside. As it jolted into action I wondered how safe they were on the roads; there were no seat belts and no rails for holding on. I nearly fell out when Nathaniel swung off the driveway and onto the grass. After bumping over the manicured lawn, I was then nearly catapulted out again when he slammed his foot on the brakes.

We came to an abrupt stop, having travelled less than fifty metres.

"What's wrong?" I asked him (other than his driving, which was atrocious!).

"Nothing." Nathaniel pulled on white fingerless gloves and jumped out.

Duke was already lifting the bag out of the buggy.

"Where exactly are we?" I asked. As far as I could see, we were still on his front lawn.

"The first tee."

"You have your own golf course?"

"Yes," he said, and pushed a small wooden peg into the ground.

Why didn't that surprise me?

"Now, how is this going to work?" Nathaniel asked me.

Honestly, I had no idea.

"Well…" I tried to think like a life coach, "You should play and I'll watch." That was a great plan as I'd get to see what the game was all about. Nathaniel was looking expectantly at me. "And…" I had to come up with something more. "I'll take notes." He was still looking at me. "And…" I was running out of ideas. "And then I'll point out where you need to make changes at the end." Thankfully, that seemed to satisfy him.

Metal sticks rattled in the bag as Duke lifted one out and handed it to Nathaniel. I picked up my clipboard and, with pen poised, waited as he stood to the side of the ball, positioning the stick behind it. He took a swing and, for a moment, held it high above his head before bringing it down in a perfect circle to send the little white ball flying through the air at great speed.

"That was fantastic!" I was genuinely impressed.

"No, it bloody well wasn't," said Duke, who was quick to point out the fault.

"It went left," Nathaniel explained.

I made a quick note: Left was not good. Duke took the stick off Nathaniel and everyone jumped back in the golf buggy.

"How do we find it?" I asked.

I imagined there was an on-board tracking device giving the coordinates.

"You watch where it goes and then you go and get it." Duke stopped just short of adding, "Doh!" I didn't know what his problem was.

I made a note and then hung on tightly as we careered down a steep slope in search of the little projectile. By the time we reached the bottom my own bottom was sore from the bumpy ride. Nathaniel and Duke walked tentatively through a patch of slightly longer grass, until finally Nathaniel found his ball. He put another coloured piece of wood underneath it. I made a note that he really should try to stay on the flatter, greener grass because it would be much easier to hit the ball. I felt proud of my profound observation and felt sure that this would be a useful piece of information.

I watched as he looked from the ball to something in a general north-easterly direction, although I couldn't see what. He wiggled his hips before taking another swing. I heard a loud *clack* as the metal stick made impact and sent it flying through the air once more. This time I said nothing but looked at Nathaniel, who proceeded to bang his stick on the ground. I took that as a bad sign.

"Left again?" I asked.

"No, it's gone wide," Duke said in exasperation, although I wasn't sure if it was with me or Nathaniel.

I wrote down that wide was also bad, before we all piled back into the buggy. Nathaniel put his foot down on the accelerator and sped off in pursuit of the ball. When we stopped, I wrote down: Driving bad! Very, very bad! This time it took longer to find the ball but eventually Duke located it in much longer grass. However, Nathaniel miraculously managed to hit it onto the green with his next shot. It was then that I realised he was aiming for another stick with a flag on it. It took him five shots to put the ball in the hole, which apparently was two over. *Over what*? I wondered. I watched Duke mark the score down on a card, which he pulled out from his back pocket.

Nathaniel wasn't happy with the stick Duke chose for the second hole so he asked for a five iron instead. I made a note: Sticks are called irons (although secretly I thought irons were used to take creases out of clothes.). I would clarify this later, preferably when Duke wasn't around. There was an uncomfortable silence as Nathaniel stood looking at the ball. I knew when he started to swing his hips from side to side that he was ready. He brought the iron down hard and I watched as the ball flew down the fairway – not to the left, not wide but straight down the green. Duke patted Nathaniel on the back and at last I had something positive to write down: five iron is good.

The ball was on flat, bright green grass which I noted was good too. From there, Nathaniel hit it close to the hole and then swapped his iron for something called a putter. He spent a great deal of time kneeling and studying the shot before giving it a much gentler tap than he had done with the five iron. The ball rolled over the green, teetered on the edge of the hole and then fell in.

"Par," Duke called out.

'Putter' and 'par' both went in the good section.

After he had teed off on the third, he leapt back into the buggy and raced up a steep incline. Holes three and four number were both par. On the fifth, Nathaniel teed off with a wood which looked different from the other sticks. The ball sailed through the air and landed near the hole. Wood went straight onto my good list. A short tap with his putter and the ball went in.

"Birdie," Duke shouted.

"Where?" I searched the sky.

"Where's what?" he asked me.

"The birdie."

Nathaniel laughed. "A birdie is one under par," he explained, as Duke grabbed the putter and shoved it back into the bag.

I made a note.

"Any particular type of bird? A hawk? A kite? A buzzard?"

"No, just a birdie," Nathaniel said, smiling. "But a two under par is an eagle."

"Oh, I love an eagle!" I made a note. "They're amazing birds. Fantastic hunters."

"And an albatross is—" Nathaniel continued.

"I know, I know! It's a big seabird with a huge wing-span." I was very proud of my bird knowledge.

"Yes, but in golf, it's a three under par."

"What's a four under par?" I was keen to know what member of the avian species came next.

"A condor," Nathaniel told me.

I concluded that all golfers must also be keen bird watchers. Duke was waiting impatiently by the golf cart.

"Next hole is a par four," Nathaniel explained. "So if I get a condor, then it's a hole in one and I have to buy everyone a drink at the nineteenth hole."

"There are nineteen holes?" *I thought there were eighteen?*

"Don't you know anything about golf?" Duke shouted at me. He didn't give me time to answer before he turned on Nathaniel. "What are you doing man? This is crazy! She knows nothing about the game. She doesn't even know how many holes there are, and you expect her to fix you?"

"That's enough," Nathaniel cautioned his caddie, who continued his rant.

"I'm your friend and I'm telling you – you're wasting your time and money. We should be working together to fix it."

"Give Anna a chance." Nathaniel defended me.

"What? To completely ruin your career? You'll be a laughingstock if anyone hears about this. You've got to get it together man."

"Just go!"

Duke had taken it too far.

"Don't worry, I'm outta here!" he shouted, and then

stormed off.

Nathaniel was upset and I felt it was all my fault. I was supposed to be helping him, not making things worse. We should've called it a day and driven back but Nathaniel was stubborn. Even though he was angry, he finished the course but it came as no surprise that there were no more birdies, of any description. I watched Nathaniel put a lot of plus signs on his scorecard and I knew that wasn't positive.

When we finally pulled up in front of the house, he asked me what I thought.

"I think... " *I think it was a disaster. I think you need to hit the ball onto the green and not into long grass. I think you need eagles, condors and a lot of birdies. I think you need a new caddie. I think you're angry and frustrated and it's affecting your game. I think I might be stuck here forever if you keep playing like you did today.* I was thinking all those things but I didn't say any of them. Instead I told him, "I think I'll drive tomorrow." My legs felt like jelly and my stomach was doing somersaults. "Your driving is awful!"

I got a smile from him.

"See you in the morning," I said, and I waved him off.

16

For whom the bell tolls

I learnt a lot about the game of golf and about caddying over the next few days. Duke had a family crisis to attend to, so I took on the role in his absence. I came to realise just how much a golfer relies on his caddie – for support, advice and guidance. It was a very important relationship. I also understood why Duke had lost his temper. He wanted Nathaniel to be the best again and he saw me as a hindrance rather than a help. I hoped I would prove him wrong.

As Nathaniel relaxed in my company his scorecard got better and, by day four, he had acquired an aviary. There were a large collection of birdies, eagles and albatrosses. I could see there was nothing wrong with his game or his technique. It was clear his mind was affecting his performance, and to fix that I had to understand the man behind the mask.

On Saturday, Nathaniel was playing a charity match at his local club. Duke was back so I was free to watch from the side-lines. It would be the first time I'd see Nathaniel play in public. A car arrived to take me to the exclusive establishment, and after my first fashion *faux pas*, Rosaria had taken charge of my wardrobe. As well as being an incredible cook, she had a fabulous eye for fashion. I felt very elegant walking into the event in the long floral dress and high heels she'd chosen for me.

Waiters circulated with trays of champagne for the invited guests. Cigar smoke and perfume filled an air that stank of social snobbery. It was very much a gentleman's club and the well-dressed women were welcomed in for one day only. Today they'd relaxed their archaic male-only membership to allow ladies to play; female celebrities who would each be paired with a professional. The golfers were posing with their famous partners when I arrived, conducting interviews with camera crews who were covering the event. Nathaniel's partner was an attractive blonde and I watched him wince as she draped herself over him for a photograph.

"Hello again little lady," I heard a loud voice say, and turned around to see Bob disappear behind a puff of cigar smoke.

"Nice to see you again Anna," Dorinda said. "That's a lovely dress."

"Pretty as a picture," Bob agreed with his diminutive wife. "I see they've paired Abigail with young Banks," Bob remarked, as he stabbed his cigar in Nathaniel's direction.

"Who is she?" I asked.

Dorinda shrieked, "You don't know who Abigail is?"

"No." (If I did, I wouldn't be asking.).

"She's in every magazine and on every TV channel. Where have you been?" She was incredulous.

"I've been out of the country," I said truthfully.

"Abigail is a reality TV star-turned international pop star. Are you sure you haven't heard of her?"

"Yes, I'm positive," I repeated. I was happy to report that she hadn't made headline news in heaven, where we still preferred choral music to pop, and where, thank God, there was no reality TV.

"She's going to be singing later."

"I can't wait," I replied, with feigned enthusiasm.

"She's also just won *Top Dancer*" Dorinda was a mine of information on the multi-talented Abigail. "Did you see that show?"

"No." Again, I was too busy wielding a sword and winning wars to watch Abigail dance her way to victory.

"I never missed an episode," Dorinda told me, her gaze trained on the all-singing, all-dancing, pop sensation.

"Well, she won't win this," Bob cackled.

I was delighted to hear that the pop princess couldn't play golf.

"It's a shame they paired her with Banks."

"I know," I agreed with him. "There's no chance

he'll win if she's that bad."

"No," he quickly corrected me. "I meant it's a shame for young Abigail. She plays off a handicap of six or so I hear." He looked impressed by this fact.

Oh my God, she's good at golf too!

"Nathaniel's a great golfer," I declared.

"*Was*, not anymore."

His words echoed what I'd told Jack at Christmas but that was then and this was now.

"I beg to differ, and you'll see just how brilliant he is today." I was very confident of Nathaniel's imminent performance.

"Okay little lady," he laughed, and held up his hands. "I hope you're right."

Dorinda was still transfixed by the bubbly blonde who was fawning all over Nathaniel.

"I've just realised that Abigail looks a lot like Nathaniel's ex-wife," she mused.

"Really?" That wasn't good. "It's been lovely to see you both again,' I said, as I excused myself. I needed to speak to Nathaniel before the match started.

"Want a little wager?" Bob called out after me.

"I don't gamble." Yet that was a lie as I was betting my entire future on Nathaniel winning again. It was time for a pre-tournament pep talk.

"Anna," he said, when he saw me walking over to him. He tried to extricate himself from Abigail's grasp but she wouldn't let go. "You look beautiful."

I looked down at the floral dress I was wearing. "Thank you, Rosaria helped."

Abigail stretched out a hand, "Nice to meet you…"

"Anna," I introduced myself, and waited for her to do the same.

Eventually she did. "I'm sorry," she giggled. "It's just that I expect everyone to know my name."

Of course you do. I had taken an immediate dislike to the pompous little pop princess.

"Do you mind awfully if I borrow Nathaniel for a minute?" I took his other arm and tried to prise him free of her grasp.

She was reluctant to let go, and I didn't want to pull too hard. With my superhuman powers, I'd probably take his arm right out of its socket, and he needed it to play. I exerted just enough brute force to win the tug-of-war.

"Hurry back partner," she pouted as we walked out of earshot.

"Thank you for that," he said.

"For what?"

"For rescuing me."

"You're welcome, but I've some bad news." He looked concerned. "I have to give you back."

He laughed.

"You're stuck with Barbie for a whole eighteen holes, but I'll rescue you again at the nineteenth."

"It's a date." He looked back at the blonde

bombshell. "Although I'm not sure I'll survive until the nineteenth!"

I took his shoulders and turned him to face me.

"Listen to me Nathaniel: I believe in you. You are a fantastic golfer. You can do this, I know you can. Focus, and don't let anything distract you." I nodded at Abigail who was looking sexy in her figure-hugging white trousers and tight white top. "Now go out there and win this." I gave him his orders and sent him on his way.

The lure of professional sports stars and celebrities had attracted crowds of spectators, who had travelled from far and wide. They gathered around the first tee, and I watched from the terraced balcony as each famous pair teed off to the sound of cheering and clapping. The loudest applause however was reserved for Nathaniel and Abigail.

The onlookers fell silent as Abigail concentrated. Finishing a perfect swing, she held her pose and we all watched the ball fly through the air. It was a great shot. She stood back and I felt butterflies in my stomach as Nathaniel took his position at the first. All eyes were on him and I willed him to do well.

He raised his hand to the home crowd who chanted his name. This was it – his big chance to show everyone that Nathaniel Banks was back. He slowly swung the driver, bringing it face down behind the ball, and then with a huge swing sent it hurtling into the air. There were audible gasps as images of spectators jumping out of the way filled the huge screens. His ball had veered sharply to the right and landed in their midst. It was a terrible start.

"Come on Banksy, you can do it," the crowd rallied behind him.

He showed his appreciation with another wave and a forced smile, but I could see his shoulders slump as he walked down the fairway. Abigail skipped along beside him, waving to her fans. One disastrous shot followed another until he finally finished the first hole three over par; a hole that Abigail birdied. I was mortified for him but there was nothing I could do.

From the clubhouse, I watched the unfolding drama play out on the big screen. I could see the anger and frustration Nathaniel felt at himself, as hole after hole he racked up an embarrassing score card. Duke shook his head repeatedly at the appalling performance. Abigail, on the other hand, played a brilliant round of golf. The brighter she shone, the further Nathaniel fell into darkness. He arrived back defeated, and in greater despair than ever before. It had been an abysmal show on home ground.

Media representatives scrambled to interview the young golfer who graciously congratulated the winners and his partner whom he said had played "An exceptional round." He brushed off his performance as "A bad day at the office. We all have them!" He tried to make light of it with the press but he wasn't laughing.

Handshakes and platitudes followed. Putting on a brave face, he walked back into the clubhouse where the other golfers rallied around him. Nathaniel Banks was popular with his peers; everyone in his profession wanted him to do well. I wanted him to do well – and not just because it was my ticket back to heaven – but because I liked him. I wanted to help him, and now I knew just how to.

17
Fighting Fit

Maria was surprised to see me at such an early hour of the morning.

"*Señor* Banks *no es* up Miss Anna," she told me in broken English.

"That's okay," I said, as I side-stepped past his housekeeper. "You might want to cover your ears," I warned her before I blew my whistle loudly.

Silence.

I gave it another long blast; the sound echoing around the vaulted ceiling. The third piercing ring finally roused a sleepy Nathaniel who stood, shirtless, at the top of the stairs.

"What's with all the noise?" he asked groggily.

"Get dressed. We're going for a run," I informed him.

"What time is it?" he asked.

"Zero Six hundred hours."

He rubbed his hand through tousled hair. I gave

another short blast on the whistle.

"Let's move it!" I ordered him.

In super quick time he appeared downstairs, dressed in a t-shirt and tracksuit bottoms. After a series of warm-up stretches we went for a ten kilometre run, which left him sweating and out of breath.

"I'll... see you... after... I shower," he managed to say, in between gasps.

"We're not done yet," I told him.

"What?" he didn't look happy with the news; his face red and flushed.

"There's still a workout to do." I reached for my whistle.

"God help me," he prayed, looking heavenward.

"He is. He sent you me."

"I'm so lucky." He didn't sound as if he meant it.

"Yes, you are," I informed him. "Now, follow me," I instructed, as I led the way to his gym. A further twenty minutes of punishing cardio and weight training left him lying breathless on the floor.

"I thought I was in good shape," he panted.

"You're definitely not." I didn't spare his feelings. "However, you soon will be. I'm making it my mission to get you fighting fit."

He raised an eyebrow, but said nothing.

"*Now* you can shower," I said, dismissing him. "I'll meet you at the first tee in thirty minutes. And don't be late," I warned, as I jogged out of the gym. I was showered, changed and waiting for him when he arrived exactly twenty-nine minutes later. "Right on time." I was impressed.

He took his bag out of the golf buggy and put it on a trolley.

"I thought we'd walk today because apparently I need the exercise."

"That's the spirit!" I ignored his sarcasm and blew my whistle.

"You don't need that," Nathaniel said, putting a hand up to his ear.

"Yes, I do. You are being drilled." I blew it again to make my point.

"I'm not in the army," he complained.

"No, but by the time I'm finished with you, you could be. You'll be in the best physical shape of your life."

"And how's that going to help my golf?" I could hear doubt creeping into his voice.

"You'll be fit - fit to fight."

He sighed and shook his head.

"You'll be physically, mentally and emotionally fit. Fit to fight, and fit to win."

I was going to use all my angelic powers to turn Nathaniel into a lean, mean, golfing machine. His stick wasn't a sword, but I was going to teach him how to wield it like one and use it to wipe out his opponents. Like a soldier he would go out and do battle on the fairways; swinging his way to victory and annihilating the opposition along the way.

"I have a plan," I announced, (and it was one I was confident would work.).

"I'm all ears," Nathaniel said, leaning on his club.

"It's called the F-Plan. First, you get fit. Then you find focus. And then, you forget them."

"I don't understand. Forget who?"

"Your fans, supporters, spectators. In fact, anyone who's watching you," I explained.

"I don't want to forget them. I love having my fans there."

"They're still going to be there, but you have to forget that they are. They're distracting you."

"They're supporting me," he pointed out.

"They're putting pressure on you."

Yet Nathaniel didn't see it the way I did.

"That was your problem yesterday, and I'm guessing that's been your problem all along. Everyone was expecting you to do well and you wanted to please everyone. It was too much pressure and the pressure got to you."

"I just had a bad day," he said, dismissing my theory.

"You've had more than one bad day – you've had three hundred and sixty-five of them in a row. This is your problem – and I can fix it – with my F-Plan."

"How can I forget them when they're standing right there?"

"Wait, you're skipping a step: Find focus first."

He looked totally confused.

"Let me get this clear – you want me to focus on the ball and then forget about everyone watching me play?"

"I didn't say focus on the ball; I said you needed to find focus. Okay then," I said, blowing my whistle. "Let's get started."

"Do you have to do that?" he asked, as he pointed to the whistle.

"Yes, I do. I've already told you – this is a drill." Besides, I liked it!

He shook his head and went to stand behind the ball.

"No!" I blew my whistle loudly. "You need to focus first!" With the lack of anything else available, I suggested he focus on me.

So he stared at me and said, "Right, I'm focused."

"I'm the only one watching you," I told him.

He looked around but there was no one else there. "I know you are," he said.

"You see only me," I said in a hypnotic voice, which I was sure would help him block out the imaginary crowd.

"Please tell me you're not seeing people Anna!" He looked worried.

I gave a short, sharp, blast on my whistle.

"Focus!"

"I see only you," he replied, pretending to be in a trance.

"Good. Now whack the little ball thing and put it in

the hole in as few shots as possible," I instructed him.

"Aye, aye captain." He stood to attention.

"It's lieutenant," I corrected him.

"Yes ma'am!" He saluted before taking aim and firing the ball straight down the fairway. It was a perfect shot.

"I don't like to blow my own trumpet (or whistle), but I told you this would work," I gloated, as we walked down the fairway.

Shot after shot, I got him to focus first before hitting the ball. Nathaniel was sceptical – he thought it was a fluke – but tallying up the score, after the final birdie putt on the eighteenth it was obvious my plan was working. I knew it to be so but it took a few more days before I convinced Nathaniel, and a few days after that before we were finally ready to put it to the test at his club.

He was playing a four ball with Duke and two other members. Nathaniel managed to arrange it so I could caddie for him. Hole after hole, he looked to me first. He found focus and it was clear – not just to me but to everyone else too – that he had regained his form. Duke walked over to me on the fifteenth as Nathaniel lined up a tricky putt.

"I didn't believe you could help him." He kept his voice low so as not to distract Nathaniel who proceeded to sink an almost impossibly long putt. "But I believe it now."

I smiled as he walked over and slapped Nathaniel on the back. I was pleased with the progress I was making but I knew there was still a long way to go. It would take time, and I didn't know how much time I had.

18
Fair Game

A few weeks later, we were making our way to Los Angeles. It was Nathaniel's first tournament, and he was under pressure to perform in front of the general public as well as his peers. There was no more time to prepare, and I just hoped all our hard work would pay off. On the flight across, Nathaniel and Duke studied the course and planned their strategy. I whiled away the time looking out of the window, searching blue sky for a heaven that was hidden from me. I couldn't see it, or the earth below me, until finally we broke the bank of white fluffy cloud and I saw a sprawling city shimmering in the morning sunlight.

"The city of angels," Nathaniel said. He was leaning over the back of my chair and I wondered if that was true. "I hope they'll be watching over me tomorrow."

I didn't know about the rest of them, but I certainly would be. As it turned out, I didn't see anyone from the heavenly realm, but the angels were indeed smiling on

Nathaniel because by the end of the first day he was only two shots behind the leader. Yoshung Orizon, who was a rising star in the golfing world, maintained his lead, and a faultless final round saw him take the trophy. However, Nathaniel kept his focus throughout, and being placed third was a great start to the tour.

I was so happy to see him smiling as he walked off the course, stopping to sign autographs for his young fans. I thought about Jack and wondered how the little boy was doing.

"That was great!" Nathaniel said, grinning from ear to ear.

"It was! Well done," I replied, giving credit where it was due. His mind had been focused on his game and he hadn't been distracted by the spectators. "But you aren't fighting," I told him. "This is a battle – you need to find your killer instinct."

He shook his head. "I don't have one."

"Of course you do. Everyone does."

"No, they don't Anna," he laughed.

This was no laughing matter.

"You need to start thinking of your stick as a sword, and your opponents as your enemy. You have to slay them and seize victory."

"Well, thank you for that very graphic visual but that's not how I play. I do the best I can and if I don't, then I don't deserve to win."

I sighed and realised the only person Nathaniel

Banks would ever fight with was himself. This was a slight setback in my otherwise perfect F-Plan. If he wasn't going to fight the competition, he was going to have to fight for himself. Either way, Nathaniel Banks was going to fight!

The weeks flew by as one tournament followed another. It was a succession of courses, crowds and hotels. Considering I had no wings, I spent a lot of time flying as we made our way back across the country. Nathaniel went from strength to strength. After Los Angeles, he came third in Phoenix and was runner up in both Atlanta and Cleveland. He had his first win in Palm Beach, followed by another in Orlando. Media interest had grown with his successes, but I was afraid headlines like, 'Banksy's Big Comeback,' and 'Banks on Course for Major Win' would put too much pressure on him. I was more determined than ever to help him focus on his game.

It was bad enough that there was pressure to please his fans who crowded the courses to watch him play, but now he knew the eyes of the world were on him too. There was so much expectation for him to do well. Jacksonville was the last PGA tournament before Augusta – the first Major of the year – and one that would really test just how well my plan was working. The press had gathered, as they did before every tournament, and the players filed in one by one to answer questions. I watched as Nathaniel sat down and took off his cap. Cameras flashed as reporters shouted questions at him.

"Dan from CBN —Your ex-wife has said she's worried you will crack under pressure again, like you did last year at Augusta. Do you think that will happen?"

Why was he bringing up his ex-wife? I could feel myself starting to get angry, but Nathaniel remained composed and replied that he was happy with his game and was looking forward to playing at Augusta.

"Do you think that your break-up and subsequent divorce was the reason you lost your game last year?" said Candy, from HBO.

"I would prefer to concentrate on this year Candy. I have a great team working with me and I'm confident that I will continue to go from strength to strength."

"Your ex-caddie has criticised some of the changes you've made to your game. What would you say to that?" Gary from NBC continued to prod.

I watched as they circled like wolves, working to bring down their prey. They were re-opening an old wound with questions they knew would upset him. Why were they doing it? It was as if they wanted to see him fail. *Leave him alone!* I screamed inside, and lights started to flicker on and off, which was apparently a side effect of 'angry Anna'.

For a second their attention turned away from Nathaniel, and I could see the fear and self-doubt on his face. While everyone else in the room looked at the ceiling, his eyes found mine and I gave him a reassuring smile. There was a loud screech before the organiser spoke into a microphone. "Thank you very much Nathaniel, and next we have Carlton Wade."

Nathaniel shook hands with the Texan golfer as he left the stage, and I caught up with him out of sight of the cameras.

"Are you okay?" I asked without waiting for a reply. "Those assholes had no right to attack you like that!" I was still furious at how they'd treated him.

"They were just doing their job."

"Their job is to report on the game, not pry into your private life. They were playing dirty. They were trying to put you off, but they're not going to! So, you pick up those sticks and you thrash your way to victory!"

"I'm scared," Nathaniel said.

Oh no! They had planted the seed of doubt and now he feared failure. I desperately tried to undo the damage they had done.

"There is nothing to be frightened of Nathaniel. You are a fantastic golfer. Stay focused, forget everything those..." I struggled to find a word strong enough to describe the horrible reporters who had upset him so much so settled on 'guttersnipes.' "Go out there and fight to win! We're at war!" I added, for good measure. It was a very inspiring team talk, even if I did say so myself.

"I'm not scared of the game Anna, I'm a little bit

scared of you."

"What?"

"Just a bit," he laughed. "You can be a little frightening at times."

Duke walked over and took the bag.

"Ready?" he asked.

"Never more so," Nathaniel replied. "See you in the field, lieutenant," and he winked at me as he walked off. "Oh, and Anna," I looked up when I heard him say my name. "Try not to kill anyone while I'm away."

I looked over at the loathsome journalists.

"Only if you kill it on the course."

"Deal."

And off he went into battle.

19

Film Star

The course was crowded, and all eyes were on Nathaniel. I had expected him to lose focus after the press conference, but he stayed calm and in control from the first tee to the last. It had been a tough field, and everyone had been on top form, their minds on the upcoming Major. I was so proud of how Nathaniel played, and I cheered louder than anyone else when he finished nine under par. I hugged him hard when he walked off the final green.

"You do realise I didn't win?" he said, as he held me close.

"It was a triumph," I told him. "I thought you would lose focus, but you didn't."

"I wouldn't call coming second a triumph."

A course official walked over and said, "They're ready for you Mr. Banks."

He was referring to the pack of press wolves and I could feel my body tense.

"It's okay, I've got this." Nathaniel reached over and gently touched my clenched fist. "Are they all still there?" he asked. "You didn't kill any of them while I was busy playing, did you?"

"No, they're all still there – for now." I assured him.

Nathaniel laughed, and I watched as he walked confidently behind the official, his shoulders back and head held high.

After dinner I lay on top of the bed and switched from one TV channel to the next as I munched potato crisps from the hotel's mini-bar. I flicked from a surgically enhanced woman with unnaturally white teeth who was advertising toothpaste, to a soap opera with overly dramatic dialogue and subtitles. I switched to another channel and saw lights flashing and heard gun shots as two cops sped through the streets of New York City in hot pursuit of a bad guy. I stayed long enough on channel 241 to hear a Fox Sports commentator report on Khayone Nikosi's win today in Jacksonville: "The South African world number two clinched victory at the final PGA tournament before Augusta," he announced. Then a picture of Nathaniel flashed up on the screen: "It was yet another good finish for the former number one golfer, Nathaniel Banks, who took second place. He seems to have finally found his form again, and if he continues to play like this, he could be on course for his first Major win in over a year. Fox Sports will bring you live coverage from Augusta, so stay tuned folks to see who will pick up the first Major title of the year. This is Ben Brown reporting," and he flashed a pearly-white toothed smile at the camera. *People on TV have really amazing teeth*, I thought as I switched again and saw Holly walk out onto a floodlit stage. The crisp packet flew out of my hand and ready salted crisps scattered all over the bed.

"What on earth is she doing on TV?" I wondered aloud, and then nearly fell off the bed when she turned around and answered me.

"I've always wanted to be an actress."

"This isn't possible…" I watched and listened as she launched into a soliloquy from *Hamlet*.

"'*There are more things in heaven and earth* Anna, *than are dreamt of in your philosophy*'."

I was left in no doubt she was talking to me and not to Horatio, or some unseen audience.

"Holly?"

"'Tis I," she bowed, theatrically.

"What are you doing?" I was incredulous.

"Shakespeare, the bard of yesteryear."

"I know who Shakespeare is. What I meant was, what are you doing on the TV?"

"It's not ideal – I really would've preferred the big screen – but here I am." When she stopped spinning around on stage, she spied the potato crisps and said, "*Mmm*, those look tasty. What flavour are they?"

Trust Holly to notice food!

"They're ready salted," I told my food-loving fellow angel.

"That's my fourth favourite flavour! My first is salt and vinegar, then sour cream and chive, then chilli," she said, counting each off on her fingers. "Then it's ready salted, barbeque, and my sixth favourite is—"

"Stop!" I neither needed nor wanted to know her top ten palate-pleasing potato crisp flavours.

She turned and walked over to a black grand piano on the stage behind her. A spotlight then fell on Holly as she started to sing a song I had never heard before. I flopped back on the bed.

"It's from *A Star is Born*." Holly enlightened me. "Very appropriate, don't you think?"

"It is actually," it was about time that she asked if I was happy being here. She'd never once asked me how I was coping with being stranded on earth.

"Exactly!" said Holly, "I'm a star waiting to be born! I should've played Ally," she told me.

"Who's Ally?"

"How do you *not* know who Ally is?" Holly said, as she jeered and shook her head, "Ally is the star!"

"The star of what?" I asked, still puzzled.

"The star of A Star is Born!" Holly was getting frustrated with my ignorance.

"Which is what?" I was now completely confused.

"Only the best, most brilliant film. It was a huge hit last year. How can you not know that? Everyone knows that. Where have you been?"

"Let me see… last year… where was I? Oh yes, I was busy doing battle with the Almighty's enemies. I'm sorry, I must've missed it," I told her.

"Lady Gaga played Ally, which was my part. I'm a much better singer and a far more talented actress," she boasted, although I seriously doubted it.

"You're an angel, not an actress," I informed her.

She completely ignored me and continued to tell me how wonderful she would've been as Ally – an undiscovered talent who is then coaxed into the spotlight by Jackson Maine. I wasn't seeing Holly's connection with the character. Firstly, she wasn't talented and secondly, she clearly didn't need any coaxing to take centre stage. I knew I was going to regret this, but I had to ask, "And who is Jackson Maine?"

"I fall in love with him in the film. He's played by Bradley Cooper, who is *so* hot!"

"I'll take your word for it." I'd neither seen nor heard of Jackson or Bradley before.

"You don't have to – I'll show you." She ran off stage and out of sight.

Was Bradley there? How did she manage that? Oh no, had she taken her crush on the actor too far and kidnapped him? Was she holding the poor man captive? I was trying to remember if I'd seen any news bulletins about a missing actor, when Holly wheeled, who I assumed was Bradley, onto the stage. Thankfully it was just a large framed photo mounted on an easel, which was reminiscent of the kind you use at funerals and memorials.

"Bradley, this is Anna. Anna, this is my beloved Bradley," she told me, as she fawned over the photograph.

I would have to get her help from whichever heavenly department dealt with delusional angels.

"He's a Hollywood heartthrob. How don't you know him? I mean, where have you been—" She stopped herself. "I'm sorry, I forgot you were busy slaying the masses."

I didn't appreciate the sarcasm, but I let it go.

"Bradley and I are in love," she swooned.

"Does Bradley know?" I was fairly certain he didn't.

"In the film, we fall in love and then as my star ascends into the heavens—"

"Where you belong," I said, interrupting her synopsis.

"My poor Bradley's starts to wane, and he can't handle all of this." I watched Holly wave her hands up and down her body, and suddenly I felt sorry for the Hollywood actor. I found her very hard to handle too!

"He had so many demons." She was starting to cry. "He tried to fight them, but he couldn't." Her voice was breaking with emotion. "He was in hell," she wailed.

Holly could make you feel like that.

"And then I lost him," she sobbed. "I lost Bradley! I

love you Bradley!" she cried out.

"Is Bradley dead?" I asked. That would certainly explain the funeral-like framed photograph.

"No, of course not!' she said, as if I was stupid. "He dies in the film." She stopped crying and sat back down at the piano.

She started to serenade the rugged-looking man who was smiling at me from behind glass. She was talking about kissing and touching and I really did not want that visual!

"Holly," I tried to get her attention.

"Holly!" I raised my voice but she was lost in the love song, so I tried one more time before I switched channels. *She is one frustrating angel* I thought as I lay back on the bed and heard a loud crunching sound, followed by a loud rapping.

"Hello?" I heard someone say as I sat bolt upright again.

"Hello?" I answered, wondering who would be banging on my door at this hour.

"Hello." Holly's face was pressed up against the glass of the TV screen. "Did you just change channels?"

"Yes."

"Well, Bradley and I were very offended." She stepped back and put her arm around his photograph. "Just so you know, it was an Oscar-winning performance. And you missed it!" she said, accusingly.

"Lady Gaga's?"

"No! Mine!" she shouted. Holly didn't believe in hiding her 'talent' behind a bushel.

"Okay," I said, in a tone I hoped would placate the histrionic diva. I hadn't seen the film; I hadn't seen her singing and I didn't know who Oscar was. It was late and there was no way I was going to ask at this time of the night. "Congratulations. Now, if you don't mind, I need to get to sleep."

"No, wait!" Holly shouted, as I picked up the remote control.

"Night Holly." I took aim at the TV.

"Stop! I have a message."

I lowered my 'weapon'.

"What is it?"

I could see her breathe a sigh of relief.

"Jack is at the academy."

"He's there now?" I'd told the little boy I'd be there too but I wasn't; I was here, in Jacksonville.

"Yes." Holly had suddenly become monosyllabic.

I wanted to know how long he'd been there and how long he was staying, but I didn't get the chance to ask before my featherless friend took a final bow and exited stage right.

"Wait! Holly! Come back!" I shouted at the TV, but the screen went black.

I picked up the remote control and pressed buttons, but Holly wasn't on any channel.

Yet again she had disappeared.

20

Fever Pitch

This was awful. I'd promised Jack I'd see him at the academy. I ran out of my room and along the corridor.

"Nathaniel! Nathaniel! Nathaniel!" I banged on his door.

"What is it? What's wrong?" He flung it open.

"It's Jack," I cried. I was so upset.

"What's happened? Is he okay?"

"No!" I wailed. "He's at the academy and I'm not there. You're not there. I promised him I'd be there. I promised him you'd be there. And we're not there! We're here!"

I could see Nathaniel breathe a sigh of relief.

"It's all right. We're going to see him tomorrow."

"Why didn't you tell me?"

If he had done I wouldn't be panicking now or standing in my pyjamas banging on his door like a crazy person.

"It was going to be a surprise."

Well, it wasn't a very good one!

He was smiling at me as he leaned against the door frame, half-naked. He had obviously been in such a rush to answer the door that he'd forgotten to put on the rest of his clothes.

"Were you having a snack?" he asked, pointing at my hair.

I reached up and realised that some of the potato crisps were stuck there. I tried to get them out.

"Here, let me." Nathaniel took a step towards me.

I shifted uncomfortably from foot to foot as he picked out crushed crisps.

"Thank you for that," I said, and quickly stepped back, feeling flushed. "And sorry for waking you. I'll let you get back to bed," I told him, as I continued to back away. "See you in the morning." I started to walk quickly back to my room.

"Anna – I think you should come in," he called out after me.

"No, no, no," I blustered and babbled. That was not a good idea.

"You don't have your key card."

"Dammit!" I'd forgotten it when I raced out of the room. I'd also forgotten to put a comb through my hair, to put makeup on and, like Nathaniel, to get dressed. I reluctantly turned around and walked slowly back towards Nathaniel who had managed to fall out of bed looking like a Greek God.

"Come inside and I'll call for someone."

I had no choice but to brush past his athletic body as he held the door open.

Please put on a shirt, I silently prayed as he called the concierge.

"Could you send someone up to open room 209 please? Miss Frost has locked herself out."

I hovered near the door, feeling very stupid and embarrassed.

"They're on their way," he told me.

"Thanks, and sorry again for getting you out of bed." I looked at the crumpled sheets and felt really awkward. "I better go," I told Nathaniel, who had started to walk towards me. My heart was racing as I tried to find the door handle. I was pressed against it, and now Nathaniel, with his naked torso, was standing right in front of me. My breath quickened as he reached out. I closed my eyes and then suddenly I was falling.

"Anna." I opened them again to see him staring down at me.

I hadn't realised he was going to open the door, which I had just fallen through! Now I was lying in the hallway, flat on my back, looking up at the semi-naked golfer and a smirking bell-boy, who had been sent from down below to let me back into my room.

"I have your key Miss Frost." He grinned inanely at me and then at Nathaniel who was in the process of picking me up off the floor.

"Are you okay?" Nathaniel asked.

"Perfectly fine, thank you. Well, goodnight Nathaniel." I brushed myself down before addressing the young whippersnapper who was wearing a royal blue uniform and a silly grin. "After you," I said, and I marched down the corridor without a backward glance.

"Did you have a good night, Miss Frost?" The bell-boy smirked as he opened my door.

I chose to ignore him and let the door slam behind me. I most definitely had not had a good night!

21

Foaming at the mouth

The next morning Nathaniel and I drove to his academy, which turned out to be much bigger than I had imagined. On the sprawling estate were two full-size golf courses, a putting green and driving range. There was also a huge club house and campus where a team of highly trained professionals helped the children attending. On-site luxury accommodation meant that their parents could stay with them while the children took instructional classes to improve their game.

Nathaniel gave me a tour of the fantastic facility that also provided specialist rehabilitation for those children who had suffered injury or who had health problems that affected their game; children just like Jack. Nathaniel Banks had made a lot of money from the game of golf, but it was clear he had also given a lot back. He had a charitable spirit and a kind heart.

As we walked around, I could see just how much the staff liked him and how much the children loved him.

Every class we went to, they vied for his attention. They all wanted to spend time with him, and he was as generous with that as he was with his money. Yet there was only one little boy I was here to see, and when we finally found him he was finishing a physiotherapy session in the indoor swimming pool.

"Anna! Nate!" He screamed in delight when he saw us.

"No running!" his physiotherapist shouted, as he charged towards us across a wet floor. Before I knew it, he'd wrapped wet arms round me and was giving me the biggest hug.

"Hello stranger," I said, hugging him in return.

"I'm so happy you're here." He smiled up at me.

"And I'm so happy to see you again. How are you getting on?" I asked Jack who was now starting to shiver after coming out of the warm water. I was looking around for a towel when I saw his physiotherapist bringing one over. She put it around his small shoulders and told us he was doing great.

"But you should get changed before you catch a cold," she told him.

I could see he didn't want to go.

"We'll wait for you to get dressed and then you can show us just how much progress you've made. How about that?"

"Okay." He smiled and happily hurried off to the changing rooms.

Lorna, his physiotherapist, told us she had been working to re-build Jack's muscle strength, which had been lost during his time in hospital, and that she had seen a remarkable improvement in a very short time.

"He's been lovely to work with," she told us.

"He's just a joy to be around," I said, and Nathaniel agreed.

Soon Jack re-appeared, dressed in white shorts and a pale blue sports shirt.

"So, young man, would you like to play a few holes?"

He looked so excited.

I watched as the master instructed his enthusiastic student. Jack listened intently and did exactly what he was told to do. It was fantastic for him to have one-to-one time with his hero. However, there were other children desperate for Nathaniel's attention too and so, after the ninth hole, he told Jack he had a lesson to take and would have to go.

"When is your next class Jack?" he asked.

"It's at three p.m. – with coach Holly."

I got a sudden sinking feeling in the pit of my stomach when I heard her name.

"I don't think I know a coach called Holly." Nathaniel confirmed my worst fears that the CIA angel had infiltrated the ranks of his staff. "She must be new."

"How about we let Nathaniel go and take his lesson and I'll come with you to your class?" I suggested, as I picked up his bag. My idea was met with a loud, "Yay!"

"I'll see you both afterwards." Nathaniel jumped in the buggy as we walked back over the beautifully manicured lawns.

"That was fantastic! I got to play with Nate!" Jack was euphoric. "I've always wanted to play golf with him. Isn't he great Anna?"

"Well, he's not yet – but he's getting better."

"I think he's brilliant!" I couldn't help smiling at his enthusiasm.

"And so are you," I told the little boy, who gave me a big smile in return. "You will be winning tournaments again in no time."

"Nate will too. You've fixed him Anna."

On the way back, Jack told me all about his time at the academy – what he'd been doing and the new friends he'd made – and he told me that his granddad Tom had come to visit him.

"I was so excited to see him! I haven't seen him in such a long time."

He must live far away, I thought, as I listened to Jack tell me that he'd promised to take him out to play golf.

"There are lots of great courses where granddad lives." I presumed Jack was going to spend the upcoming Easter holidays with him.

Suddenly, he started waving and calling out to coach Holly who was standing in front of the clubhouse, surrounded by children.

"Holly is my favourite," he said.

"Why is that?" I asked, as I tried to see if it was indeed my fellow Christmas Incident Angel who was too far away for me to be absolutely sure.

"Because she's the funniest!" he shouted, as he ran towards the other children gathered around her.

Sure enough, Holly's latest disguise was as a golfing coach, although how she had orchestrated that, I had no idea. As far as I knew, Holly knew as much about golf as I did when I first came here – a big fat nothing!

"Welcome boys and girls, parents and visiting guests." I arrived just in time to hear the start of her opening address to the class. She directed her gaze straight towards me and said, "For those of you who don't know me I'm Holly, your events organiser here at The Nathaniel Banks Academy of Golf."

The children started to cheer, while their parents clapped. I didn't do either.

"For today's fun event, we're going to need two teams – the red team and the blue team." She walked among the children, handing out red and blue sports bibs. "And for this particular challenge we need a volunteer. Can we have a show of hands?" I hadn't even moved but I heard her say, "Thank you to the lady dressed in blue."

All eyes turned to me.

"Anna!" Jack started to clap loudly.

"No, I—" I began to protest but Holly had already

joined in with Jack's applause.

"Let's give Anna a big hand to thank her for volunteering."

She walked over and took me by the arm.

"I didn't volunteer," I hissed at her, under my breath.

"Don't worry, it'll be fun," she said, as she led me over to what looked like wooden stocks once used as a means of public humiliation.

"You're not putting me in stocks," I stated firmly.

"Of course I'm not," she said, before releasing my arm and turning her attention back to the children. "Now everyone – what is the most important thing you have to learn in a game of golf?"

Lots of hands shot up in the air and there was a chorus of answers from the children.

"Putting."

"Hitting."

"Your swing."

"No, no, no," Holly told them. "It's your aim. If you can't aim the lovely little ball in the direction of the hole then you're not going to be very good at golf, are you?"

There was unanimous agreement from the children who were listening to her every word.

"So today, my gorgeous little golfers, our team challenge is all about aim – how to take it, execute it and perfect it. And just to make sure that you all try your absolute hardest, there is a big prize for the winners."

Everyone was wide-eyed, eager to know what their

reward would be.

"The team that wins today…" Holly teased her captive audience. "Drum roll please… will get to spend *all* day tomorrow with the absolutely brilliant Mr. Nathaniel Banks."

Right on cue, Nathaniel appeared beside me.

"I thought you had a lesson?" I questioned him, while the children excitedly jumped about.

"I couldn't say in front of Jack as that would've given the game away."

I was more than a little worried about what the game actually was.

"It was very good of you to volunteer," Nathaniel said.

I tried to force a smile but it ended up as a grimace.

"Okey-dokey then, let the game begin. Mr. Banks, can I ask you to do the honours and help our volunteer into position?"

"My pleasure,' Nathaniel said, and put his hand on the small of my back.

I felt a tingle run up my spine as he walked me over to the wooden contraption. He lifted up the top and Holly told me to place my neck and wrists onto the grooves. She'd tricked me! I was in the stocks and there was nothing I could do but acquiesce and let Nathaniel lock me into the instrument of punishment. I waited until he stepped back, and Holly walked over to check I was properly secured.

"You told me you wouldn't put me in the stocks!" I was livid.

"I didn't, Nathaniel did. And it's a pillory, not the stocks," she corrected, before going off to retrieve two large buckets of soapy water and two sponges.

I watched as she lined up the red and blue teams.

"Here are the rules: Each team will have two goes to hit the target. You must take aim and try your best to hit Anna smack bang on her lovely little face. You will score one point if you do, and the team with the most points at the end will win. Is everyone ready?"

"Yes!" they all shouted.

"I can't hear you! Is everyone ready?"

"Yes!" they all screamed in unison, as I did the mental arithmetic. There were twenty children in total – ten in each team – and with two throws each, I could potentially be hit in the face forty times!

Holly walked over to me. "Is our volunteer ready?"

"Yes," I said, for the benefit of the crowd. Yet as they cheered, I told Holly that when I was released from my restraints I was going to take aim with something other than a sponge. "And trust me, I never miss!" I threatened.

"Jolly good then!" she said cheerily, picking up her clipboard.

Unfortunately for me, it turned out that practically all of the kids had a perfect aim with one after the other hitting their target. I swallowed soapy water, which stung my eyes, as soaking sponges slapped against my face and fell to the ground. Eighteen out of twenty children hit me, and the contest ended in a draw.

"Well, I guess we'll have to have another round," I heard Holly tell the children, who were delighted at the thought of pummelling me again.

"No!" I spat out soapy water and Nathaniel stepped in.

"A member from each team will have one more throw to decide the winner," he suggested, in an effort to save me from the humiliation of another assault. "Choose who you want from your team to take the shot."

Each team went into a huddle to make their decision. A boy, with big shoulders and a broad back, stepped up from the blue team while Jack represented the reds. I really wanted the red team to win; so much so that I willed Jack's well-built opponent to miss. He loaded his sponge with as much soapy water as possible and took aim. I knew there was no way he would miss his target. However, just as he launched the projectile, Holly sneezed so loudly it made him jump and he missed!

"That's not fair," he complained. "I want to take my shot again!" Despite his protestations, Holly ushered him out of the way and told him not to be a bad sport.

Jack walked up and sheepishly picked up his sponge. I knew he didn't want to throw it at me. When he looked up at me I gave him a big smile.

"You can do it Jack," I encouraged him. His team began chanting his name.

He took aim and I was delighted to be hit in the face. The red team had won, and Jack would have another day golfing with Nathaniel. It had all been worth it.

Although I was still going to kill Holly!

22

Food, Flirting and Foul Play

Nathaniel dropped me back at the house before speeding off up the drive. As soon as I reached the front door, I heard Rosaria's girlish giggling. I opened it to see Leonardo – shirt open, chest bare – leaning alluringly over the stove, while she stirred a pot. For the second time that day I watched a master at work. This one excelled in the art of flirtation and I felt my stomach turn as he suggestively licked a spoon in front of the coquettish young maid.

"*Ciao bella.*" He took a well-earned break from his craft as I walked through the door. "Or maybe not... What happened to you?"

"Holly happened to me!"

Leonardo and Rosaria both looked like they had just stepped off a catwalk. Sex appeal was oozing from their every pore, while at that moment the only thing I was oozing was soapy water – all over the floor.

"I'm going for a shower," I announced, as I

squelched my way across the room, leaving puddles in my wake.

"Dinner will be ready in thirty minutes Miss Anna," Rosaria shouted from the kitchen.

I raised my hand in acknowledgement, and for the umpteenth time said, "It's just Anna."

Rummaging around in the wardrobe, I found a suitable summer dress and heels. I blow-dried my hair and put on some makeup. I was still going to pale into insignificance compared to Venus and Adonis in the other room, but at least I no longer looked like a drowned rat. Leonardo wolf-whistled loudly when I walked back into the living room, and I saw that Rosaria was now busy fluttering her eyelids at Nathaniel, who was at the door.

"I'm sorry," he said to me. "I didn't know you had company."

For a second I'd forgotten all about Leonardo until he said, "It's a pleasure to finally meet you. Anna's told me all about you." He introduced himself to Nathaniel before suggesting he join them for dinner. "Rosaria has prepared the most amazing chicken *chilaquiles*. They're the best I've ever tasted." He smiled at the young cook who turned her full flirtatious attention back to the handsome heavenly being.

"I won't intrude," Nathaniel said, still standing in the doorway. Addressing me, he continued, "I only called to see if you wanted to go to the academy tomorrow. It's

Jack's last day but don't worry. You should spend time with your—" Before he could finish the sentence I told him that of course I wanted to go.

He looked at Leonardo.

"I'm afraid I won't be able to join you." Leonardo declined an invitation that hadn't even been extended. "This is just a flying visit – to see how my little angel is getting on."

He walked over and put his arm around me. I tried to shrug it off but he kept a firm hold.

"She's doing a great job," Nathaniel assured him.

"Do you hear that angel? You're doing great." He squeezed me hard.

Stop calling me angel and let me go, I shouted in my head but telepathy apparently wasn't one of Leonardo's superpowers.

"She always doubts herself, and I'm always telling her she has to have faith – like I have in her. Isn't that right darling?"

No, it bloody well wasn't! If Leonardo didn't stop this, I was going to use one of my superpowers and Felipe him across the room!

"You see *amore* you have nothing to worry about." He squeezed my cheek before walking over to shake Nathaniel's hand, taking me with him in the process.

"I'll see you in the morning," I said to Nathaniel as he walked back to the golf buggy.

"*Ciao bello*." Leonardo waved him off.

"Let me go!" I hissed, and tried to break free of his vice-like grip.

"Dinner is served," Rosario said. We both turned to see the sexy young maid carry two plates of spicy Mexican food to the table.

"That is a feast for the eyes." He salivated at the sight. "After you," Leonardo made a sweeping bow and stepped back.

I glared at him before stomping over to the table. I had no idea what Leonardo was doing but I was going to find out as soon as I had devoured the delicious chilli chicken. It would be a sin for good food to go to waste and I was a good angel, who never sinned (except for once or twice when I got drunk. Or was it three times? Oh, and then there was the swearing and the lying, and a 'supposed' case of GBH but other than that, I was as pure and good as the day I left heaven.). That was more than I could say for my angelic cohort, who was definitely up to no good. As soon as Rosaria had left, I asked him exactly what it was he was playing at.

"I don't know what you mean." He looked hurt by my accusation.

"Calling me 'angel' and 'darling'."

"They are terms of affection, and I have a lot of affection for you." He jumped up off the leather sofa he'd been lounging on and walked over to me. I don't know how Leonardo and Rosaria managed to make walking look so sexy and seductive, but they did. He stood close to me so I could see the white alabaster skin of his chest, and smell the faint scent of a spicy cologne; the warmth of his breath on my skin.

"I must say goodnight, *mia cara*." He gently brushed his lips across the back of my hand.

"But you only just got here."

"I know, but my work here is done." He swaggered towards the front door.

"What work?" I stumbled across the room after him, finally catching up at the door.

"Say hi to Jack for me." He was being deliberately evasive.

"Wait, you didn't answer my question," I protested.

He turned around.

"I know." He was being secretive and then he disappeared out the door. "*Ciao bella*," I heard him say from the other side, and then silence.

He was gone – again!

23
A Fetal Attraction

The following morning Nathaniel arrived in a silver sports car to collect me. I sank into the soft black leather upholstery and we sped off. It wasn't long before his erratic driving started to make me feel sick. On the freeway, there was a slight respite from all the stopping and starting but when he swung off it again, I felt nauseous.

"You have to stop! Quick!" I said, winding down the window in the hope that fresh air would stop the inevitable from happening.

Nathaniel slammed on the brakes, which didn't help and I fell out of the car before being violently sick at the side of the road. He held back my hair and rubbed my back as I continued to heave and vomit.

"I'm sorry Anna."

As I gasped for breath and waited for the sickness to stop, I realised that those were the first words he'd spoken to me since we'd left the house.

"Are you okay?" Nathaniel handed me a bottle of water that he'd fetched from the car.

My eyes were watering from the strain of retching.

"No," I managed to say. "Your driving is shit!"

"I'm sorry." He tried not to laugh. "I promise I will drive *really* slow the rest of the way."

If he didn't drive at a snail's pace, I was not getting back in the car with him.

"Let's sit for a while until you feel better."

I staggered slowly towards a nearby bench, holding my sore stomach. Once seated, I sipped the water and took deep breaths of the fresh morning air. Nathaniel sat quietly beside me. Finally he asked, "Did you and Leonardo have a good night?"

"He didn't stay. He had work to do," I lied. According to Leonardo, his work here was already done. I didn't know what he meant by that and his strange behaviour the night before was still puzzling me.

"Is that how you two met?" Nathaniel asked.

"Yes, we met in a lift." The memory reminded me of the world I'd left behind. I looked up at the bright blue sky. "Everything changed that day. Nothing was ever the same again." I was no longer in the army or in heaven, and no longer an angel.

"*Wow*." Nathaniel, who'd been staring at the ground, sat up and said, "It sounds as if he swept you off your feet."

"He did," (quite literally, whenever I fell through the

189

door of the Guardians' headquarters.).

"Is he CIA too?"

"No, he's in a different department."

Nathaniel didn't pry further, and the conversation stopped again. I sat quietly beside him with my eyes closed, letting the warm rays of sunshine fall on my face. I thought about all that had happened since I'd met Leonardo; the great rollercoaster of a journey that had brought me to this point in time – to this place. I turned to look at Nathaniel.

"Are you happy Anna?" He was searching beyond the surface, looking deep into the depths of my soul, and it took my breath away.

"Yes, I am." I didn't have to think about it. I smiled at the young golfer sitting beside me on a little bench, at the side of the road, somewhere in Florida. This was where my journey had led me, and I was happy that it had brought me here. I wouldn't want to change a thing. Well, except maybe Nathaniel's driving which was horrendous! I put my hand on my stomach again and looked down.

Suddenly, Nathaniel leapt off the bench, practically taking flight in the process. I was still feeling queasy, but before I could reassure him that I was not going to vomit all over him, he started to pace up and down.

"Your sickness – it all makes sense now."

Didn't it before? I thought we'd already established he was a dreadful driver and ergo, entirely responsible for aforementioned vomiting. It was crystal clear to me that his bad driving had made me—

"Pregnant!"

I spat out the mouthful of water I'd been swallowing, spraying Nathaniel who was standing in front of me pointing at my stomach.

"What?" I wailed, as I lifted my top and searched for the tell-tale pregnancy bump. Why did he think I was pregnant? My mind was racing. "Do I look fat?" I cried. I never should've eaten all those potato crisps.

"No, no, of course, you don't!" Nathaniel backtracked but it was too late.

"You said I look fat!" I was visibly upset by the accusation.

"I didn't say you looked fat Anna." He was getting flustered. "I'm sorry. It's just that you were sick and then you said you were happy and then you held your tummy tenderly." He tried and failed to explain how he'd reached this ludicrous conclusion.

"I was holding it because your horrific driving caused me to throw up and my tummy is still sore!" I clarified.

"I'm sorry, I just thought you and Leonardo were having a baby."

It was my turn to jump off the bench.

"There is no me and Leonardo! *Urgh*! Why would you think that?"

He looked totally confused. "I just thought after last

night…" His voice trailed off.

My mind scrambled back over the events of the previous evening: Leonardo had come to see me, he'd wolf-whistled when I'd walked into the room, put his arm around me and called me darling. Leonardo fancied me and he wanted to be more than friends! The thought made me feel sick all over again.

"You don't look well." My pulse was racing, my heart was beating fast, and I felt like I couldn't breathe properly. "Come and sit down." Nathaniel led me back to the bench. "I didn't mean to upset you Anna. I honestly thought that you and Leonardo were a couple."

"Well, we're not." I would have to break it to Leonardo that we never would be. "We work together – that's all. Nothing more!" I was most emphatic.

"I'm sorry if I put two and two together and got five." Nathaniel apologised for thinking that Leonardo and I were an item and also, for being bad at maths.

"It's okay," I reassured him.

"And I'm sorry for making you sick. Can you ever forgive me?" His remorseful look was hard to resist.

"*Hmm*, I don't know. I'll think about it," I told him.

"I'll make it up to you," he teased me.

"Well, you'll have to think of something super wonderful!"

"I already have. Would you like to come with me to Scotland at Easter?"

"Not if we have to drive there," I told him.

He laughed. "No, we'll fly."

"I'm fine with flying."

"Have you ever been to Scotland?" he asked me.

"No." I hadn't even heard of Scotland! "Is it far away?'

"You don't know where it is?" He sounded surprised.

Oh no! Apparently this was something everyone was supposed to know. I was failing as a human. "Of course I do," I countered, as I tried to rescue the situation. "I just can't quite place it at the moment." That vague reply should buy me enough time to find out where it was on the interweb.

Nathaniel was smiling at me.

"I don't think I've ever met anyone like you, Anna Frost."

And I took that as a compliment.

24
Freedom!

It was Jack's final day at the academy, and I was delighted he was going to spend it with Nathaniel. I chatted to Nancy and Paul who were already preparing for their son's big comeback.

"I think your dad has plans for another trophy room," I told him.

"Granddad says that I'll soon be able to play like I used to." He was pepped up by the prospect.

I remembered what Nurse Aitkens had told me – that his paralysis could never be reversed.

"That's great!" I wanted to encourage him. "You'll be champion again in no time."

"I know I won't be, but it doesn't matter because Nathaniel *will*. Won't he Anna?"

"Of course he will," I heard myself tell him.

"And we'll watch him win the Open, won't we?"

"Yes." I couldn't say no to this little boy.

"Promise?"

"I promise." I had every intention of keeping my word; I knew it would break his heart if I didn't achieve my goal of fixing Nathaniel.

After an afternoon spent with his golfing hero, it was time for us to say goodbye.

"Keep up the good work young man," Nathaniel said, as he shook the little boy's hand.

"I will," Jack said.

"And I'll see you in New York."

I was afraid Paul was going to damage Nathaniel's arm – he was shaking it that hard – as he thanked him for all he had done for his son.

"I'll see you at the Open in June," I told Jack, who hugged me hard.

"Bye Anna. Bye Nate!" He waved us off as I warily stepped back into the silver sports car.

"I'll take it slow, I promise," Nathaniel reassured me. He put the roof down and I looked back to see Jack still waving, as we drove off down the drive.

Nathaniel didn't break his promise; now all I had to do was keep mine and make sure that he won the Open, for Jack's sake. I was more driven than ever to help him succeed after meeting the little boy again. That was the goal, but to get there he had two other Majors to play – the first in Augusta.

The following week, I flew with Nathaniel and Duke to Georgia. As always, they spent the flight discussing course conditions and planning their strategy. They had a map spread out on the table in front of them and were busy talking tactics for the tournament. On the other side of the cabin, I had a map of Scotland spread out before me and I was preoccupied charting my own course.

I was reading the guidebook Nathaniel had given me and circling in red pen where I wanted to go.

"We have to go to Stirling. There's a castle!" I was so excited. "It was built way back in 1490!" That was a very long time ago. "Can we go see it? Please?" I was beside myself at the thought of seeing a genuine, honest-to-goodness citadel from centuries ago.

"Yes, we can go see it," Nathaniel said, but he didn't seem that enthusiastic about the idea. Maybe castles weren't his thing?

I read on and circled most of Perthshire before coming across something that I knew would definitely interest him. "There's a monster!" I was practically bouncing off the seat with excitement.

I expected Nathaniel to be as excited but instead he just sat staring at me.

"There's no such thing," Duke said dismissively.

"Yes there is!"

"No there isn't!" he argued.

"Yes there is! She's called Nessie and she lives in a loch." I held up the book so he could see a photograph of the spectacular sea creature.

Duke shook his head.

"It says she's a water horse. What's that?" I asked Nathaniel.

"I don't know, why don't you ask Siri?" He handed me his mobile phone.

"What's her number?"

"She doesn't have one. Just ask the phone," he told me.

"Your phone's called Siri?" I thought that was very strange.

"No, she's in the phone."

I turned the small rectangular device over in my hand. I didn't know how it was possible that a person was inside.

He took the phone from me. "Here, let me show you: Siri, what is the capital of Scotland?"

A metallic, tinny sounding voice answered, "The capital of Scotland is Edinburgh."

"Oh, that's amazing!" I grabbed it back and proceeded to exhaust Siri of all information about my new favourite country. In the process, I also exhausted Nathaniel's battery.

"Edinburgh has a castle too." I circled the city with red ink. "And Greyfriars Bobby's grave." I circled it again. "He was a little dog who stayed by his master's side even after he died,' I told Nathaniel. "Isn't that lovely?"

"Yes, very," he agreed, although he sounded distracted.

"Sorry, I won't interrupt you again." I knew he had important work to do. "I'll be quiet."

"Thank you." He smiled over at me and said, "We really need to finish this."

"Of course, I totally understand." That was much more important than our upcoming trip. "You work away."

Unfortunately, I couldn't contain my excitement as I read about a true Scottish hero. "William Wallace," I shouted out. "Had a sword!"

My outburst made Nathaniel jump and, not for the first time, Duke just shook his head.

"And he fought in battle!" I was wide-eyed, and a little star-struck.

Nathaniel got up and replaced one small rectangular device with a slightly larger one that he put on top of my map.

"Watch this." He handed me a set of headphones. "They're noise-cancelling."

Duke smirked and I stuck my tongue out at him before settling down to watch *Braveheart*.

I clapped my hands and leapt up from my seat when I realised it was a film about my Scottish superhero, who slashed his way to victory against an invading English army.

I looked over and saw that Nathaniel and Duke were devising a battle plan, just like William and his Uncle Malcolm in the film. I gave them a thumbs up.

I danced around in front of the small screen, swinging my imaginary sword as I watched Wallace slay the marauding English army. It brought back a longing for my own sword, for the EAA and for heaven. As an angel I had been a battle-hardened lieutenant, devoid of all emotion, but as a human I was a swirling mass of feelings that I couldn't seem to control, and so when we landed in Georgia, I was in a flood of tears, swearing personal revenge on the English for killing Wallace. I would exact punishment when I got my wings and my sword back.

Fired up by the film, I thought now was the perfect time for a pre-tournament motivational speech.

"Tomorrow you are going to fight like Wallace did. You will take your stick and go into battle on the greens. Slay your opponents! Take no prisoners! Oh and maybe paint your face blue because apparently it puts the fear of God into your enemies. Which, FYI, I didn't even know."

I felt certain that would inspire Nathaniel to channel his inner warrior, spur him on to show no mercy and fight – for victory in the field – for *Freedom!* Maybe William Wallace had had an F-Plan too.

"Are you ready for war?" I shouted.

He took off my headphones, picked up his device and handed me the folded-up map.

"I'm ready to play." I hoped he was too as I watched him walk down the aisle of the plane towards the open door.

I turned back to see Duke standing up, staring at me.

"You're weird," he said, before following Nathaniel.

"*You're* weird!" I retorted.

"No, you are!" he answered back.

It was Nathaniel's turn to shake his head.

"You!"

"No, you!" We continued to bicker as we stepped out into the Georgian sunshine.

25
First Major

The Masters at Augusta drew in a huge number of spectators, and I was finding it difficult to fight my way through the masses. I had to channel my inner William Wallace as I battled on against the crowds of onlookers, hole after hole, day after day, just so Nathaniel could see me. Our ritual was working as he was one shot ahead on the final day, with only the final hole left to play.

I was walking briskly towards the eighteenth tee when I heard, *"Ciao bella!"* I turned around to see Leonardo strutting up the fairway in a lacy white shirt and tight black jeans. I watched swarms of people part like the Red Sea for the dark angel who looked more like he should be on stage at a rock concert! When he caught up with me he draped an arm around my shoulder.

"Stop that!" I said, as I shrugged him off.

"What's wrong?"

"People will get the wrong impression."

He slid the shades he was wearing down his nose and looked at the surrounding spectators. "These people are all watching the golf, so they wouldn't notice me and besides, what impression will I be giving them?"

"You know…" I suddenly felt awkward putting it into words.

"No, I don't know. Tell me." Leonardo had stopped and was waiting for a full explanation.

"That we're a—" I could feel my face redden.

"We're a what?" He prolonged my discomfort.

"We're a *couple*," he forced me to say.

"And what's wrong with that? I think we make a very attractive couple."

My worst fears were confirmed: Leonardo wanted romance. I had planned to let him down gently – explain that while I was flattered, I didn't feel the same way. To my mind we were just friends and that was all we would ever be.

"Although clearly you need to make a little more effort. Where's the outfit that Federico picked for you?"

"This is no place for Polly Pavlova!" I told him.

"I'm hearing plain and boring. To be a fashionista you need to be brave, confident – a trend-setter. Lead and others will follow!" He expounded his philosophy.

"You let me know when you are back in vogue and then I'll follow." I quipped before marching on.

It took Leonardo little effort to keep pace with me and he linked arms as he caught up moments later.

"What are you doing?" I protested.

"I'm giving the people what they want – a PDA – public display of affection."

"Well, please stop it before I make a PDA of my own!" Holly wouldn't be happy, but I felt a public display of aggression coming on.

"Are we breaking up?" Leonardo looked at me with sadness in his eyes.

"We are not breaking up because we were never together and never will be. *Aargh*! Did you just come here to annoy me or was there another reason for your visit?"

"As a matter of fact, there was. I came to offer you somewhere to stay when you're in Scotland."

The mention of Scotland and my impending trip took me aback.

"How did you—?" I stopped what I was about to say as I remembered I was being watched at all times. It was then that I noticed he had a silk tartan scarf draped over his open white shirt.

"I have a little place there that I keep for whenever I visit."

"Let me guess – a castle?" Leonardo was never understated and he had an even bigger property portfolio than Nathaniel.

"No, it's just somewhere modest that I can lay my tam o'shanter whenever I'm in that neck of the woods. You and Nathaniel are more than welcome to stay there on your *wee* trip."

We had arrived at the eighteenth hole and I wrestled my way through the crowds, pushing myself into a position where Nathaniel could see me. I looked up to see him walking towards the tee, and after quickly conferring with Duke, he took an iron and stood back. The crowds around the final tee fell silent. Nathaniel spotted me in the crowd and for a second I thought the sight of Leonardo would put him off, but he smiled before standing behind the ball. I held my breath as I watched him pivot, the club raised high above his head. Then he brought it down gracefully in a perfect arch. I heard the loud crack on impact and watched as the small white ball was sent flying into the air. A round of applause broke out further down the course that confirmed what I already knew – it was a fantastic shot.

"I take it it's going well then," Leonardo said, as I clapped and cheered with everyone else.

"It couldn't be going any better!" I told him, and we set off down the fairway to the final green. Spectators filled towering stands and a large billboard in the distance showed that N. Banks was leading the field.

"He's winning," I said proudly. "He's found his confidence – his self-belief, his faith."

"I'm not so sure your plan is working."

"Why not?" I was shocked by his reaction. "He's about to win his first Major of the year!" I pointed out, just in case he wasn't following the game.

"He has found his faith in *you*. He believes in *you*. He has confidence in *you*. But what do you think would happen if he didn't see you?"

It was then that I realised he knew about our ritual.

"You won't always be here Anna. He's going to have to learn to play like that without you."

I watched as Nathaniel studied the long and difficult putt.

"Your work here will soon be done, and you'll be gone."

The noise of the crowd drowned out the gasp I uttered at the realisation that what Leonardo was saying was true – I wouldn't be here for forever.

The ball travelled slowly over the green, teetering on the edge of the hole before dropping in. Nathaniel threw his fist in the air in triumph and the crowds went wild. He'd won.

"You have to make him see that this is all down to him and his own talent. You have to make him see that he doesn't need you. You've done a great job Anna. Now all you have to do is finish it."

"How do I do that?"

There was silence. I turned around but couldn't see Leonardo anywhere. He was gone and soon I would be too.

26

Fanning the Flames and Farmyard foul

Nathaniel was flying high after his first Major win, quite literally, at around 38,000 feet according to the captain of his private jet who had just informed us that we would shortly be commencing our descent into Prestwick Airport. I looked across at the new Masters champion. He was playing phenomenal golf, and if he continued to play in the same way he would be world number one again after the Open. It was more than I ever imagined he could achieve, and in such a short space of time too.

Now, time was running out – my time with Nathaniel and my time on earth. I had to make him see that all he had achieved so far was down to him; that he was a brilliant, talented golfer who would go on to win many more Majors. I looked across the table at the golfer whom I knew would have a stellar career, long after I had gone. *I* believed in him and before I left I had to know that he believed in himself too. I planned to find out if he did when we were in Scotland.

I also planned to visit all the places I'd circled on the map and currently read out my long list to him.

"That's a lot!" He wasn't quite as enthusiastic as me.

"Well, we have a week and you did say Scotland wasn't a big country."

"Yes, but even so I don't think we'll have time to see it all. Besides, we do have to fit in golf."

"I thought this was a holiday?"

"It is but the Open is being held in Loch Lomond in July and I want to play the course."

"I thought the Open was in New York, in June?" I was confused.

"The US Open is in June. The Open is in July."

It appeared that the organisers were not very imaginative when it came to naming their competitions.

"And which does Jack have tickets for?"

"The US Open," Nathaniel clarified.

"Erm, we might have a teeny tiny problem." I thought back to the last conversation I'd had with Jack.

"What is it?"

"It appears that I have promised Jack you will win not only the US Open but also the Open. So, no pressure then!"

He laughed. "Well, I can't let him down, and with your help, I'm sure I won't."

"You don't need my help to win Nathaniel."

"Yes, I do. We're a team."

"No, we're not." He looked upset. "Your talent alone

has got you to where you are today."

I needed to make him see that all this time he'd been doing it on his own, but before I could say another word, the captain told us that we would be landing in ten minutes. I looked out the window and caught my first glimpse of the country I so longed to see. I was transfixed by the tapestry of bright green rolling hills below as we came into land. Bonnie Scotland was living up to its name and I couldn't wait to see it all!

Our base was to be Loch Lomond. It was where the Open would be held and fortuitously it was also where Leonardo had his 'little' place.

Nathaniel handed me a small strip of tablets.

"They're travel sickness tablets, for the car journey."

The thought filled me with dread but the Range Rover Nathaniel had hired gave me an elevated view and focused my attention on the passing countryside rather than on his driving. In less than half an hour we were crossing the Erskine Bridge. The city of Glasgow was behind us and ahead was The Trossachs. Nathaniel drove slowly, allowing me time to take in the stunning scenery surrounding us.

Undulating hills rolled down to stony shores that surrounded the lochs; the same hills Rob Roy, Robert the Bruce and William Wallace had once run over. When we reached Alexandria, a tiny village on the banks of Loch Lomond, Nathaniel put Leonardo's address into the Satellite Navigation system.

"In two miles, take the next road on the right," the robotic woman's voice told Nathaniel.

"I'm sure I can find it on the map," I reassured him.

"Doris knows where she's going." It would seem he preferred to take directions from the annoying machine that continued to count down instructions.

"In 500 yards... in 200 yards... in 100 yards... in 10 yards, turn right."

I was willing Nathaniel to drive past it so I could hear Doris scream, "No Stupid! I said turn right! You've missed it! Do a handbrake turn immediately and pay more attention next time!"

Unfortunately, that didn't happen, as Nathaniel did what he was told and turned right down a narrow country road that soon became a leafy lane. Tree branches brushed against the side of the car and a leaf fell through the window, landing on my lap. I picked it up and turned it in my hand as we proceeded slowly towards our destination. According to Doris it was a mere 10 yards in front of us, on the left.

"I hope we don't meet another car," Nathaniel said, as he cautiously moved forward.

"You have reached your destination," Doris announced.

Nathaniel slowed but didn't stop as the only thing on the left was a green hedge.

"Your destination is on the left," Doris firmly reiterated.

Nathaniel put his foot on the brakes and frowned. We both stared at the metal gate outside the car window.

"We should've used the map," I said, stating the obvious.

"That's not helpful Anna," he said, as he got out of the car.

"It would've been more helpful than disastrous Doris who, FYI, has just led us up the garden path – quite literally."

We were surrounded on all sides by green fields. I joined Nathaniel at the gate and breathed in the fresh country air. Flies buzzed and birds sang as I filled my lungs with the herbaceous smell of grass and pungent aroma of cow manure.

"Would you like me to look at the map now?"

"No need, there's a farmer." Nathaniel pointed into the field. "We can ask him."

I saw a large man striding towards us, with what looked like a small pony by his side.

"Excuse me sir," Nathaniel called out, waving to the man to attract his attention.

"Oh look, he's wearing a kilt!" I was so excited to see a genuine Scottish person.

Nathaniel just looked at me.

"Sometimes Anna, I think—" He didn't get the chance to finish his sentence.

"Hello there," the man called out in greeting, as he strode towards us, his kilt swishing and sashaying with each step.

"He's speaking Scottish!" I almost clapped with excitement. I loved the Scottish accent.

Nathaniel just shook his head and asked the farmer, who had a big bushy beard, for directions to Glen Guthrie Hall.

"We appear to have taken a wrong turn. The satnav directed us down this road," he explained.

"I never trust those machines," the farmer replied from the other side of the gate, and I gave Nathaniel a look that said, "I told you so."

"Give me a map any day of the week," continued the stranger.

I didn't know who he was but I liked him already.

"Finlay Munroe." By way of a greeting he stretched out an enormous hand that was attached to an equally ginormous arm. "And this is Rufus," he said, as he introduced the huge hound standing by his side. The dog looked up at him from under bushy eyebrows and waited patiently while we introduced ourselves.

"My wife and I have been expecting you at the hall." I was delighted to hear that he was our host. "If you follow the road for another half mile, then make a sharp right by the large sycamore tree and turn left after the babbling brook, it's straight ahead. It's a very narrow road," Finlay warned us, and I saw a look of concern on Nathaniel's face which our host noticed too. "Don't worry, you won't meet anything coming the other way."

Finlay reassured us and sent us on our way.

Despite Finlay's words Nathaniel proceeded with caution along the road. Towering trees blocked out the sun and the car lights automatically came on as we turned into the road past the large sycamore tree.

"How does anyone find anything here?" Nathaniel asked, as he steered the Range Rover off road.

"I would've found it," I said, smugly.

Twigs snapped under the weight of the car as we rumbled along over the tiny track that led us to a small stream.

"This must be the babbling brook so we have to turn left here." I repeated Finlay's instructions but Nathaniel was hesitant. He glanced behind but there was no going back. The Range Rover rocked from side to side as it slid down into the stream and climbed up the deceptively steep bank on the other side. We left the darkness behind as sunlight flooded the scenic setting before us. Glen Guthrie Hall sat at the top of a sweeping driveway.

"This is Leonardo's?" Nathaniel was awestruck at the sight of the magnificent red brick building with its turrets and tall chimneys.

The driveway took us through manicured lawns peppered with unfamiliar tree species; proud sentinels whose roots dug deep into an earth that remembered ancient battles.

This was yet another stunning property in my fellow

angel's portfolio. I wondered how he could afford such expensive houses. How much money did he have? How had he made his money? These questions came to mind as I stared at the stately home.

Maybe it was family money? Maybe it had been passed down through the generations? Maybe he was descended from royalty? He did have an aristocratic air about him after all. Or maybe he had made his money by illegal means and had invested his ill-gotten gains in luxurious properties to dry clean it. He may look like a nobleman but looks can be deceiving.

As usual my train of thought took me to the dark side and by the time I reached the doorway, I'd once again demonised the dark angel.

Our footsteps crunched over gravel, leading to some stone steps under a covered archway that bore a family's coat of arms. I suddenly realised I didn't even know Leonardo's surname. I knew nothing of his past and my curiosity was peeked yet again, but before I could read the motto on the coat of arms, the large wooden door was opened and there stood Holly, dressed from head to toe in forest green tartan.

"Welcome to Glen Guthrie Hall," she trilled in a Scottish accent. "Please come inside."

I stood speechless and open-mouthed on the stone steps as I stared in disbelief at my fellow CIA agent in her latest guise.

"After you." Nathaniel coaxed me out of my

catatonic state.

I stepped across the threshold and into a home steeped in history. I walked over the soft woollen carpet that covered the huge entrance hall. It was as though I was being watched by the countless ancestors who looked down from portraits hanging on the walls; so too by once magnificent beasts whose heads had become mounted trophies, their eyes now dead and glassy.

"Are you okay dear?" I listened to the lyrical lilt of Holly's newly-acquired Scottish accent as I took in the sumptuous surroundings.

I turned to see Finlay's bulk fill the front door before large strides brought him to Holly's side.

"I see you've met my wife," he said, as he put his arm around her.

"You're married?" I asked incredulously and, not for the first time, Nathaniel looked at me strangely.

"Yes, we are." Finlay proudly pulled Holly close, and I saw her gaze adoringly up at her husband who towered over her. She then turned her attention back to me.

"Are you sure you're okay dear?" She sounded genuinely concerned. "You've gone very pale. Come here and take a seat." She took my arm and led me to a sofa in front of a blazing fire.

I took advantage of our distance from the others to accuse her. "You never told me you were *married*!" I said, through gritted teeth.

"You never asked." She smiled innocently and

pushed me down onto the soft sofa.

I had a lot of questions I wanted to ask my fellow Guardian, but it appeared they would have to wait. I had no sooner taken a seat before Holly pulled me back up.

"Let me show you lovebirds to your room." She dragged me back to Nathaniel.

"We're not—" I began to say but I couldn't repeat what she'd said.

"You're not what?" Holly made the uncomfortable situation even more so by asking.

I looked over at Nathaniel hoping he would explain, but he just raised an eyebrow.

"We're nnot—" I stuttered.

"Spit it out dear," Holly coaxed.

"We need two rooms!" My face felt as though it was on fire. I was sure my cheeks were redder than Finlay's whose complexion matched the bright red tartan of his kilt.

"Aww hen." Holly put a comforting hand on my arm. "Did you two lovebirds have a wee fight on the way over?" She didn't wait for an answer before continuing. "Well, it's time to kiss and make up." She gave me a shove and sent me flying into Nathaniel's arms.

"Come on now hen," she encouraged.

I broke free of Nathaniel's hold and turned to face my featherless friend.

"Two rooms!" I reiterated, glaring at her.

"I'm sorry hen."

Stop calling me a farmyard fowl, I wanted to scream at her.

"Two rooms aren't possible I'm afraid as we only have one available – the Wallace suite." She picked up an old-fashioned key from the reception desk and tottered off towards the sweeping staircase.

I found it impossible to believe that in this huge mansion there was only one bedroom left. I looked around but there was no sign of any other guests.

"They will be arriving later," Holly said, as though reading my mind.

There was a stained-glass window at the top of the stairs that reminded me of the one I'd seen the night of the masked ball. For a moment I wondered if Leonardo owned that magnificent mansion too. Instead of walking up the stairs, Holly led us down a corridor, past large mahogany doors. Golfing scenes adorned the walls and I thought that would make Nathaniel feel at home.

"Here we are dears." Holly finally stopped in front of, what appeared to be, the last large wooden door in the corridor. She dropped the heavy key into my hand and said, "Call if you need anything." She then turned and marched back down the long hallway, leaving us alone.

27

Floating

Nathaniel turned the key and pushed open the heavy door. An enormous four-poster bed monopolised the spacious room and a large tartan sofa and two armchairs sat in front of a fireplace. The walls were adorned with pictures of the sword-wielding Wallace and paintings of the landscape he loved; images of heather-clad hills and delicate dreamy depictions of languid lochs I couldn't wait to see. A gentle breeze blew in through the open French doors where Nathaniel stood to admire the view beyond.

"Should we go and explore?"

I didn't need to be asked twice. I ran across the room and out onto the grassy lawn that led us down to the water's edge. A small boat bobbed by a wooden pier. Nathaniel jumped in and reached for my hand. The little boat rocked from side to side as I took my seat. Nathaniel then rowed us out into the loch. I watched the wooden oars being pushed and pulled by his strong arms, as the red brick building with its turrets and tall chimneys receded into the distance.

At some point Nathaniel stopped rowing and we sat in silence, surrounded by the still waters and spectacular scenery. *This is heaven*, I thought, as we drifted across the water. Except it wasn't, really. Heaven seemed so far away.

I had expected my time on earth to pass so slowly, but it hadn't. It seemed as though it had passed in a mere heartbeat and I found myself wishing for more time here – I didn't want to leave – and yet I knew time was running out. I let my hand fall over the side of the boat and into the water; my fingers sending ripples spreading out across the surface. I looked over at Nathaniel, who I'd been sent here to help. He too was lost in thought. We drifted slowly back to shore and drifted off to sleep as the sun began to set in a crimson sky streaked with pale pinks and blues.

A sudden shrill sound woke us up.

"Ahoy there!"

Disorientated and bleary-eyed, I tried to make sense of my surroundings: a boat, a whistle and someone shouting... Oh no! We'd been shipwrecked! I sat upright then tried to stand up but there was too much swinging and swaying. Nathaniel did the same and the little boat very nearly capsized.

I looked around to see who was trying to attract our attention when I saw Holly, on the banks of the loch, waving and blowing a whistle.

"We must have jet lag." Nathaniel tried to explain the deep sleep we had both fallen into, as he rowed back to where Holly stood. She was dressed in a full-length evening gown with a yellow whistle hanging around her neck.

He helped me out of the small boat, and as he tied it back up to the jetty I said to Holly, "Isn't that a bit much?"

"Well, I did try shouting but you were both dead to the world. So, I did this," and she put the yellow whistle up to her mouth.

"Stop!" I had no desire to be deafened by the same whistle I'd last seen on an airbus on the opposite side of the Atlantic "What I actually meant was, isn't what you're wearing a bit much?"

"No. We always dress for dinner."

I thought about the clothes I had packed for our trip. I had nothing by Polly Pipping Palaver, or any other designer in my suitcase.

"It's okay, I've left you something to wear." She seemed to read my mind again. "And you're welcome. So, I will leave you love—" I would have hit her if she'd said 'birds,' but she saved herself from a thumping by saying, "Lovelies," instead. "...to get changed for dinner and I'll see you in the dining room."

"Sounds very formal," Nathaniel said, as we watched Holly walk back towards the house.

"Apparently it is, but don't worry, Mrs Munroe has taken care of it."

It was only when we got back to the room that I remembered it was a double. Suddenly, I felt awkward again as I stood by the French doors.

"It's okay, I'll sleep on the sofa."

Was everyone reading my mind today?

"Thank you." I was grateful for his understanding.

Later, I would force Holly to give me another room. All this nonsense that this was the only one! I mean, really – look at the size of the place. However, as far as the dress she had chosen for me was concerned, I was happy. Nathaniel told me I looked a vision when he came back into the room and saw me dressed in white. I looked over at him. He was leaning against the door frame, wearing a black tuxedo.

"You don't look too bad yourself," I said, returning the compliment.

"Shall we?" He walked over and held out his arm.

"We should." I was suddenly ravenous and looking forward to dinner.

We walked up the corridor, past photographs and paintings adorning the walls, until we finally reached the reception room. My mouth fell open when I found it was full of people. An army of staff in forest green tartan uniforms were greeting the arriving guests who crowded into the grand entrance hall. Guests were dressed for a formal dinner, just like us. They glided down the sweeping staircase and we followed in their wake.

So Holly hadn't been lying – there really wasn't a spare room. Leonardo hadn't told me that he was a hotelier. Maybe his surname was Hilton or Marriott? I was becoming increasingly curious about the enigmatic dark angel.

"I didn't realise he was a businessman as well as *you know what*," Nathaniel said, under his breath. "This hotel is amazing," he remarked, as we stepped inside the dining room.

Dinner was a formal affair, with a procession of waiting staff carrying plates of delicious food to the seated guests. We were shown to a table for two by the window that looked out over the lawn. Night had fallen and there was a warm glow from torch fires and lamps. Outside, staff were guided by glowing fires as they attended guests who were dressed in tuxedoes and taffeta, chiffon and silk. Ladies teetered in high heels, holding onto handsome beaus; just like I had held onto Nathaniel's arm upon our arrival to dinner.

"And how are you two love—." I looked up to see hostess Holly standing beside us. She struggled to find an alternative to lovebirds but finally settled on, "Lovelies this evening?"

Nathaniel answered, while I glared a warning at her to stop.

"We're having a great time. The food is amazing!"

By now, we had finished the first two courses; both

of us practically licking our plates clean.

"Well wait until you try the haggis. It's to die for!"

"What's haggis?" Nathaniel looked at me with the same bewildered look. Oh no! It was another one of those things everyone on earth knew about and that made me feel like an alien.

"It's stuffed sheep's stomach,' Holly clarified. I suddenly lost my appetite. "And it's served with neeps and tatties."

I wondered what part of the sheep they'd stuffed for the side dishes.

"So, what have you lovelies got planned for tomorrow?"

"Nathaniel has to play golf." I remembered the real reason we were here.

"Can't you play that anywhere?"

Nathaniel didn't look taken aback by her scolding and agreed that indeed he could.

"Good, because there's so much beauty here to see. It would be a shame to waste a second of the precious time you have left."

"We've only just got here," I pointed out.

"And soon you'll be gone," she directed that to me and her words hit home. "So, have an early night and I'll see you both for breakfast."

I wondered if Holly just appeared when there was food around. When she had left, I told Nathaniel that he should seize his opportunity to practise on the course where the Open would be held.

"No, Mrs Munroe is right. There's plenty of time for that. Right now, I want to take advantage of the time we have."

So, he was a secret lover of Scotland, wanting to see and explore the country just as much as I did. I was very happy.

"She's also right about the haggis," he remarked, as he shovelled in another mouthful of the local delicacy. "You should try it," he coaxed me, but I couldn't bring myself to. "Go on, live a little," he teased me.

If only he knew that's what I'd been doing ever since I'd first met him, and I was loving every second of it.

28

Frightening

I brought my heavily-creased map and guidebook to breakfast so we could decide where we wanted to go. I heard Holly before I saw her; welcoming her guests with a chorus of, "Good morning!"

"Did you both sleep well?" she asked, with a twinkle of mischief in her eye as she walked over to our table.

"I did, but poor Nathaniel had to spend the night on the sofa," I told her.

"Well, we can't have that!"

Finally! Holly was going to find me another room.

"I definitely want to get Nathaniel into bed." She smiled beatifically at the golfer who reassured her he was perfectly fine where he was.

"No, you're not. Don't you worry, I'll soon have you under the covers." She winked at Nathaniel who just kept shaking his head.

"That would be great!" I told Holly.

"Enjoy your breakfast," she said, gesturing towards

the beautiful buffet on display. "It's the most important meal of the day."

I thought every meal was of equal importance to my food-loving fellow angel, but apparently not. I left my map and guidebook on the table before browsing the buffet with Nathaniel; finally settling on some fruit and cereal that I planned to wash down with a large cup of coffee. Nathaniel opted for the full Scottish experience, starting his day with porridge drenched in sugar and cream. *He'll have to work that off when he got back home*, I thought.

As if reading my mind, he justified the indulgence by saying, "I'm on holiday!"

When we got back to the table my book and map had gone. I wondered if I'd mistaken where we'd been sitting but our key was still on the table.

"You won't be needing these." Holly appeared, holding my research. "Everything has already been planned."

"I'd quite like to decide for myself where we're going."

"Yes dear, I'm sure you would." She placated me, like a mother would a petulant child.

I didn't like her condescending tone and I didn't like that she was taking charge. I looked over at Nathaniel but he seemed okay with the fact that Holly was mapping everything out for us. "A car will be waiting outside for you," she announced, before I had time to protest.

The little red roadster came complete with a picnic basket and blanket attached to the boot. Finlay handed Nathaniel the keys, and I could almost feel my stomach start to do somersaults at the prospect of being his passenger.

"Don't worry, I'll drive slowly," he promised.

I picked up an envelope that had been placed on the passenger seat and opened it to find our planned itinerary.

"Go that way," Finlay instructed, as he pointed to a wide but winding driveway.

Thank goodness there was a road! I was worried we would be washed away in the small car if we tried to cross the stream again. This exit brought us back onto a country road that quickly took us onto the main road to Stirling. I was thrilled that we were going to see the castle, followed by a trip to the Wallace Monument.

We joined other visitors on a guided tour who seemed oblivious of the fact they had a world-famous golfer and an angel in their midst (despite drawing attention to myself when I started re-enacting Wallace's part in the Battle of Stirling Bridge on top of the tower.).

He was one human who could rival my sword skills, and that was saying something. Not that I was big-headed of course, but there were few others who could swing a sword like me. I was good – correction, I was great! I was the best! I continued my self-congratulatory praise on the way down the spiral stone staircase, stopping to see the legend's sword at the bottom.

"Wallace's sword was a huge five feet and four inches, and while we don't know his height exactly, it was said he was seven feet tall," our guide told us.

"Where was he born?" someone asked.

"No one knows exactly," she admitted.

As I reverentially stood in front of the relic, mesmerised by the myth, I pieced together what I'd been told about the enigmatic Scottish hero: no one knew where he had come from, he had led his army into battle and he had amazing sword skills. It was then that I realised William Wallace wasn't a nobleman – he was an angel!

The colour had drained from my face and Nathaniel asked me if I was okay. *No, I wasn't*! My mind reeled from the revelation. He was an angel who had come to earth to help the Scottish people; he had been on a mission, just like me.

I listened as our guide spared no detail in describing his gruesome execution in London in 1305, after he'd been captured by the English. I started to panic. What if the same fate awaited me? If I failed, would I be hanged, drawn and quartered? I grabbed my stomach. I'd become quite attached to my innards.

"Do they still do that?" I whispered to Nathaniel.

"Do what?"

"Kill people that way?" By people I of course meant

unsuccessful earthbound angels.

"No!" Nathaniel looked horrified.

I was relieved.

As we stepped back into the afternoon sun, I took a deep breath.

"Did you enjoy the tour?" Nathaniel knew I'd been so excited about coming here.

It had been awful to learn the tragic and terrible fate of one of my own, and a stark warning that failure was not an option.

"I learned a lot from Wallace's life and death," I told him. I learnt that if I was to succeed then Nathaniel would have to win every match, otherwise I might meet the same untimely end as my fellow sword-wielding angel.

So like Wallace, we too were going into battle. I didn't have my sword but Nathaniel had his stick. We were at war and he had to be victorious!

"I learnt that we can't fail. Tomorrow we're going to Loch Lomond."

"On a boat trip?" Nathaniel had lost focus.

"No, to play golf! You need to practise. You have to win."

"I realise now that there are more important things than golf."

Yes, there is – my life! I wanted to scream, but instead I told him, "No, there's not."

Now was not the time for that nonsense. He had to

stay focused; he had to fight!

"Yes, there is Anna. I realise now that winning isn't everything."

Oh my God! This was a nightmare. Winning was everything. Winning was a matter of life and death – *my* life (and possible death.). I had to get him to focus. I had to get him to fight.

"Anna." He reached over and took my hand. "Everything has changed for me lately, and it's all because of you."

"You're winning again, and you have to keep winning." I tried to get him to focus on the upcoming Open. "It's about winning all the way. Win, win, win!"

"I don't want to play golf," he confessed.

Clearly, he wasn't thinking straight.

"Of course, you do. It's your life!" I reminded him. *Quite frankly mine depends on it, so you better stop spouting this nonsense right now!*

"No, I want to—"

I didn't wait to hear what he wanted. I slapped him hard across the cheek. He looked stunned. He stood there staring, in silence, as I launched into a full-scale attack.

"Listen to me Nathaniel Banks – I am here to help you and that is what I am going to do. You are going to get out on that course. No more distractions. No more tourist attractions. This is not a holiday. You are not here to enjoy yourself."

He looked hurt and confused.

"No more wasting time. Tomorrow it's back to work. Losing is not an option."

I thought of Wallace and a shiver ran down my spine. I thought of heaven, my sword, the army. I thought if he failed I might never see any of them again. I thought of my possible fate. I thought only of myself.

29
Hell hath no fury

We drove back in silence, each of us lost in our own thoughts. I had had no idea what I'd signed up for by coming here and then I remembered: I hadn't signed up for this, for any of it! I'd been sent here against my will.

All the good I'd done, all the happiness I'd felt, all the joy that meeting Jack had brought me, were washed away when I'd seen Wallace's sword and heard how he met his end. They'd killed him in the most heinous way. I felt tears fill my eyes and turned my head away from Nathaniel as we pulled up in front of Glen Guthrie Hall. As soon as we stopped, I jumped out of the car and ran up the stone steps. Before I could bang on the door, Holly opened it.

"What on earth are you doing here?" She looked surprised to see me.

"Exactly! What am I doing here on earth," I cried. "I don't want to be here Holly. I want to go home."

She glanced nervously behind me to see where

Nathaniel was before pulling me out of earshot.

"Finlay?" She shouted for her husband as I sat down on the sofa. "What happened?" she asked while keeping watch for Nathaniel. "You were meant to be having a picnic, on the 'bonnie, bonnie banks' of Loch Lomond. I packed Scotch eggs and finger sandwiches and scones with homemade jam."

Trust Holly to think of food in a time of crisis. Tears were now streaming down my cheeks.

"Tell me what happened." Sounding genuinely concerned, she put a comforting arm around my shoulder.

Before I could tell her, Finlay had appeared at the foot of the stairs and Nathaniel had stepped into the grand entrance hall looking concerned and confused. He didn't understand why I was so upset. How could he? I wanted to tell him, I wanted to explain, but it was forbidden. I didn't know what punishment would befall me if I committed that cardinal sin. Tears continued to pour.

Holly jumped up from the sofa and marched over to Nathaniel.

"Now, don't you worry. Anna will be fine. It's just jet lag. I've seen it all before." She took Nathaniel's arm. "Why don't you go and have a nice game of golf with Finlay. He's a great golfer. I'll take care of Anna."

Nathaniel looked back at me. He didn't want to leave. He looked helpless. He couldn't help me. No one could.

More tears came at the thought.

"Come on laddie." Finlay put an arm around Nathaniel. "I promise I'll go easy on you. Have you ever played before?"

I watched as Finlay walked off with the professional player. Why hadn't Holly told him? Then I remembered she couldn't because she would be breaking angelic laws if she did. All these secrets weren't good. It wasn't fair on anyone. It wasn't fair on Finlay who was about to play the best golfer in the world. Or, at least, he would've been if I'd done my job right, but I hadn't, and so he wasn't. I'd failed, and I hollered again at the realisation.

Holly handed me a handkerchief.

"There, there, it's okay," she soothed, gently rubbing my back.

"No, it's not," I sobbed, and blew my nose.

"What's wrong?"

"Everything!" I cried.

"What happened?"

I tried to gulp in air between tearful convulsions. I wanted to explain but I couldn't. I looked at my featherless friend who was oblivious to the dangers of being on earth. She looked genuinely worried, and so she should be. I had to warn her.

"Wallace!" I wailed, before breaking down in uncontrollable sobs again.

"Wallace who?"

"William Wallace." How didn't she know that!

"Wallace? As in the Scottish hero? Braveheart?"

"Yes."

"I don't understand." She was confused.

"I know." I patted her knee. Poor innocent Holly, who was blind to the mortal danger she was in.

"So, tell me."

I looked at her through a veil of tears.

I broke the news to her. "He's dead."

"Yes, and he has been for the last 700 years."

"He was an angel," I whispered. "And they killed him." I expected her to be shocked by the revelation, but she simply nodded.

"You knew?"

"Well, yes. Everyone knows that" she said, in a matter-of-fact way.

"Wait! I didn't know!" I was used to failing as a human being but now I was failing as an angel as well. "Why didn't I know?" I searched Holly's face for an answer.

"I don't know dear. Maybe you're just not a very good angel." This sent me into another fit of sobbing.

"Don't you realise we're in danger?" I tried to convey the seriousness of the situation to my fellow CIA agent. "They murdered him!"

"He died a hero's death."

"Well I don't want to be a hero!" I cried.

"Don't worry, there's no danger of that! Now pull

yourself together." Holly got up and stood in front of the fireplace. "You do realise that this little meltdown has ruined everything. Do you know how much time and effort I put into planning it all? Well, do you?" I'd never seen Holly angry before.

She was marching up and down in front of the fireplace.

She was getting very worked up. "All you had to do was go out today, do a little bit of sightseeing and have a lovely picnic on the bonnie banks of Loch Lomond! But, oh no! Anna couldn't do that. Anna had to get upset and ruin everything! Why couldn't you just have gone as a tourist and then sat on your ass on the bloody bonnie bank and eaten all the delicious food I'd so lovingly prepared!"

It was all making sense now – Holly was upset about the food.

"I'd made sandwiches. I even cut the crusts off! And I made raspberry jam. I picked the raspberries myself! And baked shortbread."

I didn't know what shortbread was but I presumed it was the opposite of long bread, which I'd also never heard of but then again I wasn't the food connoisseur – Holly was. Her pacing got faster and her voice rose an octave higher.

"Finlay caught a salmon that I smoked, and shot a partridge for the pâté I made."

"I'm sorry." I mumbled an apology. I hadn't realised

the amount of effort (or sacrifice) that had gone into the execution of the picnic.

"All you had to do was sit and eat it." She had exhausted herself and now stood with her hands on her ample hips and head slumped forward. "Why Anna? Why couldn't you do that?"

"I'm sorry," I apologised again. "But I was a little too pre-occupied by a wingless Wallace who'd been ruthlessly hanged, drawn and quartered," (a bit like the poor partridge). "Forgive me, but I lost my appetite."

Holly just stared at me. I knew that was an alien concept for her. Nothing in heaven or on earth seemed to put her off food.

"There's nothing else for it. I will just have to start all over again." With that, she stomped off in what I presumed was the direction of the kitchen. "I'll see you at dinner," she called out before disappearing from sight, leaving me sitting in the huge entrance hall, ruing the day I'd ever set foot in bloody bonnie Scotland!

30

Finger Food, Frills and a Four-poster bed

A sleep, followed by a shower and a short stroll along the loch shore, improved my mood and helped me put things in perspective. I had grieved for William Wallace; I had wept and mourned for the brave, fearless angel who had given his life so that the people of Scotland could be free. A selfless, courageous act of valour and heroism, I had learnt a very important lesson from his life and death: earth was no place for angels!

I was seeing everything more clearly by the time I walked back to our room. It was obvious to me that Holly was sick, and she needed help. Her love of food had turned into an obsession that was out of control. That exhibition earlier had shown me just how bad things had become. No one got that upset over a Scotch egg and a finger sandwich. I would speak to Leonardo, when he next appeared, and he could help me organise an intervention.

As for me, I was going to put all my time, effort and

energy into helping Nathaniel win his matches and his Majors, and if I just stayed focused on the job at hand, I could get Holly and I safely back to heaven where we belonged. The sooner I got myself and my food-loving featherless friend out of here the better. I was adamant I was not going to let anyone or anything stand in my way.

I'd already changed for dinner and as I walked back in through the French doors, I saw that Nathaniel had too. He was attempting to knot his bow tie when my reflection appeared in the mirror beside him. We both stopped and stared for a moment.

"I'm sorry," I said, as I stood in the doorway.

He didn't take his eyes off me.

"I was exhausted."

"Are you feeling better now?" he asked my reflection.

"Much better," I told him, as I watched myself walk across the room. My silk dress fell over hips that swayed with each step. Only when I was directly behind him did Nathaniel turn to face me.

"I'm sorry too." He took my hand, and it sent a shiver down my spine when he raised it to his lips and gently kissed it. "I got distracted and lost focus. Tomorrow we'll get back to work."

That was music to my ears.

"But tonight we have a party to go to. Mrs Munroe delivered the invitation earlier."

I took the hand-embossed invite, but before I could read it there was a *rat-a-tat-tat* on the door that then swung open.

"Cooee, only me!" Holly strode into the room and grabbed the invitation from my hand. "There's been a last-minute change of plan," she said, with a look that told me she was still sore about picnic-gate. "It requires a slight change of attire."

She dished out the clothes draped over her arm, handing me an outfit that I was sure Polly Pipping Pavlova had designed – a flouncy pink tartan skirt with matching knee-high tartan socks partnered with a frilly white blouse with puff sleeves and a cinched pink velvet waistcoat. I looked at the beautiful dress I was wearing and the hideous outfit she had just handed me.

Why was she torturing me like this? I'd already apologised for not eating her stupid picnic!

"We're now having a Ceilidh," she announced, handing Nathaniel a dark blue tartan kilt.

"What's a kay-lee?" I was hoping it wasn't another question everyone on earth knew.

"It's a Scottish gathering, with lots of music, dancing and local fayre."

"Sounds like fun," Nathaniel said, admiring his traditional garb. "Is this my clan tartan?" he asked.

"Yes, it is. The Banks' were a hill-residing-by-the-river peoples, so you should feel right at home here. Now, don't forget your sporran." She handed him what looked like a hairy purse with tassels before turning her attention back to me.

"Unfortunately Anna doesn't have a tartan, so I took the liberty of designing one for her."

I held up the gawdy pink ensemble.

"That's so kind," Nathaniel said.

There was nothing kind about it! This was sabotage.

"A pretty pink tartan for a pretty girl." Holly pretended to affectionately pat my cheek but it felt more like a slap.

"I hate you," I mouthed to her when Nathaniel wasn't looking.

"And I can't wait to see you in it." She smiled, knowing very well I couldn't wriggle out of wearing the awful attire that was less clan and more clown. "So, we'll leave you to get changed. You're coming with me Nathaniel." She waved a key seductively in front of his face which suddenly looked pale and panicked. Before he could protest she told him she'd got him his own room.

"It's the Burns Suite, on the first floor. It has a four-poster bed and its own private balcony with views out over the first tee."

"Wait – there's a golf course here?"

"Yes, dear. Young Nathaniel was playing it earlier. He gave my poor Finlay quite a thrashing. But don't worry, he's found someone much better for you to play with tomorrow."

"We're going to Loch Lomond tomorrow," I interjected.

"There's a tournament on so the course is closed to the public." Holly dashed my plans.

"The course here is fantastic. I'm looking forward to it." Nathaniel looked very happy.

"That's great," she smiled broadly, brushing past him. "Now, come along." She called out for him to follow her, without so much as a backwards glance in my direction. "Let's leave Anna alone."

He hesitated.

"You better go," I told him, as Holly summoned him for a second time. "I'll see you soon." With that he dashed off after her, carrying his kilt.

31
A Highland Fling

After putting on the pink palaver and plaiting my hair, I pranced up the corridor in laced-up black ballet shoes. I was assuming from the footwear that there would be dancing at the Ceilidh.

"Don't you look a picture," I heard Holly say, just before I was momentarily blinded by a bright white flash as she took a photograph. "A little memento of tonight's events."

Linking arms, she then led me towards the gathering. Hostess Holly had pinned a tartan sash to her forest green satin dress and her hair had been coiffed. She was the epitome of understated elegance. This only made me feel more self-conscious as we stepped through the double doors and into the Ceilidh, which was in full swing.

The huge dance floor was a swishing carousel of kilts and skirts, swinging and swaying, as the dancers spun around with arms arched and toes pointed, jigging and jumping to the lively music. Spectators clapped and stamped their feet in time to the folk music. A fiddler frolicked about on a raised stage at the far end of the room and a feel-good, party atmosphere filled the great hall. I watched as dancers held hands and came together in a circle, following choreographed steps.

"Isn't this fun?" Holly watched with me from the side-lines.

A young man reached for my hand but thanks to my lightning-quick reflexes, I avoided being dragged onto the dancefloor.

"Don't you like dancing?" Holly quizzed me, as I took a step back to avoid any other revolving reveller reaching for me on their way past.

"I don't know how to dance," I said.

"Nonsense! Everyone can dance."

"Everyone down here clearly can, but not everyone up above," I told her.

"That's rubbish! We're always busting out moves at the office. Zelda loves a line-dance; Zachariah taught me how to tango, and Samuel is the salsa king." She started to seductively move her hips in a figure of eight. "I call him 'old snake hips'."

"We've other more important things to do in the army, like defending heaven and waging war." This left us no time for frivolous frolicking or gyrating of any kind.

"I know, you're too busy swinging your sword, blah,

blah, blah. May I suggest you stop swinging it and start dancing around it?"

"Don't be ridiculous," I retorted, as the room went dark, and a spotlight fell in the middle of the dance floor.

Two huge swords lay crossed on the ground. Finlay, who was dressed in full regimental regalia, stepped out of the shadows and into the light. Judging from the long line of medals on his jacket, Holly's husband was highly decorated. Placing one arm into the air and then the other, he stood on the balls of his feet. Another light illuminated a musician on stage who was squeezing a set of bagpipes. Taking a deep breath, I watched him blow into the pipe and the haunting note that echoed round the room was Finlay's cue to begin the dance.

I was captivated by the melodic music and amazing footwork. For a large man, he was as light as a feather on his feet, gracefully hopping and skipping over the sharp blades. I looked at Holly whose eyes sparkled with pride, and she was the first one to cheer and clap when he'd finished his Highland fling. The audience showed their appreciation by whistling and applauding their host who soaked up the adoration with Holly by his side.

I was left alone and at the mercy of other jiggers who were chomping at the bit to get back on the dancefloor. I stepped back and moved in the direction of some large round tables that would act a safety barrier. Guests enjoyed plates of delicious Scottish fayre that they had brought from the long buffet table on the far side of the room – sustenance to sustain more shimmying and shaking.

"Anna." Nathaniel, who was standing with a group of men, called and waved me over.

The huddled group parted as I walked towards them, and after introductions had been made, the conversation quickly reverted back to their shared love of golf. There was a lot of back-slapping and praising of Nathaniel whom they were delighted to have in their company.

"Anna's been helping me. I owe everything to her." He wanted me to take the credit for his sudden change in form.

All eyes turned to me. I looked at their expectant faces.

"This is all down to his incredible talent. I have nothing to do with it." I dashed any hopes they may have had that I could magically transform their games too and so they turned their attention and adulation back to where it belonged.

Nathaniel was about to argue against what I'd just said when Holly arrived and interrupted him. She wasn't alone.

"I have brought someone to meet you." I watched as my CIA cohort gently guided a young girl into the group. "Grace is a super fan." Holly continued with the introduction. "And when I told her Nathaniel Banks was staying with us, well, she was just beside herself.

Weren't you dear?"

The pretty young girl with long red hair blushed.

Nathaniel stretched out his hand. "Pleased to meet you."

She smiled broadly and her blue eyes twinkled with delight. She didn't say anything; she just stood there holding his hand, staring up at the handsome professional golfer.

Holly spoke on her behalf. "Gorgeous Grace is causing quite a stir herself on the green."

Grace modestly shook her head.

"There's no denying it," said one of the men, as he swirled ice cubes around his cut-glass tumbler. "Grace is a two-times Scottish champion." He toasted her and took a swig.

"And she's gorgeous." Another stated the obvious.

She seemed uncomfortable being the centre of attention and tried to step back, but Holly wouldn't let her. Instead she gave her a gentle push sending her straight into Nathaniel's arms.

"I'm sure you two gorgeous young golfers will be great on the dancefloor together."

"I don't think they want to dance, Mrs Munroe." I tried to intervene but no one, including Holly, was listening to me.

Everyone was watching as Nathaniel took Grace by the hand and led her onto the floor.

"You were saying?" Holly appeared beside me,

admiring her matchmaking.

"You made him do it. He didn't have a choice."

"Everyone has a choice Anna," Holly told me, before toddling off in the direction of the buffet, leaving me alone yet again.

32

A Furious Flight

The morning after the Ceilidh, I arose bright and early.
I was dressed and ready for a day on the course – to
prepare Nathaniel for his next big win. I was deploying
the power of positive thought. From now on losing was
not an option.

If everything went to plan, I would be back in
heaven's army where I belonged, and Nathaniel would
be back at the top of his game. Nothing was going to
stop either from happening.

"Morning Holly." I greeted my angelic hostess as I
ladled grapefruit into a bowl.

"Good morning Anna," she chirpily replied, helping
herself to a heaped plate of fried food before following
me to my table.

"Nathaniel will be down in a minute." I didn't want
her to sit in his seat.

"No he won't," she mumbled through a mouthful of
black pudding and scrambled eggs.

"Pardon me?"

"I'm afraid Nathaniel won't be joining you this morning. He's already had his breakfast…" She paused to dab her mouth with her napkin, before dropping the bombshell. "… With Grace. And now they're probably on their third hole," she said, looking at her watch.

The bombshells kept coming.

"He's playing without me?" That was difficult to digest.

"Yes." Holly on the other hand had no difficulty digesting it, or indeed the calorific, artery-clogging food in front of her. "Don't they make such a lovely young couple? Grace is just *gorgeous*. And a fantastic golfer. It's great they have that shared passion. It's a brilliant basis for a relationship."

My mind and stomach were doing somersaults at the same time.

"There is no relationship! They've only just met!"

"Have you never heard of love at first sight?"

"Don't be ridiculous. And stop matchmaking," I warned Holly, whose interfering was putting my foolproof plan in jeopardy.

"Why? They're both young and single."

"Nathaniel can't get distracted. He has to stay focused on his game."

"He can still play and have a life," she argued.

"No, he can't!" I was adamant.

"Yes, he can." Holly was really starting to irk me.

"And by the way, all work and no play does not keep you warm in bed at night."

"They've had sex?" I shouted, before leaping up from the table.

Everyone in the breakfast room turned and stared. I sat back down.

"Maybe they have, maybe they haven't. I don't like to stick my nose into anyone else's business."

"It's your nosiness that's created this mess!" I pointed accusingly at her.

"I don't see what the problem is. Nathaniel has met a lovely young girl – possibly the next Mrs. Banks."

"Stop it!" I shouted. "She's going to destroy everything we've worked for."

"Have you ever thought she might actually help?"

"Nonsense! She'll distract him and he'll lose, and he'll never be number one again."

"There's more to life than golf Anna."

"No, there's not! Golf is my life!" (or at least it was my reason for being alive).

I jumped up. I wasn't going to let matchmaker Holly or gorgeous Grace the golfer ruin it for me or for Nathaniel. I was going to put a stop to this.

I commandeered a buggy and hared off in pursuit of the young couple. Putting my foot to the floor, I bounced off the seat as the cart careered down a grassy bank and up the other side. Golfers on the first hole stopped playing and started to shout in protest.

"Sorry!" I waved in apology, as I weaved my way down the fairway, nearly mowing down a four-ball on the second hole.

They shouted an expletive at me but they didn't understand: I was on a mission. I had to stop whatever stupid Holly had started the night before. She accused me of upsetting her plans but she was trying her hardest to ruin mine!

There was no room in my F-Plan for flirting, fornicating or another female. I heard another f-word and it forced me to swerve sharply in order to avoid running over a golfer teeing off on the third. In fact there followed a string of f-words from the other golfers in his group as I drove on, with my foot to the floor. I was focused on finding Nathaniel and gorgeous Grace. I found it easy to forget all the players my plight was pissing off. I was going to fight to get Nathaniel back on track. Gorgeous Grace was not in my F-Plan so she could just f-off!

I tore through holes four, five, six and seven before encountering more abuse from golfers who took umbrage to the fact I was disrupting their game. Their shouting and screaming faded into the distance as I continued on down the fairway. There was still no sign of Nathaniel and Grace, who were clearly racing over the course as fast as I was.

Finally I spotted them as I hurtled over a hill on the ninth. I slammed on the brakes and watched as Grace prepared to tee off. Sunlight fell on her slender figure as she arched her back. Her club came down, connecting with the ball to take flight. Nathaniel stepped over to stand beside her as they both watched the trajectory of the small projectile. And then I watched in horror as he put his arm around the pretty young girl who had clearly turned his head.

I cursed Holly, as more cursing was directed at me.

"Fore!" echoed through the air.

I waited for another f-word to follow as I sat plotting and planning just exactly how I was going to fix Holly's big, fat mess.

"Fore!" was shouted for a second time.

Maybe they had a stutter?

"All right, I'm going to move," I called back.

I kept my eyes on Nathaniel and Grace as I pressed my foot on the accelerator. Then everything went black.

33
Fuzzy Wuzzy

"Wakey, wakey," I heard someone say. "That's right, open your eyes."

My eyelids fluttered like a butterfly's wings but I couldn't prise them open. They hurt and so did my head.

"Try again," the voice coaxed.

I made a great effort and caught a brief glimpse of Leonardo. The shock of seeing him roused me from my unconscious state.

"What happened?" I asked the dark angel, who was sitting on the bed beside me. "How did I get here?"

The last thing I remembered was my mission to rescue Nathaniel from young Grace's clutches. Yet I'd failed and had somehow ended up in bed with Leonardo. My already sore head started to pulsate with pain even more.

"Apparently, you were causing quite a commotion on the golf course." As usual Leonardo was exaggerating.

"This is all Holly's fault," I told him.

"I didn't know Holly played golf?" He looked surprised.

"She doesn't." What did that have to do with anything anyway?

"Then it wasn't her fault." He patted my hand.

"How would you know? You weren't there. She was trying to sabotage me!" I confided in Leonardo, whom I hoped would help me stop her meddling.

"Holly wouldn't do that." He didn't believe me and clearly didn't know Holly very well.

"You're delusional," I told him.

"And you're concussed," he informed me.

"How did that happen?"

"Funny you should ask..." I had a feeling there would be nothing humorous about it. "Apparently, when you were whizzing around the course like a demented racing car driver, you met with a little accident."

"I don't remember hitting anything." I desperately tried to recall if there was anything in front of me when I drove off in Nathaniel's direction. I was sure there wasn't.

"You didn't," he said, confirming what I already knew. "You were hit by a golf ball." For emphasis, he traced a semi-circle in the air with one hand and then with a *bang*, smashed it into his other hand. The loud clap rang in my ears. "Didn't you hear the golfer call fore?"

"Yes. And?" I didn't understand.

"Fore is a warning to anyone who is in the flight path of a golf ball, but because you didn't move your pretty little noggin out of the way, the aforementioned missile came crashing down and knocked you out."

I took in what he had just told me while I checked my skull was still intact. Thankfully it was, although there was a huge golf ball-sized lump.

"The swelling will go down in a few days," Leonardo said, and reassured me that the actual golf ball was not still embedded in my skull. "Just in time for your departure."

Leonardo never failed to remind me that my time was running out. I threw back the covers and sat up. My head started to pound.

"You can't get up yet – doctor's orders," he told me, plumping my pillow before laying me back down.

There was a knock on the door, and I saw Holly walk into the bedroom.

"How's the patient?" she asked, cheerily.

"Please don't tell me she's my doctor," I moaned, as I struggled to sit up again.

"Of course I'm not!" She put down the tray she was carrying and then said, "I'm your nurse."

"This is all your fault," I accused her, as she popped two tablets into my mouth.

"No, I think you'll find it was a golf ball. Now swallow," she ordered.

"I wouldn't have been on the course if I hadn't been

chasing after Nathaniel. Everything was going according to plan before you interfered. You're deliberately spoiling everything!" I was so cross.

"I'm trying to help you, not hinder you," Holly said, "and don't worry, Nathaniel will be getting plenty of practise in while you're indisposed. Grace is going to take him over to Loch Lomond."

"You said the course was closed."

"Did I?" she giggled. "Silly me, I must've got my dates wrong. Anyway, I knew how important it was for Nathaniel to play the course and as you can't go with him I suggested Grace take him. See, I am helping."

No, she wasn't!

"He didn't want to go – he was so worried about you – but I told him I would look after you."

"Now, doesn't that make you feel better?" Leonardo chipped in.

I had a large golf ball-shaped lump on my head, Nathaniel was spending all his time with gorgeous Grace and I was stuck here with Nurse Holly, so no, I did not feel better.

"Everything is going according to plan" she gloated, and then she was gone.

"I hope that will put your mind at rest, I'll be back later to check on you."

He blew me a kiss as he closed the door. I was left alone to try and process what had happened, and to come up with a new plan of my own. So much rested on my getting Nathaniel away from Grace and back on track. There was no time to rest. I tried to get up but I couldn't. I suddenly felt sleepy, and my eyes started to close.

Oh no! It must've been the tablets. Holly had drugged me! I started to formulate a revenge plan for nasty Nurse Holly but tiredness overcame me and soon I was in a deep sleep, all thoughts of revenge momentarily forgotten.

34
Farewell

I eventually awoke from the deep drug-induced sleep, with no memory of who I was or where I was. I sat up slowly and fragments started to pierce the thick fog that clouded my mind. I saw Nathaniel's face and Jack's; the latter bringing a smile to my own. Then gorgeous Grace's replaced the feeling of warmth and happiness with panic. I leapt out of bed and came face to face with a portrait of William Wallace; the image inducing dread and fear within me.

I joined the dots and remembered that I was an angel who had been sent to earth to help Nathaniel Banks. However, if I didn't stop Grace my mission would fail. A bearded Wallace reminded me of the fate that would befall me if that happened.

Holly's face appeared in my mind's eye and fear was replaced by anger. This was all her fault! If she hadn't interfered and tried to matchmake, my foolproof F-Plan would be on track and Nathaniel would be on course to winning his next Major. I had no idea what irreparable damage had been done while I'd been indisposed, but I was going to find out. I scrambled about for my clothes but couldn't find them. That's when Leonardo appeared.

"How's the head?" he asked, as he flounced into my room through the open French doors.

I'd forgotten I'd been attacked by the wayward golf ball that had crashed into my skull. I stopped the search for my clothes to feel my head. Thank goodness the swelling had gone down, and the pain had gone.

"It's fine," I told the dark angel, whose kilt swished seductively from side to side as he strode across the room towards me. He had turned a traditional garment into something sexy by pairing it with his leather boots, jewellery and his trademark white frilly shirt which was, as usual, open to expose his bare chest.

I wondered if as well as being an angel, a hotelier and a property tycoon, he was also a model who strutted the catwalks of London, Paris and Milan (when he wasn't checking up on his extensive, earthly property portfolio.).

"I like your new look," I told him.

"I would love to return the compliment but—" He turned me towards the mirror. My reflection made me scream in horror. "You look like Einstein's sister – who's been electrocuted!" He was referring to my hair, which was standing on end.

I looked around for a brush but that too had

mysteriously disappeared. I needed to shower, get dressed and sort out this mess, and I wasn't just talking about my hair. Leonardo sat back in an armchair as I flung open the wardrobe and searched drawers for my clothes.

"They're over there." He pointed to a large suitcase sitting by the door. "You're going home," he told me. Panic, fear and dread descended over me like an avalanche.

"No! I've only just got here," I cried.

"And now it's time to go," he said.

My mind, which had only just made sense of the post-concussion confusion, now struggled to make sense of what he was saying. I looked at the bed.

"How long have I been asleep?"

Leonardo got up and walked over to me.

"You've been asleep the whole time you've been here." If he hadn't had his arm around me, I would have fallen to the floor. I had lost so much precious time because Holly had drugged me. Now there was no more left.

"A lot has happened," he started to say, but didn't continue.

"What?" I wanted to know; I needed to know.

"No time for that now." He effortlessly swung the huge suitcase on top of the bed. "You need to get dressed. We're leaving in half an hour," he told me, before walking back out through the bedroom door.

I was in shock. Leonardo had said 'we'. Did he just mean the two of us? What had happened in the days I'd lost? Where was Nathaniel? And Grace? And Holly?

I got dressed and slowly walked back down the long corridor, dragging the large suitcase behind me. There was a light at the end and I could hear familiar voices. I didn't want to leave yet; there was still so much left to do. I walked past pictures and paintings of the glorious game of golf that had been so much part of my life on earth. The light got brighter and the voices louder as I neared the end. I looked up and saw Leonardo waiting for me.

"Come on slowcoach." He tried to hurry me along. "Places to go, people to see."

I looked at the fields awash with purple and green heather; the rolling hills and lochs of a Scotland that I loved but now had to leave. I knew I wouldn't see any more of its stunning landscape and that I was leaving the people I'd grown to love.

Impatient with my dithering, Leonardo came down the corridor to assist me.

"Don't keep Nathaniel waiting."

Upon hearing his name, I picked up my pace and strode into the large entrance hall where I saw him standing by the fireplace. Finlay stood with his arm around Holly, and Rufus lay like a rug at the feet of his master. The hound raised an eyebrow as I made my way across the room to Nathaniel.

"I'm so glad you're okay." He sounded relieved.

"You had young Nathaniel very worried," Finlay told me. "But I told him you were in good hands." He squeezed his wife's shoulder. "Holly took good care of you. Didn't you dear?" He looked at his wife with affection and she smiled up at him in return.

"It's lovely to see you back on your feet hen," she said.

No thanks to you, I thought, as I glared at her.

"That was a nasty wee bump to the head you had. Who thought golf could be such a dangerous game?"

I wanted to scream at her. *It wasn't golf that knocked me out, it was you!*

"It really isn't, Mrs Munroe," Nathaniel interjected, in defence of his sport.

"Maybe Anna didn't hear them calling fore?" came another's voice.

I looked around to see Grace sitting on the sofa.

"Grace stepped into your shoes when you were incapacitated," Holly informed me. "She spent all her time with Nathaniel on the course. And off it." Holly was delighting in filling in the blanks. "Didn't you hen?"

I turned to see the young girl smile shyly up at the golfer. I had no idea what had happened in the days I'd been unconscious, but it was obvious something had.

"She's been an angel."

And then it all made sense: my papers had gone

through and heaven had sent someone else to help Nathaniel. Not only had I been knocked out but I'd also been replaced. I knew I'd asked for it (not to be hit on the head or drugged by Holly), but I had asked to get back to heaven and now I was going.

"I'm afraid it's time." Leonardo pulled me away in the direction of the door.

"Wait!" My protest was futile as he led me straight outside. "I didn't get to say goodbye," I cried, and turned to go back inside.

"You can't go back." Leonardo stopped me and then my tears came. "I thought you'd be happy to be going home?"

"I am," I sobbed. I closed my eyes and tried to think happy thoughts. I tried to think of the army and swinging my sword but all I could think of was Nathaniel and Jack.

"You've had a really miserable time," Leonardo said. "Don't worry, you'll be back home soon."

"Great." I was still weeping.

The truth was it hadn't been all that bad. In fact, a lot of it had been brilliant. A car stopped alongside and Leonardo opened the door.

"We're driving back?" I asked, as I sat down in the seat.

Leonardo leaned in. "Of course."

I settled back and braced myself for a long drive. I didn't know how many miles it was to heaven, but it must be a lot. I wondered why he wasn't getting in.

"Just waiting on one more." He, like everyone else, seemed to be able to read my mind.

It had to be Holly. On my way back to heaven, at last I'd be able to wreak revenge on my fellow CIA angel for all that she had put me through. I was just in the process of making a long list of her misdemeanours when she slid into the back seat.

"My plan worked." She sat beside me, a smug look on her face.

"You planned to crack open my skull and overdose me with meds?" I accused my assailant.

"Absolutely, and it worked a treat. Finlay's a great shot." She winked.

I couldn't believe what I was hearing. I felt angry but also hurt and betrayed.

"You tried to kill me."

"Well, I had to do something. You were ruining everything," she said, defending her murderous behaviour.

I had no idea what she was talking about. I'd been focused on doing my best to help Nathaniel.

"So, you deployed Grace?"

"Yes, and she did a fantastic job."

I wondered if the gorgeous angel was also a Guardian?

"Well, she's not finished yet," I pointed out. Nathaniel had to maintain his form and win the next forthcoming Major.

"Her work here is done," Holly told me. "She's going home, just like you."

How could that be? Clearly when I'd been lying unconscious I'd missed a lot more than I thought. Now I had a long car journey ahead with an angel who'd tried to assassinate me and one who'd breezed in and succeeded where I had failed; not to mention Leonardo, who harboured secret feelings for me, which were in no way reciprocated. I needed air. I opened the window and leaned out.

"Time to move things along." I came face to face with Leonardo, who looked mischievous.

I quickly sat back in my seat and closed the window. I really needed to explain how I felt about him, once and for all. Meanwhile, Holly had disappeared again, but for once I was glad. However, my joy was short-lived when I heard the car door open again. I was expecting the company of angels but instead Nathaniel got in.

"Ready for home?" he asked.

I thought I was going back home to heaven; that my time here on earth was up? I was completely confused!

"Not really," I answered honestly.

"I know you were so looking forward to seeing Scotland, and I feel terrible that you didn't get to do that, but we'll be back again, and I promise we'll go visit all the places you didn't get to see."

"I'd like that," I told him, but I knew it was a promise

he wouldn't be able to keep.

My time was coming to an end and in fact I thought I was leaving right now. As it turned out, I was to remain here for a little longer, but I had no idea how much longer. Holly, Finlay and Rufus stepped outside the hall and stood on the stone steps. Leonardo followed behind with his arm around Grace. I watched as he pulled her close. If he thought that was going to make me jealous he was very much mistaken. He was such a flirt!

They all waved as the black limousine drove off down the driveway. I looked back and watched as the red brick building with its turrets and tall chimneys faded from view. Only then did I look forward.

35
First Steps

As we flew back across the Atlantic, Nathaniel launched into a list of the leading names in golf who he would be playing against in the upcoming PGA. No amateur players would be competing in this second Major – only the *crème de la crème* of the golfing world. I listened as he assessed the strengths and weaknesses of his competitors and plotted how best to approach the field. I couldn't help but smile: he was making a battle plan.

"Do you realise you're preparing to fight?"

"You're right, I am." He smiled too.

"You still haven't told me what you thought of the course at Loch Lomond."

"It was great," he enthused. "I shot an eleven under par on the first round. Still, Grace nearly beat me. If I hadn't birdied the last two holes, she would've won."

"Good for Grace." I felt myself tense at the mention of her name. "I'm so happy she could help you," I lied. I hated the interloping, golf-playing little angel who had swept in and stolen my thunder, not to mention my job!

"She knew the course like the back of her hand and gave me some great pointers for the Open."

"So, do you feel better prepared?"

"Absolutely! I have a really good feeling Anna that this is going to be my year. Just wait and see."

I would love to wait here and watch him win all the Majors. I wanted to see him lift the Wanamaker trophy, the Claret Jug and the US Open trophy. I'd been doing my homework and knew the names of the silverware that came with each tournament. Yet I wasn't sure just how long I had left. I remembered my instructions: 'you are going to help a young man in despair, who has lost his confidence, self-belief, hope and faith.' I looked across at the now self-assured player; a young man who was looking forward and with a conviction in his ability, and faith in his future. I had done my job.

"I've always believed in you Nathaniel. I'm so happy to see you believing in yourself again."

"It's all thanks to you."

I was prepared to take some of the credit, but not all.

"I only helped you remember who you are – the best golfer in the world."

"I'm not number one yet," he reminded me.

"But you will be." He was ready to reclaim his number one ranking.

He had come so far in such a short time; our journey together seeming to have passed in the mere blink of an eye.

"Here's to slaying the competition in Wisconsin," I toasted.

He lifted his glass of champagne.

"I'll do my best."

That was all me or anyone else could ask of him.

There was enormous pressure on Nathaniel to perform in the PGA. He was pitched against the elite of his profession, and he needed to go out there and show the world that Nathaniel Banks was back!

I gave him a fighting pep talk before sending him in to face the world's press. He deflected every tackle with dextrous aplomb and took the jibes in good humour. He exuded confidence, and soon the questions went beyond this Major to the next.

"Are you going to do the double?" one reporter asked.

"Do you think you will add the Claret Jug to your trophy cabinet?" another said, referring to the upcoming Open.

"No golfer has won all four Major titles in the same year since Bobby Jones. Could you be the first golfer since 1930 to do the Grand Slam?"

Nathaniel had inspired in the press the same faith he had found in himself. They believed he could do it and so did I.

"I am very happy with my game but I'm not looking that far ahead. I'm focused on this tournament, going out today and playing to the best of my ability. Thank you ladies and gentlemen." He stood up and confidently strode out of the room.

"That went surprisingly well," he said, as he put on a white glove. "See you at the first tee."

"No Nathaniel, not today," I told him.

"What's wrong?"

"Nothing. You don't need me to be there."

"I do," he panicked.

"No, you don't." Perhaps I should've told him in advance rather than springing it on him at the last minute, but it was too late for that now. Duke was waiting for him and he was due to tee off.

"I can't do this without you." Self-doubt crept in and threatened to undo all the good work we'd done.

"Of course you can," I reassured him. "Besides, I'm going to be watching every swing and every shot."

"But I need to see you."

Duke called out, "We have to go."

"You don't have to see to believe," I told him. "I promise you, I'll be with you every step of the way."

He closed his eyes for a moment, and when he opened them again all trace of doubt and fear had disappeared from his face.

"Nathaniel!" Duke shouted.

It was time to go.

He stood up straight; his shoulders back, confident, proud and self-assured.

"Go out there and show me, and everyone else, just how great you are."

He jogged towards his caddie but turned back before he reached the door.

"Promise?"

"Every step of the way." I wished him good luck as he disappeared from view.

36
On form

"Canapé?"

I took my eyes off the coverage to be confronted by Holly, who was carrying a tray of rather delicious looking mini *vol-au-vents*.

"What are you doing here?"

"Well, I thought that was obvious." She pushed the platter under my nose.

I didn't know why I was surprised to see her or by her latest guise. I was becoming accustomed to her turning up like a bad penny and I shuddered to think what her ominous presence meant. I had a sense of foreboding as she force-fed me a shrimp-filled pastry tart before indulging in several herself.

"*Hmm*, delicious," she said, her mouth full.

Holly thought all food was delicious. Satiated with shrimp, she stopped one of the other servers and swapped trays before proceeding to consume several sweet snacks. I turned my attention back to the screen.

Hospitality Holly stood beside me, happily munching away as we watched Nathaniel make a particularly difficult chip onto the green. I held my breath as I watched the ball land, rolling slowly towards the hole before dropping in.

"Looks like Grace's tuition is paying dividends." Holly's irksome remark infuriated me.

"That has nothing to do with Grace!" I was incensed at the mention of her name.

"Okay," Holly said, taking a step back. "No need to be so touchy."

"All *my* work is paying off." I suddenly became very territorial over Nathaniel.

She refused to concede that Grace had played no role in it or give me the credit for the hard work I'd put in. "Well, whosever it is, it is paying off."

Nathaniel's name appeared at the top of the leader board. Holly had set down the tray and was looking for a member of staff serving beverages.

"Bubbles," she called out, and a young man pranced over carrying a tray of champagne. "Would you like one?" she asked.

"No thank you. I'm not a big fan of bubbles."

She frowned and waited for the young server to walk on.

"That wasn't very nice," she scolded me. "Bubbles is so sweet and lovely."

"I'm sorry." I thought she had been talking about the

drink, not the waiter!

"I'm going to check and see if he's all right. He's a very sensitive soul," she said, before walking off.

I was happy to turn my full attention back to the coverage. Hospitality Holly didn't make another appearance and I wondered if she'd just turned up for the food.

There were a few nail-biting moments on the first day as I watched Nathaniel search me out in the crowd. Remembering I wasn't there, he lost confidence on the first tee and struggled to find focus. Yet he soon got into the game and into his stride. By the seventh, he was smiling at the camera and waving to the crowds who were now friends rather than foes. Encouraged by their cheering and clapping, a faultless first round saw him leading the field which was where he stayed right up to the final day.

"I want you to come out on the course today," he said, as we walked back to our rooms after breakfast. As the leader, Nathaniel was the last to tee off.

"I think this tournament has proven you don't need me," I reminded him. "You're doing great!"

Great was an understatement. Unless anything went disastrously wrong, Nathaniel Banks' name would be engraved onto the Wanamaker trophy later today.

"I know I don't need you, but I want you to be there," he told me. I hesitated and so he added, "To see me win. In person."

"Okay then," I agreed.

It would be good to be out on the course again soaking up the atmosphere. It wasn't quite the same watching it from the hospitality screens backstage. So, just before noon, I walked out with Nathaniel and Duke.

"Remember the F-Plan." I was about to recite it when he stopped me.

"I have a new F-Plan – focus, fantastic play and four Majors."

I couldn't argue with that. "Firstly, go out and win your second."

"I will! Just watch me."

"I won't take my eyes off you," I told him, before stepping into the crowd of surrounding spectators.

After a quick huddle with Duke, he took the driver and stood behind the tee. He looked from the ball, down the fairway, and back to the ball. Positioning his stance, he raised his club high above his head, never taking his eye off the ball. I watched a perfect swing send it in a textbook trajectory, straight towards the green. He hadn't looked for me; he'd stayed focused on his shot and I felt incredibly proud. Duke was smiling broadly as he retrieved the driver. It was only then that Nathaniel scanned the crowd. I clapped my hands when he found me, and he smiled before walking off with his caddie.

As I walked with the herds of onlookers from hole to hole, I couldn't help but wonder how long it would be before heaven came a-calling. There was really no reason left for me to be here.

Nathaniel extended his lead with every hole he played. There was never any doubt that he would win and there was chanting, cheering and huge celebration after he made his final putt on the eighteenth. He hugged Duke and threw his cap high in the air.

I couldn't have been happier for Nathaniel, who stopped to sign photographs for his fans, as he walked off a champion. I wondered if Jack had been watching his hero's triumphant second Major win. Next month he would be there in person to hopefully see him win his third. I couldn't wait to see him again.

"We did it!" Nathaniel picked me up and spun me around.

"*You* did it." I felt light-headed when he put me back down.

"Let's celebrate." He took my hand and led me into the hospitality tent.

His peers and members of the press immediately gathered around so I let go of his hand as he was swept away on a congratulatory tide. Turning back, he reached out for me, but this was his triumph and his time. I raised my hand to reassure him. I would wait until they had sung his praises and rejoiced in his victory.

"Would madam like a glass of champagne?" A rather indignant Bubbles appeared at my side.

"Thank you, that's very kind." I felt obliged to accept.

The young waiter gave me a hard stare before turning on his patent heel and striding off.

Hospitality Holly reappeared dressed in her staff uniform, a gold crest emblazoned on her navy jacket.

"I think you've made a great success of your first mission."

Seeing Nathaniel succeed was a double-edged sword as I would soon be picking up mine again.

"Our boy won!" She grabbed a flute from another waiter. "Cheers," she toasted, as she clinked my glass.

He wasn't ours! He was mine, and I told her so.

"All the early starts, long hours, the tournaments and games were all worth it. All our hard work has paid off."

I didn't remember Holly doing any of those things. In fact, the only thing she had done was change her disguise and stuff her face. I was about to point that out but I didn't get the chance.

"Finlay will be so happy to hear that he's won." The mention of Holly's husband brought back a longing for the small country I'd so wanted to see. "We'll have to celebrate when you come visit for the Open in July."

I was shocked to hear that I was still going to be here then.

"You'll love it in summer. It's the perfect time to sightsee and the perfect time for a picnic. Won't that be nice?"

I was reminded of what happened the last time I refused to eat finger food on the bonnie, bonnie banks of Loch Lomond – she very nearly fractured my skull!

I looked over at Nathaniel who was surrounded by well-wishers. I'd done what had been asked of me. I didn't know what else I could do.

"Shouldn't I be going home?" I asked Holly.

My question was met with silence and I realised that she was gone.

37

A Floral Dress and a Flash

Next on the golfing agenda was the US Open. This was the tournament I was most looking forward to. I was going to keep my promise to Jack whom I couldn't wait to see. Exhilarated from a second Major win, Nathaniel and Duke were more relaxed than they had been before on the flight to Mamaroneck.

"Shouldn't you both be plotting and planning?" I didn't want them resting on their laurels.

"It's a golf tournament, not a bank heist." Duke was his usual surly self.

"All done," Nathaniel reassured me.

"Are you sure you shouldn't do it again?"

"We have this in the bag," Duke snapped.

"And pride comes before a fall," I retorted.

Nathaniel put a stop to our bickering by reassuring me that he wouldn't let Jack down. He had guessed the real reason for my anxiety.

The small population of Mamaroneck had tripled

overnight, thanks to the spectators and members of the press who had all gathered there to see the world's best golfers compete for the prestigious US Open title. As the favourite, Nathaniel was receiving plenty of airtime as the media speculated if he could take his third Major. There was no mention of last year's performances (or lack of them.); no mention of his ex-wife, his state of mind or loss of form. There was no more doubt. Nathaniel Banks was back on top, and the world's press were betting on him to win. Everyone wanted to see him lift the cup; none more so than me and Jack.

The black Sedan, which had been sent to chauffeur me to Winged Foot, joined the long line of cars waiting to deliver invited guests to the prestigious event. I sat in the back and silently prayed that Nathaniel would stay focused and give another stellar performance on the course. I looked out the window at bright green immaculate lawns where course officials were already shepherding the flocks of spectators into position.

Winged Foot's grand clubhouse was an imposing Tudor scholastic-style building. I stepped out of the car and walked under a bricked portico into the historic building that had a long association with the US Open. I entered an elegant entrance hall and continued through an arched opening, framed by two tall ferns. Well-dressed guests stood in groups watched over by a painting of a former golfing star, who from his prime position above the fireplace, kept a close eye on all who entered.

Wafts of cigar smoke rose up from high-backed leather armchairs and ladies sipped coffee from delicate bone china cups. I leisurely wandered from room-to-room while being mindful of the time. Nathaniel had an early tee off and I didn't want to miss it.

Through huge arched windows, sunlight flooded into a mahogany-panelled room. Two chandeliers hung from the ceiling, illuminating names etched onto display boards affixed to the wall. Taking centre stage was a huge silver cup on a carved plinth. The trophy was surrounded by tables and chairs where the well-heeled guests would sit to watch the coverage from the comfort of the clubhouse on the huge screens that had been erected around the room.

I closely studied the incredible craftsmanship of the piece, observing a winged victory on top of the silver jug, engraved with a laurel wreath that wrapped around four golfers; the names of all previous winners etched into the base. I slowly walked around the spectacular silver cup and into a cloud of smoke.

"Well, howdy doody little lady," Bob greeted me.

"Bob!" I choked.

"Look Dorinda, it's young Nathaniel's girl," he drawled loudly.

I could feel my face flush.

"You look beautiful Anna. Doesn't she Bob?" Dorinda admired the long pale pink dress Rosaria had helped me choose. The maid had also curled my hair, spent an inordinate amount of time putting on my makeup and generally fussing over me.

Apparently all her hard work had paid off.

The huge Texan agreed before poisoning me with another puff.

"There's your boy's name." He jabbed the short stubby cigar at the base of the stunning piece of silverware.

I wish he'd keep his voice down. He was attracting attention and hushed whispers passed between curious guests at nearby tables who nodded in my direction.

"Nathaniel Banks, 2016," he boomed, causing more onlookers' heads to turn. "That was before he completely lost it – crashed and burned – fell from grace."

"Well, he's back on top now." That put a stop to Bob's rant.

"All thanks to you," he announced.

Inquisitive guests now looked on with interest. Thank heavens they didn't know my name!

"Anna!" a voice called out. It was Jack.

He ran towards me and wrapped his arms around me.

"Is this your boy?" Dorinda asked.

"This is Jack. And *these* are his parents." I introduced Paul and Nancy as they finally caught up with their son.

"Pleased to meet y'all." The loud Texan shook hands with the family. "So, young man, are you a big golfing fan?" he asked Jack, who was still holding onto me.

Jack enthusiastically nodded his head.

"And who do you support?"

"Nathaniel Banks," he said, proudly. "He's the best golfer in the whole world!"

"Well now, you are a big fan," Bob chuckled.

"I love him." Jack was utterly devoted. "Just like Anna does."

A woman stood up and took a photo with her phone. Her action prompted another to do the same and this then alerted a lone reporter who stealthy moved around the tables towards me. When he raised his camera I made my excuses, and hastily retreated from loud-mouth Bob. With Jack in tow, we made our escape outside.

"What's wrong?" he asked.

"I just needed some air," I told him, as I took a deep steadying breath.

More guests milled around chatting. I nervously glanced back to see if we were being followed but there was no sign of the reporter and I breathed a sigh of relief.

"Look Anna, it's Nate." Jack pointed to the big screen. "Quick," he said, and he grabbed my hand.

He pulled me through the crowds and back inside to a packed upstairs terrace. Pushing his way to the front, we jostled into a prime position to watch Nathaniel tee off.

I was so happy to see him smiling and waving to the crowds who were cheering him on. Jack was shouting from the balcony and waving wildly. It was as if Nathaniel heard him because he looked up at that moment, and upon seeing us he waved before then stepping up to the tee.

"He saw us! He saw us!" Jack was ecstatically jumping up and down beside me.

The crowd fell silent, and I held my breath as Nathaniel readied himself for the shot. A beautiful swing sent the ball on a perfect trajectory. Jack was shouting with joy and the spectators were chanting, "Banksy! Banksy!"

Nathaniel looked up at us again. Jack was cheering and I was clapping my hands in congratulation. He waved before setting off after the ball, causing heads to turn. I stepped back from the edge and into the crowd. Reaching for Jack's hand, we jostled our way through the throng of people.

"That was brilliant! I know he's going to win!" Jack announced with confidence. He had complete faith in Nathaniel and his enthusiasm was infectious.

I was so preoccupied I didn't see the furtive photographer hiding behind the fern until it was too late. He jumped out in front of us and I was momentarily blindsided by a flash. I stood motionless, like a deer caught in headlights, as I watched him leave with his prize.

"Bugger!" I swore.

Jack and I located Paul and Nancy sitting at a table, avidly enjoying the game. After his fabulous start, Nathaniel played a fantastic round and had secured a good lead by the end of the first day. He met us for an early dinner, whereupon Jack proceeded to recount every detail of every shot he had made that day. Every sentence ended with, "You're brilliant."

"Stop or you'll give him a big head." I leaned over and warned him.

"But he is brilliant," he asserted. "Isn't he Anna?"

"Very brilliant," I agreed, and Nathaniel smiled.

"Well, if I'm going to be brilliant again tomorrow, I'm going to have to have an early night."

"And so will you," Jack's mum told him.

"No! I don't want to go to bed," he protested.

I looked over and saw his eyelids were starting to close but still, he refused to give in to the tiredness.

"Yes!" she insisted. *"Early to bed and early to rise makes a man healthy, wealthy and wise."* She quoted the proverb and for emphasis added, "Just like Nathaniel."

Reluctantly he acquiesced, but not before asking me if we could go out and watch Nathaniel on the course tomorrow. I looked at Nathaniel for his answer.

"I would love that," he said.

"Please Anna!" Jack was looking at me with big brown eyes that were hard to resist.

"Of course we can."

38

From strength to strength

I couldn't sleep when I went to bed. I was worried about being photographed by the paparazzi again and afraid that the other guests would reach the wrong conclusion about Nathaniel and me.

I switched on the TV and flicked through the sports coverage. Nathaniel's face appeared repeatedly with every news channel's coverage of the US Open. They all reported on his fantastic first round and excitedly speculated on a third Major win. I watched replays of different shots and putts. He really was brilliant, just like Jack had said. He was totally focused, in fantastic form and ahead of the field. If he continued to play that way he was on course for his own F-Plan of four Major wins in one year.

I awoke bright and early on day two, as did Jack. He wanted to get out first thing to secure a prime spot and as Nancy and Paul had opted to watch from the comfort of the clubhouse, I was in charge of taking him out on the course.

"Can we go now?" he asked, through a mouthful of soggy cereal. He repeated the question shortly afterwards while eating a piece of toast.

"When we're finished," I promised; his parents having just told him the same thing.

He gulped down every morsel of the morning meal as fast as he could, never taking his eyes off me. Like an expectant puppy, he jumped up at the first sign that I was ready to go.

"We're too early." I tried to calm his eagerness. Having no desire to stand by the first tee for an hour just waiting, I took him backstage to see Nathaniel instead. Surrounded by so many of his golfing heroes was like being in seventh heaven for Jack. He pointed to different players, shouting out their rank and form, not caring that they could hear him. Thankfully none of the golfers took offence at his brutally honest appraisal of their performance and position. Making a beeline for his superhero, he greeted him with his trademark line, "You're going to be brilliant!"

It made me smile.

"I'm going to do my best for you," Nathaniel told Jack who was delighted by the compliment.

Jack was dressed in a polo shirt and chinos and I watched as he put his hand in his pocket, aping his idol. They say that imitation is the greatest form of flattery and this little boy was doing everything possible to be just like Nathaniel.

"Okay mister, I think we better go and find a prime spot to watch Nathaniel be brilliant."

As I turned to go, I came face-to-face with the same photographer from the day before. He gave me a fright and I jumped back.

"Can I take your photo?" He was the epitome of polite professionalism.

I said, "No," at the exact same moment Jack shouted, "Yes!"

He proudly posed beside Nathaniel, and I could see the photographer's smile turn into a sneer as he took their picture.

"And now a family photo." He turned to me.

"We're not a family," I informed him, standing my ground.

"Oh, I'm sorry. I thought you were together?" He raised an eyebrow.

I glared at the scheming reporter who was just digging for a story, and folded my arms. There was no way I was giving him any information or the picture he so desired.

"Please Anna." Jack pleaded with me.

Begrudgingly I went to stand on the other side of Jack.

"That's not working," the sneaky photographer said. "If you stand here..." He moved me like a chess piece to Nathaniel's side. "Then if you stand in front..." he said, placing Jack where he wanted him before moving back. "That's better, but if you could just put your arm around your girlfriend."

"I'm not his girlfriend!" I told the puppet-master, who pressed the button.

Red-faced and raging, I grabbed Jack's hand.

"Good luck," he called out to Nathaniel, as I dragged him in the direction of the door.

Glancing back, I saw the photographer write something down in a notebook. My heart was racing.

"Everything will be okay Anna." Jack squeezed my hand.

"I know." I reassured him but I couldn't ignore the gnawing doubt that it wouldn't be.

However, the feeling of anxiety faded as we followed Nathaniel around the course. Jack made no apology as he wiggled and weaved his way through the waiting crowds at each hole, pushing us to the front. Spectators were forgiving of the young boy but a little less so of me. Unlike Jack, I spent the entire time apologising for usurping their prime position. Secretly though I was happy when he did it. It felt like old times and Nathaniel and I fell into our former routine.

Before each shot, he found us in the crowd. Although now he did it just because he wanted to, not to keep his focus. No one clapped or cheered louder than Jack, and as I walked with him from hole to hole, I forgot about the artful photographer.

He told me how well he was playing. He was defying science. No one believed that he would ever play again at the same level. Yet here he was. I listened as he told me about the competitions he'd just won, and how he planned to take back his title from Jordan, his biggest rival and best friend. He'd fought to overcome so much in his short life. Jack was a fighter; he had faith and I had no doubt he would win that battle too. I believed he would grow up to be just as brilliant a golfer as Nathaniel.

Together, we supported Nathaniel the whole way round and he performed even better than the day before. He extended his lead by four shots, and after he made his final putt, Jack ran onto the green before I could stop him. Nathaniel picked him up and they both punched the air in victory. Every news channel reported on the story with headlines like, 'Nathaniel Banks shares joy with young fan,' and 'Young boy congratulates golfing hero.'

The press even managed to interview Jack, and when one reporter asked him if he thought Nathaniel would win the US Open, he didn't hesitate: "Yes, because he's brilliant!"

39

With a click of the fingers

The next morning Jack wasn't at breakfast.

"Are you coming out on the course today?" Nathaniel asked me, as I sat down at the table.

"Definitely."

"Good." He smiled. "Yesterday meant a lot to me."

"Me too." I felt I was back where I belonged.

"Although today you'll be on your own." He must've seen the look of panic on my face and reached over to take my hand. "Don't worry, there's nothing wrong with Jack," he reassured me. "He's doing his own round of interviews. The press is much more interested in talking to him than to me now." He sat back and smiled.

That wasn't a bad thing, I thought.

"So, I hope you've been working out because you're going to have to push your own way to the front."

"I've done it a few times before, I'm sure I'll manage." It was my turn to offer reassurance. "After all, I don't want to miss you swinging your way to victory."

"Cheers to that," he said, as he drank the last mouthful of coffee. "See you at the first." He gave me a kiss on the cheek before dashing off.

Just like the crowds, support swelled for Nathaniel on the penultimate day of the tournament. With every shot he was coming ever nearer to lifting the trophy. I thought I would have to force my way to the front but spectators stepped out of the way, which I considered strange, but I didn't have time to wonder why; I was too preoccupied with watching Nathaniel.

Every move he made was like a beautiful dance – the mesmerising swing of his hips, the flexed muscles of his bicep as he held the club high above his head, the arch of his back and the curve of his body. I couldn't take my eyes off him so was oblivious that other eyes were on me. I was in a world of my own until I was paid another visit from the one up above.

"This way." Course official Holly guided the tsunami-like mass of spectators. She was wielding her favourite instrument of torture – the yellow plastic whistle. I covered my ears as she pursed her lips, nearly deafening those unfortunate enough to be standing nearby.

"Keep to the left." She corralled the crowds like cattle into her cordoned-off corridor. "Please be quiet," she bellowed. "We don't want to put anyone off their game," she overemphasized by pointing towards the nearest green. Dressed in a fluorescent jacket emblazoned with her new job description, she ordered everyone to, "Tiptoe to the next tee."

I pity help the next players, I thought, as I pulled my cap down and positioned myself in the middle of the moving masses in an effort to avoid detection. They wouldn't have a hope of concentrating with the racket Holly was making. She continued to holler orders punctuated with a shrill, sharp blast of the whistle and I was happy when I heard her voice fade into the distance behind me.

There was a delay on the seventeenth and I nervously waited for the players to finish the hole. Nathaniel looked relaxed, whereas I had taken to biting my nails as I watched and waited for him to take centre stage. I didn't want him to falter or fail. His closest competitor had narrowed the gap, so the pressure was building; he couldn't afford to drop a shot. However, confident, calm and in control, he stepped up to the tee.

I willed him on to win as I watched the familiar ritual that I hoped would result in a fantastic shot. He took a second to make eye contact. It was a look that reassured me he had control; that I should have the same faith in him as he now had in himself. He wanted me to believe in him – trust him. It was a look that took my breath away; a fleeting moment but in that moment all my anxiety disappeared. I didn't even have to wait for him to hit the ball to know it would be a perfect shot. As everyone else watched the small ball fly into the air,

Nathaniel turned to face me.

There was something in his eyes – a declaration and demonstration of all he could do; a look that reassured me he was in charge. No words were spoken but I knew he was trying to tell me it was over; that I had done my job and he was back on top. It was a bittersweet expression as it meant he didn't need me anymore.

I smiled and nodded before stepping back.

"There you are." I turned to see a red-faced Holly. "It's like finding a needle in a haystack," she panted, exhausted from pushing and shoving her way through the crowds. "I thought I'd lost you." She gasped for breath.

No such luck! I didn't know why Holly was here but I had learnt that an appearance from her never ended well for me.

"I have to give you this." She unclipped a white envelope from her board and handed it to me.

We stood like two islands in a stream as spectators washed around us.

"Move along." She managed to find enough breath to give one last blast on her whistle.

"What is it?" I had a feeling she was the bearer of bad news.

"It's good news." She clapped her hands in excitement. "Read it! Read it!" I normally only saw her this enthused by food.

I tore through the official seal, took out a sheet of

white paper and read the short letter. It informed me that my mission was over and I was being summoned to a meeting. The letter was signed by my colonel and commander-in-chief and was addressed to Lieutenant Anna Frost. It appeared my request had been granted.

"Isn't that great?" Holly stood to attention and saluted me.

"Yes, fantastic news." Yet I was fixated on the finality of the words, 'your mission is over.'

"This is exactly what you wanted. I thought you'd be thrilled."

"I am," I lied, trying to process what this meant for me and for Nathaniel.

"When am I leaving?" There was no mention of a time or date in the letter.

"I don't know but I'm sure it will be soon. You know how quickly things move up above. One minute you're here and the next…" Holly clicked her fingers "*Poof*! You're gone. No more earth, no more boring golf, no more flying without wings, and no more Nathaniel Banks. You'll never have to see him again."

I couldn't speak; I just kept staring at the letter. That's what this meant – I would never see Nathaniel again. I walked in a daze to the eighteenth hole, still holding the summons in my hand. The last time I'd stood in front of the colonel I had been dismissed, deported and deployed in a heartbeat. It was happening again. I heard my heart beating in my chest. I was still alive, but for how much longer?

I missed Nathaniel playing the final hole but the rapturous applause told me he'd won another day's play. He was twenty-four hours away from taking his third Major. I wanted to be here to see that happen. One more day was all I needed –

40
Forewarned is Forearmed

Jack was busy telling everyone at the table about the interview he had just done.

"I told Amelia, the interviewer from Fox, that Anna and I were going to watch Nathaniel win the US Open tomorrow." He smiled at me across the table. "And the Open."

I didn't know if I'd still be here to see either now.

I sat, at what could be my last dinner, trying to memorise everything in case I suddenly disappeared during the night. I wanted to remember Jack's voice, every feature of his face, the colour of Nathaniel's eyes, the way a dimple appeared when he smiled. I worried that they would fade from my memory when I was back in heaven and I would forget everything. Like me, they would be gone forever.

"If I win tomorrow, will you help me hold up the cup?" Nathaniel asked his most ardent fan.

Jack was dumbfounded.

"One day, you're going win the US Open," Nathaniel told him. "I thought you should get a little practise in."

Jack nodded in earnest and Paul reached over to shake Nathaniel's hand.

"One day, you're going to be champion," Nathaniel told Jack.

One day seemed so near and yet so far away; one day soon I would be gone. I just prayed that day wouldn't be tomorrow. I wanted to be there to see Nathaniel and Jack lift the spectacular trophy, but I didn't know how many days, hours, minutes and seconds I had left here.

I was both surprised and delighted when I opened my eyes the following morning and realised I was still on earth. Thoughts of how little time was left were still preoccupying my mind when I joined Jack, Paul and Nancy on the course. Everyone wanted to see the live action of the last day; soak up the atmosphere from the side-lines and watch Nathaniel win the US Open for a second time.

He had maintained his lead going into the final day – now all he had to do was continue that way and the title was his. The pressure didn't seem to faze him. In fact, he thrived on it and was playing even better than before. One birdie after another appeared on his score card; he was flying higher than the real thing.

I nervously kept watching for Holly as we walked from hole to hole but there was no sign of the heavenly course official. Leonardo however appeared on the ninth, swaggering towards me with his trademark open white shirt that today had been teamed with a pair of skin-tight tartan trousers. I let Paul, Nancy and Jack walk ahead before confronting the dark angel.

"What are you doing here?" I hoped it wasn't to escort me home.

"Like everyone else." He made a sweeping gesture. "I'm here to watch your young man claim victory."

"No other reason?" I was suspicious of his motives.

"Absolutely not." He gave me his most charming smile. "Cross my heart and hope to die," he vowed, as he traced a finger over his bare chest.

"You're already dead." The gesture was of no comfort to me.

"You have a point," he said, draping his arm around me. "And so do I."

I knew it! He had an ulterior motive. He was going to push me into some hidden lift and send me on my way. I tried to shrug him off but he kept a firm grip on me.

"The point is, my darling girl, you did it!" He squeezed me close. "You came, you coached, you conquered," he complimented. "You followed orders. You helped him find faith. You gave him hope. You helped him win. You were a triumph. It was a victory."

Then why did it feel like I'd lost?

"Up above are very pleased with you. Just between you and me, I think you'll be getting exactly what you wished for," he whispered conspiratorially and winked. "Lieutenant."

I had wished to be back in the EAA ever since I'd been unceremoniously pushed out and sent to earth on a mission via the Guardians. I'd dreamed of donning my uniform again, wielding my sword and leading the legions. Having my rank reinstated should have made me deliriously happy, but instead my stomach was churning and I couldn't focus.

"I think I'm going to be sick." I had to take a breath.

"You do look pale. Here, let me." Leonardo guided me off to the side.

"It must've been something I ate." I gulped in the air, hoping the sensation would soon pass.

"You have to be careful with this foreign food," Leonardo cautioned. "Not to worry, after Scotland that won't be a problem."

"Scotland?"

"Yes, you have one more job to do before you leave," he told me.

"I'm not going now?" I wanted to make absolutely sure I had understood him correctly.

"No! Whatever gave you that idea?"

"Well, you." His being here had given me that impression!

"You'll have time at the Open to say your goodbyes to young Mr. Banks."

"So, I'm going to Ireland too?" I had found out the

Open was being held there.

"No, you're going to the Scottish Open – the one before the Open."

The golfing world really needed to get a bit more creative with the names of the competitions. It was downright confusing when they were all called the same thing!

"So, just to be clear, I'm going to the Open in Scotland but not the Open in Ireland?"

"Correct, and you needn't worry about packing. Federico has sent some of Palava's new creations for the occasion which are just divine."

I was sure that there was nothing heavenly about them. No doubt I'd be dressed like a big tartan haggis.

"And I've popped something in your wardrobe for later."

"What's happening tonight?"

"The celebration dinner. Honestly, Anna, do keep up."

I was finding that difficult. Apparently, I was going to celebrate Nathaniel's win, I was going to Scotland and then I was going home. Another wave of nausea forced me to clutch my stomach. It took a moment for the sickness to pass and in that moment, Leonardo had gone.

41

Feeling Flashy

I caught up with Jack, and together we cheered Nathaniel on. Along with everyone else at Winged Foot, we watched him take the US Open title. I felt so proud and privileged to see him reach a new high in his career. I thought back to the bridge, and every footstep from then on that had brought us both to this place – this moment in time – this victory. I was so thankful to have shared his journey.

I watched Nathaniel punch the air after he made the final putt, and everyone cheered loudly. I watched Jack's pure joy as he walked back onto the green holding Nathaniel's hand. After paying tribute to the other players, Nathaniel picked him up and each of them took a handle, lifting the silver cup together. It was so emotional to watch.

"One day Jack will win this," he told the assembled press.

After the presentation, Nathaniel and Jack were taken

away for another round of interviews and I was left alone. I went back to my room and took a long soak in the bath before getting ready for Nathaniel's celebration dinner. Leonardo had left a figure-hugging full-length black satin gown and a diamond necklace, together with a note: 'It's your turn to shine.'

I picked up the stunning piece of jewellery, which must have cost a fortune. I put it on, and not for the first time wondered how Leonardo had acquired his earthly wealth. There was a knock on the door as I did a twirl in front of the mirror and in walked Rosaria, swinging a hairdryer in one hand and a makeup case in the other.

"Oh, Miss Anna! Your dress is amazing! We just need to fix your hair and," she drew a circle in the air to indicate my face.

I let her get to work and after forty-five minutes I looked fit to walk the red carpet.

"Wow!" I was overwhelmed by the transformation.

"Time to go." Rosaria handed me a pair of strappy stilettos and shooed me in the direction of the door.

The competitors had been joined by their respective wives, girlfriends and partners, and everyone mingled at the prestigious Winged Foot clubhouse. Due to their hectic press commitments, I'd agreed to meet both Nathaniel and Jack at dinner.

"Well little lady, it looks like your boy is back on form." Beefhouse Bob, who was dressed in full Texan regalia, bellowed before striding across the room to me.

"And my oh my has he hooked a beauty." He whistled in appreciation.

"You look sensational Anna." Nathaniel had appeared at my side.

"Gorgeous," Dorinda added.

I felt overwhelmed by all the attention.

A gong rang, signalling the start of dinner. I held onto Nathaniel's arm as we joined other guests waiting to be seated. The large round tables in the mahogany-panelled room were now elegantly dressed for the grand occasion. We were shown to the top table; above us, the podium platform where the US Open cup was proudly on display. We joined Duke and his wife Sue, as well as Paul, Nancy and Jack, and the club chairman and his wife and daughter.

Jack was very quiet when I took my seat beside him.

"Did you get to do more interviews?" I asked him, and he nodded. "And did you get to hold the mic?" I knew he liked that.

Another nod but he remained silent.

"Is anything wrong?" I quizzed him.

He hadn't taken his eyes off me since I'd sat down but hadn't said a word.

"You're all twinkly." He seemed transfixed.

"It's the diamonds." I stroked the expensive necklace.

"You're sparkly," he told me.

"That's what happens when light falls on diamonds,"

I explained.

"Breathtaking," Nathaniel said, admiring the spectacular statement piece I was wearing.

"Leonardo wanted me to wear it tonight," I told him, which caused him to raise an eyebrow.

I couldn't fathom how he had acquired the exquisite piece of jewellery or how he had amassed his earthly fortune. Yet it was a mystery I fully intended to solve before I left this world which, quite frankly, didn't give me long.

The light I felt radiating from me suddenly darkened in line with my thoughts when I remembered how little time I had left. Saying goodbye was not going to be easy. I tried to push those thoughts to the back of my mind because contrary to what Leonardo's note had said, this was Nathaniel's night to shine.

After a fantastic celebratory dinner, the chairman took to the stage and the spotlight fell back where it belonged - onto the champion golfer beside me. As he introduced the three-times Major winner and US Open champion everyone stood and clapped while Nathaniel took to the stage. He thanked the chairman, the club, the organisers, sponsors and his fans for their support. Then he personally thanked Duke.

"I couldn't have done it without you buddy. We're a team."

His usually stern-faced caddie raised a glass and looked quite emotional.

"And there are two other very special people here tonight who I would also like to thank."

Nathaniel looked at Jack.

"I'm sure you all know Jack by now and I think you'll agree he's been the star of this tournament." A round of applause broke out for the blushing little boy. "He is such an incredibly talented young golfer and one day he's going to be standing on this stage, holding this amazing trophy." Whoops of joy and applause echoed around the room at Nathaniel's prediction.

"But what you might not know, is that I met Jack when he was in hospital when he was recovering from a brain tumour." This announcement silenced the crowd, except for a few audible gasps of shock. I put my hand over Jack's and held it there as Nathaniel continued. "He was a champion golfer before he got sick, and he will be again; not just because of his incredible talent but also because of his fantastic spirit."

I felt tears welling as I squeezed Jack's hand.

"I don't know if any of you noticed, but last year I lost a few games… here and there." Light-hearted chuckles broke out among the diners. "It wasn't until I met this inspirational young man that my game turned around. He believed in me and he taught me to believe in myself again; he taught me how to fight for what I wanted. So Jack, this trophy is for you. You might have to build another shelf Paul!"

Jack sat with his mouth open; his father was in

complete shock.

"I couldn't have won it without you, or without—"

I knew the spotlight was going to fall on me. I shifted uncomfortably in my seat, waiting for him to say my name, when a high-pitched screeching made most of the guests cover their ears. I saw him mouth my name as someone dashed on stage and unplugged his microphone. The equipment appeared to have malfunctioned.

"Ladies and gentlemen, please be upstanding and raise your glasses for Nathaniel Banks, your US Open Champion," came a familiar voice over the sound system.

The chairman dashed back onto the stage to present Nathaniel with the trophy he had so kindly gifted to Jack, who was whooping and hollering for his hero. Part of me had wanted to hear what he was going to say about me, but angels shouldn't draw attention to themselves. Fingers would point, questions would be asked and up above wouldn't be pleased.

I was here undercover. I had to stay in the shadows and tonight I had Holly to thank for keeping me there. I didn't know if she had blown her deafening yellow whistle into the microphone, but her announcement had saved me from an embarrassing situation.

I couldn't stop the tears as I said goodbye to Jack the next day.

"Why are you crying Anna?"

I couldn't tell him that I might never see him again.

"Nathaniel won and we'll watch him win the Open too." He reminded me of a promise I could no longer keep.

"I have to go back to work Jack and it's going to take me far away." I hoped he would understand.

"But you promised." He knew how to weaken my resolve.

"I know I did, and I don't want to break that promise, but I'm going to be far away."

"You promised!" He wasn't listening, and his bottom lip was trembling.

This was terrible! There was no way I could let him down. I was sure God would understand and give me the day off from fighting evil.

"I promise I'll come back – just for you." That made him smile.

He hugged me hard, and I left him to say goodbye to Nathaniel while I wiped away tears that continued to fall. It had been so difficult saying goodbye to Jack and I dreaded having to say goodbye to Nathaniel, but that was what I would have to do in Scotland. We had an early flight so I would have time to see the sights before the Scottish Open started. Then I would have to leave him and the country I had come to love so much.

42

Feeling Frisky

This time when we landed we didn't need Doris's help, and Nathaniel had no fear of the narrow road that led to the dark forest. He didn't flinch when the Range Rover rocked down the slope, through the stream and up the other side, bringing the impressive red brick building with its turrets and tall chimneys into view.

When we pulled up in front of the stunning stately home, I remembered the family coat of arms. I was on my way up the stone steps to investigate who Leonardo had inherited his fortune from when the door opened, and Finlay came out to greet us. He stood right in front of the crest and his huge frame blocked my view.

"Welcome back to Glen Guthrie Hall," he boomed. "It's not often we get return visitors."

I couldn't understand why; it was so beautiful. Finlay reached for my bag. "After you," he said, waiting for me to enter first which deprived me of the chance to look at the plaque. I would have to continue my sleuthing after we'd checked in.

"There you are!" A portly Mrs Munroe walked towards us, arms outstretched in welcome. "My little love— lovelies!" She was at it again. "You've picked the perfect time of the year to come back to us. The sun is out, the flowers are out and the guests have just checked out, so there are two rooms."

I was so happy!

"But the midges are also out and the wee beasties bite," Finlay warned us.

"Nonsense! I think I've only seen one all year," Holly contradicted her husband. "I'll take you up to your rooms and then you can go explore our beautiful country," she said, as we followed her up the sweeping staircase.

"You're back in the Burns Suite." Holly opened the door for Nathaniel. "And don't worry, your lovely Anna is right next door in the Campbell Suite."

I was delighted to hear that I too was being treated to a suite.

"They were lovers you know." Holly looked from Nathaniel to me. "They had a brief affair and planned to run away together but before they could, poor Mary died of a fever." She punctuated the sad story with a reverential pause before continuing. "A distraught Robbie wrote *To Mary in heaven* for her because that's where the angels took her." Holly let that fact register with me before continuing the tragic tale. "They had the briefest of affairs but remember – it's better to have loved and lost than never to have loved at all." She kept her eyes firmly fixed on me as she spoke.

I wasn't sure where Holly was going with this, but I was going to my room. I took the key and stepped into the love-inspired suite, closely followed by my hostess who was still quoting poetry written by the bereft bard.

"So, what happened to Robbie?" I imagined him not being able to live in a world without his true love. "Did he die of a broken heart?"

"God no! In the end, he died of a fever too. He fell out of a pub drunk one night, fell asleep on the side of the road and died, right before the birth of his twelfth child."

"He fathered twelve children?"

"I'm afraid our Mr. Burns had an eye for the ladies. He racked up quite a few notches on his bedpost before he met his untimely end, but not before he wrote some of the most beautiful poetry the world has ever seen, inspired by Mary's loss. Isn't that romantic?" Holly lay back on my bed and ran her hand through the delicate voile that fell around the four-poster bed.

"No, not really. I'm amazed he found the time to write anything at all, what with all his shagging and childcare demands. He should've showed some loyalty and mourned her passing."

"He did." Holly defended the sex-mad poet. "He missed her but he was a man, not a saint. Men have needs." She mouthed the word 'sexual' to emphasise her point.

"*Urgh*!" I didn't want to talk about sex, especially not with Holly.

"I should know; Finlay has a huge appetite."

I covered my ears and turned away, but she sneaked up behind me and pulled them away.

"He's insatiable. We can hardly keep our hands off each other."

"Please stop," I begged her.

"Morning, noon and night." She informed me that sex, like food, came in three courses.

It did however explain her lengthy absences during my time here on earth. The amount of time she spent frolicking with Finlay, along with the inordinate amount of time she spent feasting on food, left me wondering how she managed to get any CIA work done at all.

"Well, don't let me keep you." I nodded towards the door.

"He's away getting the car ready for you." She dismissed the idea with a wave of her hand. "So…" She turned her full attention back to me. "When are you going to tell Nathaniel?"

"Tell him what?" I absentmindedly answered, as I tried to decide what to wear for our jaunt out.

"You know." She winked.

I realised the point she was trying to make.

"Oh, that." I was leaving and, like Mary, was going

back to heaven. "It's going to ruin things if I tell him."
I wanted to enjoy what little time I had left.

I was hoping to tell him just before I vanished in a
puff of smoke or Leonardo shoved me into the nearest
lift and I went up, up, up and away.

Holly was swinging her hips from side to side as she
walked across the room. She reached inside her ample
cleavage and brought out a small key.

"This is the key to heaven." She caressed it before
handing it to me.

She sashayed back to a door I had presumed led to
the neighbouring suite.

"All you have to do is open it."

It wasn't a connecting door at all but a portal – an
exit. Once I'd told Nathaniel, once I was ready, all I had
to do was turn the key. I looked at the closed door.

"Heaven is waiting for you on the other side of this
door."

I put the small key safely in my pocket. I'm afraid
heaven's door would be staying locked for a little while
longer.

43

A Flight of fancy

Over the coming days Nathaniel and I visited quite a few of the red-circled locations on my map. We went in search of Nessie who sadly didn't make an appearance. We visited an art gallery, a gothic cathedral and an old war ship. Mostly we managed to remain incognito, but when we reached Edinburgh we noticed there was a lot of finger-pointing. When people recognised Nathaniel, they whispered and giggled, pointing cameras and taking photographs. Finally, when someone started to film us, Nathaniel took my hand and told me it was time to go.

We weaved in and out of the tourists and locals who filled the bustling back streets of the old town.

"I don't understand," I said, as we stopped to catch our breath.

"Look! It's Nathaniel Banks! And Anna!" A girl shrieked, pointing at us.

This wasn't good. Heads turned as we took flight

again, making a beeline for the car that was parked near the castle. Nathaniel ran ahead, not realising I had stopped. I stood in front of a newspaper stand and my face stared back at me from the front cover of a magazine. Nathaniel's was on another, and the headlines insinuated that I was the reason he had picked up his game – that 'love conquered fear'.

I was frozen to the spot, not able to look away, as I read on.

'Who is the mystery woman in Nathaniel Banks' life?' read one headline.

The whole world was asking who I was. This was a cataclysmic disaster! I was an angel who was supposed to remain anonymous but somehow I had managed to ruin everything.

"No, no, no!" I was shaking with shock, trying to absorb it all.

Nathaniel had jogged back to me.

"What's wrong?"

All I could do was point. I put my hand over my mouth and shook my head. This was a nightmare. The reporter from the US Open had clearly sold his pictures to every magazine, and while we were busy sightseeing the story had broken.

"This is awful,' I said.

Nathaniel grabbed a handful of the publications.

"Keep the change," he told the vendor, who would've preferred a photograph.

There had been quite enough of those taken. He took my hand and coaxed me out of my catatonic state.

"Anna, we have to go."

I nodded and only felt safe when we were back in the car and on our way back to Glen Guthrie Hall. We didn't speak on the way back; both of us lost in thought, trying to process the implications.

"I'm sorry," was all I could mutter. "This is terrible."

He reached over and took my hand as we came to a stop in front of the stone steps.

"No, it's not."

"Back so soon?" Mrs Munroe quizzed us, as I leapt out of the car.

"Anna," Nathaniel called after me. "We need to talk."

I ran inside, up the sweeping staircase and straight to my suite, collapsing on top of the bed. I was dizzy, I felt short of breath and my heart was racing. There was a knock on the door and Holly marched in, carrying an armful of the malicious magazines. She dropped them on the bed and then sat down beside me.

"Well, well, well." She licked her finger as she turned the pages, each plastered with images of Nathaniel and me. "This is interesting." She studied each one intently.

"It's a lie!" I sat up to see Holly wagging her finger.

"The camera never lies." She then flicked over to reveal a full-page spread of shots.

"I was set up. He stalked me and secretly took those photos."

She peered closely at the page. "It certainly looks like you didn't notice he was there. It looks like you only had eyes for Nathaniel."

I jumped up and started to pace up and down, biting my nails.

Holly stood up too. "The truth is, the whole world will now want to know who Anna Frost is."

I was forbidden by a heavenly decree from telling them or Nathaniel.

"The truth will set you free," Holly continued.

"The truth will get me in big trouble. The truth will get me booted out of the EAA for a second time. I'll be charged with breaking angelic law. I'll be sent somewhere worse than the CIA!" I still struggled to come up with anywhere worse but wherever it was, that was where I was going.

"It's time to tell the truth."

Holly wasn't in her right senses (clearly too much food and sex had addled her brain.). Had she forgotten it was a cardinal sin to tell anyone you're an angel? That was the truth – I was an angel – sent here to help Nathaniel. I couldn't tell him that!

"It's time, you have to tell him," Holly persisted, as she picked up the offending publications and walked towards the door. "He's waiting for you."

I nervously paced up and down. Nathaniel deserved

an explanation, but what could I say? That I had briefly breezed into his life to get him back on track and now it was time to leave? That was the truth; I was leaving. The best thing I could do was just leave before I undid all the good that had already been done.

I reached for the key to heaven's door. I wanted to say goodbye to him, but I couldn't. I didn't know what to say. The one thing I did know was that I couldn't tell him the truth. I looked from the bedroom door to heaven's door. I had to make a decision and choose between them.

"I'm sorry Nathaniel," I said, even though he wasn't there.

I put the small key in the lock and turned it quickly before I changed my mind. *This is the right thing to do*, I reassured myself, as I stepped through heaven's door and straight into Nathaniel's arms.

"I wasn't ex…expecting you," I stuttered, stepping back.

"I heard the lock."

I looked around the room which confused me. This definitely wasn't heaven. I looked at the key. Maybe I had turned it the wrong way? Then I looked at Nathaniel, who was looking directly at me.

"We need to talk," he said.

I had been trying to avoid exactly that and now I was stuck. There was no escape.

Dammit!

44

Fleeing the scene

"I'm sorry," I started to apologise. "I didn't mean for any of this to happen. It's the press, making up stories. None of it's true."

Nathaniel had walked to the window and was looking out over the loch.

"It is true Anna. Everything changed the moment I met you in Central Park. You're the reason I'm playing the best I've ever played."

"The truth is you could always play that way. I just helped you to remember how."

"The truth is I couldn't have done it without you. I never got to thank you at the dinner. I had a whole speech planned. There's so much I want to say to you Anna." He turned around. "I never told you this before but I was in a really dark place that night. I didn't know how I was going to go on. I was in despair."

Just like it had said.

"I'd lost my wife, my best friend. I was losing my

career. I was losing everything that was important to me or that I thought was important. I was praying that night Anna, for help from up above and they sent me you. You're my angel Anna."

Holy shit! How did he know?

"You are heaven-sent."

God, I was in trouble now! It was my turn to pray. *I'm very, very sorry God but in my defence, I didn't actually tell him. He figured it out. So, please don't punish me.*

"You've given me hope. You've helped me believe again, in myself."

Do you hear that God?

"You've given me faith."

Yes, what a result!

"And hope."

I had ticked every other box so surely that should count for something at my trial? Oh no! I hadn't thought about that. I was going to be prosecuted for crimes against heaven. What was the punishment for treason? I remembered what they did to Lucifer. Suddenly, I felt faint and then I was falling, into darkness.

"Wakey, wakey," I heard a voice say, as I regained consciousness.

My whole body was violently convulsing but when I opened my eyes, I realised it was just Holly shaking me.

"That's right hen, open your eyes."

I obeyed just in time to see her raise her hand and

slap me hard on both cheeks.

"Ouch, that hurt!" I cried, as she yanked me to my feet.

"There now, isn't that better?" She brushed me down.

"Are you okay Anna?" Nathaniel looked worried.

"Of course she is," Mrs Munroe answered for me. "Her blood sugars must be low. What she needs is good food and fresh air."

Food was Holly's answer to everything but it wasn't mine. What I needed was to find heaven's door.

"I've prepared a lovely picnic for you both," she said, as she tried to usher me out of the suite.

Oh no, not the dreaded picnic; the one thing that had upset her so much before! I was worried what would happen if I didn't eat Holly's stupid finger food, but I was also worried what would happen to me if I didn't get back to heaven. I was caught between the devil and the deep blue sea, and I worried I'd be seeing Satan if I didn't sort this mess out.

"Wait." I broke free of her grip. "I'm feeling much better."

I was still holding the key; all I needed was to quickly find the door.

"Are you telling me that you don't want to have a picnic?" She stood with her hands on her hips.

"Of course not." I quickly shoved the key into the lock of Nathaniel's wardrobe door and flung it open.

"What are you looking for?" Nathaniel was confused.

I couldn't very well tell him the truth.

"Nothing." I raced over to the only other door, turned the key and ran through.

"Call of nature?" Holly asked, as I stepped out of the bathroom and scanned the room. Maybe it was hidden? Under Holly's eagle-eyed gaze I walked slowly back towards them, gently running my fingertips over the walls as I went, trying to feel for a secret doorway. I knocked from time to time, but the walls were solid.

"Ready to go?" Holly held onto the only door that was open to me.

I purposefully took my time.

"This way," she ordered, as I loitered, looking for any other possible exit.

Finally, I stood in front of my fellow CIA agent who was listing the delicacies she had lovingly prepared for us.

"And you won't be needing that." She grabbed the key from my hand, storing it safely back in her cleavage.

I glared at her.

She launched into a Scottish song as she shepherded us down the staircase towards the front door. "*For ye'll take the high road, and I'll take the low road, and I'll be in Scotland afore ye.*" She continued on. "*For me and my true love will never meet again, on the bonnie, bonnie banks of Loch Lomond.*" This was apparently to be the precise location of our picnic. "Such a sad song." Holly felt the need to explain its story. "The poor soldier would never meet his beloved again."

Nathaniel made the mistake of asking, "Why? What happened to him?"

"He met the hangman's rope instead," she replied, miming the method of his demise.

I reached up and put a protective hand over my neck. Was Holly trying to tell me that's what would happen if I didn't consume her mini quiche and sausage rolls?

She waited until I got into the car and Nathaniel started the engine.

"Enjoy!" She waved us off, and I had no choice but to take whatever fate had in store for me on the bonnie, bonnie banks of Loch Lomond.

45

Finger Food and Feasting on flesh

The afternoon sun fell on still waters. Across the loch I could see the turrets and tall chimneys of Glen Guthrie Hall and I wondered if Holly was watching us through a pair of binoculars. She had given Nathaniel precise instructions, and I had no doubt we were right where she wanted us.

I waited as he laid out the tartan blanket and unpacked the vast array of tasty treats – finger sandwiches, Scotch eggs, a pastry-topped pie and jars of pickles and preserves followed by strawberries dusted with sugar and a bowl of fresh cream.

I stood on the heather-clad hill and looked out across a timeless landscape. I was standing on the same ground as heroes of old; sons of Scotland who had fought for freedom – the players who once passed this way, now phantoms of the past. They were gone and soon I would be too.

"Champagne?" Nathaniel asked.

I nodded even though I didn't feel like celebrating. He popped the cork and I watched bubbles rise up as he filled the flute.

"Here's to the future." He raised his glass.

I may not have one, but a sparkling career lay ahead for him.

"I hope it brings you everything you could wish for," I said, as I raised mine in return.

"It already has Anna."

At least I could leave happy, knowing that he had found success again. His star was shining bright and he was going from strength to strength. I felt sure there was more success to come but I wouldn't be here to see it. My time was coming to an end and soon I would return to heaven where I belonged (or at least I would when I finally found the door and extricated the key from Holly's ample bosom.). I shuddered at the thought.

"Are you cold?" Nathaniel didn't wait for me to answer.

He draped his jacket around my shoulders, and for a moment I could feel the warmth of his body and hear his heart beating.

"I'm scared Anna."

I was scared too; scared of telling him the truth. I was scared of being punished for breaking angelic law, of being flung out of heaven and spending the rest of eternity in hell (which I considered to be even worse than spending it at the Guardians.). I was terrified at the thought that I was leaving; that I would never see him or Jack again. Most of all, I was terrified that time was running out.

"I don't want to lose everything again," he said.

When I first met him Nathaniel Banks was in despair, but then so was I. I'd been stripped of my rank and I'd lost my career. The army was my family. I understood how it felt to lose everything you loved. He was frightened that all he'd worked for, all that he'd achieved, would just disappear again. Yet I knew it wouldn't because he was focused, fit, fighting, and playing fantastically. He was right on course to win four Majors.

"You can't let fear hold you back." This wasn't in either of our F-Plans. "You know what you want, it's within your grasp. All you have to do is reach out and take it."

I watched the fear fade from his face as he walked towards me with a determined look. He stepped on sausage rolls, smashed Scotch eggs and squished finger sandwiches as he strode across the tartan blanket. Holly was not going to be happy! The next thing I knew, he had taken me in his arms.

"*Ouch*!" I cried out.

"*Oww*!" Nathaniel echoed.

"It hurts!" I was hopping around now, as I felt teeth pierce my flesh.

"Midges!" Nathaniel was flailing his arms.

We had been ambushed and were under attack by host of flying insects with razor-sharp teeth. The pain was excruciating.

"We have to get out of here." Nathaniel told me to grab one end of the picnic blanket while he took the other, and we unceremoniously hurled it into the boot before slamming it shut and speeding off towards the hall, leaving the blood-sucking battalion in our wake.

An eruption of red spots covered our arms, and I lifted the hem of my dress to see that they had also feasted on my flesh from the knees down. Abandoning the car in the drive, we stumbled through the open front door, spotty and sore.

"Did the wee beasties get you?" Finlay appeared with Rufus at his heels.

"Midges?" An incredulous Mrs Munroe marched over.

"Yes, it was a plague of biblical proportions."

Nathaniel quite literally put the fear of God in me, and I was expecting hail, fire and brimstone to descend from the heavens next.

"And what about the picnic?" Holly, as usual, was only concerned about the food.

Never mind that God's wrath had left me covered in a modern-day equivalent of boils!

"It was ruined," I told her, and I thought she was going to explode with anger.

Finlay jumped to our defence. "That's no one's fault

but Mother Nature's!" He sent a very grumpy Holly off in search of salve to soothe our sore skin.

"Mrs Munroe went to so much trouble and she really wanted us to have a picnic today," Nathaniel mused, as we watched her stomp off in a huff.

"Well, it's best not to force these things. I'm a firm believer in letting nature take its course," said Finlay. I feared for him as he obviously had no idea just how precious finger food was to my featherless friend.

46
Face to face

I needed time to breathe calmly and to think. I covered myself in soothing cream and chose clothes that would protect me from another potential plague before walking outside, alone with my thoughts. I wandered around the estate, making sure I kept away from the golf course. The last time I hadn't eaten Holly's picnic she tried to smash open my skull with a golf ball before drugging me! Unsurprisingly, I had no desire to spend my last few days on earth concussed or comatose so I decided to avoid her at all costs.

Golfers were arriving for the Scottish Open and Nathaniel and I would join them in the morning, at the hotel. After that, he would go back to Miami and carry on with his career and his life while I went back to heaven's army. I knew one day I would come back to earth, but it would be to some war-torn place to do battle. I would never see here again and that made me incredibly sad.

My wanderings took me over manicured lawns, down to the stream and through a forest filled with foxgloves, nightshade and mistletoe, which grew on a great oak. I came to a brick wall that I thought marked the end of the path, but hidden behind an arched and weathered wooden door, secluded from view, was a secret garden. A tiny gravel path meandered through beds of white, yellow and pale pink wildflowers, past beautiful begonias, bushy hydrangeas and climbing clematis. I watched a wasp nestle in a native thistle; a bumblebee, blackbird and bullfinch blended with the fluttering of tiny butterfly wings, as they flitted from flower to flower. A stone angel sat on top a small fountain and another angel sat under the shade of a tall tree.

"Leonardo!" I exclaimed when I saw him leaning against the broad bark of the tree, his tousled hair falling over his loose-fitting white top. I studied the fine features of his face as he remained focused on his drawing. I was mesmerised by the pencil that dashed and darted over the paper.

"It's so beautiful here," I said, as I took a seat on a nearby swing suspended from a bough.

"It's my little piece of heaven on earth." Leonardo smiled as he sketched.

I thought of all that he owned – the magnificent penthouse, the stately home, priceless works of art and luxurious furnishings – but they all paled in comparison to the divine natural beauty of this spot.

I swung like a pendulum as the time ticked by. I looked up to see the sunlight filtering through a latticework of limbs that stretched high up into the sky. Tiny orbs danced over twigs that twisted from branches bursting with green leaves. I was reminded how the seasons marked the passing of time; what blossomed in the spring would bloom in summer, but a change in the autumn would leave the branches bare by winter.

Finally Leonardo stopped and stood up to hand me his sketch. When I looked down, I saw the familiar features of my face staring back at me. He had captured me perfectly as I was that day and, unlike the leaves above me, I would never change. I saw myself then as others saw me. I saw beyond the dark hair, high cheekbones and full mouth. I saw an ethereal, otherworldly look and the ghost of a smile hinting at a secret I could never tell.

"It's perfection." I was in awe of the portrait.

"I've had a little practise in the past; drawn the odd angel here and there." This piqued my curiosity but before I could quiz him about any other talents he may be hiding, he asked me if I'd said my goodbyes.

"Not yet." I kept staring at my picture, which was now frozen forever in black, white and shades of grey. Time alters everything but I would never age.

"There's no time like the present," I heard Leonardo say. "You should do it now."

I realised then that time had run out.

I should've been prepared but I wasn't.

"I thought I was going to the Scottish Open?"

"There's no time for that now. You must say your goodbyes tonight. We are leaving for New York in the morning."

"Aren't I going home" I was confused.

"You are, but you have one more thing you have to do first," he told me.

"And what's that?"

"All in good time, my angel." He draped his arm around me and led me back down the garden path towards the arched doorway. "First, you must bid *adieu* to your young man."

Leonardo leaned against the weathered frame and watched as dejected, I walked back along the path. I slowed my pace, in an effort to delay what I now knew was inevitable, saying a final farewell to Nathaniel, who was waiting for me inside the impressive hall.

47
Forbidden Fruit

For once, I wanted to see Holly at the top of the stone steps. Or Finlay standing by the fireplace. Yet my path from the secret garden to the Burns Suite was clear, with nothing and no one to delay me. I stood outside the door and readied myself for the task at hand. My legs were like jelly and my heart was thumping.

Pull yourself together Anna, I told myself.

I stood up straight and then knocked on the door. When Nathaniel opened it I marched inside and announced that I was leaving. There was no room for sentiment so I didn't sugar-coat my announcement. Nothing was going to change the facts and I decided it was better to get straight to the point.

Nathaniel didn't say anything; he just sat down on the bed and rubbed his hands through his hair.

"I'm sorry but it's work," I explained, as briefly as I could.

"I thought *I* was your work?"

"You are – you *were* – but you've no need for me anymore Nathaniel. My work here is done."

"You said you were coming to the Scottish Open."

"I know and I'm sorry, but I've been called back."

"To where?"

"I can't tell you that."

"I thought you'd left the CIA?" He was becoming agitated.

"I can never leave." I tried to explain that I wasn't making a choice – I was following orders.

"You're freelance. You can decide what work you do."

The truth was that I couldn't – I had no free will but I couldn't tell him that of course.

"You can't go. I need you."

I stood still as he paced back and forth in front of me.

"You don't need me anymore Nathaniel. You are a strong, confident man with an incredible talent and a wonderful career ahead of you."

"Please." He reached for my hand. "Just come with me to the Scottish Open."

I was finding it hard to stay strong and stand firm.

"It's not possible." I had told him the truth. He dropped my hand before taking the picture that I still held on to.

I watched him walk over and sit down on the bed. He was staring at the portrait.

"Who did this?" he asked, never taking his eyes off

it.

"Leonardo – a little while ago."

"It's fantastic."

"Apparently he's quite a good artist."

"He's better than good – he's a genius!"

"Well, I wouldn't go that far." I certainly wouldn't be passing on Nathaniel's praise as Leonardo's head was big enough already without him hearing that he was some sort of art protégé. I didn't know anything about drawing, but it appeared he was above average.

"It's like he can see inside your soul."

"I can see you have this strong outer shell that protects you from the world. You need that because of your work in the CIA."

It wasn't tough enough to protect me from Holly!

"He's shown that behind your tough exterior, there's a vulnerability."

Holy crap! He was seeing everything!

Nathaniel stood up and walked towards me, looking from me to the sketch, comparing and contrasting.

"I can see in your eyes that you're conflicted. You have to go but you want to stay."

This was really freaking me out. I tried to keep my composure. I shook my head in an effort to deny it.

"You follow orders. You are dedicated, obedient and professional. But there's something you're not telling me." He studied the sketch, and I felt myself begin to sweat under his interrogation. "A secret…"

I snatched the sketch from his hand.

I walked out the open doors and onto the terrace. I needed fresh air to calm myself, and natural light to look at the drawing properly. I stared at the portrait. My hand was trembling as I tried to see what he had seen.

Nathaniel was standing beside me with his hands in his trouser pockets, looking out over the first tee.

"I know what it is." He was smiling now.

"You can't possibly know."

"I didn't know before, but I do now." He looked pleased with himself. "Leonardo told me." He took back the drawing.

"You can wipe that smug look off your face for a start," I snapped, as I plucked the offending portrait from his grasp. "You don't know."

I scanned the drawing to see if there was a halo or any other clue that I was a celestial being. I held it up to the light to see if Leonardo had written some secret writing that said, 'This is Anna, an angel and former bad-ass lieutenant in heaven's army.' As I had suspected, there was no such clue. Then how was Sherlock here figuring all this out? Did Nathaniel have a hidden talent he wasn't telling me about? Was he a detective in his spare time?

"No one would guess the work you do from looking at that sweet, angelic face."

I panicked – did he really know my true identity?

"I know that you are—" he began to say, as he turned

towards me.

"Stop!" I didn't want him to say it because if he did, there was no going back. If he actually voiced it, then everyone in heaven would know that I'd blown my cover and I would be in a lot of trouble.

"It's okay." He stroked my hair.

"No, it's not! No one can know." I felt tears begin to form.

"I want the whole world to know!" Nathaniel shouted out.

"Are you crazy?" Was he trying to get me killed?

"Yes, I want to shout it from the rooftops. Anna Frost is—"

I reached up and put my hand over his mouth. If he kept on with this I'd have to forcibly shut him up, even though Holly had warned me no more superhuman demonstrations of strength.

He took my hand away from his mouth before leaning down and whispering in my ear, "In love with me."

"No, I'm bloody well not!" I was indignant. That was not what I was expecting to hear. Besides, how dare he say that! "I thought you were going to tell me that—" I stopped myself just in time.

"Tell you what?"

"It doesn't matter," I said, dismissing it quickly. I was just relieved he didn't know I was a celestial being. "And what makes you think I'm in love with you anyway?"

"Your eyes." He held up the drawing. "And the way you look at me; the way you're reacting now."

"Bollocks!" I denied it.

Mr. Banks was suddenly making it very easy for me to say goodbye. Having no desire to stand here and listen to this any longer, I reached out my hand formally. "Nathaniel, it has been my pleasure to help you and I wish you all the best for your future, but it's time for me to leave." He looked bemused as he took my hand and shook it.

"Miss Frost, the pleasure has been all mine," he said, with a smile.

Aargh, men!

"Goodbye." I turned and marched off in the direction of the bedroom door.

"Anna." He stopped me just as I reached out for the handle. "I forgot something."

I turned around to see my portrait fall to the floor, and he pulled me into his arms. His lips found mine. I tried to resist – to push him back – but he held me close. Then I stopped resisting.

48

Farewell to Love

I awoke to see Nathaniel standing with a towel wrapped around his waist; the water from his wet hair dripping down his toned torso. I covered myself with the bedsheet before sitting up.

"Morning beautiful." He sat down on the bed. "I'm sorry, but I'm afraid it's me leaving you now." I was reminded of my imminent departure. "But this isn't goodbye," he said, as he held my hand.

"It *is* Nate" My job, who I was – all meant that I would never see him again. "There's something that I want to tell you before I go." I wanted to explain and to make him understand I didn't have a choice.

"Don't say another word." He silenced me by putting a finger to my lips. "I understand Anna that your job is classified. I don't want you to say anything that will get you into trouble with the powers that be, up above. I know you have a job to do. And so do I." He leapt off the bed and started to get dressed. "But we will be together again."

A brief affair – like Burns and Campbell – was all this could ever be.

"You'll miss me, you'll write a poem, then you'll forget me and move on." I remembered randy Robbie, who said he was mourning Mary but then ended up in bed with half of Scotland!

"Whoa! That is not going to happen. Firstly, I'm not a poet, and secondly, and more importantly, I will never forget you. Fate brought us together and it's fated that we will be together."

Well, technically it was celestial orders that caused our worlds to collide. A relationship between a lieutenant in God's army and a professional golfer was not going to work.

Then I had an idea: what if I got a transfer back to the CIA? Maybe then our relationship could possibly work! The thought raised my hopes. If Holly had a husband here, and Leonardo spent most of his time on earth, then surely so could I? I jumped up and ran to the desk.

"What are you looking for?" Nate had finished dressing and was now getting his bag ready.

"A pen and paper," I told him, as I rummaged in the drawer of the large desk where Robbie reportedly penned his poetry.

"Are you going to write a poem about how much you'll miss me?" Nathaniel teased.

"No," (I wasn't a poet either.). "I'm going to write a

letter to Santa."

"What? Why?"

"I want to give him plenty of time."

"Duke was right," he told me, as he pulled me to him. "You are weird Anna Frost but… I love you." Before I could say a word, he kissed me. "Don't ever forget that."

There was a knock on the door, and I heard Holly tell Nathaniel it was time to go. I didn't want him to leave; I wanted more time. He held me even closer before stepping back.

"I have to go," he told me. "I have an F-Plan to finish. I have to play fantastic golf and win those four Majors. But there's something else that I'm going to fight for – something I want more than any Major or tournament or trophy."

"What's that?" I looked up at him.

"A future with you, Miss Frost."

There was another knock and we both looked at the door.

"Until we meet again." He picked up my portrait. "I'm taking this with me. This is not goodbye."

I could feel tears stinging my eyes and I was too emotional to speak. He blew me one last kiss before stepping through the door, and I was left alone in a world I didn't want to leave.

49

A Freudian Slip

I struggled into my clothes and scribbled my letter to Santa before stuffing it into an envelope and addressing it to the North Pole.

"Housekeeping," Holly called out before barging in. "Well, well, well. What do we have here?" She feigned shock and surprise to see me in Nathaniel's room.

I ignored her as I searched for a stamp.

"Crumpled sheets and a fallen angel with bed hair… let me see now… if I've got this right… there's been an affair!"

Inspector Holly wanted all the salacious details of what happened the night before.

"I'll tell you, if you tell me," she persisted.

I didn't want to know what happened between Holly and Finlay!

"I'm not saying a word." It was no one else's business, especially not Holly's. "But there is something that you can tell me."

"Anything. I've had a lot of experience in that department. I could write a book on the subject. Actually, I have. It's called the Kama Sutra. Would you like to read it?"

"No! And it's nothing to do with that! I want to know how you and Finlay got married."

"We went to a church. Finlay wore his kilt and I had a big, puffball styled white dress."

"Yes, but *how*?" I didn't need to know the finer details of her day.

"Well, the priest asked me, 'Do you take this man?'"

"That's not what I meant." I stopped her from regaling the entire wedding ceremony. "I want to know how, as an angel in the CIA, you were able to marry a human here on earth?" As was so often the case with Holly, I had to be spell it out.

"Are you getting married?" She sounded excited. "Did Nathaniel propose? Can I be your matron of honour?"

"No, no and definitely no!"

She looked annoyed that I'd rejected her, and possibly Nathaniel too.

"A bridesmaid then?" she asked, sulkily.

"No nuptials, no getting hitched, no tying the knot." I felt the need to reiterate the point that I would not be walking up the aisle anytime soon. "I just want to know how you can have a relationship here on earth with Finlay, while still being a celestial body."

"It's one of the perks of being a Guardian. Everyone knows that."

Why didn't I then?

"Can you post this for me?" I handed Holly Santa's letter.

"It's summer!"

"I know, but I want to get my request in early. Send it first class please."

Leonardo was waiting for me downstairs; it was time to go. I had made up my mind that I wasn't going to tell him about what happened last night. He was harbouring all these deep feelings for me and I was afraid it might break his heart. The dark angel, wearing his trademark tight trousers and white shirt open to the waist, sauntered seductively towards me twirling a pair of sunglasses in his hand as I walked down the sweeping staircase.

"*Bonjour, ma chérie*," he greeted me, taking my hand and kissing it before stepping back to stare at me.

He was making me feel self-conscious, and I wondered if I had food stuck in my teeth or in my hair (it wouldn't have been the first time if I had!).

"What's wrong?" I asked, thinking I should try to find a mirror.

"I don't know." He peered closer as he pondered. "I can't quite put my finger on it. There's a faint blush to your cheeks and a light in your eyes. You look... glowing."

"It must be the Scottish air." I made light of his observation while realising too late that, like crumpled sheets, a glow and sparkly eyes were also a giveaway.

"You look blooming, like a beautiful flower whose raised their pretty head to the sun." He extolled virtues I wasn't sure I possessed.

I really would have to be honest with the amorous angel about my lack of romantic feelings for him, although if I simply told him about Nathaniel, I could avoid that awkward conversation all together. I weighed up my options as he continued to wax lyrical about my beauty. Having finally exhausted his encyclopaedic knowledge of mushy metaphors, he walked back towards the door.

"Did you tell him?" Leonardo asked conspiratorially, linking arms with me.

"No, there wasn't time to say goodbye," I lied. The truth was I just couldn't actually say the words.

"There is always time. Time stays long enough for those who use it. Don't worry, the most beautiful words of love can be conveyed just as well by a silent look," he said, staring at me.

I didn't know if he was accusing me of loving Nathaniel or if this was his way of trying to say he loved me. It was all too confusing at this hour of the morning. I continued outside, Leonardo joining me on the stone steps.

"What do you see?" he asked, as he pointed upwards.

Above me, the sky was blue and speckled with wispy white clouds. Beyond that, out of sight, I knew was heaven.

Instead I said, "I see a beautiful, bright summer's morning."

"Look at the light and admire its beauty. Close your eyes and then look again," he instructed me. "What you saw is no longer there and what you will see later is not yet," he said, cryptically.

"Did you swallow a Shakespearean book last night?" I seriously hoped he wouldn't continue with this philosophical gibberish all the way back.

"William Shakespeare is not responsible for those words of wisdom." He was staring expectantly at me.

Well I didn't know who wrote it, and I had no intention of asking Leonardo for fear he would launch into another rendition of profound ramblings.

"Aristotle?" I said the first philosopher who came to mind.

He sighed and shook his head.

"Socrates?"

"No, try again."

"Plato?" I offered up another wise man.

He shook his head. Clearly there was a philosopher-sized hole in my knowledge.

"The person was an Italian," he said, trying to coax the cogs of my brain into action.

I searched my mind for a potential candidate.

"Plutarch?"

"No, he was Greek."

Dammit! "Cicero?"

"Right country but wrong man." He sounded weary now.

"Aurelius? Seneca?"

I fired off names but none of them hit the target.

"I'll give you a clue: he was a Renaissance man." Leonardo seemed to think that would clinch it.

"Oh, I know, I know!" I put up my hand, confident I had cracked the conundrum. "Machiavelli!"

"No!" Leonardo sounded frustrated. "The man in question was a highly talented scientist, an inventor, an engineer!"

Despite the clues, I was still had no idea.

"He was also an architect, cartographer and botanist." Leonardo continued to list the many skills this mystery man apparently possessed. "Any idea now?"

"I'm afraid not." Although, I was amazed he had found the time to be philosophical as well!

"He is revered as one of the greatest painters of all time."

I knew nothing about art.

"Da…" Leonardo prompted me, and then I got it.

"It all makes sense now! That's why your sketch was so good. You got your drawing talent from you dad." He looked baffled. "Sorry, your da."

"Oh, *mon Dieu*." He started a conversation with God,

in a language I didn't understand, before turning his attention back to me. "Da Vinci!"

"Never heard of him," I told Leonardo, who looked like he was about to pull all the hair out of his head in frustration.

"He painted the *Mona Lisa*!" He was pacing up and down. "One of the most beautiful paintings in the world!"

"I haven't heard of moaning Lisa! I'm no art expert, but I would have painted a smile."

"She is smiling!" He was shouting now. "Everyone has heard of her painting. Where have you been?"

I told Leonardo what I'd also told Holly numerous times before. "I've been busy doing important army work and lately, I've been trying to fix a broken golfer. I'm sorry, but I haven't had the time to waltz around art galleries!" (or read deep and meaningful drivel written by Daddy Vinci, who sounded a little too clever for his own good.).

"I have to go." Leonardo opened the car door.

"I'll be right with you." I hoped he wasn't going to bore me with a résumé of Mr know-it-all Da Vinci on the way back.

"You're staying," he snapped.

I'd obviously offended him by not having heard of moaning Lisa or his dad.

"I thought there was something else I had to do before I left?"

"There is – you have a promise to keep," he told me. "Jack is on his way."

That was great news; the thought of seeing him again raising my spirits.

"Where are you going?" I asked a weary-looking Leonardo.

"To the chateau." He closed the car door with a bang.

"Bye then," I called out, as the black limousine pulled away.

50
Fading away

A penthouse, a stately home and now a chateau? Mr. Vinci Senior must've made a lot of money but then again, he did do a lot of things. The family crest confirmed what I already knew: Papa Vinci had owned this impressive residence and passed it down to his son.

He probably put his architectural talent to good use and designed it himself. As a botanist, with knowledge of plants and trees he wouldn't have needed a landscape gardener either. I wondered if he'd invented something important that everyone used, like a toothbrush or a kettle or a car? That would have made him a lot of money. One thing was certain: he hadn't made his money from drawing or painting pretty pictures. I mean, how much does a small piece of canvas with a dollop of paint cost to buy anyway?

Leonardo was apparently enjoying the fruits of his father's labours on his earthly visits, flitting from one luxury property to the next on the pretext of celestial business. I wanted to know what it was he *actually* did as far as I could see, all he did was float around and flirt. He was a playboy with too much money and time on his hands; a rebel with a roving eye and a rockstar lifestyle.

"Has Leonardo left already?" Holly made me jump; I hadn't heard her come outside.

"Yes. The lord had left the building." And was en route to another of his palatial properties.

"And did he give you your orders?"

"Yes," I answered absentmindedly, as I was still thinking about Leonardo's luxury lifestyle.

"You know what you have to do then?"

"Yes." Leonardo had told me Jack was on his way, and for once these were orders I was looking forward to fulfilling. I was determined to keep my promise to the little boy.

"I know this is going to be difficult for you." Holly put her arm around my shoulder in comfort.

I was going to watch Nathaniel win the Open with Jack – there was nothing difficult about that – so I shrugged her off.

"If you need me, I'm here to help."

At last, a Guardian who remembered her code of conduct and job description!

"When will he be here?" I asked.

"Next Wednesday."

I didn't understand. Why couldn't I go with Nathaniel to the Scottish Open then? I still would have been back in time to watch the Open with Jack – he was only a few miles away.

"You can't leave Anna," Holly told me when I suggested doing just that.

"Am I a prisoner?"

"You said your goodbyes to Nathaniel. He thinks you're on a secret mission, which you are, or at least you soon will be."

So, I was a prisoner.

"There's a plan Anna. You have your orders. Execute them."

Holly's choice of words reminded me there was a punishment for insubordination and failure. As much as I wanted to see Nathaniel, I would follow orders and stay under house arrest until Jack arrived.

I was delighted he was coming over to watch Nathaniel here, but I couldn't understand why we couldn't go to Ireland to see him. I presumed it was to maintain the pretence that I was doing actual undercover secret service work, rather than being in the heavenly CIA. However, it wasn't Christmas, there was no incident, and at this moment in time, I wasn't an angel.

Hostage-taker Holly had confined me to my 'barracks' (which were rather beautiful). I passed my days watching TV coverage of the Scottish Open, shouting at the screen if Nathaniel missed a shot or screaming with joy when he did well. Thankfully, there were more of the latter.

Sometimes Finlay joined me or even Grace, whom I now realised was a rather lovely and sweet young girl. She was extremely attentive to the residents who arrived on an almost daily basis; it now being the high season. Grace was kind and caring, and I felt momentarily guilty about the way I had acted.

She would've been perfect for Nathaniel – a kind and caring wife with a passion for the sport he loved. Instead, I did what I do best: I went into battle and fought for him. I hadn't realised at the time that I had wanted Nathaniel for myself yet still I had been driven by instinct. My head didn't know then what my heart obviously did and poor Grace didn't stand a chance. However, I should have let nature take its course. If Nathaniel had wanted me, he would have chosen me. I should have trusted that – I should have trusted *him*.

As well as watching Nathaniel lift another trophy, I spent a lot of time remembering and reflecting. Was Nathaniel just another trophy for me? The way I felt about him made me realise this wasn't the case at all.

He had taught me that life was beautiful and precious; something I now wanted and desired. Ironically in heaven, as an angel leading legions I didn't give life a second thought. I just fought one battle after another – a continuous war with evil – and that's all I saw on earth: all that was wrong in the world. All the times I had visited earth, I had seen only despair. I had been blind to the love, kindness and beauty of life and had forgotten that it really is wonderful.

Meeting Nathaniel and Jack had changed everything; they had changed *me*. Thoughts turned to the little boy whom I had cared for from the moment we met. I would never be a mother but if it had been possible, I imagined having a son like Jack. I wanted to help him in any way I could. It wasn't duty or orders that bound me to him; it was an unconditional love that I felt for the little fighter who had overcome so much in his short life. He had bravely gone into battle and never given up. I was so proud of him, and I wanted him to have the same success as Nathaniel.

Jack was fearless, just as I too had been as a lieutenant. Yet as Anna Frost, I battled daily with an unfamiliar enemy. I worried for Nathaniel and Jack. I was frightened that I might never see either of them again when I returned to heaven – that I would forget how I felt, and my memories would fade. I was scared of how I would feel when I became a lieutenant again because now I wanted to have a life, not take one. I wanted to be a wife, not a warrior. I didn't want to go into battle to fight or wield a sword anymore.

I had all these thoughts during my time at the hall, which I spent wandering by the loch, walking in the secret garden, and through the forest as I waited for Jack to come.

51

Floppy Ears

Finally, the day had come. Jack was arriving just in time for the start of the Open. I stood with Holly, Grace and numerous other members of staff in the grand entrance hall. A fire still blazed in the hearth even though it was summer. I heard the coach pull up outside and we all readied ourselves to welcome the guests. As the door opened, in came Jack who ran straight into my open arms.

"Anna!" he screamed in delight.

Finlay shepherded in the rest of the visitors who were checked in by the waiting staff and shown to their rooms. I looked around for Paul and Nancy, but I couldn't see them.

"Where are your parents?" I asked him.

"They couldn't come," Jack told me.

That's strange, I thought. He really was too young to be travelling on his own, especially with his underlying health conditions.

"Don't worry Anna, I told them you would take care of me."

Holly came over with her clipboard.

"Welcome to Glen Guthrie Hall young Master Jack." Mrs Munroe told him he would staying in the Burns Suite. "This was where Nathaniel Banks stayed just before the Open."

"Did he?" Jack was thrilled to hear he was being given the same room as his hero.

"Anna knows the way." Holly ticked Jack's name off her register. "Speaking of the brilliant Mr. Banks, he's due to tee off so you'll have to be quick. You don't want to miss that," she said, winking at him.

Jack dashed off, darting in and out of his fellow travellers who looked weary and in need of a rest. I stumbled over suitcases and made my apologies as I tried to squeeze past staff who were busy taking visitors' details and filling out forms.

"Hurry Anna!" Jack was now halfway up the stairs. He led and I followed even though I was the one who knew the way.

Jack raced ahead and was standing outside the Burns Suite by the time I had managed to drag his suitcase up the stairs.

"Found it," he smiled proudly.

"Clever… boy." I was out of breath.

I handed him his teddy bear as I fumbled with the key, finally managing to open the door. Jack pushed past me. Fresh linen had been put on the four-poster bed he was now jumping on, and the pillows had been re-plumped. There was nothing to suggest what had happened between Nathaniel and I in this room. I stood on the spot where he had first kissed me while watching as Jack whizzed excitedly around the room before running out onto the terrace. Memories of a different kind of love would be made during Jack's stay.

"Anna look! There's a golf course." He was pointing excitedly. "Please can I play?"

"Yes, you can." I would ask Finlay to take him out later. "But first things first: we have an Open to watch." I reminded him of his reason for being here.

"Nate!" he screamed, and ran out the bedroom door, shouting for me to hurry up.

I don't know if it was a child's sixth sense, but he naturally found his way to the TV room and had taken up a prime position in front of the screen by the time I arrived. Hugging his stuffed bunny whom I learnt was called JR (an abbreviation for Jack Rabbit), he finally settled down to watch his hero step up to the tee.

The Open was being held in Portrush, a coastal town in Northern Ireland. A camera panned out over the sea and a long stretch of white sandy beach. The sun shone and we could see crowds of spectators lining the length of the golf course. Nathaniel walked confidently onto the course and stood behind the ball. Firmly focused, he swung the club high.

I watched the arch of his back; the sway of his hips and the flexing of his muscles reminding me of the night we had shared. They awoke a desire and longing for his touch, which I might never feel again. I lost concentration from time to time as my mind drifted from the present to the recent past, but I could always rely on Jack to let me know how Nathaniel was performing on that first day. Other guests filtered in and out of the room, momentarily stopping to catch up on the action, but only Jack and I remained vigilantly watching the big screen for the duration of the game.

"I thought you might like something to eat?" Grace put down two hot dogs covered in ketchup.

"My favourite!" Jack reached for a frankfurter.

"How's he doing?" Grace asked.

"Brilliantly," enthused Jack, through a mouthful of half-masticated meat.

"Why don't you sit down and watch it with us?" I extended the invitation to the young girl who happily accepted. "Grace is a very good golfer," I told Jack. "Don't tell anyone, but she nearly beat Nathaniel!"

"No way!" He spat out some sausage in surprise.

Grace laughed. "Yes way!"

"Maybe if you ask her very nicely, she might take you out for a game of golf."

"It would be my pleasure Jack." The young girl didn't even wait for him to ask. Grace stayed with us for the rest of the day to cheer on Nathaniel, who had a narrow lead by the end of the day's play.

In between cheering for Nathaniel, Grace and Jack happily chatted about all things golf which gave me an opportunity to focus solely on the man of the moment. This was Nathaniel's fourth Major which, if he won, he would be world number one again. A fourth victory would also make modern day history as he would become the only golfer ever to take four Majors in a year. He had already shown the world he was back; now I wanted him to show them that he was the best – that he was brilliant.

By the final putt, I could see Jack struggling to keep his eyes open. The journey here had been a long and tiring one, and he was sound asleep before the applause had even stopped. Finlay carried the little boy upstairs and I then tucked Jack into bed. Holly had given me the key for the interconnecting door which I left open. I also switched on a light so he wouldn't be scared should he wake up during the night. I stroked his hair and kissed him goodnight.

"Sweet dreams my angel," I said, as I put JR in bed beside him.

The next morning when I woke up, I saw two glass eyes staring back at me and a pair of floppy ears. Jack's head popped up behind JR's.

"Morning." I smiled and Jack bounced off the bed in excitement.

A night's sleep had re-energised him and he dashed

back and forth from his room to mine while I got ready for the day ahead.

"You're going to see how good I've got," he told me, as he chewed his toothbrush.

Grace was due to take him out on the course to play the first nine holes before we watched the second day's coverage of the Open.

"Breakfast first." I would need caffeine if I was to keep up with jumping Jack!

"Ready," he declared, as he ran off down the stairs. He found his way to the dining room and was already seated at our table by the time I arrived a few moments later.

"And what time do you call this?" Hostess Holly met me at the dining room door.

"The middle of the night." It was still dark outside.

"Dawn is breaking, the birds are singing, and Grace is ready to go."

I looked over at our table and a fresh-faced Grace waved back. Where did they get their energy from?

"A nice hearty breakfast is what you need." Holly prescribed her remedy for everything.

There was no one else in the dining room at this ungodly hour, although a large buffet was laid out for the guests when they did arrive. Jack had taken a plate and was piling it high with sausages, bacon, eggs and beans.

"That's a good boy." Holly encouraged him. "You

need to keep your energy up."

He was already hyper; he didn't need fatty foods to give him any more energy.

"I'll just have coffee," I told Holly, but she wanted me to have more.

"Try some black pudding. It's made from pork blood, fat and oatmeal," she elucidated. "It'll put hairs on your chest!"

I nearly vomited at the thought of it, and I neither needed nor wanted hairs there. By the time I'd finished protesting that I only wanted coffee, Jack had finished his breakfast.

"I'm ready to go," he said, tugging on my hand.

I really needed caffeine to keep up and I was grateful to Grace who offered to take him on out to the course.

"I'll catch you up," I promised, and Jack told me to hurry before skipping out the door holding Grace's hand.

"Where does he get all his energy?"

"He's making the most of his time here," Holly smiled. "He doesn't know it yet, but he's got a big surprise coming tomorrow."

Holly didn't elaborate, and I wondered idly what she meant as I sipped coffee in the now empty dining room and watched a beautiful dawn breaking outside.

52

Mr. Fantastic

Finlay had joined Grace and Jack on the course.

"Watch me Anna." Jack made sure I didn't miss a single stroke.

Grace gave him helpful pointers along the way; correcting his posture and adjusting his swing. I told him how wonderful he was and cheered in encouragement. Rufus looked disinterested in the game but stayed at his master's heel, flopping down and patiently waiting each time it was Finlay's turn to take a shot.

"Brilliant!" he boomed, as Jack made a tricky putt.

"That was fantastic!" I clapped the little boy who was bursting with pride.

I was genuinely impressed with Jack's progress since I last saw him play, and there was almost no sign of the paralysis that had threatened a career in the sport he loved. Light fell on the future star as the sun rose higher in the sky; the sunlight falling on Grace's auburn hair.

Bathing us all in a golden ray, we walked from the ninth, Finlay's kilt swishing from side to side, back to Glen Guthrie Hall.

"I only hope Nathaniel plays as well as you did today." I put my arm around Jack and pulled him close. "You were brilliant!"

Holly had left drinks and snacks for us to enjoy as we watched the second day's play. Jack spent most of it shouting support and jumping up and down, while Nathaniel methodically executed one amazing shot after another. He was indeed brilliant and managed to extend his lead by four shots.

Towards the end of the game Jack started to yawn and, just like the previous day, his eyes began to close. He sat on my knee for the final few holes. He was fighting a losing battle to stay awake, but he still wanted to know how Nathaniel was doing. I gave him a running commentary as he nestled his head into my shoulder.

"He's just about to make his final putt," I whispered, as I stroked his hair. "It's a lot like the one you made today. He's lining it up… he's tapped the ball… it's rolling towards the hole. Everyone is waiting and watching, hoping it's going to go in." I held my breath as the ball rolled over the green. As it fell into the hole, I heard Jack's soft breaths that indicated he had fallen into a deep sleep.

I let him nap on my lap as I listened to Nathaniel speak at the post-match press conference. Excitement was growing as he drew ever closer to making history.

"I'm taking nothing for granted," he told the reporters. "It's still anyone's tournament."

There was a handful of golfers still in contention; a bad round for Nathaniel and a good round for one of them could turn the tables in their favour.

"But I'm focused. I shot a fantastic round today and I hope I'm on course for a fourth Major win." He smiled directly into the camera as he said, "I have an F-Plan."

"And is Miss Frost part of that F-Plan?" a voice queried from among the pack.

I could see the question had caught him off guard and for a second, he froze. Suspecting they had found a weakness, the reporters saw their chance to attack.

"This is a very important tournament. Is Miss Frost not here with you? Are you no longer together?"

I felt panic set in as they planted the seed of doubt. All this negativity could put him off his game. I was angry with the reporter but also worried. What if he believed them? What if he thought I had abandoned him, that I didn't care? They bombarded him with questions about me until he finally raised his hand to silence them. He pulled the microphone closer.

"Miss Frost is not here and I'm not going to speak about our relationship, except to say that in answer to your question…Miss Frost is very much a part of my F-Plan."

"Thank you Mr. Banks, that's all I wanted to know."

I watched as Holly wrote something in her reporter's notebook, using a long white feathered quill.

I slept as soundly as Jack that night and I dreamt for the first time since I'd been on earth.

I was back in Central Park. It was spring and everything was bursting into life. There was light and laughter and love. I wandered along paths where children played hide-and-seek, and passed by lovers who walked hand in hand while joggers and cyclists hurried on by.

I stopped to listen to birdsong and smell the bouquet of blooms bursting forth from colourful herbaceous borders. I was looking for something I'd lost as I walked over old ground, and footsteps from the past took me to the angel of the fountain.

"Please help me," I asked the celestial statue, who had always watched over me.

Then people started to stare and point at me. I panicked. They knew I didn't belong here; that I was different. I started to run and didn't stop. The people disappeared and I was alone again. I ran away and hid in the forest. It was dark and I was afraid, but then I heard someone call my name and Jack found me.

"Close your eyes and count to ten," he told me, before running off again.

It was my turn to seek. I could hear his laughter but try as I might, I couldn't find him. He wasn't on the carousel or by the lake; he wasn't in the zoo or in the play park. He wasn't anywhere a child should be. I was getting upset when Holly appeared, dressed as a clown.

"It's all just a game," she told me. I didn't know whether to laugh or cry.

She handed me a red balloon and I continued with my search. High and low – in every nook and cranny of a park that I knew so well – I sought to find what was hidden from me; what I had lost.

People re-appeared, reaching out to me as I ran over Bow Bridge, back along the path. Leonardo was leaning against a tree trunk, waiting for me.

"It's time," he told me, and he reached for my hand.

We walked together under cherry blossom that floated like confetti from powder-pink trees.

"This is your wedding day." The dark angel was dressed in a black tuxedo, and hand in hand we walked down the aisle. There were seats either side. I looked down and saw I was wearing a wedding dress.

"No!" I cried out, as I awoke and sat immediately upright.

"Anna?" Jack was standing by my bed. "Are you OK?"

"No." I was still disorientated but I didn't want to worry him so I corrected myself. "I mean, yes. I'm fine. I was just having a bad dream," (although the thought of marrying Leonardo was a nightmare of hellish proportions!). "What time is it?"

Jack was dressed and ready to go.

I looked at the alarm clock: five a.m.

"I'm ready for breakfast," He had been up with the larks, eager to play another round of golf.

"It's very early." I felt like I had actually been running around Central Park all night and would have loved to be able to go back to sleep.

"But I'm ready. Come on Anna." He tugged at my arm. "Get up!"

I begrudgingly got up and five minutes later was following him in a sleep-deprived stupor down the stairs.

"There he is – the final member of our four." Finlay's loud voice echoed round the empty breakfast room.

I remembered Holly had said Jack would have a surprise, and now someone had come to see him. When the man sitting beside Holly stood up, Jack loudly exclaimed, "Granddad Tom!" His scream made me jump back in shock.

Now it made sense why Paul and Nancy weren't with him; he was coming to visit his grandfather. The little boy lost all interest in food and Holly had to practically force-feed him a battalion of soldiers dipped in yolk.

"You need your energy to keep you going. You have a busy day ahead."

He kept pushing the food away, but Holly was persistent.

"Remember, an army marches on its stomach. Isn't that right Anna?" She took the opportunity to remind me that I would soon return to the EAA.

"It's the most important meal of the day, so eat up Corporal Jack."

"Aye, aye captain," he saluted.

"Actually, it's lieutenant." I winked at him as he washed down his toast with warm milk.

As Jack had rightly said before, his granddad lived in a place with great golf courses, and he was as keen as Jack to get out on the green. Finlay sung Jack's praises, as did Grace who was very loving and protective of him. She was like the big sister, he never had.

"Didn't I say you would soon be playing like you used to? By the sounds of it, even better than before, although I don't think that's possible," said his granddad, proudly.

"I am granddad! I have a better swing and I putt better too."

Before Jack could list any more of his improvements, his granddad said, "Why don't we go so you can show me just how great you are?"

"He's not great," I told everyone at the table. "He's brilliant!" Jack stood up with his shoulders back and his head held high as everyone nodded in agreement.

As the sun rose, Jack and his granddad walked outside hand in hand, happily chatting to each other as they went.

"He's doing so well." I stood with Holly, as Finlay and Grace left to join the other two.

"He's a little trooper," said Holly. "He has a great spirit and Grace has been so good with him."

Previously, I would have been angry with Holly for insinuating that Grace was better with him than me, but not anymore.

"She has been amazing," I agreed. I was happy he was in safe hands. "I can't believe that I will never see him again."

"That's life, lieutenant."

Jack's life, like Nathaniel's, would go on here on earth while I returned to the army.

There was so little life left. Tomorrow was the last day of the Open and by then I would have fulfilled my orders.

It would be time to go.

53
A Final Fling

Victorious, Jack marched back towards Glen Guthrie Hall, excited to see how his hero would perform on the penultimate day of the Open. We could see from the TV coverage that a strong wind was blowing on the links course and it had started to rain.

"Irish weather." Tom passed comment on the inclement conditions. "I hope the boy is not a fair-weather golfer."

"Nate will be great!" Jack enthused, as usual.

However, as Nathaniel stepped up to the first tee, I wasn't as confident. He looked worried and I had a bad feeling as his club crashed down. We all watched the ball struggle against the wind before it landed in the rough. Nathaniel banged it off the soggy ground in exasperation with himself. It was not a good start.

There was none of the usual banter or smiling and waving as he walked ahead of Duke. His mood, like the weather, had taken a turn for the worse and it was affecting his play. Another bad shot followed, and I could see his frustration. He finally finished the hole two over par.

"Come on Nate!" Jack continued to cheer him on with the same unwavering enthusiasm.

I willed him to find focus as he stood talking to Duke before taking a five iron for the second. I remembered five irons were good and was hopeful he would get back on track. However, I was misguided; much like the ball that landed amongst a group of soaking spectators. This was terrible and soon the commentator questioned if fear had raised its ugly head. "Is Nathaniel Banks having a crisis of confidence?" he asked the audience.

Each awful shot fuelled speculation that Nathaniel had lost his form, and predictions that soon he would lose the tournament and the chance to make history as well. I took to biting my nails and pacing back and forth, as I watched him drop from first place to fourth on the leader board, and then down to tenth. To make matters worse, the other players in contention for the trophy had improved their game, with Elliot Jones from England taking a healthy lead. It was painful to watch. Tom left to play another round of golf with a friend of his, who was also staying at the hall. Finlay left on the pretext he had work to do, and Grace excused herself too. Only Jack and I endured Nathaniel's humiliating fall from grace.

"You have to fix him Anna!" Jack pleaded with me.

"I can't." I wanted to but how could I? He was there and I was here. There was nothing I could do.

Holly came in carrying a tray of food that she piled onto the table in front of us; plates of cocktail sausages, mini hamburgers, chocolate cake and ice cream. Grace followed behind with a large jug of fruit juice but neither I nor Jack had any appetite.

"So, how's our boy doing?" Holly asked.

"Not good. Not good at all." I was frantically trying to think of a way to help him.

"He's being very mediocre," Jack confessed.

"Are you two not cheering him on loudly enough?" Holly managed to imply Nathaniel's poor performance was our fault. "Shall I get us all some pom-poms?" she suggested, and Jack's eyes widened. "I'll get them if you eat," she bargained with him, so he picked up a sausage and ate it quickly. "Good boy," Holly praised him. "You need to keep your strength up for all the cheering you're going to be doing soon."

"Nathaniel can't hear us from here," I said, stating the obvious. In fact, he didn't even know we were watching.

Holly ignored me and left. Jack took her advice and shouted encouragement at the TV.

"Come on Nate, you can do it!"

Unfortunately it didn't work, and he missed a very easy putt on the seventh, putting him twelve over. The rain had stopped just as he was stepping up to the next tee and Holly returned dressed in a cheerleading outfit, carrying a large box. She was wearing an orange top emblazoned with a large blue 'N' on the front, and her hair was pulled into bunches on either side of her head. Handing Jack a pair of tinsel pom-poms, she led him and Grace in a chant.

"Give me an N! Give me an A! Give me a T! Give me an E! What does it spell? Champion!" she screamed.

Clearly spelling wasn't Holly's strong point. Her chant didn't even rhyme but it didn't matter because Jack loved it. He danced about in support of his favourite golfer, waving his blue tinsel pom-poms as well as shaking a rattle he'd found in the box.

Nathaniel was nearly halfway through and I did some quick calculations. If he continued to play like this, it was over for him; there would be no coming back. I prayed for help. Maybe I couldn't help him, but someone else could.

Please God. Please help him. I prayed because I didn't want him to lose. He had fought so hard to regain his confidence and his self-belief. He had told me he didn't want to lose everything again and I remembered his despair before. I was afraid of what it would do to him if it happened again.

Duke, who would have every right to be angry and stomp down the fairway, instead looked concerned. Not for the first time, he put a comforting hand on Nathaniel's shoulder. It seemed something had happened but I didn't know what. I felt so helpless. It was horrible to watch and so I turned away from the TV screen.

"This is most unorthodox," I heard the commentator say. I looked again and saw someone tall and dark-haired step out from the crowd.

I walked over to the TV to make sure what I was seeing was real.

"What has he handed him?" the commentator asked.

"It can't be," I gasped, as Leonardo gave Nathaniel an envelope.

Opening it, Nathaniel read what was written on the piece of paper within. As Leonardo turned towards the camera, he smiled.

"What did it say?" The commentator was as curious as the rest of us.

Nathaniel began to get emotional. What had Leonardo done? I was furious with the dark angel who had just made a bad situation even worse. He had sabotaged Nathaniel and any hope he had of recovering from this catastrophic day just because he was in love with me. I was raging with him!

"Focus Nathaniel!" I shouted. "You can do this, I know you can!"

Jack started bouncing up and down and waving his rattle. The crowd fell silent as Nathaniel stepped up to the tee. His stance changed and he eyed the ball with a steely resolve.

"Yes!" I said, seeing him truly focus for the first time that day which was no thanks to Leonardo!

It was clearly our cheering that had done the trick. He finally broke his duck, and from the eighth hole to the eighteenth, more favourable feathered friends filled his score card. An extremely exuberant afternoon of cheering left Jack exhausted while for Nathaniel he now stood a chance of winning. Thankfully Jack stayed awake long enough to see a condor on the sixteenth, which whether a fluke or decreed by fate, was fortuitous timing. While fortune favoured Nathaniel, others in the field began falling back. It was still all to play for on the final day.

I cradled Jack as once again he slept in my arms as I watched Nathaniel step in front of the camera. There was a barrage of questions about his abysmal performance earlier in the day. Everyone, including me, was desperate to know what had caused such a sudden loss of form.

"I am a professional and I try not to let my private life affect my performance, but that can be very hard at times, and earlier on in the game, it was impossible. I had some bad news today about someone I love very much – someone who taught me how to fight. I know it won't bring them back, but I'm doing this for them."

There was a cacophony of sound and speculation but Nathaniel said no more. He simply stood up and left the room.

I knew it! I knew that Leonardo had interfered. He'd told Nathaniel that I was going back to the army and that he'd never see me again. He probably told him that he and I were going to get married too, according to my dream. I was livid!

That night I watched over Jack, who had fallen into a deep and peaceful sleep on the bed. There was a serenity in the quiet time between dusk and dawn but still, I couldn't sleep. I was scared to close my eyes in case I dreamed again; the last person I wanted to see in the flesh or in a dream was Leonardo. I had been right about him all along – he was a demon double agent. I should have trusted my instincts.

My mind recalled my time here and all that had transpired. I was so grateful for every moment I had spent with Nathaniel and Jack. I sat on the bed beside the little boy and stroked his hair. Tomorrow would be a difficult day; it would be so hard to say goodbye. Sleep finally found me but when I awoke, he was gone.

"Jack!" I called out, but there was only silence. "Jack!" I repeated.

I was meant to have been watching over him, looking after him, and I'd fallen asleep on the job. I had failed as a Guardian.

I ran out onto the terrace. Dawn was breaking; light pinks and blues streaking the horizon. I looked out across the fairway and that's when I saw him: a small figure walking over the hill in the distance. He wasn't alone and I strained to see who he was with. Sensing he was being watched, Tom turned and doffed his cap in my direction. I waved to his granddad from the balcony with a feeling of immense relief.

Much later than usual I made my way to the dining room. It was full of guests at this hour. Yet I sat alone sipping my coffee, staring out the window at the lovely landscape and loch beyond. Holly flopped down on the chair opposite and dropped two tablets into a glass of water, which fizzed as they started to dissolve.

"Big night?" I asked my featherless friend.

"As a matter of fact, yes." She pushed her sunglasses down to the end of her nose so she could see me better. "And where were you?" she asked, as she peered over them.

"Watching over Jack."

"Well, you missed a great shindig." Holly looked as if she had continued boozing and boogying into the early hours of the morning.

"I didn't know you were having a party?"

"I left an invitation in your room," a hungover Holly informed me.

I hadn't left Jack's side all night which would explain why I hadn't seen it.

"We always hold it the night before guests check out." She picked up her glass of what I supposed contained soluble headache tablets. "Bottoms up," she said, before gulping it down in one.

I looked around the room at the other guests who also looked in need of sleep.

"What time is check out?" This was my subtle way of asking when I was going.

"It's different for everyone." Holly leaned her head back and took a deep breath. "It's going to be a *busy* day." She stood up.

"What time is Jack leaving?"

"Didn't Leonardo give you a time?"

"No." The demon dark angel hadn't told me anything, so I had no idea what time Jack's flight was or even who was taking him to the airport.

Holly sat back down. "This is what is happening today…" My fellow Guardian angel then proceeded to tell me exactly what to expect, and when.

I tried to digest what she had told me as I walked in a daze back up to my room. A beautiful gown was draped over the bed and I picked up my invitation to, A Final Fling:

Before the final curtain falls

In this our final act

Let's say a final fond farewell

And make a final pact

To forgive ourselves and others

For footsteps in the past

On the fated road we followed

From our first breath, to our last

Put on your festive finery

Family and friends now flock
So, come now Cinderella
Tick, tock, tick, tock.

Time had run out. I let the invitation fall to the floor as I fell to my knees and wept for the fairytale ending that would never be.

54

A Fanfare

Hungover Holly was decorating the room with posters, banners and balloons, assisted by a very willing helper, Jack, who was busy with poster paints. Guests who were still in the party spirit from the night before, enthusiastically prepared the room for another celebration.

The live TV coverage had already started, although the star of the show (and the reason we were all here) had yet to tee off. Grace was teaching Granddad Tom how to cheerlead. I didn't want Jack to see me upset or to know just how sad I was feeling, so with my shoulders back, I forced a big smile as I walked into the room.

"Anna!" he shouted, as soon as he saw me. "Look what I'm painting." He held up his poster for me to see.

"That poster is exactly what it says here – brilliant!" I told him. "Do you need any help?"

He nodded. "Can you do the stars?"

"Absolutely. What colour should I do them?"

"I think blue."

"Good choice." I squeezed out a bright dollop of blue paint from the tube and got to work. "I wish Nathaniel could see this," I said to him. He was putting so much love into what he was doing.

"Me too. But the man said he would tell him that we were cheering him on."

"What man?"

"The man I saw on the golf course earlier with Granddad. He is going to tell him we're watching him today."

One of the golfers must be flying over to watch the final day's play, I thought.

"Leonardo's going to bring me back a signed cap!" Jack was so excited.

I didn't know what devilment the dark angel was up to now, but whatever it was, he better not distract Nathaniel today or there would be hell to pay!

There was a media frenzy on the final day and all eyes were on Nathaniel. Before yesterday, they all had faith he would take his fourth Major. Now, however, memories of the previous year when his personal life had impacted so detrimentally on his game, were at the forefront of everyone's mind. He had lost everything then and I didn't want to see that happen again.

As soon as Nathaniel appeared on screen, everyone in the room started clapping and cheering. Jack stood up, waving his poster and shouting, "Go Nate! Go Nate!"

His granddad also joined in by chanting, "Nate is great!" as he punched the air with a pom-pom.

I watched as he walked out through the gathered press pack; camera bulbs flashing as probing questions were fired at him.

"I want to say something." The reporters fell silent, and he stared down the camera. "I know you're watching Jack. This game is for you buddy." Nathaniel's personal message sent Jack into an excited frenzy as he jumped around the room, grinning broadly, as Nathaniel went into battle on the golf course.

Others may have speculated if he would win or lose today, but not me. I knew before he even reached the first tee that he was focused and ready to fight. He was driven to succeed by a force greater than fear – love. He was doing this for the love of a little boy who had touched his heart and changed his life; an inspirational and beautiful boy with a passion for life and an infectious love for golf.

There was a joyous feel in the room. We ate sweets and crunched crisps as we chanted and cheered in support of Nathaniel. Pizza was washed down with lemonade and there was candy floss and cakes a-plenty. Jack had missed the party the night before, but today was as much about him as it was about Nathaniel– indeed, it was a celebration of him – and I was delighted

Jack had such a fun-filled final day. However, by the end of it, his excitement and exertions had taken their toll and once again I saw his eyes grow heavy. He valiantly fought it all the way; so determined was he to stay awake long enough to see his hero take his final putt.

There was never any doubt in my mind that Nathaniel would win. He played each hole with a steely determination, slaying the competition as he swung and slashed his way to victory. I couldn't have been prouder.

As deafening cheers rang out in our room, out on the course the crowds of spectators erupted into rapturous applause, and the commentator congratulated the four-times Major winner. I watched Nathaniel punch the air in celebration. As he stood looking heavenward, I could see tears flowing down his cheeks. The day had drained Jack; all the shouting, cheering, clapping and dancing. He was exhausted and he came to sit on my lap.

"He did it Anna!"

"He did. You can go to sleep now." I stroked his hair as he rested his head on my shoulder.

Nathaniel walked off the eighteenth a champion, and as always, he found time for his fans. He stopped to sign photos and books for the boys and girls whom, just like Jack, had believed in him. I looked at him, victorious and saw that my work here was done. He had successfully beaten all of his demons and I was confident they would never raise their ugly heads again.

Just as I was thinking about hellish dark angels, Leonardo suddenly appeared on screen, swaggering over to congratulate the champion golfer. Inaudible words were spoken between the two men before Nathaniel took off his cap and signed it.

"Leonardo has your cap for you," I told Jack, but his eyes had closed. He was dead to this world.

"Come here laddie." Finlay gently lifted the sleeping child into his strong arms, and we left the party.

I followed behind him as we walked down the long corridor, past bight, colourful pictures and paintings of different golf courses. Among the wall hangings were family photographs and framed cartoons. Finally, Finlay reached the last large wooden door; the room where Nathaniel and I had first stayed together. He lay the little boy down on the bed and left.

I stood at the open French doors and looked out at the landscape of a land I had come to love. I breathed in the air as I listened to the tick tock of the clock on the wall. It was nearly seven p.m. There was just enough time for me to change and then, at eleven minutes past the hour, it would be time to go. I watched the hands slowly count down. The time had come; I took a deep breath and walked over to the bed.

"Jack, wake up." I coaxed him out of his deep sleep.

He struggled at first but then he opened his eyes.

"Hi." I smiled down at the little boy who took a moment to register where he was.

"Anna?" He sat up, rubbing his eyes.

"It's time to go."

"Where are we going?"

"We're going home. Are you ready?" I reached out for his hand.

"Yes, I am."

At exactly eleven minutes past seven, that evening, we left the room and stepped back into the long corridor. We walked slowly past the large wooden doors, back towards the entrance hall. I could hear voices and could see the light, but I took my time as I wanted to look at the pictures once more. Tom was calling to Jack and I could feel the little boy tugging at my hand.

"Hurry up!" This time it was Leonardo's voice I heard.

We were getting ever closer.

"Come on Anna," Jack said, pulling me along.

I looked back one last time. The light was all around now. I saw Tom opening his arms to receive his grandson. I let go of Jack's hand and he ran to his granddad who covered him in kisses.

"This is for you champ." Leonardo put the signed cap on top of Jack's head. "Nice wings," he said, as walked towards me.

I shifted uncomfortably from one stilettoed foot to the other as he admired my feathers. I straightened my white pencil skirt as I fluffed them up for effect. They were rather magnificent.

"Bye Anna." Jack turned to me and waved.

"Bye my angel." I blew him several kisses as he walked off into the light with his beloved Granddad.

55

A Flop

Leonardo came to stand beside me – a vision in leather and lace - looking like he didn't belong in heaven.

"You look as hot as hell in that uniform Miss Frost."

"Isn't it time you were going back there?" I confronted the demon who had tried to destroy all my good work with Nathaniel. I stabbed a finger in his chest. "*You* tried to put Nathaniel off his game by poisoning his mind with lies!"

"And what, pray tell, were they?" He raised an eyebrow.

"That we – you and me – were in love and going to get married."

"I'm sorry, but I don't remember proposing." In my haste to accuse him I had forgotten that had happened in my nightmare and not in reality. "And I'm sorry my dear Anna but I'm not in love with you. I love you – as a friend and a colleague – but that's all. There will never be anything more."

Oh my God! Leonardo was having to let *me* down when it should have been the other way around!

"I'm sorry if you've been harbouring such feelings for me all this time."

I stood opened-mouthed, too shocked to say anything.

"But don't worry, there is someone out there for you. Someone much better than me."

Well, that wouldn't be hard!

"Admittedly, I am the whole package – tall, dark, handsome, multi-talented, charismatic, charming and incredibly sexy – but you will find someone who is much better suited to *you* than I am; someone who is right for *you*."

Wait a minute – was he implying that he was out of my league?

"I completely understand why you fell in love with me."

"I did not!" I cut him off, having finally regained my ability to speak. I wanted to continue to say, "You arrogant, self-opinionated, big-headed pig!" However, apparently my use of foul language had been curtailed by the reappearance of my wings. *Bugger! Shit! Damn! Fuck!* Luckily I could still think them!

"It's okay. It can be our little secret. I won't tell a soul. Cross my heart and hope to die."

If he kept talking, I could arrange for that to happen.

"Just to be crystal clear – I am not, or ever have been,

and never will be, in love with *you*. Ever!"

"Methinks the lady doth protest too much." He winked at me.

"I don't love you!"

"Yes, you do."

"No, I don't!"

"I think you do."

I was about to condemn him and his thoughts back to hell where he belonged, when Holly appeared munching a large slice of cake leftover from the party.

"It would've been a sin to see it go to waste. Want a bite?"

"No, thank you." I politely declined, and my thoughts immediately turned to Nathaniel. I wondered if he was celebrating his fourth Major win, if he'd heard about Jack or if he was missing me. I was just wondering if I'd ever see him again when Holly handed me a rolled-up piece of paper.

Opening it, I read: 'Lieutenant Anna Frost, report to the boardroom immediately.' It was signed by Colonel J.W. Cole.

Leonardo and Holly both stood to attention as I turned and tottered off in high-heeled stilettos.

"Looking good lieutenant," Leonardo called out after me, as I stepped into the lift accompanied by Amadeus Wolfgang Mozart on my way up to the boardroom.

He was busy conducting his own concerto, and I listened to the diatribe of direction he was giving to the imaginary orchestra as I prepared for what was to come. Usually his music calmed me, but not today. The lift came to a stop and the doors opened. The petite composer stopped flailing his arms and waited for me to get out but I was reluctant to leave. I stood staring at the open door.

"Off you go!" Mozart then directed me out of the lift.

I squeezed past the diminutive maestro with his wild hair. I then took a moment to preen my feathers, checking that they were all in place as I did so. It was a delaying tactic as I stood in front of the boardroom door. At last, I could postpone the inevitable no longer.

"Come in lieutenant," Colonel J W Cole called out, when I knocked.

I straightened my pencil skirt, stood tall and sashayed into the room. Like before, he was sitting between two of the angelic hierarchy whom I was in no doubt would make the final decision about my future.

"Lieutenant Frost!" The colonel looked shocked at the sight of me, and shifted in his seat in obvious discomfort. "Where is your uniform?"

"I'm wearing it sir." I stood to attention in front of my superiors. "In case you've forgotten, I'm a Guardian – CIA division."

"Quite. Well, I have your transfer papers here so you can take that off right now," he blustered.

"I think that would be inappropriate colonel."

My commanding officer was losing composure and

turned to his superiors for support, but the pair remained silent.

"And I would like to withdraw my request for a transfer. I think my talents are better suited to being a Guardian than a lieutenant."

"You are an officer in the EAA. You are suited to wielding a sword and fighting evil!" The colonel thumped his fist down on the desk in front of him.

At that moment, the door burst open and in walked evil personified.

Oh God! He was sure to make this worse.

"Gentlemen." Leonardo bowed to the board. "In Anna's defence," he began.

What was he talking about? I wasn't on trial.

"I think she has done a pretty good job as a Guardian. There were things she could've done better but it was her first time."

This was sounding more like a condemnation than a commendation. I glared at Leonardo who was now walking towards me.

"*Get out,*" I mouthed silently.

He smiled and put his arm around my shoulder.

"I'm sure she'll do better next time."

I shrugged him off.

"With respect, I did great this time. My performance as a Guardian was exemplary."

Leonardo sneezed to cover what he then said, "Swearing, drinking."

"It was a successful mission. Mr. Banks has returned to his former glory. He's a four-times Major winner. He is the world number one."

"But he's still in despair," Leonardo informed me and the board.

"Wait – what? Why?" I was shocked and concerned at first, and then cross. Why was Leonardo saying and doing this?

"He formed quite an attachment to our Anna. There was a little bit of a romance. She may have, rather stupidly, stepped over the line – let it get out of hand."

He shouldn't be telling them this, I thought.

"But I'm sure we've all had an office romance at one time or another." He winked at the colonel who was seething with anger at Leonardo's impertinence. "We can't help who we fall for. Even Anna herself has fallen prey to this. Just between us, she has fallen head over heels in love with me."

My face flushed a bright shade of red, although whether from embarrassment or fury, or both, it was hard for me to tell.

"It would break her heart if she was taken away from me, so I'm here to plead her case – to remain as a Guardian."

I stood there reconsidering my future yet again. The army, or anywhere that was far, far away from Leonardo, was looking good right now!

The colonel was shaking his head and a superior,

who was dressed in a white suit, spoke on behalf of the board.

"Have you anything to say Miss Frost?"

"Yes sir, I do. It is not true – I am not in love with Leonardo. And I *never, ever, ever* will be in love with him." I hissed as hysteria set in.

Leonardo, who was now sitting on the edge of the desk casually swinging his leg over one side, whispered to the other suited superior, "I rest my case."

"I have been nothing but professional. I was sent on a mission and it was successful." I wanted to add that I should be getting a medal or a promotion – I was that good – but decided against it. "Just like when I was in the EAA."

"Which is where you belong!" The colonel was exasperated that my future was still open for discussion.

One of the heralds held up his hand and silenced him.

"It appears you failed to fulfil your orders," he said, addressing me.

"But sir, I did an amazing job!"

"I have heard enough Miss Frost." He wasn't going to let me defend myself. This was awful! "Your orders were to help a young man in despair. Your young man is still in despair."

Leonardo nodded solemnly.

"No!" I cried. It wasn't true; I had left him happy. This was all Leonardo's fault. He must have said or done something to change that.

"I'm sorry Miss Frost, your request for a transfer is denied."

"No, wait!"

They weren't allowing me to transfer back to the Guardians. I'd never see Nathaniel again or be able to help him. I was distraught and then I was dismissed without further delay.

56
The Fall

One minute I was standing in front of the board and the next I was lying flat on my face. The ground below me was moving and I realised I was lying on top of someone. I looked down at the bare chest framed by white lace.

"Get off me!" I squirmed and struggled to stand up.

"I think you'll find that you're on top of me." Leonardo was loving this compromising position and therefore doing nothing to help.

"What have you done?" I demanded.

"I got you the transfer you wanted. I thought you'd be pleased?"

"Well, I'm not. You told my superiors that I'd failed and that I was in love with you!" I screamed.

"I thought you loved Nathaniel?" Holly suddenly appeared to pour more fuel on the fire.

I was definitely going to apply for another transfer, if only to get away from these two! I glared up at my CIA cohort who was chomping down on a chocolate-chip muffin.

"Love has nothing to do with it." I punched Leonardo in frustration as I said, "*He* told the colonel and the higher-ups that I'd failed. I never fail!" I punctuated my point with another punch. "Never!" Failure had never been in my F-Plan. "I had a blemish-free record until you barged in and ruined it with a pack of lies!"

"May I remind you an angel never lies."

Yes, but a demon does. He looked all sweetness and light, feigning innocence, but I wasn't fooled by any of it.

"And FYI my dear Anna, love has everything to do with it. Someone great once said, 'A life without love, is no life at all'."

"What does that mean?" I was not in the mood for listening to the profound rantings of anyone – great or otherwise.

"A lot. Now, as much as I love you sitting on top of me, I really need to get up. Do you mind?"

I'd forgotten I was still on top of him. I stood up and straightened my skirt. He reached out his hand for me to help him up, which I ignored, turning instead towards the Guardians' office door. I marched through it with my shoulders back and head held high. Contrary to what Leonardo thought I'd done an amazing job, and I was expecting some sort of accolade as I walked back into the office.

However, no one even looked up from their desks let alone congratulated me, which I was a little taken aback by. Then I saw Zelda teetering towards me with her arms outstretched.

"Anna!" She grabbed me and held me in a vice-like grip, pushing my head down onto her ample bosom. "Anna, Anna, Anna," she said repeatedly, as she patted my head. "I forgive you."

"For what?" My voice was muffled by her huge breasts.

"For failing." She shoved me backwards and I wobbled, trying to steady myself after this unexpected reaction.

"But I didn't fail."

She linked arms with me and dragged me along.

"I understand how difficult it is to be a Guardian. Not everyone can do it; not everyone is suited to the job."

Being a soldier was difficult. Leading an army into battle was challenging. It required skill, expertise and talent, but babysitting, on the other hand, wasn't hard at all which was why I had excelled at it. Why couldn't anyone see that?

"Nathaniel Banks is now on top of his game, all thanks to me. He's the best in the world."

"Yes dear, and bravo for that. But he's still in despair."

"I don't understand."

"I know you don't." We reached my desk and Zelda

pulled out my chair, pushing me down into it. "Why don't you write up your report and let's see if you can figure out what went wrong with your F-Plan."

I was trying to comprehend what was happening. This wasn't what I expected – I thought I'd return to a hero's welcome. I thought Nathaniel would be happy after he won, and that I'd be allowed to go back to earth.

Aha, that was the answer! I would go back down and sort all this out.

"You're on desk duty," Zelda pointed out, halting my idea in its tracks. "Another member of your team will take over this case."

Leonardo and Holly turned up at that moment like two proverbial bad pennies. Holly's entire attention was currently taken up by a box of chocolates, so it was Leonardo who offered to help Nathaniel. He wasn't even on my team!

"This was my mission. I want to go," I protested.

"There is no 'i' in team," Zelda told me.

Maybe not, but there was more than one in 'stupid' and 'idiot,' I thought, as I looked at Leonardo and Holly.

"Leonardo will finish this," she reassured me.

The dastardly dark angel would undo all the good work I had done. Before I knew it, Nathaniel would be playing awful again and he'd end up spending another Christmas Eve in Central Park. I couldn't let that happen!

"Okay everyone, back to work." Zelda handed me a

398

piece of parchment and a feathered quill. "Make sure you include every teeny, tiny detail," she told me, before turning on her heel.

Zelda might look like an angel on top of a Christmas tree, but she meant business. I walked over to the large round hole. Below was Central Park – the beating heart of New York City. I put my hand up to my chest but there was no heartbeat.

Leonardo joined me. We had been here many times before. He stood in silence beside me as my eyes wandered over the weaving paths. It was summer and the park was in full bloom. Native New Yorkers brought deck chairs and picnic blankets with them to soak up the sun. Tourists took trips round the park in horse-drawn carriages, and a baseball match was being played. From the top of the fountain, my angel watched boats bobbing along in the water.

"What do you see?" Leonardo asked, kneeling to get a closer look.

I saw reflections of the surrounding skyscrapers in the glassy waters. I saw dogs on leads, or chasing balls, bounding happily along beside their owners. I thought of Lucy, the lovable Labrador, and little Ella Wella. I heard screams of delight as children played hide-and-seek and I remembered my own childhood as well as my time with Leonardo. They brought back memories of happy times.

I saw a wedding ceremony taking place at the Ladies

Pavilion where a couple were exchanging vows in front of family and friends. Another wedding party stood in the Dene Summerhouse and a bride and groom were having photographs taken at Turtle Pond. A newlywed couple shared a kiss under the Wisteria Pergola where I had dreamed that one day I too would be married.

I saw life and laughter and love so why then did I feel so sad? I reached up and realised a tear was running down my cheek. I didn't think it was possible for an angel to cry.

Finally, I found Bow Bridge. A young couple stood with their arms around each other, looking down at the pool of water below. I could see the reflection of their faces in the water. They were excited, happy and looking forward to a future together. I remembered Nathaniel's F-Plan was to have a future with me.

Leonardo had said he was in despair. What if he thought that I was never coming back? Supposedly I was carrying out CIA work, so if he never heard from me again he would think I'd been injured or worse and like Mary Campbell, I'd been taken to heaven, which ironically was the truth.

Then panic set in. Robbie Burns professed to loving Mary but still jumped into bed with half of Scotland. I didn't want Nathaniel to have lots of sex, in a vain attempt to console himself. I didn't want him to be with anyone else full stop, let alone sleep with them. He was mine and I was his; we were made for each other.

Admittedly we were made in different realms, but I wouldn't let that stop us. I was going to move heaven and earth so that we could be together.

I was failing *him* by not fighting for *us*. I had to find a way back to tell him that I wanted a future with him too. I didn't want to be in the CIA or the Guardians or the EAA. I wanted to be with him – for forever.

My mind was whirling. How was I going to escape heaven? I'd been sentenced to the tedious task of penning up my report which would take ages. What was worse, Zelda was going to send Leonardo to find Nathaniel and finish the mission. There was no telling what damage he might do. I had to put a stop to that. I had to find Nathaniel.

I couldn't forget the life I'd had or what was waiting for me on earth. I just had to figure out how to get it… Then an idea came to me.

Leonardo looked at me and again asked, "What do you see?"

I looked the dark angel in the eye and said, "I see my future."

With that, I jumped off the side and fell down.

57

Featherless

To fall was the fastest way to get where I wanted to be. With the wind in my face, I felt like I was floating free as I fell down. Finally, I would be with Nathaniel again. My future was within my grasp. There was a flurry of feathers and then everything went dark.

My eyelids fluttered open as I regained consciousness. I was lying facedown on the ground, looking at a pair of familiar dusty leather boots. I groaned. What was he doing here?

"Go away!" I told the dark angel.

His face appeared before me.

"I was expecting a thank you for saving your pretty little feathered ass from being splattered all over Central Park."

"I'm not on earth?" I sat up and looked around. I was in a cell. "I'm in prison?" I couldn't believe it.

"It's for your own safety," Leonardo explained, rationalising their reasoning for locking me up. "After what happened we don't want you trying to hurt yourself again."

"I wasn't – I was going back down to find Nathaniel."

"Well, why didn't you just use the lift?"

"Because I wasn't allowed to go back."

"So, let me get this straight: you were disobeying orders?" Leonardo, as usual, was not helping.

Holly appeared dressed as a prison guard, brandishing a large ring of keys. She made a great fuss of finding the right one before opening the cell door.

"And how's the prisoner?" She came in with a tray of bland food that even she wasn't tempted to eat.

"I'm locked up. How do you think I'm feeling?"

She walked up to me and stared directly at my face.

"I'm guessing by the red cheeks, gritted teeth and wild eyes that you're not happy. Am I right?"

This was not a game.

"Let me out of here!" I tried to snatch the keys from her, but her reflexes were lightning fast.

"Now you better behave or I will have to restrain you." She dangled handcuffs in front of me.

"This is ridiculous! I've done nothing wrong. All I was trying to do was get back to Nathaniel. You said yourself he was in despair." I tried a different tact. "Please, you have to help me. I need to fix this."

Leonardo and Holly exchanged a look.

"I have my orders. I'm going to see Nathaniel,"

Leonardo reminded me.

"What are they?" I was desperate to know what was going to happen.

"I'm afraid that information is classified. I can't tell you anything until you are acquitted – at your trial."

"There's going to be a court case?" I was horrified. This was going from bad to worse.

"Don't you worry Anna, I'll be defending you," Holly told me. I banged my head off the bars in frustration. That was it then, I would never get out of here. By telling me that, she was handing me a life sentence while at the same time taking any hope of a life away from me. I was doomed.

I was left in limbo as Leonardo went off to see Nathaniel. I had no idea what he was going to say or do, but I imagined the worst. Every minute was torture. I paced up and down the cage that trapped me. Light radiated from the bars – everything was light, bright and white – but I felt only darkness. It might have looked like heaven but it felt like hell.

Barrister Holly sat outside at a desk, preparing my defence. She didn't inspire confidence and I had no faith in my counsel who planned to plead temporary insanity.

"I'm just going to tell the truth," I told her repeatedly, but she didn't listen.

"That would be a bad idea," she cautioned me.

"And why's that? Aren't angels meant to tell the truth?"

"Yes, but technically you're not one at the moment. You lost your wings when you took a nosedive," she told me.

"I'm not an angel?"

"I'm afraid not." Holly put a hand of comfort through the bars and reassured me. "Don't worry Anna, I'm going to get them back for you."

From then on, I started to form my own defence. It was foolhardy to rely on my feathered friend to free me. I was formulating a new F-Plan that I was confident would work.

58
Foul Play

The day of my trial finally came. I sat in front of the familiar long white table and faced my judges – six superiors in white suits. The jury sat opposite and members of the EAA and Guardians filled the courtroom. I sat beside Holly, who was dressed in a white wig and long white robe. The other desk was empty, and I wondered who would be prosecuting my case. Leonardo flung open the door and flounced in, wearing a long black robe.

"You're late, Mr. da Vinci," one of the superiors said, as Leonardo took his seat at the prosecutor's table.

My mouth fell open in utter shock. How could he betray me like this? I glared at the dirty double-crossing demon who had the absolute cheek to wink at me.

I tossed my head and turned to my only hope – defence lawyer Holly – who at that moment was busily dunking a biscuit into her morning cup of coffee.

Dear God, I was doomed!

"Shall we begin?" The most senior higher-up brought the courtroom to order by banging his ivory white gavel on the table. "We are here today to decide on Miss Frost's future."

Well at least I apparently had one, which was a good thing, I thought.

"I am inviting her defence attorney to take to the floor."

Holly stood up with a handful of soggy biscuit that she somehow managed to manoeuvre into her mouth at the last minute.

"Your highnesses," she said, as she addressed the superiors. "Friends, Guardians, fellow angels – lend me your ears." She started her defence by unashamedly plagiarising Shakespeare. "I am here to defend this wretched creature."

Excuse me?

"Who has, over the course of the last six months, broken not only angelic law and human law but God's own law too."

There were audible gasps from me and every other angel in the courtroom.

"I know." She was sagely nodding her head. "Pride, envy, gluttony, *lust*." She lingered on that particular sin before continuing, "Anger, greed and sloth. Sadly, Miss Frost has fallen prey to them all."

"I have not!" However, in front of judge and jury, I was about to commit the cardinal sin of choking the life out of Holly!

"Silence!" the superior ordered me.

"She's used foul language, she's been jealous, vain, and she's enjoyed the sins of the flesh." This wasn't a defence – it was a death sentence! "Anna came to us from the EAA, and it was clear to us that the army had broken her sweet spirit."

I looked at the colonel who in turn was glaring at Holly.

"I put it to you that they are culpable. They are responsible for her atrocious behaviour and they should be on trial – not her."

Holly took a bow. I couldn't believe what I was hearing. What exactly was she saying?

"*I'm sorry,*" I mouthed to my commanding officer while miming that she was crazy.

"My turn." Leonardo leapt up and took centre stage.

I braced myself for the damning evidence he was about to present.

"It's true that Miss Frost, during her time on earth, did fall prey to temptation but she was human after all." He paused to give weight to his opening statement. "Her orders were to help a young man in despair and, in the line of duty, she went above and beyond. Why, she actually jumped off a bridge trying to save him. Quite heroic, don't you think? I'm afraid I disagree with my esteemed colleague. I think Miss Frost worked tirelessly with young Mr. Banks, who did indeed regain his standing and his success on the fairways." He mimed hitting a golf ball. "She fought, just like the army taught her." I saw my colonel sit up straight, with his head held high. "It is not the army who failed her, but Anna herself. "

For a second it was all going so well. It wasn't fair that I had two prosecutors and no defence. I was about to point that out when Holly called her first witness to the stand.

"Milordiness, I am calling Ms Zelda Zolliner." I watched as the diminutive buxom blonde raised her right hand and swore to tell the truth, the whole truth and nothing but the truth which seemed a bit of a pointless exercise as she was an angel and therefore had no choice but to do that.

"Can you please tell the court what a pitiful, sorry state this poor angel arrived in."

"Objection!" Leonardo jumped in. *Bloody right*, I thought. *There was nothing sorry about me.* "Leading the witness."

"Overruled," the superior said. "Please answer the question Zelda."

"Of course, Frank," (Zelda was on first name terms with the higher-ups.). "Miss Frost arrived a very angry angel."

I'd been yanked from a job I loved and sent against my will to the Guardians – I wasn't angry, I was furious!

"I thought the spirit of Christmas would help Anna

adjust to her new role, so she became a Christmas Incident Angel and Holly took her under her wing. It was her idea to send her to earth straight away."

"She had no appreciation of Christmas music or food, and who do you think I blame for that colonel?" Holly chimed in.

The colonel was red-faced with rage and I didn't blame him.

"We are a caring organisation whose job it is to help others, unlike the army, who tend to want to kill them." Holly ploughed on, doggedly.

"Anna's mission was to help a young man in despair and, in my opinion, she did a great job," Zelda told the superiors.

"With my help," Holly piped up. She looked at me and said, "As *her* superior I tried my best to keep her on the straight and narrow, but it wasn't easy. No, sirs. In fact, I deserve a medal for what I had to put up with."

She looked hopefully at the line of suited superiors who said nothing, and offered nothing.

"Your witness Mr. da Vinci." It seemed that the judges had heard enough from Holly and frankly so had I.

"Anna was sent to earth to help a young man in despair. Her previous life and work gave her a greater understanding and empathy with our subject. In my humble opinion she was the perfect angel for the job."

Leonardo sat back down, and Zelda was dismissed.

Well, that went much better than I thought; no thanks to my incompetent counsel who was doing her best to get me sent to hell! Holly stood up and addressed the jury.

"After first losing her orders and then trying to mug the young man in despair, who was terrified and traumatised after being attacked by my defendant, she ended up in hospital. I am now calling my second witness, Mrs. Iris di Maggio."

"I thought Iris was a human?" I whispered.

"She was but she's not anymore," Holly told me.

Iris, I was to discover, had lost none of her razor-sharp wit and she was still being brutally honest.

"I knew she was CIA," she announced, before even waiting to be asked anything.

"Did Miss Frost tell you she was working for a covert agency?"

"No, she told me she was here to protect Mr. Banks, but I knew." She pushed her heavy-framed round spectacles up her nose.

"So, she confided in you? She told you the reason she was here on earth? Isn't that against angelic law?" She asked the court. "And didn't you in fact address the defendant as 'angel', implying you knew she was a heavenly being?"

"I didn't know," Iris said, but Holly ignored her and pressed on.

"To sum up: having only just arrived on earth, Miss Frost held Mr. Banks up at gun point and then informed

the first human she met that she was indeed heaven-
sent."

"Iris." Leonardo sauntered over to the witness. "May
I say how lovely you're looking today."

I watched as Iris fell under his charming spell.

"Did Anna tell you she was an angel?"

"No."

"She told you that she was there to help Nathaniel
Banks, which she could've done as a human. Correct?"

"Yes," Iris agreed.

"Thank you, Mrs di Maggio."

"What are you doing?" I hissed at Holly, as Leonardo
helped Iris down from the stand.

"My job," she smiled.

"You're meant to be defending me!"

"Do you want a biscuit?" she asked, as she began
dunking another digestive.

If she went on like this for much longer, I was going
to sit with Leonardo who was doing a much better job
of defending me than she was. After a slurp of coffee,
she then called Snowflake to the stand.

"She's an angel?" I was shocked.

"Oh yes. She's a very good agent and a very
convincing human. No one ever suspects her." She
raised an eyebrow at me before rearranging her papers
and wig.

"Agent Snowflake, how long have you been a nurse
on earth?"

"My first mission was the Crimean War. I did the two World Wars…" She counted off on her fingers as she tried to do the mental arithmetic.

"A long time then." My impatient barrister didn't wait for her to finish. "And as a trusted, experienced and successful secret agent, in your opinion, did Miss Frost draw unnecessary attention to herself and therefore put her identity and the identity of those in her team – you and me – at risk?"

For a start I didn't know Snowflake was on my team and as for Holly, she was missing in action for almost the entire time I was in the hospital.

"Anna certainly drew Jack's attention." She smiled at me. "He loved her and—"

Holly abruptly interrupted her. "A simple yes or no will suffice."

Snowflake didn't know what to say.

"Um, yes," she was forced to confess.

"No further questions," Holly said, and sat back down.

'WTF?' I wrote on a piece of paper and pushed it over to her. I watched as she tried to figure out what it meant. Then she had a lightbulb moment.

"Oh, yes," she said.

"What?"

"Was That Fruitful? The answer is yes."

I gave up. Leonardo meantime had swaggered over to the young nurse/angel.

"You mentioned Jack. Can you tell the jury a little bit about him?"

Snowflake was happy to. "Jack was a patient and Anna was great with him. They formed an immediate bond. It's very difficult for a child, being away from his parents. Jack trusted Anna."

"Would you say she helped him?" Leonardo asked.

"Absolutely. She was amazing."

I smiled at the young nurse, and my thoughts turned to Jack whom I missed very much.

"Thank you." Leonardo sashayed back to his seat.

"I'm going over there." I tried to get up but Holly kept a firm hold of my arm.

"Have faith, this is going great." She gave me a thumbs up before calling flight attendant Felipe to the stand.

I banged my head on the desk in renewed despair.

"*He* was an angel?" I couldn't believe it.

"No, don't be silly."

"Then what's he doing here?" I was confused.

"Sudden passing," Holly said, and stood up.

Felipe still sounded hysterical as he took a seat and asked, "Where am I?" He looked disorientated.

Holly stepped up. "Welcome to heaven," she said, before consulting her notes.

His eyes were wide as he took in his surroundings, trying to decide if she was joking.

"I'm dead?" he cried out, and started to sob.

Leonardo interjected. "Your honours, I don't think this witness is fit to testify."

Felipe rambled on. "I was walking down the street. Then everything went black. My head, it was hurting…" He was trying to piece together what had happened to him.

Holly interrupted him mid-sentence. "I'll be super quick your holinesses. His testimony is important to my client's case."

After a quick consultation, the head judge nodded and said, "Proceed."

"You were walking down Hollywood Boulevard, had a blackout, hit your head off the curb and now you're here," Holly explained to the young flight attendant, whose lip was trembling.

"So, I'm really dead?"

"Oh yes, very."

"But I was walking one minute and the next I was gone." He was trying to make sense of what had happened.

"Yes, it happens. Don't worry, we'll get you into orientation in a sec, but first, I have a few questions. Do you recognise the defendant?" Holly pointed to me.

Felipe had been looking at me before but without registering who I was.

"It was her!" he screamed. "She killed me!"

This wasn't good and it also wasn't true. I expected my defence counsel to point that out. Holly came over and stood behind me. She put her hands on my shoulders.

"Are you saying that Miss Frost was responsible for your sudden passing?"

He was crying uncontrollably now.

"Ever since she attacked me, I have had these headaches." I could hear the gasps of shock resonate within the room.

"Can you please tell the court exactly what happened."

"Well, you know, you were there – you saw it happen," he said to Holly, who was nodding in agreement.

"Yes, yes I did but please, in your own words."

Encouraged by Holly, Felipe, now appealed to judge and jury by giving a step-by-step account of the incident that occurred on the plane.

"This skinny, scrawny specimen hurled a grown man through the air. Would you say that she drew attention to herself, for her very unhuman-like behaviour?"

"Oh yes, she is a demon!" Members of the jury scrambled to make notes.

"No more questions."

Yet I had one and this time to avoid any confusion, I wrote plainly and simply, 'What the hell??!!'

"Yes dear, that's where demons come from and go to," Holly said, as she patted my hand.

"Felipe, can I get you anything? Tea? A glass of

water?" Leonardo asked him.

"Oh no, thank you." The witness was suddenly very demure.

"Are you feeling better now?" Leonardo soothed.

"Much, thank you." He was fluttering his eyelids at the handsome angel who was leaning over the stand.

"Your head doesn't hurt anymore does it?" He stroked Felipe's hair which he obviously enjoyed.

"No, no, it's fine now, there's no pain," he reassured Leonardo.

"I'm so glad to hear that. And lovely haircut by the way." My prosecutor unashamedly flirted with the witness. "I just want to go over a few things and get them clear: you say that Miss Frost was responsible for your untimely demise, is that correct?"

"Yes sir."

"So, Miss Frost was on Hollywood Boulevard this afternoon, when you died?"

"No."

"Then how is she responsible?"

"I had been having these headaches ever since she venomously assaulted me." He continued with the histrionics by pointing accusingly at me.

Leonardo was busy reading a document.

"I have your autopsy report here. It says that you have suffered migraines all your life. Is that true?"

"Yes, but—"

Leonardo silenced him. "'Yes' is quite sufficient. It

also says that your cause of death was blunt force trauma to the cranial frontal lobe, caused by a fall, when you tripped. I put it to you, that your passing was the deadly combination of the new high heels you were wearing and a broken paving stone and that they, and not Miss Frost, are responsible for your sudden death. With regard to the incident on the plane, I believe you tried to forcibly remove Miss Frost from business class. The unfortunate incident that then occurred was because she was acting in self-defence and was unaware of her own strength which is a common side effect of deployment on earth," Leonardo concluded, dismissing Felipe in the process. He turned his back on the flight attendant who was escorted from the court.

Hooray! Leonardo had saved me!

Holly stood up.

"Miss Frost was sent to save a young man in despair – a young man who had lost everything. It was her role as a Guardian to protect him and help him through a very difficult time in his life. His wife had left him for his best friend. His career was going down the toilet. He was falling from grace and that's when an angel of the same name stepped in and fixed him. Can I call Grace to the stand?"

"Wait! What?"

My outburst caused the most senior official to bang his gavel.

"Silence Miss Frost! If you can't respect the court,

then I will have you removed. Do you understand?"

"Yes, sir."

Grace took the stand.

"Ladies and gentlemen of the jury, may I introduce Grace Hepburn? On earth she was taking the golfing world by storm. Then tragedy struck – or should I say it was lightning – which struck a tree during a storm that brought our beautiful Grace back home again. However, not before she helped young Mr. Banks. Please Grace, can you tell the jury exactly what you did?"

Grace looked uncomfortable.

"I didn't do anything. It was all Anna. She helped Nathaniel."

Holly laughed. "Come now, there's no need to be modest. Tell everyone how you took Mr. Banks out to play the course at Loch Lomond, the same one where he would later win the Scottish Open – all thanks to you."

"I played the course with him, but he didn't need my help. He played fantastically well. He never stopped talking about Anna and telling me how much she had helped him."

Holly interjected. "But I want to talk about all the good *you* did."

"Honestly, it wasn't me, it was all Anna."

"My witness." Leonardo walked over and pushed Holly out of the way. "You are gorgeous Grace." He made the young girl squirm uncomfortably at the attention, but he continued with his charm offensive regardless. "So beautiful both inside and out. Tell me, did Mr. Banks ever tell you that?"

"No." She shook her head to emphasise her point.

"You spent a lot of time together when poor Miss Frost was concussed and comatose. She had her skull smashed in by a golf ball and was drugged by her defence attorney," he told the court.

Holly's latest dunked biscuit fell into her coffee as she listened to Leonardo.

"Did anything happen between you and Nathaniel, romantically?"

"Absolutely nothing."

"Thank you, Grace, you may step down."

"He was – he *is* – in love with Anna." Grace wanted to set the record straight.

Holly stood up.

"Wait – are you saying that Miss Frost, an angel, who was sent to earth to help a vulnerable human, abused her position of power? A position of trust and responsibility? I put it to you that she took advantage of him, seducing him for her own sexual gratification."

Grace looked shell-shocked, with no idea what to say in response.

"No further questions milord." Holly took her seat.

"You're fired!" I told her and I crossed my arms.

"And I am ready to sum up," she told the court.

59

Final Judgement

"I have one last witness I would like to call," Leonardo requested.

"This is most unusual Mr. da Vinci," a superior said.

"But most relevant to Miss Frost's case."

"Very well." They granted him permission to call Jack to the stand.

I watched as the little boy was led in, and I stood up to object.

"Anna!" He broke free and wrapped his arms around me.

I hugged him hard as I addressed the judges.

"With respect, a courtroom is no place for a child. Jack has been through quite enough in his young life. He shouldn't have to answer questions as well."

"I want to Anna." He smiled up at me. He didn't realise that I was trying to protect him. "Please Anna. I can do this."

"The child agrees." The chief judge slammed down

his gavel. "Now can we please move things along?"

I reluctantly let him go. Holly moved to stand up but not before I gave her a stern warning. "Do not say or do anything to upset Jack or I swear there will be hell to pay!"

"Hello Jack." She walked over to the little boy.

"Hello coach Holly." He sat up straight, smiling at her.

"Jack and I met at Nathaniel Banks Academy of Golf where we put Miss Frost in the pillory and fired wet soapy sponges at her face. Happy times..." she told the court. "I had arranged for Jack to meet Mr. Banks—"

Jack quickly corrected her. "No. Santa did."

"Sorry, yes I mean Santa." There were chuckles from some of the jurors. "He arranged for Jack to meet his hero in the hospital; the same hospital Miss Frost had been admitted to after attempting to mug Mr. Banks just before she jumped off a bridge. And what happened when you met Miss Frost?"

"Anna told me her secret – that she was here to fix Nate."

"She told you the reason she was on earth?"

"Yes." He sounded so proud to have been entrusted with the secret. "She had come to help Nate be brilliant again, and she did it."

"So, you knew Anna was an angel?"

"Oh yes." He nodded in confirmation.

I was shocked!

"Thank you Jack, you've been very helpful."

I smiled over at the little boy who had sealed my fate. The jury was certain to find me guilty now of breaking angelic law.

Leonardo began his questioning.

"How did you know Anna was an angel?"

"Because I asked for her to come," he told the prosecution.

"I'm sorry, I don't understand?"

"I prayed,' he told Leonardo. "To God." He felt the need to add this just in case there was any confusion. "I asked him to send me an angel because I was scared."

"Of being in the hospital? Of being sick?"

"Of being alone, of leaving my mum and dad and of dying. I was frightened." I hadn't realised any of this. "But then Anna came, and she made everything okay."

"And how did you know that Anna was your angel?" Leonardo asked.

"Because I wasn't scared anymore."

I wiped a tear away.

"Thank you, Jack." Leonardo ruffled the little boy's hair before Tom came to take him down from the stand. My prosecutor addressed the court officials. "As you can see, Miss Frost is not a good angel—"

"No, she's a brilliant angel!" Jack blurted out.

Leonardo bowed to the little boy and I blew him a big kiss as he was led out of the courtroom. I was glad he wouldn't be there to hear the dark angel tell everyone how awful I was. That would only have upset him, and I didn't want that.

"As I was saying…" Leonardo resumed his statement. "Miss Frost is not a good angel – she is a brilliant angel, just like Jack has said."

My mouth opened in surprise.

"Miss Frost is a fighter, and may I say colonel, the army taught her well." The colonel looked proud of this compliment. "She loved the EAA and she missed it. That was all she wanted when she got to earth – to have her sword back and return to the job she loved; leading the legions into battle and slaughtering the masses. Isn't that right lieutenant?"

I sounded like a bloodthirsty mass murderer when he put it like that!

"She fought with the same zeal and vigour to fix young Mr. Banks; drilling him and putting him through his paces with military precision. He ended up swinging his stick almost as well as she did her sword. Anna Frost is a fearless fighter who lets nothing stand in her way."

I looked at the colonel who looked incredibly proud.

"So, I put it to the court that this brilliant warrior should be allowed to return to the job she loves the most. Give her back her sword and let her lead God's legions!"

Yet I didn't want to lead His legions; I didn't want to go back to the army at all. I wanted to go back to the life I loved, not the job I loved before I fell in love.

"Objection your honourablenesses." Thank the Lord

Holly was protesting. "I think I have made it very clear to the court that the army destroyed my client with all its slaying and slashing, not to mention how much she has annoyed me over this last year constantly talking about it. Honestly, if I have to listen to Anna bleating on one more time about how busy she had been fighting evil, charging into battle, wielding her great big sword, blah, blah, blah…"

The colonel had turned beetroot red, and was clearly enraged.

"Anna Frost belongs with us; we're her family now. She's a Guardian (albeit not a very good one), but I promise you I will work with her day and night to help her improve. I will never leave her side. I will dedicate every waking moment to helping her become the Guardian I know she can be. We are her future."

At that moment I was ready to go to hell – or wherever else they wanted to send me – if it meant not having to spend every waking hour with Holly!

"Have you anything to say Miss Frost, before we pass judgement?"

"I do your higher-upness." I stood up. "The prosecution is right," I began and I heard Holly gasp. "I did want to go back to the army. I loved being a lieutenant; I loved my sword. I couldn't ever imagine doing anything else that I loved more. But then I became a Guardian."

"Ha! Told you!" Holly pointedly looked at the

colonel.

"Admittedly at first I hated it." The Guardians gasped. "I didn't like the uniform." I saw each one look down at their tight white trousers and dresses.

"What's not to like?" Holly promptly opened her robe and flashed the entire courtroom, showing off her voluptuous figure that was squeezed into a tight white skirt and top.

"I didn't like the music, or the idea of going to earth to help anyone. But all that changed when I joined the CIA. I'm sorry colonel." I addressed my commanding officer directly. "I don't want to transfer back to the EAA. I don't want to be a soldier anymore."

"I was right, and you were wrong." A smug Holly childishly taunted my commanding officer.

"And I don't want to be a Guardian either."

"Say what?" Holly nearly chocked on the celebratory chocolate she had just rewarded herself with.

"I'm very grateful that I was given the opportunity to be one; just like I was very grateful to have served in God's armed forces. Both organisations do wonderful work and are full of fantastic celestial beings."

This seemed to placate the whole courtroom.

"The EAA taught me how to fight and that's what I'm doing now – fighting for what I want, and the future I want. In the CIA, I found that future."

"So, you want to continue to be a Christmas Incident Angel?" Holly surmised.

"No. I want to be a human."

There was an audible drawing-in-of-breath and shocked whispers between members of the EAA. Guardians gasped, and an incredulous colonel sat with his mouth wide open.

"Order! Order!" Head Judge Frank banged his gavel to silence the room.

Holly was on her feet and floundering as she hastily shuffled through papers until she found the one she was looking for.

"I'm pleading insanity. My client is not in her right mind! Please strike her request from the records."

The room fell silent; all eyes on me.

"Holly told me I'm not an angel—"

"For the time being," she interrupted. "I also told you I was going to get your feathers back. So, if you would kindly sit back down and shut up, I'll get on and do that!" She was fuming.

"I'm a human, of sound mind and body," I told the court. "Someone great once said that a life without love is no life at all." Leonardo nodded in agreement. "I don't want to live without love, and I love Nathaniel Banks."

"The human you were sent to help?" one of the higher-ups asked.

"Yes, sir. I was sent to fix him, and I thought I did. I came up with an F-Plan. I drilled him, just like Leonardo said, and got him fit to fight. I taught him to find focus and have faith in himself."

"And did this F-Plan of yours work?" a curious official asked me.

"Yes. He started to play fantastic golf. In fact he won four Majors."

Everyone looked suitably impressed.

"I fought so hard for him to see a future, and finally he did – with me – and then I left him." I felt so guilty that I had abandoned him. "Now he's in despair again and so am I. He probably thinks that I'm dead," (which I was of course.). "Or that I've run off with Leonardo."

The dark angel seemingly smouldered with sex appeal as he stood up and looked seductively in my direction.

"For the record, the last time I saw Mr. Banks I left him in no doubt about my relationship status with Miss Frost."

Well, that wasn't comforting!

"Which is?" The head judge and everyone else wanted to know.

I braced myself for the lies Leonardo was about to tell the court.

"I know this will be hard for you all to believe, but Anna and I are just work colleagues. And, I hope, friends. We have never had a sexual relationship." His admission sent shock waves reverberating around the room. There was a stunned silence.

I was dumbfounded and deeply disturbed that they thought we ever had! How could they?

"Trust me, no one was more surprised than me. I am fully aware of how utterly irresistible I am."

 I looked around the room and it was clear from their faces that the big flirt had fumbled with quite a few feathers.

Head Judge Frank looked directly at me. "Have you anything else to add Miss Frost?"

"I just want to be with the man I love."

"May I remind you that you are an angel."

"I don't have my wings," I pointed out. I took a deep breath. "And I don't want them back."

I saw the higher-ups share a glance with each other at my announcement. A feather would have been heard dropping, such was the silence as I stood in front of judge and jury. I knew what I had said was a flagrant disregard for my feathers and that was forbidden. I was in no doubt that I had sealed my own fate. I looked around the room and saw that the colonel had taken off his hat and was holding it to his chest. The soldiers I had fought alongside looked shell-shocked while the Guardians I had known for such a short time, looked similarly bereft. Leonardo cradled his head in his hands and Holly sat beside me in stunned silence.

I had no idea what fate I was facing for the crimes I had committed in heaven and on earth. It was true: I had broken both angelic and human law. I thought over the journey that had brought me here, to this time and place. I hadn't planned for any of it when I was first sent, featherless, to Central Park to fix Nathaniel Banks. I didn't foresee that as I walked over footsteps of my own past my heart would take flight; that I would find what I'd always been looking for – a love so great that I could fly without wings, fall from the greatest height, and forfeit my feathers just so we could be together forever.

Holly reached over and squeezed my hand. I smiled at my food-loving fellow angel. I was happy for her that she had Finlay and her feathers. Yet for me, there was no future if Nathaniel wasn't in it.

Head Judge Frank brought the court to order for a final time.

"Miss Frost."

I stood up straight.

I had fallen in love with Nathaniel and had no remorse and no regrets. I was ready for whatever punishment they were going to exact because I knew that I would do the same again in a heartbeat.

"You are sentenced to…" I closed my eyes and held my breath as I waited for the sentence to be passed. He banged his gavel and then I was falling. I was falling down.

60

The future for Frost

Faces flashed in front of me as I fell far down. I expected to end up in the fiery pits of hell and be greeted by Satan and his sidekick, the dark double agent who had successively seduced half of heaven. Yet I stopped falling and started floating instead as I landed on familiar ground. I looked up at the starry sky and surrounding skyscrapers. I found myself standing in satin slippers in Central Park.

I spun around, sending the full skirt of the fabulous frock I was wearing swishing out. I felt my chest and found my heartbeat. I was alive!

"Thank you," I said, to the heavens and the angels that I was sure were watching me. Now all I had to do was find Nathaniel.

Soft snowflakes started to fall and ahead, framed by an arch, I could see my angel of the waters. The words to the hymn, *Hark the herald angels sing* echoed around the vaulted ceiling as I ran through the Moroccan-tiled arcade and under the watchful gaze of the winged bronze angel who stood on top of the fountain, a group of carollers sang. I, like others, stopped to hear the heavenly choir sing.

"What are they doing here?" I was shocked to see soldiers, superiors and Guardians standing side by side.

"Fairytale of New York!" someone shouted from the crowd, who had no idea they were listening to an actual host of angels.

Leonardo stepped out and under the light of a lantern, he started to sing. Bare-chested and wearing breeches, the onlookers went wild for the lothario who only had eyes for me.

I hated to break it to him as he serenaded me but this definitely wasn't our year – and if he'd come all this way just to declare his undying love for me, he was wasting his time. I loved Nathaniel. Why couldn't he get that through his thick head?

Then Holly stepped out, wearing a tight-fitting bodice, bustle skirt and belted out the next part of the duet. I was just imagining how intolerable a Broadway Holly would've been, when I heard them confess that they had kissed?!

What? Holly and Leonardo had been a couple! I looked around expecting others to share my disbelief, but everyone seemed oblivious. I turned to the choir who surely would be as surprised as I was by the revelation, but it would seem not.

The colonel was swaying beside the superior who had sentenced me earlier. Dressed in a velvet frockcoat, Frank doffed his hat to me and I'm sure I saw a twinkle in those old blue eyes. Snowflake stood beside Sebastian who waved a frilly cuff, and I was in no doubt that the flamboyant couturier was responsible for the vast array of crinoline, cravats and corsets on show. Zelda conducted the choir (who looked like they'd just stepped off the streets of Victorian London) as the two divas took centre stage and began to brawl. I listened in horror as insults flew back and forth. Holly was furious and there wasn't even food involved. Maybe she'd turned to food for comfort after Leonardo had taken her dreams and crushed them under his very expensive boot?

Holly hurled a final insult at the dark angel, who clearly had left a trail of broken hearts and ruffled feathers in his wake.

"He's waiting for you." Zelda, who looked like a fairy, waved her wand in the direction of Bow Bridge.

I had been lost in the *Fairytale of New York* but now panic set in. It was Christmas Eve and Nathaniel Banks was in despair. I charged along the path, which weaved its way around the lake. History was repeating itself. He thought I was gone and never coming back and unlike Randy Robbie, who consoled himself in the arms of other women, my Nathaniel was so heartbroken he couldn't live without me.

I picked up my pace and full skirt, hoping and praying that I would get there in time. The bowed arch of the cast-iron bridge came into view and I could just about make out the figure of a man.

"Wait!" I waved but I was too far away for him to see me.

I sprinted as fast as I could, losing a slipper along the way. Stumbling onto the bridge, sweating and shoe-less, I was stunned to see it wasn't Nathaniel but Santa who stood waiting for me.

"No!" I cried.

"Normally people are pleased to see me," said the man in the red suit.

I pushed past him and looked over the edge. There was no sign of Nathaniel in the deep dark waters below. I'd come all this way; given up my feathers, my friends, my sword and my home for the man I loved, and I was too late. He was gone.

"I have something for you Anna Frost." The big, bearded man picked up his sack.

"I don't want it." I fell to the ground and wept.

"Are you sure?" I looked up again and saw Nathaniel standing with my slipper. He knelt down and put it on my foot. "It's a perfect fit," he said, before pulling me up and into his arms.

I thought I was too late; I thought that he was gone. I thought I heard sleigh bells, and then he kissed me and I thought of nothing else.

61
Finale

These last few months had been a whirlwind and I was so grateful for the time I'd been given. I had loved every second of my time here and I never wanted it to end but that is the one certainty of life: one day it all comes to an end and this was my last day as Anna Frost.

"Have you any regrets?" the dark angel asked, as he stood beside me dressed in black.

The tears sprung to my eyes. I was so emotional, I couldn't speak so I simply shook my head.

"Are you sure?" Holly stood in front of me, with her hands on her hips. "You can't think of anything?"

"Erm, no."

"Really?" Her voice had risen several octaves in disbelief. "What about me?" She was getting very agitated and I wondered if her blood sugars were low. I looked around for something sweet to pacify her.

"Don't you feel any guilt about leaving me?"

The simple answer was, "No."

"We were a team. We were good together. No wait." She started crying now too. "We were great!"

"You still have Leonardo." I tried to console a hysterical Holly with that thought, as well as a cupcake.

"I don't want Leonardo," she cried, but took the conciliatory cupcake.

"Anna has made her choice. Now she has to live with it," Leonardo said.

I stood up straight, with my shoulders back and head held high.

"I'm ready," I told him.

"It's not too late. You can still change your mind!" Holly was frantic.

"No, I can't," I told my food-loving former colleague.

The next thing I knew, she'd pulled me to her and held me in a massive bear hug. "I'm going to miss you Anna Frost." She was quite literally squeezing the life out of me.

"*Mon Dieu*, what are you doing?" Sebastian came to my rescue. "Get off her!" He was hitting Holly with his handheld fan. "You are ruining everything, you crazy woman!" The French couturier was livid. "Look what you've done to her feathers!" He slapped Holly before fixing and fluffing until everything was perfectly preened and in place.

"*Voila*!" He stepped back to admire his handiwork. "Now you look heavenly."

"Divine," Holly mumbled, through a mouthful of cupcake. I wasn't sure if she was referring to me or the frosted fancy.

"A beautiful angel." Leonardo stood beside me.

He looked handsome in his tailored tuxedo, which he'd agreed to wear just for me. It was after all the most important day of my very short life. Felix took a seat at the black grand piano and started to play.

"The maestro that is Mendelssohn," Leonardo enthused.

Sebastian was busy wrenching the cupcake out of Holly's hand, as I turned to the tall, dark angel. Another wave of emotion washed over me, and I just about managed to thank him before the tears came to my eyes again, and this time I allowed them to flow down my cheeks.

"What is it with all this crying?" Sebastian flounced over, flapping his fan. "Stop it." He snapped his fan shut and wagged it at me. "Rosaria!" He clicked his fingers and she appeared in front of me. He encircled my face with his fan. "Sort this mess out. Quick! Quick!" He clapped his hands.

Rosaria reapplied my makeup while a flustered Sebastian continued to fuss around me.

"Finally, we are ready! Now, go!"

I turned to Leonardo. There was still so much I wanted to say to him but there was no time left.

"*Allez*! Come on" The excited couturier ushered us

into position.

I took Leonardo's arm and looked down the long arched tunnel ahead of us. This was it – there was no going back.

Cherry blossom fluttered and fell like confetti as I walked beside the dark angel. Holly walked ahead of us, stepping in time to the slow march. Old friends and new sat either side of the petal-strewn pathway. They stood as I passed, and I smiled at the famous faces who were unaware they were in the company of angels.

Snowflake stood beside Beefhouse Bob whose large frame eclipsed that of his diminutive wife. Zelda and the colonel looked so proud, while Mozart looked miffed that Mendelssohn was getting all the attention.

As I walked down the aisle, Sebastian's feathered couture creation was gaining admiring looks from all the gathered guests (although it might easily have been my handsome escort who was attracting all the attention.). Both Leonardo the lothario and my matron of honour Holly were revelling in their starring roles, and neither had any qualms about upstaging me! I watched as Holly swung her hips, and Leonardo winked and waved to pretty guests (causing quite a few to swoon on sight), as I walked towards Frank.

Dressed all in white, my superior addressed the congregation.

"We are gathered here together to join Anna Frost with…"

"Nathaniel Banks," Leonardo prompted the celebrant who appeared to have forgotten my groom's name.

"Friends," he addressed the congregation, "I have listened to Anna Frost plead her case and I was left in no doubt that this," he waved a hand in Nathaniel's direction, "is what she wants."

"Why? What has he got?"

It was matron of honour Holly who told him, "A big mansion in Florida; an Academy of Golf; four Major trophies."

Frank silenced her.

"He has a beautiful angel…'

Oh dear Lord! Not again!

This was no time to enrage the Almighty. I glared at Frank.

"Who has fallen…"

What? Now he was telling God and everyone else that I was just like Lucifer!

"In love with him.'

"He," Frank raised his voice and pointed at Nathaniel. "He would have nothing without Anna Frost, who charted every step they took along the fairways."

At last! I was getting the credit I deserved for Nathaniel's success on the course. Technically, it was Duke who did all the plotting but it was *my* F-Plan that put Nathaniel back on top again.

"Anna Frost had a distinguished career. She was dedicated and decorated. She was exemplary in all she did."

"Well, I wouldn't say that," I heard Holly mutter under her breath.

I was warming to Frank's unconventional ceremony. 'And, then she met *him!*"

For a moment, it was all going so well.

"Anna Frost had an F-Plan, to help him find focus and faith, play fantastic golf, win four Majors. But this fearless fighter never foresaw that she would find so much more. She found friendship with Holly and Leonardo…"

I looked at my food-loving and flirtatious fellow Guardians who had been with me every step of the way.

"She fought hard for a future with the man she fell in love with…"

"And finally now, the end is near…"

"I love you Anna Frost," Nathaniel told me.

I was wearing a fabulous feathered frock, surrounded by family and friends. I thought back over every footstep that had brought me to this time, this place.

"Anna Frost," my superior addressed me.

I had no regrets and if I could, I would do it all again but there was no more time.

"I sentence you to…"

I felt the fairytale. I felt love. I felt life…then, I felt them all slip away…

And in that moment, Anna Frost was no more.

Acknowledgments

I would like to thank Kirsty Jackson and her amazing team at Cranthorpe Millner Publishers, Victoria Richards, Shannon Bourne, Michelle Spowage, Sian Reece and Donna Borg for all their help.

And thank you to my wonderful family: my mum, Jamie, Joshua, Darcey and Lionel for all your love and support.

Love always
xxx